THE BEGINNING
BERLIN GOTHIC

Berlin Gothic was first published in 2011 by Berlin Gothic Media under the same title. Translated from German by Edwin Miles. Published in English by AmazonCrossing in 2013.

Published by AmazonCrossing
PO Box 400818
Las Vegas, NV 89140

ISBN-13: 9781477807347
ISBN-10: 1477807349
Library of Congress Control Number: 2012916376

THE BEGINNING
BERLIN GOTHIC
JONAS WINNER

TRANSLATED BY EDWIN MILES

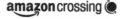

London may be the city of money, Paris the city of love, Rome the city of ruins, and Moscow the city of snow . . .

But Berlin is the City of Fear.

It is a gaunt and haggard fear that has no object, a fear that afflicts people like a disease; it hollows out their bones and their thoughts. It is a fear that paralyzes them, that poisons their laughter, cripples their imaginations, and warps their best intentions. It is a fear that has always abided here, stemming from deep beneath the city, where a gap, a tunnel, a shaft opens down into the depths of the earth to tap an emotion at the center of the world that exists nowhere else with such raw purity.

The fear is reaching a culmination, wrapping itself around the heart like a net; like a spiderweb, it inextricably binds the people of Berlin tighter and tighter. The fear drives them before it, makes their voices more constricted, more shrill. The fear makes their eyes bigger, their vision increasingly unstable, their thoughts increasingly erratic. The fear clutches like a steel fist and crushes like a vise; it steals their breath away and draws their faces long. The fear burns them until, showering sparks, they scream and rage and go insane. It sears them until, ablaze, they lash out wildly, anything to not burn away helplessly. They are already more dead than alive, but still smolder with enough heat to set anything they touch on fire.

1

It's looking at him. It's an eye and it's looking at him.

Till's diaphragm clenches. He sucks in air, drawing it into his body through his teeth with a hiss.

The eye blinks.

Till tries to say something. A rattling sound escapes his mouth. "Tschschsch, tschschsch . . ."

An eyelid comes down, half covering the eye.

Till jerks his line of sight upward. Past the eyelid, the shaved eyebrows, the forehead. Stops at a bump. Snaps back to the eye, then across the face to the other eye.

He hears a chuckling sound. The eyes seem to flash.

He looks at the forehead again. Above the other eye, too, is a bump, a . . .

"Horn." His voice sounds like it's coming out of a drain.

The head in front of him nods.

"A horn?"

Nod.

Till has raised his head instinctively, and now lets it sink back to the mattress.

The face before him smiles. The lips part and a tongue appears. A young woman's tongue. It glides over her lips.

Till turns his head aside, horrified. Her tongue is *split* down the middle; it has two tips.

"No, look," he hears the woman say. He turns back. She stretches one tongue tip upward, the other downward, comes closer. The tips curl and curve.

Till feels how his palms press into the mattress. He is suddenly aware of a searing heat shooting through his body.

No, he wants to shout, *please don't! Don't come any closer.* The tips of the tongue are writhing before his eyes. She lowers her head; the horns enter his field of view.

"You wanna feel?" she whispers.

"No." The word rasps in his throat. "I . . . I'm not feeling so good . . . it's so hot."

Her head jerks up and her eyes appear in front of his again. "Don't you like me?"

"It's not . . ." He feels dizzy. "I . . . a glass of water, can I?"

"HEY!" A voice slices between them. The girl leaning over Till backs away.

"Hey! Is anyone there?!" The voice cuts loudly across the dimly lit room. The woman turns to the other figures Till now sees are crowding behind her. They are all trying to catch a glimpse of Till over her shoulder. She holds her hands open in front of her as if to ask the others what she's supposed to do.

"He's awake," she whispers.

"Oh, yeah?"

A massive torso pushes past her. A man looks into Till's eyes. "How you feelin'?"

Heat blasts through Till; he feels like he's lying in an oven. "Hot. I'm burning."

"It'll pass." The man's cheeks are striped with finger-wide scarification marks. "It's the stitches. But you don't have to worry."

What stitches?

"Ungh . . . ," Till manages.

The man over him moves back a little and nods toward the other side of the room. With effort, Till manages to turn his head in that direction.

What he sees there scorches his retinas like a branding iron. The body of a woman is strung up horizontally, hung on large meat hooks from the ceiling. The hooks have been driven through her bare flesh, then attached to twelve nylon lines from which she is dangling. The skin and the tissue beneath each line are distended from the weight, stretching nearly four inches out from her body. Her head lolls back on her neck. Her forearms and lower legs, free of hooks, hang limply. Her body slowly rotates in the parched air.

"IS ANYONE THERE?!" The voice again, pounding through the semidarkness—but the figures gathered around Till just whisper and touch one another on their synthetic horns and scars. They don't seem to hear the man shouting.

Water. The thought throbs in Till's head. *I have to drink something.* But he can't move; he feels as if he's encased in concrete. His eyes move downward. He wants to see why he feels so hot, but his body is hidden beneath a blanket.

"You should stay still for now," says the man beside him who tugs at a chain pulled through his own ear. "You're not done yet."

What? The dizziness sweeping through Till intensifies. "What . . . what do you mean, 'not done yet'?" His voice sounds as feeble as a dying bird.

"You can't drink anything yet, but it's not gonna take much longer."

"What have you done?"

The man's dark eyes above him are laughing. "It's beautiful. You'll love it."

"Love what? Please . . . *what?*"

The man exhales, the fumes from his overwide mouth moist and heavy. Now Till sees that the corners of the man's mouth have been sliced to make the opening bigger. When he smiles, the flesh opens all the way to his back teeth.

"Whaddaya mean, 'what'?" The man stretches his mouth a little wider.

"What you've done," Till breathes.

"Don't you know?"

No, no . . . Till's head lolls right to left.

"We've modified you . . . you'll like it."

Modified . . .

Modified . . .

2

TODAY

The rain crashes down as if floodgates in heaven have opened. It's night; the clouds hanging low and heavy over the city, dumping water in cascades, seem only to make the night darker. Through the raindrops tumbling and spilling earthward, Butz just barely makes out the officer standing at the side of the road; he's waving to him. Butz slows his speed, pulls over to the curb, and rolls down the passenger-side window.

"It's just down here, Mr. Butz," the officer yells at him through the window. Raindrops stream over the shiny visor of his cap and fall into the car. "You can leave the car with me; I'll park it a bit farther down with the others."

Butz leaves the key in the ignition, shoves open the driver-side door, and jumps out. In seconds, his jacket and shirt are soaked through. He dashes around the car to the trunk, jerks it open, and takes out an umbrella. As he snaps it open and slams the lid of the trunk, the car is already moving again. Butz looks around.

From under the rim of his umbrella he can make out another officer—also under an umbrella—standing on the sidewalk and looking in his direction. Butz splashes through the water rushing a half-inch deep over the asphalt. A flash of lightning silently illuminates the facades of the apartments lining the street.

The man waiting for him calls out, "I'll show you the way, Inspector"—then the thunder booms overhead. The roar of the rain intensifies; the thunderstorm seems to be reaching its peak.

In silence, they walk a few paces past the house that Butz stopped in front of. On the next lot, instead of another apartment block, there is only a wooden fence. Entrance gates wide enough for large trucks to roll through stand open.

The officer turns to Butz. Butz nods and they enter the construction site.

Butz has driven by this fence once or twice in the past few months. But he never realized the size of the building site on the other side. It extends as far back as Invalidenstrasse—the street parallel to where Butz left his car, a good hundred and fifty yards north—and stretches across a frontage wide enough for five or six apartment blocks. The site has already been excavated with heavy equipment for the foundations. In a flash of lightning, two steel machines slant out over Butz's head—massive cranes, already standing in the pit. The unrelenting rain streams down the sodden gravel ramp leading into the hole. With every step Butz and the officer make as they descend, the windowless wall of the bordering apartment block to the right seems to loom higher and higher.

Butz wipes a hand across his face as he walks. It's as though he's been pushed underwater, it's that wet. He raises his eyes. Down below, at the lowest point of the excavation, he can see the pale headlights of several cars sliding over the first concrete foundations, already laid.

"Is the emergency doctor here?" He has to yell to make himself heard over the noise of the rain.

The officer in front of him stops and looks at him. "Not yet, but he'll be here any second—the ambulance, too. You're the first, apart from some of our guys."

The headlight beams cross and swing apart again, then come to a standstill, focused on one point. Butz sees a driver's door swing open; a black silhouette climbs out and takes a few steps in the direction indicated by the headlights.

He stumbles on.

A clap of thunder rips through the air. Butz flinches, slips in the streaming mud on the ramp, and catches himself. The officer leading is already ten yards ahead. Butz only catches up with him when they pass the cars at the base of the pit. His shoes are caked with mud, his pants saturated. He moves past the cars to the men gathered at the spot where the headlight beams converge.

Her face is almost white with the light of the headlights shining on her. Her hair hangs in heavy strands over her forehead.

She wears a tight T-shirt and over that a shiny jacket. Jeans. Flip-flops. Her body is lying half-propped against the embankment that leads back out of the pit. Butz pushes between the officers and kneels beside the woman. His hands sink to the knuckles in mud as he braces against the ground.

"I checked her vitals; there's nothing left." An officer squats next to him and shouts over the rain into Butz's ear.

A siren can be heard in the distance, drawing closer.

The woman's eyes are aimed directly at Butz and seem to be floating in the water running over her face. With the tip of his right index finger, he lifts a corner of her jacket. The T-shirt underneath shines blackly, as if a bottle of ink has been tipped over it. At the level of her navel, a spot the diameter of a cork catches Butz's eye. The cloth of the T-shirt is torn open right there. Butz pinches his eyes closed and has to swallow hard for a moment. He was staring straight into the wound. Numb, he turns to the officer. The wailing of the siren subsides.

"That's still lying there." The man awkwardly indicates something in the mud two steps away from the woman.

A rechargeable electric drill.

"Looks like it was rammed into her stomach."

Butz nods, shifts his weight forward, and looks at her face for a moment.

The drone of the rain seems to pull away from him slightly. Behind them, the engine of the approaching ambulance can be heard, then the clack of the vehicle's door.

Butz's heart skips a beat. Her lips!

His eyes flick back to hers.

In the same moment, the emergency doctor frantically pushes past Butz. He shines a tiny flashlight directly into the woman's pupils. Through the rain, Butz sees them contract.

"She's alive!"

The man beside Butz throws up his arms and waves to the ambulance, which has stopped farther back. The blue light on the roof flashes to life and begins to rotate again. With a loud shriek, the siren begins to wail.

And as everything around him starts to move, Butz kneels in the mud next to the woman—her ice-cold hand in his.

3

TODAY

She's propelled to her feet. She's got the little Leica in her hands and snaps off a shot as she rises. Arching above her, Lubajew's massive back strains against the ring ropes and for a second she thinks they'll snap under his weight. Then his body is flung back into the ring. She catches a flash of Frederik's face over the Russian's shoulder. His eyes are nearly closed, his lips stretched over his mouth guard. His head is tilted and she can see his scalp through sweat-soaked hair—then his body tenses and his left arm reaches back, just as Lubajew flies forward. There is a crunch; she clasps the camera to her chest, clicks. The Russian's head twists. He has his back to her, and she sees his lower jaw shoot forward. Something hits her in the eye. She raises the Leica in her right hand, clicks, wipes her eye with her left. Frederik lands a second right to his opponent's head.

Claire looks at her hand; it's smeared with blood. She sees a fine trail of spray angled across her shirt. Above her, the Russian bellows. She takes a step to one side; behind her she hears yelling from the spectators whose view she's blocking by standing. She ignores them. The pictures are sensational. Instinctively, she selects a larger aperture to throw everything out of focus, apart from the two boxers. Frederik looks like a dancer now—a bloodthirsty dancer. He goes after the Russian, hitting him in the throat, ears, mouth, neck. Claire sees the referee's arm forced between the two men, but Frederik is unstoppable.

It's as if he's become part of the Russian, slamming his right fist into the man's side like a piston, over and over.

Claire raises the camera to her eye. Through the lens, the scene looks flash frozen: hard, black-and-white contrast; the low angle; the white shirt of the referee, who clutches at Frederik's shoulder. Lubajew staggers back. They're climbing over the ropes in the opposite corner. Lubajew falls. Claire sees the Russian's body slam onto the mat, bounce. He raises one arm. Frederik crouches over him like a tiger, his right fist poised to strike. The Russian's head is rolling from side to side. Claire squeezes the shutter. Lubajew's eyes are swollen shut; the skin under his ear is split open. She smells the odor of copper rising from him.

Frederik rocks back—his arms in the air. Three men have reached him. The referee's face is twisted in an expression of indignation, his mouth moving incessantly. Claire looks at Frederik: he's dancing. Stretched high over his head, his gloved fists clap to the rhythm of the crowd chanting his name. Everyone jumps from their seats; Claire feels herself being pushed forward as the throng crowds the ring. Someone jolts the arm holding the Leica just as she clicks off a shot. Heads shove in front of her, the smell of sweat stings her nose.

She lets the camera hang on the strap around her neck and grabs the lowest of the four ropes. Her sneakers find a grip on one of the empty seats. She pushes off, ducks low, and is standing in the ring.

Frederik has his arms wrapped around the men trying to lift him up. His head swings around; his eyes glint. She laughs. His chin tilts upward. Claire presses herself against the ropes and edges along, circling the group soaking up the audience's acclaim in the middle of the ring. No one pays attention to her; no one stops or questions her. The roll of film in the Leica is finished and she takes out a digital camera. Then she is standing only two steps away from him. This is the shot she will later use for the cover of her Berlin book: Frederik's head partially cut off by the frame, his naked torso towering in front of the observer like the chest of a rearing horse. His mouth is slightly open, twisted, high on victory, and his gloved hands are angled over his head. Looking directly at the observer, his face sliced by the camera, one eye gleams brightly.

"Everybody out! Come on, people. Just a few minutes. That's how she wants it. Come on now." His voice reverberates in the low concrete room. He's wearing the championship belt; a doctor has swabbed his cuts superficially. The victory, the force of the impact of Lubajew hitting the mat under Frederik's fists, it all still seems to be coursing through his system.

He smiles at her. "Okay."

Okay, thinks Claire.

She doesn't know the names of the men crowded around him. His trainers, friends, brothers, managers all jabbering loudly, filling the room with noise.

She sees how they bow their heads when he tousles their hair with his huge mitt, how they try to catch his eye, how they treat him with respect.

"Out!" he shouts, and laughs.

A frail, dried-out-looking old man is the last to leave, shuffling out of the changing room. Then Frederik turns back and faces her.

"You sure this is a good idea?" His eyes gleam. "This ain't exactly a beautiful spot."

Steel lockers line the wall. Benches, sports bags with his promoter's logo. It's exactly what she's looking for.

"Sit down." Claire has reloaded the Leica. "This is what I've been waiting for."

"Oh yeah?"

She purses her lips, buries her face behind the camera. He drops onto a bench and looks uncertainly in her direction. Through the lens, his features are reduced to the bare essentials. There's something mischievous there—something candid, almost noble. She squeezes herself into the farthest corner of the changing room, letting the sudden silence work on both of them. She wants the uproar that surrounded him until a moment before to drain away first.

Frederik breathes out, leans back against the wall. "And now?"

She looks at him over the camera. "That's fine, Mr. Barkar. Fabulous." She crouches on the floor and frames the whole room in her viewfinder. Through it, she sees an endless expanse of floor; the ceiling is as wide as the heavens above.

Click. Clickclickclick.

She sees him stand. Click click. She leans to the side, framing him vertically. He moves toward her. His boxer's boots, laced almost as high as his calves, fill half the image. Claire angles the camera upward and the neon light behind his head shines directly into her lens. It happens so naturally that she isn't surprised at all. His arms come down, grasp her waist—she feels herself being lifted up. She doesn't need to think twice. For a moment, she's floating, then her legs encircle his hips and her feet lock together behind his back. With his torso he pushes her back gently against the cement wall; his hands grip her thighs, his eyes seem on fire. She feels like a doll—and at the same time senses how every press of her thighs shoots through him like an electric shock. He reaches under her skirt with both hands and pulls carefully, and the seam of her panties bursts. She presses her naked skin hotly against his body.

It has begun.

My God.

My God, what have I done?

Me.

Me?

Isn't this how it had to be? *Wasn't it unavoidable? Did I have any other choice? Wasn't it necessary, inescapable, inevitable? Wasn't it a force of nature, a thrust, a surge, that I was practically tied—nailed!—to the front of?*

He *was the one who started it. Without him, none of it would have happened. Without him, the night that's devouring us now never would have fallen. It's not me dwelling in the heart of the night.* He *is the one who set it all in motion.*

Till.

If Till hadn't run away from Brakenfelde, things never would have gone this far.

TWELVE YEARS AGO

Till ran. He knew that if they went in now and found his bed empty, they'd sound the alarm in an instant. The sun was already below the horizon, the sky not yet completely black, but down below in the trees he was running through, it was already dark. The fallen leaves rustled and the ground was springy under his feet. Every step was a small victory, a leap in the right direction. Away from the home; it was behind him now—he would never go back!

Whack! A thin branch whipped him in the face. He ducked, ran around the tree, hurried on. He had left the main road that led back to Brakenfelde and slipped into the underbrush, heading cross-country. It was safer here.

Spit collected in his mouth as he stumbled on, and he balled his hands into fists. He had sworn to himself never to cry again—never again—but the tears were practically boring into the back of his eyes.

He fought against it but was utterly overwhelmed by the pain that had been waiting subconsciously in ambush for him. In spite of himself, Till's bottom lip edged forward and tears fell on his hands. He ran on, gritting his teeth, telling himself that he had made a vow—but the insides of his little body were churning up.

Trembling, he threw his hands over his face; it was soaking wet.

Armin was gone—that was it. And that's why he had run away.

****

"Hey, Tillster? Everything cool down below?"

He could still see Armin lying on his bed, arms crossed behind his head, and how he looked at Till as he came into the room.

"Everything's cool—what's the matter?" Till had replied.

"What's the matter with what?" Armin had his eyes glued on the ceiling again.

"Well . . . with you."

"Don't know."

"Maybe we could work on our boat," Till had said, trying again from square one.

"Hmm." That was all Armin had said: "Hmm." But they used to spend hours talking about their boat, a real sailboat, without a cabin but with a real mast.

"So that's it for the boat, then?" Till had asked—and in the sound of his own voice he could hear how much he was getting on his brother's nerves with all these questions.

"Don't know," Armin had answered.

Till lay down next to him on the bed and stared at the ceiling, too. "What's the matter, Armi?" he asked. "Are you sad?"

Armin hadn't answered. Till turned his head and looked at Armin; his brother's face had turned deathly pale. Armin gave Till a look, as if he wanted to tell him something, but then just shook his head and looked at the ceiling again.

They'd had no more time that evening. Dirk showed up and bitched that Till should have been downstairs ages ago; it was past bedtime. Till had stuck it out a little longer, but then Dirk started raising his voice and Armin said that it really would be better if he went. So he finally had no other choice. He got up and marched downstairs to his own room . . .

. . . not suspecting for a second that he'd never speak to his brother again.

****

Till's gaze swept across the tables set up outside of the restaurant. They were all vacant, but one table had a plate of noodles drowned in red sauce, piled up at least an inch over the edge of the plate. Still steaming! He squinted his eyes to peer inside the restaurant. Through the window, he could make out the hazy outlines of more tables and chairs. But there was no one in sight. He looked back at the plate on the unoccupied table.

He'd spent the night in the forest and awoke in the morning in a pile of leaves. Freezing, famished, and afraid, he'd come here—to Alexanderplatz—by train, knowing that homeless kids sometimes hooked up here. But he hadn't seen a single kid who didn't look like he knew exactly where he belonged. And now all he saw was the plate on the table outside the restaurant. The entire enormous public square around Till seemed to converge on this one plate.

The waiter who'd just been eating the pasta had been called inside the restaurant by another employee—and had simply left the plate sitting there. Abandoned. Hot. And it smelled delicious!

As if driven by an unseen hand, Till began to move, his head turned stubbornly to the left as though what held his attention was something on the other side of the square. Should he sit and bolt down the noodles? No way! If the waiter saw him, he wouldn't just stand around and wait for Till to finish up then clear away the empty dish.

One last step and Till had reached the table. No one was paying any attention to him. He grabbed the plate, turned, and marched back into the square with his loot in his hands.

Local trains clattered into the station, and passersby hurried about their business; the sun shone from a deep-blue sky above the city.

Something hit him on the back of his head. Till instinctively drew his head down between his shoulders. It couldn't be; it wasn't possible!

He felt a second blow, this one even harder than the first—a knock that rocked his head sideways and made him so mad that he wheeled around.

In front of him stretched the black vest of the waiter.

He acted without thinking, pushing the plate of noodles into the man's belly. He saw worms of spaghetti squirming from the sides of the plate, then spun around and ran. He could hear the shouts and footsteps of his pursuer right behind him.

Till could barely feel his feet touching the ground. It was almost as if he were floating through the air. There was no heart thumping sluggishly in his chest, no lungs to feel small and crushed, no legs hanging leaden from his body, and no feet that had to roll from heel to toe. All there was was a will, a power, an urge pushing him forward. He was flying, floating; his movement interrupted only by the tips of his toes delicately touching ground again and again as they catapulted him ahead—five, ten, forty yards at once with their incredible thrust.

Weightless and unfettered, he crossed the space in front of the television tower, its tip already bathed in sunlight. The ground under his gliding feet seemed to contain the last remnants of the cold, moist night.

And then, the soundless, euphoric sense of being borne along was ripped apart. His own ragged gasping finally reached him. He heard the thudding of his legs striking the ground like wooden poles, his hammering heart, his wheezing lungs. As much as he had soared at first, he now battled forward clumsily. There was no longer a tailwind to lift his wings and carry him forward; instead, he was dragged down by a force of gravity seemingly multiplied by ten.

Till felt his backpack dancing on his back and sensed that the man behind him was reaching out to grab him. He saw the busy road that cut the square in two up ahead, coming closer with every step. He'd already made it to the parked cars, was past them, the Spree River, the cathedral, the linden trees in front of him when suddenly his feet lost touch with the ground beneath.

A sharp pressure in his side—a delayed screech, a crash, and a piercing pain in his chest—then a blow, as if the asphalt itself had reared up to hit him in the head.

Then everything was silent.

A car tire: Till was looking right at it. Behind that he could see the suspension and the undercarriage of the car caked in black. He saw a pair of women's shoes with medium heels appear on the other side of the car, descend to the asphalt, and disappear from view again.

Till rolled onto his back. There were forms bending over him.

They looked quickly this way and that and their mouths moved, but he couldn't make out what they were saying or if they were actually saying anything at all. Two men—one younger, one somewhat older—and a fat woman with a coarse face. Then a hand was laid on his shoulder, a touch like a butterfly landing, and he smelled a scent he had never smelled before.

The face of a woman came between him and the sky he was looking into. She looked frightened, and her hair hung so low that it almost brushed his forehead. A thin chain dangled around her neck. She wore lipstick and her lips were moving, but he couldn't hear what she was saying. There was just a distant noise that made it seem as if someone had stuffed his ears with cotton.

Till smiled and saw the woman's face brighten a little. She looked up at one of the men standing over her.

". . . still on hold, they have to pick up soon," seeped through to him, and he noticed for the first time that she had a cell phone pressed to her ear.

He gasped. "What?" His voice boomed in his ears.

"Take it easy, kid," he heard someone behind him say.

He turned his head and found himself looking into the genial face of a man kneeling behind him on the ground. "We're calling an ambulance." Till jerked upright and managed to brace himself with one arm, his head almost colliding with the woman's as he did so.

"What for? I'm okay!" They'd find out who he was in a second. They'd send him back! Till saw the woman giving him a puzzled look.

"I don't need a doctor!" He jumped to his feet. His legs trembled but he took no notice.

Just then, the expression on the woman's face changed.

"Yes, Julia Bentheim here," she said into the phone, also rising to her feet.

"No!" Till was close to tears. This couldn't be happening! He couldn't manage it a second time; he wouldn't be able to run away again. Couldn't she see that? "Please, Mrs. Bentheim, really, I'm fine It's just . . ." he rasped.

"Wait a moment," she said into the phone and looked at him. "You can't take an accident like that lightly—" A long blast of a horn interrupted her. Only now did Till notice that they were standing in the middle of the street in front of the car that the woman had climbed out of, and that they were blocking traffic.

The jam extended up the street behind the woman's car. Through the windshields of the other cars Till could see the perplexed, pleading, resentful faces of the drivers.

"You can't just send the kid off in the shape he's in," the man who had been kneeling behind Till spoke up. "He needs to be examined!" He looked the woman up and down skeptically.

"Yes." She nodded her head. "He does, of course . . ." She looked at Till. "I have to make sure that you're okay. Try to understand." Till sensed how pale he must look. The hunger, the night spent in the forest, the shock of the accident. He would have liked to just lie back down on the asphalt and go to sleep.

"No, hold on," he heard the woman say into her phone. "I'll call back in a minute." She slipped the phone into the pocket of her loose-fitting pants and leaned toward him. "You don't want that? No ambulance?"

He shook his head. "I'm okay, really." The blare of car horns ripped through the air.

The woman took his arm. "Let's get you off the street first. I'm holding up traffic." He nodded, trotted between the parked cars to the sidewalk, listened to the woman behind him talking to the crowd. Then he felt her hand once again touching his shoulder.

"I can't let you go in this state." She had followed him and now looked back at her car, which the other vehicles had begun to drive around. "Do you have a phone? No, wait, just give me the number and I'll call your mother." She pulled out her phone again. "I need to sort this out now."

Till exhaled. "It's okay, Mrs. Bentheim, honestly. I'll just sit on a bench for a bit and I'll be fine."

"It's probably the shock." She smiled.

Horns started blaring again. The traffic flowed around the woman's car for only a moment before jamming up again against the oncoming vehicles.

"Come with me," she said, and pointed to her car. "Jump in, okay? I have to get off the street." Till glanced at her car. A Jaguar—he'd already registered that—an old-fashioned model. He could dimly make out the figures of two children peering out at him from the backseat.

"You can sit up front," he heard the woman beside him saying, "Okay?"

He looked at her uncertainly.

"I'm driving him to a doctor," she said, gesticulating to the passersby who'd stayed behind, waiting between the parked cars. "Well, come on." She smiled at Till and it was clear to him that she wouldn't be able to just drive away even if she'd wanted to.

"Okay." Still somewhat dazed, he let her lead him back to the street. He'd never been in a Jaguar before. An old XJ, he guessed, probably with a real Daimler emblem on the back. The woman pulled open the passenger door.

"Can we get going again, Mama?" he heard from behind. The face of a young girl appeared from the backseat. She was slightly older than the other child, who sat next to her in a second child's seat.

"In a minute," answered the woman and smiled at Till. "We'll get going again in a minute, Claire."

****

Julia Bentheim looked at the pale boy sitting beside her in the passenger seat. It was obvious that he wasn't as unscathed as he'd like her to believe.

"Still in one piece?" She wheeled the heavy auto forward, rolling slowly past the parked cars. The boy seemed to be thinking it over.

"What's your name?"

"Till."

"Till who?"

"Till Anschütz. Mrs. Bentheim?"

"Mm-hmm." She was concentrating on the traffic.

"I don't want you to take me to a doctor."

Julia sighed. "Listen, Till, it's probably best if I give your mom a quick call." She turned to face him for a moment. "Then we'll see what happens after that, okay?"

Till stared fixedly straight ahead.

"Don't you know her number?" He shook his head without looking at her.

"What about your father?" No reaction.

Julia turned to the front again. "Well, then. This is what we'll do. I'll take you to a hospital, right now. It's better that way." She regretted having canceled the ambulance.

"My mother's at work, Mrs. Bentheim," she heard him murmur beside her. "I don't want to bug her, you know? It's really important she doesn't get disturbed at work, 'cause she needs the job. If she hears I'm in the hospital, she'll just drop everything and come. She'll lose her job—and then what?"

Julia hesitated. How was she supposed to know that?

"Then she'll be crying again 'cause we won't be able to pay the rent anymore. And we'll get kicked out of the apartment. And it took a long time. She was so happy when we found the place." He leaned forward and lowered his voice. "Okay, it's just a little place on the second floor, but my mom has a little balcony. She's so happy to have a balcony! She's planted all her flowers there and she spends all her free time out there. We even use it for playing Parcheesi." He leaned back again. "But she always says if she loses her job, we won't be able to afford it anymore!"

"But she wouldn't lose her job just for collecting her son from the hospital." Julia stopped; the traffic light in front of her was red.

When she turned to him, Till looked her straight in the eye. She waited in vain for him to reply. But all he did was shrug his shoulders; then he grabbed the door handle and pulled it.

"You don't understand." He shoved the door open.

"What if our pediatrician takes a look at you?" He turned back. "I just have to be sure you're okay." Julia looked at the traffic light. Still red. "But I have to get home, too; the girls really need something to eat."

"Listen, Till," she said, and looked at him again. "We'll swing by home quickly first. That's down in Dahlem, but it's not that far away anymore. Our pediatrician can check you over there and if nothing's the matter, we don't need to say a word to your mother about it, do we? How about it?" She saw the boy mulling it over.

"Dr. Trimborn is just the guy, right?" said Julia, glancing at the backseat.

"Right," came the immediate reply.

She looked at Till again. "Can you do that? Do you have someplace you have to be?"

For the first time, it struck her that he could use a shower. And his shorts and blue pullover certainly didn't look as clean as they might. Would it be imprudent to take the boy home with her?

"Nah," said Till. "That's okay."

"Great!" She smiled. The boy did have a particular charm.

Till leaned over to the door, which was still hanging open, reached for the handle, and slammed it closed again. At the same time, a horn sounded behind her. The light was green and Julia sped away.

Beside her, Till reached for the seat belt and pulled it diagonally across his chest and clicked the buckle.

A thought suddenly shot through Julia's mind: *He's buckling himself onto me.* But she was so relieved to have finally found a solution that the thought didn't trouble her for long.

TODAY

The emergency doctor's eyes flare at Butz over the face mask. "No. I don't think so." His eyelids close.

Butz can barely make out what the man says. Sirens are screaming in his ear and the men around him are shouting to each other.

Someone shoves him aside.

"Can I ride along? In the back?" Butz has grabbed hold of the doctor's sleeve again.

"No. Out of the question."

"Look, the woman's dying . . ." Butz dodges to one side. Two paramedics have laid her on a gurney; metal rods clatter, wheels fold away, rails click into place. They slide her into the back of the ambulance.

". . . you said so yourself." The rain drips from Butz's glasses. The man in front of him is no more than a blurry form. "I have to talk to her. She may still be able to tell me something."

The doctor turns away. "Do what you have to do." He springs into the ambulance and holds out his hand. Butz reaches out . . .

The ambulance motor roars to life; in dull pulses its flashing lights illuminate the place where they found her—the officers, the mudhole they're still standing in—washing it all in an uneasy glow.

Butz's fingers close around the emergency doctor's hand, he pushes off with his feet, and the back door of the ambulance slams shut behind him.

He can sense the driver hitting the gas, can feel the flat vibrations of the driveshaft under his feet. A low, intermittent beeping penetrates the wall of noise around him.

His eyes flick around the narrow interior of the vehicle: monitors, cables, tubes. An assistant doctor fits an oxygen mask over the woman's mouth and nose, pressing the device onto her face. The emergency doctor throws back the thermal blanket covering her and Butz turns his head to avoid seeing the injury.

As the doctor begins to treat the wound, the woman's body begins to tremble. The two doctors exchange a look. Butz notices the emergency doctor nod to his colleague, who removes the transparent mask from the woman's face. Butz leans his face close to hers; his cheek is almost touching her lips—he can sense them moving.

"Hhhhhrggg." More a breath than a sound.

"What?"

Butz turns his head and finds himself looking into wide-open eyes whose shine now has something dazzling about it, like a lightbulb just before it burns out. Instinctively, he pushes his hand under her head, as if by doing so he could somehow stop her from slipping away.

Just then, the ground gives way and Butz is thrown against the wall of the ambulance with a thud. The engine howls and the ambulance lurches to a stop.

The assistant doctor bangs open the back door of the ambulance, allowing the rain to whip inside. The pit opens blackly below them; they've made it only halfway up the ramp. The ambulance has sunk into the muddy track, the wheels scrabbling in the muck.

Butz looks at the woman again. The noise of the racing motor seems to be coming from directly behind his eyes. He feels her hand touching his arm—then the glow in her eyes is washed away by a cloudy wave.

Butz presses himself back against the wall of the ambulance to make room for the emergency doctor. The beeping sound transforms into a steady tone.

In the same moment, the tires once again take hold in the soft earth and the ambulance leaps forward. Butz's gut clenches and he sinks his mouth into the crook of his arm.

The assistant doctor glances in his direction. Butz nods, yes, he wants to get out. He pushes behind the doctor to the back door, which is still hanging open, and jumps out into the night. The rain descends on him in glowing, white strands from what seems to be an infinite height. The ambulance has stopped again; the siren has been switched off, the blue light extinguished. Around Butz everything is black except the yellow rectangle, the interior of the ambulance, glowing in the darkness. Inside, the two doctors are shutting down the still-blinking equipment, the strangely motionless, shrunken body of the young woman still lying between them.

****

"Think you could let me borrow that?" asks Butz, nodding toward the heavy flashlight held aloft by a cop's bent arm. "They're about done." He indicates the officers whom the young cop is illuminating as they set up a floodlight.

Clicking, whirring, crackling—then the blinding beam from the floodlight's halogen lamp washes the ground between the vehicles with light. The cop shrugs and hands Butz the flashlight.

"There's a Starbucks up top. I saw it coming in." Butz takes the flashlight. "Go get yourself a cup of coffee." He points the light toward the back of the excavation. "I'm going to poke around here till you're done, then I'll let you have this back." Without waiting for an answer, he stomps away, heading in the direction he has indicated.

The rain has finally let up. In the pool of light that moves ahead of him over the ground, Butz can see tire tracks, puddles, and some concrete structures already poured. He takes care not to stumble, moving slowly away from the spot where the body was found. Outside the glare of the floodlight, the night sky shimmers a deep blue. The voices of the officers milling around where she had lain slowly sink away into the night's hum. At the edge of the pit loom the silhouettes of the apartment blocks on the adjoining properties—some still with firewalls left from wartime—their blank facades only broken high up on the fourth or fifth floors, where tiny postwar windows have been chiseled out.

Butz wanders on, lighting up the ground. The woman's death has hit him hard. He doesn't know what he's looking for; he only knows that he's not ready to leave the pit where she was found, not yet.

He comes to the cement foundations of a basement, low walls already poured.

Concrete pillars jut at regular intervals, rebar struts reaching up to the night sky like bony fingers, thin and crooked. Butz plays the light over the cement and notices that the basement walls seem to have been built to just under three feet high. Beyond the walls is the embankment, sloping a good twenty-five feet above him to street level.

Butz resolves to make a wide arc and return to the other officers, from his vantage point just small figures standing in the glistening light from the halogen floodlight. He begins to make his way along the side of the foundations. The rain has washed mud down from the embankment, heavily in places. Here and there small streams still trickle down the slope.

Butz slows his steps and turns around. He plays the flashlight uncertainly over the ground. There! He stops with the beam aimed at a black shadow about halfway up the earthen embankment.

What is that?

He slides the flashlight into the side pocket of his jacket, sets both hands on top of the wall of the concrete basement, and pushes off.

The rough surface of the cement cuts into the meat of his hands, and then his foot finds a grip on the top edge. He kneels, then stands.

Carefully, he takes the flashlight out of his jacket pocket, shining it into the shadow that appears to be bored into the embankment less than ten feet over his head.

Butz reaches high with the arm holding the flashlight. Then he sees it. A fine trickle of water shoots out of the shadow. It comes straight out of the embankment—from a shaft driven horizontally into the earth.

$$****$$

"The rain must have opened it up!" The site manager is a tall, heavy man in his midfifties. Butz looks practically skinny next to him. "I've never seen that shaft before." The manager shakes his head. "It's not on the plans, either."

The beam of light from the flashlight dances across the blueprint that Butz and the site manager are holding between them. An occasional raindrop splats onto the paper.

"This shows the adjoining buildings." The site manager points at the floor plan with a meaty index finger. "Could the shaft be part of the sewer system?" He looks at Butz. Butz frowns.

"You think there's a connection with the dead girl?" The site manager takes the plan out of Butz's hand. He's been there only a few minutes, since the officers called him on his cell phone.

Butz looks up at the tunnel and hands the manager the flashlight. "Could you shine the light on it for me?" He climbs on top of the concrete wall again.

"What's the idea?" The site manager shines the beam from the flashlight directly into Butz's face. "You want to go climbing around here? In the middle of the night?"

"Just looking."

"But you can see the rain's washed everything down," the builder's deep voice rattles. "You can't see a thing in the dark anyway! Come back down—what the hell, man?"

Butz jumps off the low concrete wall and lands softly in the loose soil of the embankment on the other side.

"Anything happens here and it's my goddamned ass on the line!" he hears the manager grumbling behind him.

"Settle down; of course it's not." Butz feels his hands sink into the mud as he starts to scramble up the bank. "Put some light on it, at least." The light from the flashlight slides up past Butz, over the ground, and comes to rest on the mouth of the shaft, now directly over his head.

Butz straightens up and looks into the opening. For a moment, he has the impression of cool air wafting from the tunnel.

"Can you see anything?"

Butz turns. The site manager is standing in the foundation of the basement below, looking up.

"Not yet."

Butz fishes a pocket flashlight from his jacket, snaps it on, and aims the beam down the shaft.

The passage is no more than three feet high, the same across. No cables, no lamps, no masonry. A tunnel dug into the earth without the slightest protection, the floor glistening and moist. The rain has seeped through and collected on the floor of the tunnel. From there it trickles in a small stream to the end of the passage and out to the outside world.

It's as if someone has taken hold of Butz's hair and jerked his head back.

He hears something. With a jump, he's inside the opening. Ducking low, on all fours. Every muscle in his body tensed.

"Are you crazy? Inspector!" The site manager's voice reaches him from below.

Butz ignores him. He clamps the flashlight in his mouth, which lets him move ahead on all fours and still light the way.

It's not the sound of trickling water. Not traffic. Not some blast of air. It's a rustling, scraping, snuffling sound.

He scoots into the passage. Now he can hear it clearly. It sounds like a pack of dogs, all crammed together, squirming in the tunnel.

He feels his head bump the roof of the tunnel as he scuttles along.

The site manager's voice rumbles behind him, as if from another world.

Butz suddenly stops.

What's that?

He holds his breath.

Silence.

Something flashed. Up ahead. A long way ahead.

Didn't it?

The light from his flashlight wavers. Butz shifts his weight to his left arm, takes the flashlight out of his mouth with his right hand.

He stabilizes the beam. A hundred feet ahead, the passage turns a corner.

"Pfffsssslsssspfffff."

"Hello?"

Rats. And if it *is* rats . . . ?

Butz instinctively aims the light at the floor of the shaft. The water drains between his legs, but there are no creatures in sight.

"Anyone there?"

Nothing.

He looks around. He's about sixty feet into the shaft. Behind him, he can see the mouth of the tunnel and the night, a curtain of glittering points: raindrops, reflecting the beam from his flashlight. It has started to rain again.

Butz exhales and listens to the distant murmur of the rain. For just a moment, time seems to stand still.

Then he notices the little rivulet of water in the middle of the tunnel. It was as thin as a pencil, but now it practically covers the entire width of the passage.

It's as if someone shoves him to the right—the tunnel wall next to him collapses along a six-yard front.

"Aaaarrhh!" Butz's own cry propels him forward.

How could he have been so reckless?

Now he's flying. And the tunnel's walls around him are giving way. He's no longer scrambling on all fours; he's running, bent low, his back scraping the tunnel roof. He pushes off from the side walls with his hands, first left, then right. And can feel the sodden earth around him sagging together.

The stream he's running through is transforming into a gullet of sludge.

"It's slipping! Butz! It's caving in!" The site manager's voice rings loud. Butz pushes off, sets himself for the jump from the tunnel mouth—then, as if it has arms, the mud reaches out for him, grabs him by the feet, rolls over him from behind, and presses his head into the floor of the passage. He can see the earth sealing the exit, the full weight of the mass pressing his face into the ground. The palms of his hands are squashed against his eyes, mouth, and nose, as if crushed by a steamroller . . . At the very last second, he manages to throw his hands in front of his face.

It is completely still. Completely dark.

The palms of Butz's hands are pressing into his face. He can't get any air.

Hmmm hmmmmhmhmhhmm . . . the life is flowing out of him. He's got a minute, maybe two . . .

He can't think. All he can do is push against this pit of no return. Panic.

The pressure on his chest.

The blood in his brain feels like it's boiling.

He presses his hands together in desperation and pushes them back into the dirt. He manages to get them a fraction of an inch, a hairbreadth from his face, forcing a rift in front of his nose, his mouth, his eyes. There!

Butz sucks in air like an industrial extractor through the tiny slit he's formed—his eyelids are lifting from the pressure . . . huuuuuhuuuuh . . .

Farther, farther—a little farther, he draws strength from his success. He is able to use his forearms now, pushes up with all his might—and goes stiff. His desperate exertion has made the muscles in his shoulders cramp and burn.

Huuuhuuuuh . . . huuuuhuuuuuh . . . huuuuuh . . . he's getting dizzy. It's not enough. The gap is too small!

The palms of his hands are still touching the tip of his nose. But the air Butz is sucking into his lungs is already hot; he's breathed it out so many times already. Hot, sticky, poisonous, just the dregs his body has thrown away but he has to inhale it again and again, over and over like a starving man.

His mind drifts. How much longer? A minute? Less?

He's going to die in this mudhole.

Suddenly, another thought seizes him. Why didn't he say good-bye to her properly that morning? He'd thought about turning back, but didn't. *Why not?*

Butz feels his eyes grow moist. He should have told her! He should have taken her in his arms, held her tight, not let her go. But he'd screwed up.

Don't they have an excavator here? Isn't there a single fucking crane on this whole damn site?! Can't they just rip the bank apart and push this goddamned mud off me?

The site manager saw this thing bury him!

Huuuhuuuuh . . .

Butz coughs, chokes. Droplets of saliva catch and hang in the tiny gap he's breathing through.

They can't just let him perish here in this mud.

He feels every muscle petrify, feels the sweat covering his back. But the muck has him in its grip, pressing deeper and deeper into his ears, pushing harder into his sides, his temples, his scalp.

It's his own fault, no one else's, that he never told her. That he never told her how much he loved her.

And now it's too late.

And MAX? If it was Till . . . then what about Max?

Oh, really?

Him too?

And Tom and Dick and Harry and Mary?

Did everything happen because of something you, in truth, were responsible for?

But Max . . . it was through Max that you got to know Till, wasn't it? Max was your friend, my dear. It was with him, with Max, that you spent the afternoons, the nights, the weeks of summer. It was with Max that you traveled, with Max that you drank, talked, laughed. It was with him that you tried to find a way, an opinion, an attitude—a clear view of things!

And now? Now he's supposed to have nothing more to do with any of that?

. . .

Sometimes I can barely remember what he looked like. It's been so long . . . so much has changed . . . I've changed . . .

Then I see him in front of me again: the smooth hair, nearly black, how it stuck out behind his ears; his pale, penetrating eyes.

Max.

Max Bentheim.

6

TWELVE YEARS AGO

Tick tick tick tick tick tick . . .

Max Bentheim stared at the timer perched on top of the grand piano. Just under forty minutes to go. But he wasn't going to let them get him down. It wasn't the first time he'd had to practice the piano and it wouldn't be the last. So it didn't make sense to get so worked up about how unbearable, horrible, unbelievable it was. He tried to convince himself that all he had to do was tink around on the keys a bit and the time would fly by.

He cautiously raised his hands and touched the surface of the keys, but didn't strike them yet. The black-and-white band stretching in front of him sometimes looked to him like a venomous snake that he tried to appease with all his might, but the snake was ruthless and went on biting him.

Tick tick tick tick tick tick . . .

Thirty-eight minutes to go. He tapped on the keys gingerly with his fingertips. The sound wasn't bad. Max glanced up at the sheet music set out for him on the music stand. What would happen if he just ignored the score? Maybe that was the problem. How was he supposed to play music dreamed up by some composer hundreds of years before? Why not follow the music he sensed in himself instead of slavishly repeating a melody that someone else had come up with?

Tick tick tick tick tick . . .

Apart from the ticking of the timer, the house was absolutely quiet. Lisa was probably painting a picture in her room; his mother was still out, picking up Claire and Betty from Gran's. And his father? Out in the guesthouse, as usual.

Max let his fingers dance in the air for a while. No one would hear him. He pulled himself together and his fingers fell heavily onto the keyboard, drawing out a beautiful, rich sound. Satisfied with this initial result, he spread his hands left and right on the keyboard. A sparkling, funny tune; Max's mood brightened. This was okay.

He let his fingers wander back to the middle of the keyboard, this time using the black keys as well to make the sound come out a little more warped. Then he jumped to the left with both hands together, now more springing than running, making the music stronger, angry, almost enraged.

"Now contrast!" he murmured to himself. And as if on command, his leaping hands came back to earth, now more crouching, sweeping together across the keys to the right, the music softer, gentler, more delicate.

Max pressed on both pedals with his feet; the individual notes blurred and blended.

"Fantastic! Now the variation."

He focused on letting his hands follow their own creative urges, each independent of the other; the right the rhythm this time, the left more melodic. And for one moment, he truly had the feeling that his hands would know best what they had to do. He could just lean back and listen to what they were playing for him—as if they had actually separated from him, allying themselves to some higher spirit that knew how to send them down paths that Max Bentheim alone never would have followed. But then the moment vanished. In its place came the realization that no one but he himself could tell his hands—his fingers—what they had to do. No one but he himself could have any idea of where this journey was going or of how this piece of music was supposed to develop. It was a task whose complexity left Max confused almost as soon as he became aware of it.

He tried doggedly to find a way back to the clarity that he'd just felt so distinctly, the clarity that he'd really heard—not just imagined—in the music he'd been creating. But the more desperately he tried to pull himself back and the more energy he put into trying to surprise himself by once more making that fabulous music, the more dissonant the sounds he brought forth.

"Play through it," he implored himself. "Take what's still in the air and give it a meaning completely new and unexpected, by making sounds that only reveal their true significance later on!" He lashed at the keys, desperately seeking a way out of the ugly hole, but he just dug himself in deeper. With every jarring note he hit, he irretrievably lost the courage that he knew—knew only too well— he would need in order to master the task he had set for himself.

And he kept telling himself over and over that he would not let himself be beaten down. Until, suddenly, he realized he was no longer just hitting the keys with his fingers, but pounding them with his hands, with his elbows even. His forearms and his wrists were hurting and the wood was groaning under the impact. His playing had transformed into something like a battle—a struggle, a spasm, a collapse.

Something banged behind him.

"Are you playing loud enough?!" he heard a girl's voice scream, and spun around.

Lisa was standing in the doorway. She had slammed the door open so hard that the wood had crashed into the wall.

"What? Already done? But you were just getting started!" She glared at him.

Tick tick tick tick tick tick tick . . .

Max glanced at the timer. Thirty-one minutes to go.

Still, he'd made it through seven minutes.

Lisa sniffed. "Just tell Dad you want to stop playing the piano!"

"He'd never let me." Max was still a little out of breath from his exertions.

Lisa approached him, took his hands. She turned the palms up and examined his forearms where his sleeves were rolled back. His skin was red from pounding on the keys.

"Of course he'll let you," she said, releasing his arms. "You just have to tell him the right way."

"Can't *you* tell him?"

"Nah."

Her answer didn't surprise Max. He slumped forward on the piano stool with his back curved. In his head he replayed the notes that his music had begun with. This time, just playing them over in his mind and not trying to pound them out, he succeeded in developing the piece at just the point he'd turned in the wrong direction minutes before.

This time, instead of getting lost in increasingly discordant noise, it swung to a crescendo of effects and surprises that seemed to go straight to the ceiling and beyond.

Max looked up. He wanted to call to his sister and tell her that through his improvisation he may finally have found the right way to come to grips with the piano. But the room around him was empty again.

Lisa had left him alone.

✳✳✳✳

When Mrs. Bentheim turned the car onto the shady estate where the Bentheims' white villa stood, Till's first impression was of a veranda with massive columns, trees with outstretched branches, and a flight of stairs curving in a grand arc to a windowed porch.

Till was reminded of antiquated plantation manors in the American South. Although he knew the houses only from television, he had always loved them. He imagined the atmosphere at once shaded and sultry, with the distant roars of alligators in the air. In the upper stories of the splendid houses, beautiful women under enormous fans dreamed up intrigues to play their bullnecked husbands against some man lying beneath a classic car behind the house, pulling the engine apart.

Mrs. Bentheim pulled the Jaguar to a halt in the driveway.

Curious, soaking up the details of the building and the front garden, Till followed her from the car to the front door—through which the two girls from the backseat had already disappeared. Wicker chairs and an ornate sofa with a worn silk cover stood on the veranda; some distance to the right, an overgrown hedge hid the neighbor's house from view. Off to the left, the sunlight vanished among the tree trunks of a bordering wood. Alongside the natural stone path, which appeared to lead past the house to a garden behind, was a rectangular pond where pinkish-gray, almost oily-looking fish darted between water lilies.

"Koi," Till heard Mrs. Bentheim say. She was next to him and must have noticed him looking at the fish.

She squatted at the edge of the pond and stretched a hand down to the water. The fish, gliding over one another, swam to her and nudged their noses against her fingertips.

"Mom?"

Till looked up. A girl, older than Claire and Betty, perhaps as old as Till, was coming toward them across the grass. "Where were you?"

"Till, Lisa. Lisa, Till." Mrs. Bentheim stood up again beside him.

Was he supposed to shake the girl's hand?

Till glanced rather uncertainly up at Mrs. Bentheim, but she had turned to her daughter and explained to her in a few words what had happened.

"Come on, Till, we'll call the doctor. How are you feeling, by the way?" She looked at him again.

"Fine." And he was feeling fine, very well indeed. It's just that everything was happening so fast, he was starting to feel a little dizzy.

"Why didn't you want the ambulance to come?"

Till turned around, his mouth full. Behind him, Lisa stepped gracefully into the kitchen.

"Ah, it was nothing. It didn't even really hurt." Till swallowed.

Mrs. Bentheim had led him to the kitchen when he'd hinted that he was a little hungry; a woman whom Mrs. Bentheim had introduced as Rebecca warmed up some soup for him.

"And then you didn't want my mother to call yours." Lisa climbed onto the bar stool on the other side of the elevated table and looked pensively at Till, her pretty mouth closed tightly.

"So what?" Was she trying to interrogate him? Till forced himself to stay calm. The doctor would get there soon and after the examination he'd be on his way again, in any case. She didn't have to worry that he'd break her dollhouse.

"If someone ran into me with a car, I'd definitely call my mom."

That didn't warrant a reply. Till reached for the ladle protruding from the soup tureen and filled his bowl again.

"So, where do you live?" Lisa wasn't letting up.

Till frowned. "Do you really want to know?"

"Sure."

"Why? Why do you want to know that?"

Lisa looked at him thoughtfully. He'd turned the tables and she hadn't expected that.

"Just because."

Till sighed. "Pass the bread?"

The basket, with a few slices of white bread, was closer to her than him. Lisa pushed it across the table without taking her serious gaze off him, which made Till nervous.

Her light-brown hair hung at shoulder length; her lightly tanned face looked so full of life, so graceful, that he practically had to force himself to lower his own eyes before he lost himself completely in hers.

He reached for a slice of bread, dunked it in the soup, and took a bite. He didn't have to chat with her, did he? He could just sit here and eat.

"Mom's totally worried that you've done something to yourself. But if you ask me, you don't look like anything hurts too much."

Till had to grin. *Sheesh, it was nothing, really. A little bump, that's all. They shouldn't get themselves so worked up.*

"You know what?" He looked at her finally. "I didn't want your mom to call my mom because . . ." He knew this was it, the chance he had to take. This was the acid test; he had to do everything just right.

". . . because my mom is dead." It seemed to him that the words had tumbled out of his mouth like toy blocks. *Because my mom is dead.*

Lisa eyes widened.

"I didn't want the emergency guys to come because they would have sent me back."

"Back where?"

"To Brakenfelde."

"What's *that*?" Lisa sounded like she had some inkling it was a place she didn't want to have anything to do with.

"A children's home."

"You live in a home?" she whispered, and Till could tell she was whispering because she didn't want anybody to hear.

He stuffed the rest of the bread into his mouth to delay his reply. When he looked closely he could see a vein pulsing at her throat. He wondered whether it had been pulsing like that before.

Probably because Lisa was wondering if she shouldn't get up and go tell her mother after all. But she just went on sitting there, looking at him.

"Are you going to kick me out now?" Till's eyebrows pulled into a defiant frown. That's what she ought to do. And if she did, it didn't make sense to waste any more of his time here, did it?

But instead she asked, "Why would they send you back?"

"Because I ran away."

She swallowed. "What are you going to do?"

"Dunno."

"Till?" It was Mrs. Bentheim's voice.

He turned around and saw Lisa's mother enter at the doorway. "The doctor's here. Coming? He can look at you right away."

Till glanced at Lisa, who hadn't taken her eyes off him. He didn't say anything, just smiled. He was only eleven, but he knew how mischievous that looked. He slid deftly from the stool and walked over to the kitchen door.

"Sure thing, Mrs. Bentheim. You didn't really have to call the doctor. But okay . . ."

He could see that what Lisa's mother most wanted to do was tousle his hair. But then she didn't.

✳✳✳✳

Brrrrrriiiiiiiiingggg!

The timer rang.

Max sighed and slammed the lid down over the keys of the grand piano. He'd just sat there without moving for the last few minutes anyway. Another successful hour of piano practice! He jumped off the piano stool and strolled jauntily out of the room.

When he reached the entrance hall, he noticed that a number of people had gathered in the living room. Curious, he sauntered through the sliding door and over to the others, then stopped short when his eyes fell on a boy sitting on the sofa, his chest bare, being examined by Dr. Trimborn.

Who's this?

Max looked to his mother, who was sitting in an armchair opposite the sofa and watching the doctor's movements with concern.

Dr. Trimborn seemed satisfied with the outcome of his examination because he nodded at the boy encouragingly. "You can get dressed again." Then the doctor turned to Max's mother. "How fast were you going when it happened?"

"There was a lot of traffic. I was barely moving."

"Well, I think Till here had a guardian angel watching over him." The doctor turned back to the boy, who was in the middle of pulling a long-sleeved T-shirt over his head. "But you did the right thing, calling me. You can never tell."

Max hesitated. Was he mistaken, or was Till's T-shirt rather dirty?

"All four tip-top otherwise?" Dr. Trimborn tossed the stethoscope he'd been using on Till into his old-fashioned doctor's bag, which was standing next to him on the table.

"Just fine." Max's mother stood up, then noticed her son. "Right, Max?"

He grinned. "Just fine, Doc."

"Well, great. See you later, kids," said Dr. Trimborn to the group, grabbing the handle of his doctor's bag.

Max noticed that the boy was looking at him intently, but was careful not to return the look. Instead, he looked over to Lisa, who was sitting in an armchair farther back. He tried to signal her inconspicuously to let her know that he wanted to know who the boy was. But Lisa didn't seem interested in Max anymore, because without giving him a second glance, she jumped from her chair, walked to the door that led outside, and pulled it open.

"Would you like me to show you our garden?" She looked straight at the boy, who had begun to rummage—rather aimlessly, Max thought—through a small nylon backpack, while Max's mother and Dr. Trimborn slowly made their way out of the living room toward the front door.

The boy looked up. "Oh yeah. Super."

'Super?' Where did this one escape from? thought Max.

"You coming, too?" Now Lisa was looking at him.

Max hesitated.

"My name's Till." The boy had stood up from the sofa and come over to him; he was holding out his hand.

"I know." Dr. Trimborn had just said the name.

Max stuffed his fists in his jeans pockets rather than shake Till's proffered hand. This was how Max always preferred to deal with such situations. Or was he being too unfriendly? He was just about to take Till's outstretched hand after all when Till shrugged and stepped past him and through the door leading to the garden, where Lisa was already waiting for him.

✳✳✳✳

"What's Dad working on?" Lisa's shout dragged Max out of his thoughts. He had followed his sister and Till out to the garden and let them get a few steps ahead of him across the grass. Now they were standing by the hedge that separated the back of the property from the rest of the garden. They were looking in his direction.

"No idea." He strolled toward them. "Mom said it was nothing for kids."

Lisa laughed. "Again?"

Max had to smile. "I asked her, but she clammed up. It's too spooky; she reckons I'd get nightmares again. I could read it when I'm old enough, she said."

He noticed the look Till gave Lisa and stopped when he caught up with them.

"He writes novels." Lisa smiled at Till. "Stuff kind of like *Phantom of the Opera, Dr. Jekyll and Mr. Hyde, The Mountains of Madness . . .*"

"D'you know those?" Max looked at Till, well aware that he was the first of the two to engage the other in conversation. But Max was interested now.

"Uh-huh." Till had pursed his lips a little.

"So, what do you like reading?" Max didn't take his eyes off him.

"My brother used to tell me about stuff he thought I should read."

This came as something of a surprise to Max. "Can't you tell what you like to read yourself?" But even as he spoke, he had the impression that a strange shadow, a kind of vulnerability, had come over Till's face . . . and he decided to soften the edge in his voice.

"How'm I supposed to know if a book's any good if I've never read it?" Till said, eyeing him.

Max frowned. True enough.

"Did you ever read one of your dad's books?" asked Till.

Max looked at Lisa for a moment. No, he never had. They weren't allowed. And it was getting worse—now they weren't even allowed to know what he was writing *about*. His father used to tell them he was writing a story about the North Atlantic, or about robots, or about a creature that couldn't die. But these days he just shook his head when Max asked what he was writing about. They weren't even allowed to see the pictures on the covers of the books his father published! His parents kept the copies of his books all the way at the top of the bookshelf in the living room, where neither Max nor Lisa could reach them. One evening, not so long ago, when their parents were at dinner with friends and Rebecca was busy washing the dishes in the kitchen, Lisa had insisted that they look at the books anyway, just once. They had pushed the low coffee table in front of the bookshelf and put a chair from the dining room on that, and then Max climbed up. But when he'd slipped out the first book and glanced at the cover, he understood why his parents hadn't wanted the children to look at them.

He still wasn't sure what the picture on the cover was meant to show. More than anything else it had resembled a worm, a strangely hairless animal that seemed to have fallen victim to some kind of painful cramp, because a web of muscle and sinew was drawn over its face, distorting it into a grimace of torment and decay. It was an image that had repelled Max, and when he passed the book down to Lisa, she had dropped it instantly.

Max closed his eyes to slits and looked at Till. "Is there anything you *wouldn't* read?"

Till smiled. "Well, I doubt I'd read everything! I don't have that much time. Only good stuff, stuff you can really get lost in." He seemed to think it over for a moment. "The ones that make me forget everything around me, that's what I like. Then it's like you're flying through the book . . ." His eyes were shining. "Reading a book like that, it's like a dream, isn't it? That's what I always look for when I think about what I should read next."

Max nodded. "Okay, sure, but I mean . . . are there books you'd prefer not to touch at all? Because you're afraid they'll give you bad dreams or something?"

"You mean, be afraid of a book?" Till grinned and looked at Lisa. "What can a book do to me? I can close it anytime I want, just stop reading—then it's done."

Lisa tried to say something, but Max cut her off. "Are you so sure about that? I mean, are you so sure it's really finished if you close the book?" Max swallowed. "It can keep going in your head. The people who were in the book, they're still in there, in your head, kind of. You know what I mean?"

He saw that Till was looking at him with suspicion, but there was curiosity there, too. "What do you do if they don't stop, if they keep on . . ." Max's voice grew hushed. "I don't know . . . if they keep screaming . . . keep killing . . ."

Max noticed that Till grew more serious, saw how Till seemed to sense that Max wasn't just saying these things for fun.

"Oh, come on," said Till. "They're just characters in a book. Even if you can't get 'em out of your head, they can't do anything to you! It's like when you dream. When I wake up from a dream, I know for sure that it was just a dream—"

Max interrupted him. "Sure, but then you'd still be scared of the dream . . ."

"Of the dream? Really? Isn't it that you're scared of *falling asleep again*, scared that the dream will keep going?" Till frowned. "I'm not afraid of the dream . . . getting me when I'm awake . . ."

"No?"

Till shook his head. "So I figure there's no reason to be afraid of a book, as long as you don't go and open it again. That's how I see it, anyway."

For a moment, the three stood together silently in a circle. Max knew that the guesthouse where his father was working was behind them, on the other side of the hedge—but he deliberately didn't look in that direction.

"I don't know . . . ," he started again, and looked at Till. "What you dream and what's in the real world . . . I don't know if it's so easy to keep them separate." He stuffed his hands in his pockets. "I don't dream about things that are *only* in dreams. I dream about that house back there, for instance," he said, with a nod toward the guesthouse, "and that's really there. It's the same with what's in books. How do I know it's just a story, that the people who the book's about aren't also here in *real life*, I mean, in the same world as me, in a way?"

He knew that what he was saying came across as a little strange, but when he saw how Till folded his arms he had the feeling Till could follow what he was saying.

"But that's always clear," said Till calmly. "There are books that an author has *thought up*, which means the people who the book is about are *only* in the book, in the world of the book, and *not* in the real world.

"And there are nonfiction books, about things that the author *didn't* make up, about people who really lived and things that really happened."

"Right. But how do you know which characters are real and which ones are just made up? Because the author told you?"

"Yeah, why not?"

Max's eyes widened and he fixed Till with his gaze, then threw himself into what he really wanted to say. "Are you sure you can always trust the author? How do you know you're not making a mistake when you trust him? How do you know he's not out to trick you? What if an author says that his characters were really alive, when he just made them up?" Starting with a prickling in his arms, Max could feel a kind of agitation spreading through him.

"And what if the writer says he's just *thought* the characters *up*." He cleared his throat; a stubborn scratch had crept into his windpipe. "But it's a flat-out lie and the characters really lived . . . or are even still alive!"

Till had clearly never considered this possibility.

"You mean," said Till slowly, "that you're afraid of a book because it could be that the writer *says* that he just made up the story . . . but it really happened. Or it's still happening."

Max nodded. "Could be, right?"

Only now did he notice that during the last part of this exchange, Lisa had turned and moved a short distance away from them. He saw her drift through the small gap in the hedge at the back of the garden.

"Lisa?" He cast a glance at Till, who was also watching her.

"Does it keep going back there?" Till pointed with his thumb at the gap in the hedge, where Lisa had just disappeared.

Max nodded.

"Where to?"

To my dad's guesthouse, thought Max. "Want to see?" He tilted his head a little to one side.

Till grinned. "Yeah?"

When they came out on the other side of the hedge, Max saw Lisa already heading for the guesthouse set at the end of the property, fifty yards beyond the hedge.

"You don't want to go, too?" Till nodded in her direction.

"Nah, not interested," Max replied curtly.

"How come?" Till was looking steadily at him.

"Maybe another time," Max murmured, surly, as he observed how Lisa stood on the small terrace and knocked on the glass door of the guesthouse. Till and Max had stopped at the hedge, but the slight rattle of the glass door still reached them.

A moment later, the door opened and a ray of reflected sunlight swept across the grass. But there was no one to be seen in the doorway. Lisa stepped into the building without turning back again and the door clanked softly shut behind her. Shuddering slightly, the glass mirrored the darkening afternoon sky.

****

Max knew the process. He sat next to the mirror on the dressing table and watched as his mother got ready to go. He knew that his mother was aware of him there watching her, but it didn't bother either of them. He just wanted to spend a little time close to her before she and his father went out. She leaned close to the mirror again and again, going over her eyelashes, doing her lips with a tiny brush without making much difference to their color, dabbing on subtle eye shadow, trying on earrings by holding them up to her earlobes and turning this way and that, checking the effect on her reflection in the mirror. She normally finished the routine by puffing a little perfume behind her ears, but she hadn't yet reached that stage this evening.

"Did you work on your piece?" His mother paused with the mascara brush poised in midair and looked at him inquiringly.

Max flinched. He'd been hoping the subject wouldn't come up. "I was practicing just now . . ."

"And? Is it working out?" She pushed the brush thoughtfully into the mascara tube and slowly withdrew it.

"More or less," said Max.

Till had said his good-byes to them a good hour earlier, insisting that Rebecca just drop him off at the subway station and suggesting that he might come by again in the next few days.

"Your father wanted to hear it today, before we leave." Max's mother closed her eyes slightly and pulled the little black brush carefully through her eyelashes.

"But why? Can't it wait till tomorrow?" Max looked at his mother suspiciously as she went on applying mascara, unperturbed. "Or did you tell him he should be paying more attention to my piano lessons again?"

"No, Max, I did not." She purposefully put the brush back into its tube and reached for her perfume.

The moment had come. She raised the glass atomizer and squeezed the bulb. The fine scent swirled around her shoulders. She removed the white cloth that she had thrown over her shoulders as protection from her makeup and tossed it without looking among the pots of makeup. From under the cloth appeared the two straps of her evening dress, taut against her skin.

"Have you already put out my suit?"

Max raised his eyes and his stomach gave a lurch. His father had come through the door into the bedroom.

"It's hanging on the wardrobe." Julia had only half-turned her head to her husband, without looking away from the mirror.

"Hi, Max."

"Hi, Dad."

Xavier Bentheim stepped over to the freestanding wardrobe, where the suit hung on a coat hanger behind the door. "Think you can play me that piece you've been practicing?" He threw the suit onto the bed.

Max cursed himself for getting caught in the bedroom. If he'd stayed in his own room, his father would no doubt have forgotten about it.

"I . . . " He broke off.

Bentheim gave him an inquiring look as he buttoned his shirt.

"Okay, I'll go to the piano room." Max stood up and brushed past his father and out of the room.

He stared at the piano keys. He was trying hard not to let his rising panic get the upper hand. Why hadn't he made more of an effort that afternoon? Why hadn't he told his father to wait till the next morning to listen to him play? Why did he always do everything wrong?

Max laid his fingers carefully on the keys but didn't trust himself to press down on them. A jarring note now would just make it worse. Maybe he'd be lucky, he tried to encourage himself; maybe the art of playing had seeped into him earlier after spending so much time sitting at the grand piano. When his father came in, he'd simply start playing. It didn't need to be perfect; he just had to surprise him with the first notes he played.

"So, begin," he heard behind him, and his father—now fully dressed in a trim, striped suit, a light coat over his arm—entered the room. "Just a few bars, Max. You can play it for me again tomorrow morning in peace and quiet."

He crossed through the room to the piano and stood where he could look Max in the eye.

Max stared at the keys.

"Please, begin." His father's voice had grown soft.

"Yes," Max whispered, "soon . . ." A sharp prickling sensation crept along his hairline. It took all his power to force his fingertips onto the keys. *You don't need to be afraid,* he berated himself. *He'll be thrilled. He'll grab you from this piano stool and twirl you around the room.*

Then the first note he hit rang in his ear. Max's fingers cramped up; his heart felt like it would explode. He hunched forward, raising his hands in the air as he did so. He just didn't want to hit another false note.

Beside him, his father's silence gaped like an abyss.

Max looked up helplessly.

Bentheim had bowed his head, his eyes not leaving his son. All the color had drained from his face, which towered gaunt and pale above the white shirt visible under his suit.

"I can't," whispered Max, and lowered his eyes.

His father suddenly stepped up behind him and with one arm against Max's left, one on the right, reached for the keys. No, he didn't so much reach for the keys—he attacked them. The grand piano answered with a deep scream, rebelling under the man's hands. Max's father's fingers were racing over the keys. On both sides, Max saw the pale-skinned hands with their grid of raised veins dragging a veritable flood of sound out of the instrument. It was not the music Max was supposed to play, but it was also not completely different. It was bluster, thunder, inside which Max could recognize his piece as an embedded motif, a reverberation, infinitely deeper, more powerful, more secretive. It seemed like the echo from some massive mountain—rebounding, resounding—minutes after someone had yelled out the pitiful original. Max sensed his father's head above him, could hear his quiet breathing as he concentrated on the grand piano. It was as though his father were dancing with the instrument, building on the modest fundamentals of the piece with a mountain range of complex, grand sounds that came rumbling down on Max.

Max was already thinking he couldn't stand it any longer, braced himself to jump up, when the stream of notes suddenly stopped. His father straightened up behind him and his voice, the threat in it modulated to a delicate tremor, sliced into Max's ear. "I will not put up with the fact that you don't *try*."

"Dad, I . . . really . . ." The tears were flowing over Max's cheeks. "I did try, the whole afternoon . . ." But his father grabbed Max's head and turned it so that Max was forced to look into his pale face.

"I will not accept that nothing interests you, that you can't do anything, that you don't know anything." His father's voice was clear—almost too clear—too distinct, too nice.

Max lowered his head, but didn't dare avert his eyes. "I'm sorry," he stammered, hazily thinking about how pathetic he must look when he pleaded for leniency.

His father's face tightened and Max saw the wretchedness of his own expression reflected in his father's disgust. Then something flew at him, hitting him in his eyes, on his nose, on his lips.

Bentheim pushed him away and Max pitched forward, arms first, onto the grand piano's keys. The strings responded flatly from the other side of the wood cladding. His head buried in his arms, Max heard the hard soles of his father's dress shoes receding over the parquet floor.

But he didn't look up. His face was burning with shame and wet from his father's spit.

TWELVE YEARS AGO

"Changed? Changed how?" Xavier Bentheim steered the Jaguar through the evening traffic, heading for the city center. It was raining, and the rear lights of the other cars were smeared patches of color through the windshield.

"I can't put my finger on it exactly." Julia narrowed her eyes slightly and glanced over at her husband from the passenger seat. "I—" She interrupted herself and started again. "Let's talk about it another time."

"Are you serious?" Xavier didn't take his eyes off the road.

"Xavier, it's not something we can talk about now. Let's talk it over in peace tomorrow. Not in the car."

"I can stop a moment."

"No, better keep going. Felix will already be waiting for us." Xavier's eyes seemed to Julia to have become a shade darker. "Don't get upset. It's nothing. I'm probably just imagining it."

Xavier smiled and kept driving. "So, which is it? Have I changed or not? I mean, this is a serious matter, isn't it? You marry a certain person because you love the person the way they are, right? But if he now goes and changes . . . then, of course, the question arises whether what you loved has vanished." Xavier gave her a mischievous look. "Or have I got that wrong?" His eyes were smiling.

"I love you, Xavier." Julia raised her hand and carefully swept a strand of hair from his forehead.

She was probably mistaken. Changed? He'd changed? What was that supposed to mean? Probably . . . no, it was just the work on the new book, that's all. It was affecting him. He'd already hinted in that direction himself, more than once. But that wasn't something she wanted to talk about just then. She was right to say they'd be better off discussing it another time.

Without warning, she tapped him lightly on the cheek with the hand she'd just used to move the strand of hair. "Come on, hit the gas, we should be there by now!"

Several cars were already waiting at the entrance to the Quitzow company's massive edifice when Xavier turned the Jaguar onto the side street between Unter den Linden and Gendarmenmarkt, where the building was located. Xavier maneuvered the car to the end of the line and stopped. Through the wipers slapping back and forth, Julia saw a man with a huge, burgundy umbrella approaching the cars pulling up one after another. He was opening doors and leading the guests to the entrance, shielding them from the rain with his umbrella. Valets were waiting to jump behind the wheels of the idling cars, and would speed off to make room for the next one.

Xavier had been under contract with Felix von Quitzow for only close to a year, and this was the first opportunity Julia had had to visit the company. However, she knew the building well from the outside. She had often walked by the place and wondered what was hidden back there, behind the imposing walls and windows several yards high. Even the entrance was set well above street level.

According to Xavier, a student of Schinkel had designed the building a century earlier and built it as the main branch of a successful Berlin bank. Following the crash of '29, which had taken the bank down with it, the bulky but still impressive building had lain empty for decades, right through the Nazi and Cold War eras, until Felix had acquired the place as a dilapidated ruin some years earlier and gone to considerable effort and expense to repair it.

Somebody opened the door on Julia's side. "May I show you to the door?" The wide face of the man with the umbrella was looking at her.

Julia threw her coat around her shoulders, climbed out of the car, and ducked under the umbrella. A fine rain sprinkled her face. The man next to her carefully took her by the arm and led her around the car. Only now did she realize that a red carpet had been laid on the sidewalk in front of the entrance, shining darkly now that it was thoroughly saturated from the rain. Then Julia was standing in the building's open lobby, where golden light from old-fashioned glass candelabras replaced the damp, deep-blue shimmer of night.

"Did you get wet?" Xavier slipped his hand under her arm and they ascended the stairway leading up from the lobby.

Julia smiled and shook her head. No, it was nothing.

She was glad now that she had spoken up earlier in the car, and had said that she was worried about the changes she had seen in Xavier.

An oak double door at least twelve feet high opened from the landing into an auditorium that seemed larger than the nave of a church. The babble of a hundred guests, standing in different groups, rose to the deep-red ceiling. Julia, dazzled by the energy and opulence around her, stepped into the hall on Xavier's arm.

A young woman approached Julia to take her coat, and she barely had time to hand it over before she heard Xavier calling behind her.

"Come on!" He signaled to her, looking excited, as if he could hardly restrain himself from pushing his way into the throng. "Felix is back there; I want to say hello!"

Julia nodded. Together, they weaved their way through the crowd of guests.

Felix von Quitzow was short, about the same height as Julia, and perhaps in his late forties—a few years older than Xavier. He wore a bespoke and extraordinarily elegant suit.

His face was finely chiseled. He wore his hair short, and when he looked at Julia she had the feeling that his pale, almost too-large eyes were examining her.

"Xavier! Julia!" He came to meet them, beaming with delight. He smiled pleasantly at the guests he had to push through to reach them, shaking hands with one or two as he passed.

He took Julia's hand, pulled her gently to him, and touched his cheek to hers. *One or two kisses?* Julia was still wondering when he'd already released her and turned to Xavier. "Simply marvelous you were able to make it." He looked at Julia. "You've never been here before, have you?"

Julia smiled. "The building is magnificent."

"Wait until I've shown you my apartment." Felix's eyes flashed and he pointed at the ceiling. "Up top, the penthouse. A friend of mine, an architect, Manteuffel, do you know him? He designed it for me." He looked at Xavier again. "But you must have seen my place?"

Julia also looked at her husband. It struck her that Xavier still seemed elated. "Of course, my friend, of course," he said. Then he caught Julia's eye and she thought she saw the distracted smile, which had been on his face just a moment before, get swept aside by a faint breath of vigilance. But Felix had already taken her by the arm.

"Maja Oetting, Julia Bentheim," she heard him say, and when she looked at Felix again, a slim young woman was standing at his side, regarding Julia pleasantly.

"Maja's been helping me in the office since the start of the year," Felix explained as Julia and the younger woman greeted each other. "And now I hardly know how I'd get through the day without her."

"Lovely to meet you." Maja beamed at Julia. "Do you also write, like your husband?" Maja's face wore an expression of innocence so pure and at the same time so seductive that Julia was momentarily disconcerted.

"No," said Julia, and glanced at Xavier. "And sometimes I'm very glad about that when I see what he goes through." Even as she spoke, though, she couldn't stop herself thinking, *But why doesn't he say hello to Maja?* Had he already seen her today? At the same time, she realized that Felix had turned and was pointing out someone behind them to Xavier, causing Xavier to turn around as well.

"Really?" Maja's eyes shone. "When you read what your husband writes, you get the feeling that it all just comes so easily to him. It's as if all he has to do is sit at his desk and the sentences write themselves."

"You should tell him that—he'd be happy to hear it."

"Felix was thrilled to get Xavier on board," Maja continued brightly. "Xavier Bentheim—that's the future. He said it over and over."

As Maja was speaking, it occurred to Julia that Felix in the meantime had led Xavier a few paces away from them. Felix was speaking incessantly in his idiosyncratic way, underpinning his words with small, crisp gestures, talking the whole time to Xavier, who had bent down to the smaller man and was listening closely to him.

"Did you work at another publishing house before you came here?" Julia looked back at Maja, whose eyelids lowered a fraction over her velvet pupils.

"I was studying," she said. "Felix is a friend of my father's."

She's not even twenty-five, thought Julia. "And now you're helping him out in the office. Congratulations."

"Felix exaggerates." Maja's lips parted slightly, revealing flawless white teeth. "I'm something like his assistant, but I don't have a permanent position. He gives me different things to do, but I'm just starting to learn how the company works."

And you sleep with him, Julia heard herself thinking. Just then another young woman came over to Maja and touched her on the shoulder.

Maja turned around and her face lit up. "Hello!" She bent forward and the two women kissed each other fleetingly on the cheek. The new arrival was somewhat taller than Maja and had long black hair that hung loosely over her shoulders. Over her thin dress she wore a much-too-short jacket. As the girl swept her eyes quickly over her, Julia got the impression that the girl deliberately would not look her in the eye—her line of sight falling instead a fraction of an inch lower at the level of Julia's cheek.

"I just wanted to say hello. Have you seen Henning?" The girl had turned back to Maja.

"He was here earlier, asking after you." Maja pointed past Julia toward the end of the room, where a wide door led into another hall. "He's probably in the map room."

The young woman nodded, glanced again at Julia—again, not directly—then moved past them gracefully, heading in the direction Maja had indicated. But in that precise moment, when she glanced at Julia and Julia smelled her perfume, it came to her that *that* was what was slowly changing Xavier. It was the company that Felix surrounded himself with, the women that came and went.

****

An ancient scene stretched across the entire two thousand square feet of the ceiling. Devised by the artist to incorporate hundreds of figures, it was a labyrinth of bodies, expressions, and gestures. Staring upward, Julia would have loved to know what story the fresco told—but she was not able to decipher the pictorial tale.

She lowered her gaze again. She almost had the impression, walking through the building, that she had stumbled into a baroque palazzo from old Rome. She'd lost track of Felix and Xavier almost an hour before and had gone off to look around the building a little. Above the map room she'd found herself in a hallway where only catering staff were milling about, and from there she had found the hall with the fresco on the ceiling.

"Excuse me." Julia squinted a little to help her eyes adjust to the dim glow created by the floodlight aimed at the ceiling. Farther back in the room, five or six people had gathered on sofas and arm-chairs around a low table.

"I'm looking for Mr. von Quitzow." Julia took a step toward the small group. It struck her that none of them was speaking. Moving closer, she saw that a young woman had her head nestled in the lap of a young man, and he himself was ensconced deep in the cushions. A dog lay on its side in front of the table and looked at Julia—but not one of the guests reacted to her question. Their breathing quietly filled the room.

"And my husband, Xavier Bentheim, maybe you've seen him?" she tried again. The woman's eyes locked onto Julia's face and fol-lowed her every move. Julia was about to address her directly when the woman's eyelids slowly sank over her eyes, stopping about half-way, then slid back up again bit by bit, though her eyes did not open again completely.

Julia swept her eyes over the other guests. An older man with a bald head and his shirt unbuttoned, a gold chain glittering underneath, had let his chin sink onto his chest. A fine strand of spittle dripped from the corner of his mouth. Next to him, draped over an armchair, was a young man, maybe twenty years old, his pants low enough on his hips to show his boxer shorts beneath, and under those the hint of a tattoo.

But when Julia saw the young man's face, she started with shock. His face was deeply marked, as if cut with a knife, the furrows slicing past the corners of his mouth.

"They must have taken drugs. They were completely out of it. They were hardly aware I was even there, but they weren't asleep, either. They were caught up in some sort of weird dream state, like they were in a reverie and taken off to some weird, toxic fantasy worlds in a room with a huge fresco on the ceiling. Haven't you seen it?" The words were almost bubbling out of her.

Xavier narrowed his eyes and smiled, a little confused. "What? I don't understand. Where *were* you?"

Julia had finally found him. She had fled the hall with the painted ceiling, then wandered through the building. It was only when she asked a waitress from the catering service where Felix was that she had been led here, to a rooftop garden. She was only able to reach it through a room with an indoor pool.

"Julia!" Xavier had come to her with outstretched arms as she entered the roof terrace.

"Nice of you to join us." He took her by the arm, but instead of leading her to the group he'd just been standing with, he guided her instead to the terrace railing, which offered a stunning vista over the city. "Fantastic view, isn't it?"

Julia nodded and looked over at Felix, who was also on the terrace, but who had stayed with the group that Xavier had been a part of a moment before. As Felix's eyes met her own, Julia suddenly had the feeling that he was slightly put out that she had tracked them down, and that he was trying to hide his irritation behind a smile.

"You'll have to show me that hall with the fresco later." Xavier looked at the empty glass in Julia's hand. "But you've got nothing to drink—should I get you something?" He seemed to her to be making an effort to keep his voice very mild.

"Ah, so that's the idea." She smiled at him. "Are you looking for an excuse to abandon me again?"

"Nonsense!" He laughed. "Did you have a nice chat?"

Julia loved it when Xavier laughed—but her feeling of unease increased.

When she'd arrived on the rooftop he'd been chatting away with the others, in a great mood. Everyone had a glass in their hand, the men with crossed arms, the women young, fresh from the hairdresser, bare shouldered. Then she appeared and Xavier's face looked like he was trying to decide the most appropriate look for this exact moment.

She glanced over to the two women that Felix had remained with. They looked to her like wildcats, sizing her up with arched eyebrows, as if questioning whether Julia had any right to be there at all.

"Maja looked after me and introduced me to one of her friends." Julia looked at Xavier again. "What were you all doing out here?"

Xavier calmly looked out over the city and sipped his drink. "What do you mean, what were we doing? We were talking."

"What about?"

Xavier grinned. "About? I have no idea. No, wait, Gellert said he wasn't sure which project he should tackle next."

"You can't come up with anything more vague than that?"

Xavier frowned. "What's the matter with you? Should we get going?" He leaned toward her slightly. "Are you annoyed about Maja?"

Maja. He spoke her name in such a matter-of-fact way. And in the same moment, she felt his hand upon her arm. She sighed.

"Are you okay?" Xavier looked at her tenderly. But it seemed to Julia that with every step he took toward her, his true goal was to paint another coat over what he was thinking.

Then his face was near hers and filling her whole field of vision; his lips, at once dry, cool, soft, and a little hard, brushed against hers. He kissed her tentatively on the mouth.

Julia closed her eyes. What had she been thinking? Everything was fine. He loved her; they had just been talking about it in the car. They were together; they were an impregnable fortress. But just then she felt a wet, sticky liquid trickle onto her upper lip and seep down between her mouth and Xavier's. She drew her head back sharply, with a movement simultaneously abrupt, horrified, and confused. She opened her eyes and saw Xavier in front of her, grasping his mouth in alarm, his hand flecked, his lips bloody. He fished in the vest pocket of his jacket, pulled out a handkerchief, and held it under his nose. A dark-red blotch formed within seconds.

"Xavier?" Dismayed, Julia reached out and touched his arm.

But Xavier pulled back from her and turned away—not, it seemed to her, to hide his face from Julia, but to check if the others had noticed.

Julia caught Felix's eye. He had taken a step away from his group and was looking over at them, ever vigilant.

"Bentheim?" Felix's voice was clear, sharp, and loud. "Anything the matter?"

"Let's just go," Julia whispered to Xavier. The shock had cut into her deeply.

But it was too late. She saw Felix heading in their direction.

"Everything's fine here." Xavier turned to Julia again, wiping the blood from his nose with the handkerchief. His whole bearing expressed the effort he was making not to let anything show.

"Glad to hear it." Felix tilted his head slightly to one side and smiled at Julia as he joined them. "Your husband is so sensitive, Julia. Sometimes I'm almost afraid for him."

Why can't we just leave? Julia's eyes pleaded when she looked at Xavier. But he seemed to be oblivious to her again.

"But my sensitivity, as you call it, is exactly what you want me for, Felix," she heard Xavier retort, his voice unusually brittle.

"Yes, but not like this." Felix shook his head. "Not at the cost of your health, my friend."

"What do you mean, health?" Julia looked at Xavier in confusion. "I don't know what . . ."

"He's exaggerating," Felix nearly hooted. "He doesn't know what limits are. Didn't you know that?"

Julia saw that Xavier's face looked tired, almost aged—sunken in on itself. "It's . . . it's nothing," he practically stammered. "I'm really okay."

"Well, then . . ." And with that, Felix walked—no, pranced—back to his other guests, clearly more than satisfied with the impression he'd gotten of Bentheim.

In the same moment, Xavier's nose erupted again, this time with such force that the blood nearly flooded the front of his shirt.

He lurched away as Julia, appalled, reached for his arm. She looked into Xavier's eyes and saw something there that she had never seen before, something animal-like, injured, maimed.

"We . . . ," he choked out, his voice flat and frail, ". . . we can't go yet, Julia. He's got me over a barrel."

And before she could catch him, he collapsed onto the stone slabs of the terrace.

TODAY

A food trolley clatters in the distance. The squeak of orthopedic shoes. The song of a bird now and then.

Butz keeps his eyes closed. His head reclines on a large, soft pillow. He can feel his hands resting on a clean sheet.

He sits bolt upright. Gasps for air—feels it come with flooding relief, filling his lungs. His chest rises almost as high as his chin; his arms are forced outward from his body; his head lifts. He relishes the oxygen he sucks in, feeling the air flowing through his veins, how it energizes, refreshes, permeates. He laughs and purses his lips to feel the air as he breathes it out again.

He sinks back onto the pillow, his eyes open now. Above him, a neon lamp on the ceiling glows behind metal slats.

He turns his head to the side. Beside his bed is a nightstand and on it is a plastic cup and a carafe of water.

His gaze wanders out the floor-to-ceiling window on the other side of the nightstand. He can see a tree outside, the branches heavy with leaves.

They got him out. The mud had squeezed into his mouth, had seeped under his eyelids. He had felt the vibrations as the heavy equipment had pushed the masses of earth aside. He'd prayed, fearing that the excavator's shovel might smash his skull.

He had felt the air suddenly come through the last layers of muck, had stretched out his arm and broken through, heard the voices of the men, felt them dragging him out.

He hears a clicking behind him, but he is too weak to turn around. Heels clack. Then she moves into his field of vision.

His face tightens. He sees her step up to the bed. Cautious, catlike, her hand reaching out for his arm.

His eyes graze her face. How beautiful she is.

"Claire." His voice rattles like a tin can.

"Yes."

He tries to sit up but she pushes him gently back onto the mattress.

"Claire." He can't get his voice under control and feels its shakiness affecting every inch of his being. "Claire, I . . ." Butz lays his head back on the pillow and looks up at her. Knowing that she has come for him is so delightful that it actually hurts—and he finally finds the words he has been looking for. "I love you, Claire," he whispers. Maybe it sounds banal—but it's the truth. He doesn't know how else to say it.

Her eyes are on his.

"Will you marry me?" He can hardly believe that he has really said it. But he has been too close to death to go on resisting the urge to ask her.

But she hesitates. And Butz turns away.

No one says anything, but he is churning up inside. Pushing fifty and he's never asked a woman to marry him. Here, in a hospital? What an idiot! How could he let himself be so deceived by his own weakness?

Butz feels Claire sit next to him on the mattress. "I'll think about it, okay?" he hears her say.

Butz nods without looking at her. Of course. No hurry.

But he knows he's screwed up.

"There was something about her." Butz exhales, searching for words. "She reminded me of another case."

Claire has not answered his question, whether she would marry him. Now it hangs between them, and every moment that passes without an answer is almost unbearable. Is he supposed to try to convince her? Should he resign himself to the idea that she'll turn him down? Hasn't she already given him her answer by *not* saying yes? Butz knows that Claire feels it the same way, as an ordeal she is putting him through. He knows that it is afflicting her, that he is afflicting her.

He forces these gnawing thoughts aside.

"Someone rammed a drill into her stomach, Claire." He tries to focus on the case. "That isn't—how can I put it—it deviates from the norm. I mean, from the criminal norm, you know? It's about a lack of inhibition, ruthlessness, senselessness, too." His gaze drifts to the window. "It's not so long ago. Three, maybe four weeks. A body in a parking lot, a colleague of mine had the case. He showed me the photos."

He hears Claire sigh and suspects she is wondering if she really wants to listen to this. But it also seems that she does not want to interrupt him—maybe to avoid the conversation returning to the other subject.

"When I saw the woman down in the pit, when I saw what someone did to her . . ." Butz's hands closed into fists on the bedspread. "I'll spare you the details, but the first thing I thought of was the woman from the parking lot. I thought that perhaps both women had gone through something similar. Whoever did it went for the stomach of the woman on the building site." His eyes meet Claire's; her face has gone very pale. "And in the parking lot, it was the face."

"Yeah, okay." Claire seems tense.

"Yeah."

Butz stays with his thoughts. When his colleague had shown him the photos from the parking lot, he'd felt like it was the first time he'd seen such madness. It had hit him hard, really hard. And he was happy when his colleague had taken the photos back.

"What do you think? Some lunatic trying to cause chaos in Berlin?" Claire looks at him.

Yeah . . . yeah, that could be it, of course . . .

"I don't know. When I saw the photos from the parking lot, my first thought was that it wasn't a normal case. At first I pushed them to pay more attention to it at headquarters. But . . ." He buries his face in his hands. "I don't know why. There were a thousand things. For whatever reason, I put it on the back burner. Convinced myself it wasn't so urgent, not so out of the ordinary."

He notices that she starts, suddenly distracted, and he lowers his hands from his face.

"Claire?"

Now he hears it, too. The buzz of a cell phone vibrating. Claire reaches into her jeans pocket, takes out her phone, and peers at the display.

A look of confusion crosses her face, Butz notices. "Text?"

"Hmm." She stands up and goes to the window, her face turned away from him.

Butz sighs. Shouldn't he be feeling better by now? There's no lasting damage, no injury, no broken bones.

He throws back the blanket and swings his legs down from the mattress. He feels momentarily dizzy, then sits on the edge of the bed. Claire still has her eyes on the display of her telephone.

"I think I'll try and talk to a doctor."

Claire turns back to him, her face tense.

"What's the matter?" Butz smiles.

"Does something hurt?"

"I'm fine. I . . . I just can't lie around here forever."

"You want to get up?" There's something in her voice; she sounds harassed.

"But nothing happened. I'm feeling fine!"

She steps closer to him. "I don't think it's a good idea, Konstantin."

He laughs. "I love it when you worry about me."

Love. There's that word again.

He gives himself a shove and stands up. "What was the text just now?" Or is she behaving so strangely because he wants to get out of bed?

"Sorry," he adds quickly, "none of my business." He smiles. "Maybe I haven't got it quite as together as I'd like yet."

She nods. "They'll make you sign a waiver saying you're leaving at your own risk."

"Whatever, doesn't matter." Butz, still a little unsteady on his feet, gropes his way over to the wardrobe, where he thinks his things have been put. "I just want to get out of here."

✳✳✳✳

"He's sick."

The man behind the metal desk in the construction site's office trailer doesn't let Butz out of sight.

"But he was here yesterday. I spent a long time talking to him . . ."

"Are you doubting my word, Inspector? Excuse me, but I'm telling you: the site manager is sick. He called in early this morning. What am I supposed to do?"

They are both wearing the yellow safety helmets mandatory on the site. In all the confusion the day before, no one had taken any notice of helmets.

Butz touches the short, hard visor of the helmet with his fingertip, pushing it back a little on his head, and casts a glance at the engineer supervising the work.

"Fine. Sick. No problem." Butz smiles. "In any case, I'm not here to talk about the site manager." He can feel how the accident is still with him, deep down, but he's not going to let it distract him. "What concerns me is the tunnel I was looking at yesterday."

The man behind the metal desk has his hands flat on the desktop in front of him and is looking calmly at Butz.

"We have to examine that passage," Butz insists, but the man is already shaking his head.

"You haven't seen the spot my people dragged you out of yesterday, have you?" he asks.

"Not yet—" Butz starts, but the other man interrupts him.

"Sorry, Inspector, but we can stop right here. I'm glad they managed to avoid more damage than was done last night. But you can't get into that shaft anymore."

"Why not?"

"The whole bank collapsed. What do you want us to do? Just put three days' work on hold and rip the embankment apart?"

For a moment, Butz feels like he can't get any air.

"Besides, we already had to pour there."

"Pour what?" Butz forces himself to breath calmly, feels the sweat break out on his forehead.

"Concrete." The man smoothes an eyebrow. "The rain isn't letting up. The ground is completely saturated. Digging out the embankment—to get you out—meant destabilizing the entire slope. Do you know what it means if the embankment—we're talking twenty-five, thirty feet—if it comes down on the foundations that have already been laid?"

His blue eyes look calmly at Butz. "We had to raise the sides of the foundations as fast as possible to avoid even bigger complications. And that's just what we've done."

The ground vibrates as the front-end loader passes, barreling down the ramp into the pit at high speed. Butz sees the driver's face through the plastic window of the cab as it flies past. The man ignores him completely.

Butz moves on. When he gets to the end of the ramp and the concrete basement, he sees it. Last night, he'd still been able to see the embankment beyond the sides of the basement. Since then, formwork has risen fifteen feet above the foundation.

"But the next block already has a building on it." He can still hear himself trying to convince the engineer. "We can't get to the tunnel from there, either."

"Come back with a court order telling us to tear down the wall again, Mr. Butz, and we'll do it. Until then . . ." And with these words the engineer led him to the trailer door. "Please understand that I have to push ahead with the work. And the wall we've just put up as fast as possible and at considerable additional cost, well, I have no intention of tearing it down."

Butz watches as the workers guide a hose that shoots a stream of cement as thick as a man into the new forms. The engineer's explanations had sounded plausible enough, but he can't shake the feeling that all this could have been avoided. That it might have been possible to dig out some sort of access to the tunnel—instead of sealing it off forever.

9

TWELVE YEARS AGO

Brakenfelde.

Lisa lay on her back in bed and looked out the window of her room. The night sky was only just showing the first glimmer of dawn, but she couldn't sleep. She had woken up when she heard her parents' car pulling up. But her thoughts were not on her parents. She was thinking instead of the boy she'd met the day before.

Till.

Lisa regretted not stopping him when he'd left. She would have liked to find out more about him. More about Brakenfelde, the home he'd been in, and above all, why he'd run away, as he said he had.

She heard her parents come up the stairs to the second floor, where the bedrooms were, and turned her head so she could see the open door of the younger children's room.

Her mother was just passing by. She glanced into Lisa's room and stopped.

"Hey." Her mother's voice was very soft.

"Hi, Mom."

"You should be sound asleep." Julia entered the room and approached her eldest daughter's bed.

"Were you gone the whole night?"

Julia smiled. "Uh-huh."

"So, how was it?"

"Nice. Nice. Your father wasn't feeling well for a little bit, but he's fine now."

Lisa noticed how her mother looked down at her and she reached out one hand from under the blanket. Julia took her hand and held it tightly, and finally sat on the edge of the bed.

Lisa looked at her. Only now did she notice that her mother's eyes seemed red.

"Were you crying?"

Her mother's lips contorted slightly, and Lisa could hear her swallow.

"What's the matter, Mom?"

Her mother let go of her hand. "You should really sleep now, baby."

But I can't sleep was all Lisa could think.

"Okay?" Her mother looked at her.

He ran away from Brakenfelde, Mom. But Lisa knew it was better to keep that to herself.

"Okay." She curled up and lay on her side with her face turned to the wall. She felt her mother kiss her hair, then heard her stand up and leave the room.

Where is he supposed to sleep if he's run away from the home, Mom? That's what was making Lisa so restless. Till had no home. So where did he sleep?

****

When Till awoke, he was freezing. He threw on his pullover, then dug a transparent rain poncho out of his small nylon backpack and pulled that on, too. Through the branches he had used to build his hut, he could see out into the forest, where pale strands of early-morning sunlight were beginning to filter through.

The previous evening he had made his way from the subway to the Grunewald forest. He quickly discovered a suitable small clearing; on one side a slight rise protected him from the path that led past, and on the other side a patch of conifers covered his back. In between, the trees thinned, and at the edge of the clearing someone had stacked a pile of branches and sticks. Till found the strongest branch, then jammed one end of it into the lowest fork of a tree at the edge of the clearing; the other end he'd jammed into the fork of the tree next to it, which was close to the same height. Then he'd taken some smaller branches and leaned them against the ridgepole—alternating between sides so the projecting ends crossed over. He had managed to close the gaps in the walls somewhat with branches torn straight off the conifers. Finally he had lined the ground with fallen leaves scraped together from around the entrance.

With the rain poncho over his sweater, he climbed out of the hut. He'd eaten nothing since the soup in the Bentheims' kitchen.

His thoughts returned to the Bentheim family. Would he see them again? Could he show up there today? Or would it be better to wait a day and go first thing tomorrow? The more Till thought about it, the more uneasy he felt. He didn't want to get on the family's nerves by showing up too often. A degree of restraint was what was needed. But when it came to the Bentheims, how was he supposed to restrain himself? They were all he had.

He angrily kicked aside a branch. Bullshit! He was not dependent on them! He could do what he wanted.

But he did think they were really nice, Max and Lisa, so he would try to visit them soon. After all, it was summer vacation and they hadn't gone away, so maybe they'd be happy for a break from the routine. But if they acted strangely to him, if they acted maybe cool or snobby, then he'd just move on. He didn't need them.

Defiant, he reached for his backpack, swung it onto his shoulder, and set off.

"Nice." Till turned back to Max, who had stopped in the doorway that opened into Max's room.

It had been no problem at all. Rebecca had opened the door for him, then called out to Max when Till asked for him. And it had been obvious that Max was happy to see him back.

Max gave Till a look, then locked the bedroom door behind him and stuffed his hands in his pants pockets. "Lisa said you sleep in the forest."

Till sighed. So she'd told after all. But in a way it was good that she had. Till hated the thought of lying to Max.

"Yep, that's right." He narrowed his eyes. Evidently, it wasn't such a big deal for Max to know about it.

Till thought he saw something flash in Max's eyes, something like curiosity mixed with a little admiration.

"So, how is it?"

"Okay."

"Have you got a hut or something like that?"

"Just a few sticks for a roof. I'll show it to you if you like."

Max thought it over. "Is it far?"

"About two hours on foot."

"We could take the bikes. Lisa'll let you use hers, for sure."

Till nodded. *Sure, works for me.*

But then Max himself nixed the idea. "Maybe later."

They were silent for a moment and Till wondered if he shouldn't act as if sleeping in the woods was the most natural thing in the world and simply move on to the fun part of the day—playing. But Max still seemed to be thinking through the practical ramifications of what Till had just confirmed.

"It's supposed to rain again tonight. Is the hut watertight?"

Till shook his head no.

"You can sleep in the shed in the garden if you want," Max said.

Till looked up in surprise. "For real?" But then he thought of all the things that spoke against it. "But it won't work. If your parents find out . . ."

"They don't need to know anything about it." Max looked at him. "It's pretty rough, but no one'll bug you there. And the house where Dad works is out of sight from there." He pulled his hands out of his pockets and crossed his arms. "There's water there, too. But if you don't want to . . ."

"No, fantastic!" It was just what Till needed. "Have you ever slept in the forest? I spent the whole time just thinking about how to get through another night."

"So, why'd you run away from that home?"

Till swallowed. "Because of my brother. They . . . he . . ." It was hard for him to talk about Armin. "Do you really have to know?"

Max dropped his arms. Till could see that he was embarrassed to have grilled him like that. Max turned to the wardrobe that stood beside the door and pulled it open. "Let's go and check out the shed, okay? You'll need blankets." Max pulled out two thick wool blankets lying on the bottom shelf, then glanced up at Till.

"Something to change into, too?"

Till shook his head. "Nah, don't . . ."

But Max had already pulled out two white T-shirts and a pair of jeans. "Everybody has this stuff. Not even my mom will notice it's mine." He threw the clothes to Till.

They smelled of laundry detergent, clean and fresh. The stuff they'd used in Brakenfelde never smelled that good.

Till walked through the garden with Max, each carrying two large bags. Max had insisted that Till, as he put it, be "decently outfitted." So they had gone into the kitchen and gathered cans of fruit, beans, ravioli—things you could eat cold if you had to. Then they had to have a can opener. Till also needed water and bread, cookies, too, and Max insisted that he take nuts with him and even packed in a stick of butter and half a sausage. Then, of course, he needed a knife for that, and a cutting board and a plate—and the pile of equipment they were putting together rapidly grew so large that they had to start a new bag. Rebecca, looking in on her way to the pantry, was told by Max—in a tone that forestalled any questioning—that they wanted to have a picnic in the garden. And, in fact, she didn't probe any deeper, leaving the two boys undisturbed.

The third bag was filled with such useful things as a flashlight, new toothbrush, toothpaste, washcloth, and towel; last but not least, Max fished out from the storeroom an air mattress complete with air pump.

When they stepped into the shed with their stuffed bags, Till immediately saw that it was perfect. The wooden shack wasn't even nine feet by twelve feet, and seemed to be used by the Bentheims only in winter to store their garden furniture. But in summer, the tables and chairs were strewn about on the lawn and the shed was empty.

Max pumped up the air mattress and Till set up house. In one corner he assembled a kind of kitchen, and on an old wooden shelf in another corner, he stacked his new clothes.

Perfect. He grinned from ear to ear. Max grinned, too.

****

"Dad!" Claire had been eating her soup in silence and only now and then looking over at Till, her eyes wide as saucers. But now she jumped to her feet. Lisa instinctively turned her head. Her father, a tall, slim man, had just come through the door.

He stroked little Claire's hair then went to Lisa's mother, leaned down, and kissed her. Then, holding Claire's hand, he swung his eyes over the children. "Hi" was all he said. "Good stuff?"

Lisa nodded with the others. She was excited. Till had reappeared that morning. Until now he'd mainly been playing with Max, but they were all having lunch together.

"Come and sit." Her father gave Claire a pat, then looked at Till. "You must be Till," he said and took a step toward him, offering him his hand. "My wife mentioned you were eating with us today."

"Good that you could make it, Xavier," Lisa heard her mother say. "Didn't you want to have a word with Max?"

"Now? Here?" Her father sat down.

"I thought it would be a good time, now that one of Max's friends is here." Lisa's mother pushed the bowl toward her father so he could help himself.

Lisa cast a glance at Till and had the impression that he wasn't exactly okay with the family discussion.

"Yes, maybe." Her father's gaze fell on Max. "How old are you now, Max?"

"Twelve, Dad. You know that."

"Twelve, right," said her father, digging into the bowl. "Maybe today's really a good time to talk about it again."

Talk about what? Lisa was genuinely curious.

"I'm just starting eighth grade, Dad," said Max. "Graduation's still five years away. That's tons of time—"

"I know how far away it is, Max," his father interrupted, his voice suddenly taking on a sharper edge.

Lisa instinctively ducked her head and looked at Max. The grin he'd been wearing had slipped a little.

"So . . . " Her father was now totally focused on his son. "What is it that I want to discuss with you?"

Silence settled over the table. Lisa looked at her mother, who seemed strangely stiff, as if she did not entirely approve of the way the discussion was going.

"Max?"

"I . . . I'm not sure, Dad," Max croaked out.

His father's reply came back as hard as a super ball flung at a wall. "What it's about is that I can't see—and you won't tell me—what it is in life you feel *drawn* to."

Silence.

"Do you understand?"

Nod.

"I can't hear you, Max!" And this time, her father's voice sliced through the room like a knife.

Lisa looked at Max and saw tears brimming in her brother's eyes. His lips quivered and his face was suddenly pathetically sad. It was as if all hope had been driven from the boy's slight frame in a single stroke.

"Y-yes," he stammered. "Yes, I understand, Dad."

"You see, that's the problem." Her father's voice was suddenly gentle again. "I can't see which way you're leaning. Everything seems equally important to you. Sometimes you do this, sometimes that, sometimes nothing."

Silence settled over the table again.

"Which is why I've been thinking something over," continued her father after a while. "Why don't we set ourselves a deadline? Until the end of summer, the end of summer vacation."

Max looked up. "Till the end of summer, what?"

"By the end of the vacation you will have figured out what you would like to do when you're an adult."

Max lowered his eyes. "Okay, fine."

Lisa saw her father look over at Till. "Now, you're probably thinking we go at it like this here all the time," he said, "but that's not the case."

"Why does he have to decide now what he's going to do in five years?" she heard Till ask, his voice low but firm.

An uneasy feeling came over Lisa.

"I mean," Till continued, and his quivering voice betrayed how upset he was, "there's enough time to do it later, too."

"Is that so?" Her father took a deep breath. "Of course, at first glance . . ." He seemed thoughtful. "But look at the people—I mean, the people who really achieve something. In sports, in chess, in ballet, whatever. Every single one of them set themselves a goal early on and then stuck to it, not looking left or right. This one starts to play the violin when he's four, that one starts his first company at eleven, another wins a math competition when he's eight."

Till looked at him, his eyes wide.

"Some people may find that stupid or sad, but it is true," continued Lisa's father.

Max hadn't raised his eyes from his plate again. But Lisa's father wasn't paying any attention to him. He was now completely focused on Till.

"And when you look at it closely, then you'll see who's responsible for the fact that these people are able to reach such dizzying heights of achievement. It's not so much the individuals who actually do it, but . . ." He swept his eyes around those at the table.

No one said anything.

"Their parents, naturally," he said, completing the sentence.

Lisa swallowed. *Was that true?*

"The *parents* are the ones who encourage their children," her father continued. "*They* are the ones who give them the chance to make something out of their lives. Which is why"—and here he turned to Max again—"I would say, it's very simple. You choose what you would really like to do, we support that, maybe find you a teacher, sign you up for a few courses. And in the end you'll thank me for doing things so rigorously right from the start because you'll find that there's no one who can hold a candle to you in your special field."

"Yeah, that's it. That's what it's about," Lisa heard Max's voice croaking. "That no one can hold a candle to you." *He looked rather helplessly toward his father.*

He doesn't want to provoke his father, she told herself, hoping fervently that he would take Max's remark the right way. *He only wants to show that he has understood.*

"Then it's also about me." Till had found his voice again. "About me not holding a candle to Max, isn't it?" He looked at Lisa's father tensely.

"Don't you want to be better than him?" her father asked in reply, and Lisa had the feeling that her father was looking at Till a little more attentively than a moment before. "Hold on," he quickly added. "Don't rush with an answer. Think about it a moment. When you run a race, when you play chess, when you argue. Don't you want to be right, to be better, to win?"

Lisa saw a grin on Till's face. "Maybe you're right, Mr. Bentheim, but I still don't want him to do badly."

"Of course you don't. I know that putting something so bluntly doesn't sound very nice, but I think it's best to call a spade a spade. And it's a fact that we have to measure ourselves against others. Of course, I'd prefer not to have to rip into Max like that and just let him go on daydreaming. But that's not how it works. As a father, I'm responsible for him doing something with his life, or else he'll turn around in ten years and accuse me of not caring about him enough."

Her father turned back to Max as he continued speaking, but it seemed as if the son he was speaking about was no longer present.

"Anyway, it's probably a waste of time trying to push Max to reach a decision. A gift or a talent that would be worth supporting, well, it basically shows up on its own—or not at all. Right, Julia?" He looked to his wife, but she just shook her head, and Lisa had the impression that she, too, was fighting back tears.

Her father glanced at Max again. "And what if nothing appears?" He seemed to think about his own question for a moment, then continued with some emphasis. "He'll spend his whole life stumbling and fumbling from one thing to the next, staggering, lurching, and bumbling his way along, until he has battered and scraped himself half to death and is so bruised and sore that no one will want anything to do with him."

Shocked, Lisa looked at her brother, whose face betrayed how completely crushed he was. He was crying. There was no holding back anymore; there was no hesitation and no hope—only bottomless despair. It was as if Max had fallen into a chasm he could never climb out of again. Just then there was a clatter and she watched as Till sprang from his seat and—ignoring everyone else—ran around the table to Max and held him tightly in his arms.

"Yeah!" Claire's voice chimed in brightly and she hopped down from her chair and went and squeezed herself against the two boys, as well.

Lisa looked at her father. All this talk had obviously taken its toll on him. His veins bulged blue at his temples and it seemed to her that the bones of his skull were visible under his skin.

10

TWELVE YEARS AGO

What was it Max had told him? "He works at night," he'd said. "He locks himself away in the guesthouse for entire nights. I've never seen him writing and never read one of his books. Sometimes I'm not sure it's even true. I mean, that he writes books at all."

Till threw back the wool blanket he'd pulled over himself, rolled off the air mattress, and crawled on all fours to the wooden door of the shed. Cautiously, he pushed it open.

It was the middle of the night. The garden lay before him, black as coal. Silently, ducking low, he crept to the hedge that screened the back of the property from the house. Looking through it he could see the lights of the guesthouse gleaming.

He darted through the gap in the hedge, heading for the guesthouse, ready to flee at any moment if Bentheim's figure suddenly appeared.

But everything was quiet.

Till lay flat on the ground. He wanted to give the light spilling out through the open window and the glass door the smallest possible surface to illuminate. He crawled on, pressing himself as close to the earth as he could.

"I'm still wearing pants, belt, shoes, but my torso is bare . . ."

It was Bentheim's voice. Steady and low, now insistent, now soft, full of suggestion and promise. No doubt about it, the voice was coming from the guesthouse.

Pushed by the urge to understand better what the voice was saying, Till crept even closer.

"I turn around, my head twisted toward the mirror to see my back. As I do so, I feel my body temperature chill by several degrees. Beneath the skin stretching across my stomach and chest, with breathtaking speed, a small wavelike movement resumes. At first I think I'm mistaken—but then another wave has already begun, rippling across my back."

He's reading aloud. Till turns his head to the side so he can hear better. He's working on one of his books.

"A small elevation," he heard Bentheim's voice go on, "no bigger than a bean . . . no bigger than a mouse. There! Now two waves meet and cross, rolling across my chest from opposite directions, as if two tiny creatures are moving rapidly over my body, under my skin. My eyes flick to my face in the mirror. I have my teeth clamped together, my cheekbones protrude, the lips stretch back, baring teeth. My breath comes in short bursts, as if I'm hauling a massive load up a flight of stairs."

Inch by fraction of an inch, Till raised his head and peered through the glass door into the illuminated room. One of the bookshelves lining the walls must have been built to extend into the room; there was no wall visible beyond the edge of the shelf, only the room's ceiling, projecting a short distance farther into the background.

Till crawled a little to one side to get a better angle. Bit by bit, the dim room behind the bookshelf came into view.

He was sure that Bentheim's voice was coming from there. For a moment, the mullion of the glass door blocked Till's view into the room. Then it slid aside, and Till could see that Bentheim was sitting in an armchair behind the bookshelf. He was bending over a stack of pages balanced on his knees.

". . . screw up my eyes to be able to see the crawling motion under my skin better. The one tiny bump has transformed not just into two or three; every time it circles my trunk, the creature seems to divide again; there are already eight or ten waves swarming over my body—and I realize that it is not only the mouse-size bumps that are moving, but beside them, behind them, between them run myriad smaller, finer ripples that I had not seen at first. Now that my eyes have adjusted to the dim light, I can see that my skin is far from a still surface plowed now and then by one of the ripples; oh no, *everywhere*, even when stretched tight, it is being traversed incessantly, undermined, burrowed, riddled by a constantly changing, flowing motion, by waves of all sizes, frequencies, and lengths. From bumps as big as a child's fist down to a scurrying that makes me think of an insect nest, it's as if an entire colony of ants has pushed, eaten, and gouged its way under my skin. A teeming and scuttling infestation that, with growing horror, I realize is not restricted to my torso but has also gone beyond, migrating up my neck, flowing around my ears, making the hair on my head rise and fall, boring across my forehead, dropping down the ridge of my nose, digging under my eyelids. Even my reflection in the mirror seems to have lost its solidity, becoming something hazy and unsteady. A reflection—and when I see it, I press a fist between my teeth to stop myself from screaming—that is starting to melt together as the waves reach my pupils, transparently traversing them like gelatinous earthworms, causing my eyeballs to flicker in their sockets."

Bentheim paused and stared at the sheaf of pages on his lap. He sat there motionlessly for a moment, then let himself sink slowly back in his chair. Till impulsively pushed himself a little higher, scanning Bentheim's face, until now bent low over the pages, for the waves he had just been reading about. But the man was too far away. From where he was, Till could not make out if Bentheim's skin was being plowed by bean- or mouse-size ripples. Then Bentheim slowly raised his head.

Till looked down at himself instinctively. He was lying on his stomach but had pushed himself up, bracing with his hands. The light! The light coming through the glass door was on him!

He dropped silently onto the lawn and pressed his face into the grass. A musty, earthy smell rose to meet him. He didn't dare to breathe.

"I drop to my knees and wrap my arms around my body, as if their pressure might squeeze away this whirring and buzzing under my skin," he heard the voice continue. "But the ripples and the bulges move along my arms and it seems to me almost as if the bumps are getting bigger, as if the creatures have ceased to merely scuttle and have started jumping. First a twinge, then a tearing accompanied by excruciating pain, a leaping and hopping until it seems I can take no more, for I see in the mirror that I have begun to tremble, my head pulled in deep between my shoulders, my feet crossed at the ends of crooked legs. I sink to one side, slow as a falling tree, my legs pulled convulsively into my stomach, chin pressed against my chest. My neck projects sharply; the spasmodic groaning has given way to dull panting. I lean my head back, and the face staring at me from the mirror looks gray and tired. It surges and throbs, deformed by a dancing agitation at once lifeless and frantic. My eyes, hollow and contorted with pain, look back at me, shot through with this scrabbling that turns them into two jellyfish, two blobs of glop. At the same time, I see my mouth—the lips likewise throbbing, rippling—I see it slowly open, as if I want to laugh at being so hopelessly overpowered. But what comes out is not laughter; it is a groaning, moaning, croaking that intensifies a hundred times, a hundred thousand times, as my mouth stretches wider. Already it seems as if the lips must rip apart, because my jaws, my mouth, opens wider and still wider, until it is gaping at me from the mirror like some terrible abyss. A chasm, the groaning coming in short, sharp bursts from within, a sound that must have its origin in my pain and the strain it puts on my body to tear my jaws so gruesomely apart. A void that seems to have only one purpose, to swallow me up, to suck me out of the room I am lying in—and with the helplessness of a child paralyzed by fear, I throw my arms over my face and wait to be wolfed down the gullet that opens before me . . ."

Again, the voice broke off. Till heard the rustling of the paper, then the legs of the armchair scrape over the timber floor.

Footsteps.

Till pressed his hands to the back of his head in fright. What was he still doing here?! How could he have screwed up like this? Why hadn't he crept away while Bentheim was still immersed in his text?

The footsteps stopped.

For a second, nothing happened. Then they started again and Till heard the hollow wooden sounds give way to the crunch of the stone pavers on the front terrace of the guesthouse. A moment later, the sound of the footsteps was swallowed by the grass. Till rolled himself onto his back.

The figure of Max's father loomed blackly between him and the night sky he was staring into, his face lit dimly by the light coming through the glass door.

"I was just leaving. I'm sorry, Mr. Bentheim. I didn't hear what you were saying." The words came bubbling from Till's mouth.

"What are you doing here, boy?" Bentheim snapped at him. With a quick, hard movement, he grabbed Till and jerked him to his feet. Till felt like he was being torn out of his T-shirt. "Is Max here, too?"

Till's head jerked left and right—*No, Max isn't here, it has nothing to do with him, it's all my fault, Max just wanted to help me out.*

"Speak!" Bentheim bawled—as if the force of his bark could make Till function by remote control.

"It's not Max's fault, Mr. Bentheim," he jabbered. "I asked him if I could sleep in the shed, I was going to take off in the morning anyway, it was just for one or two nights. I didn't do anything; I'll get my stuff and go now. I'm really sorry, but you can't blame Max."

Then the faith that he was saying what he wanted to say left him again, and he was afraid he'd fall down right there on the grass at Bentheim's feet from the near panic he was feeling. He was afraid that the man might simply kick him in a rage because Till had not answered him quickly enough, the first kick in the stomach, then in the face.

But instead, Bentheim looked at him calmly. "Go to the shed and wait for me there," he finally said.

Till nodded. *Yes. Yes, I'll do that.*

With fitful, erratic steps, Till ran back to the shed then pressed himself into one corner, the blanket wrapped around him. He felt as if a block of ice had dropped into his stomach.

Thirty minutes later, the shed door opened with a soft squeak. Till drew the blanket around him and stared into the darkness. The door swung open. At the top of the door frame, he could see the dark blue of the night; below rose a black silhouette. "We were wondering why you came back to us today," said the silhouette.

Till shivered.

The silhouette pushed through the doorway. Till thought he could actually smell Bentheim. The man let himself drop into a garden chair that Till and Max had brought into the shed. His face was invisible in the darkness.

"Forget what you heard, understood?"

Yes. Of course.

"It was nothing. A passage I'd written. I'm not going to use it; it's no good. I didn't get it right; I don't like it and I don't want to hear about it again, ever."

"Yes."

"Do you understand?"

"Yes."

Till heard the man exhale.

"Don't you have any parents, Till? What are you doing here?"

Bentheim would call the home. They'd come for him. It was over. They'd take him back to Brakenfelde. Back to his room, back in his bed. Back to the house where . . .

"I ran away, Mr. Bentheim. From the home."

He stared at Bentheim's form. The man sat in the chair without moving.

"How long ago was that?"

"One—no, two days ago, including today."

"What about your parents, Till. Can't they take care of you?"

"My mother passed away. And my father, I don't know."

Bentheim's chair creaked. "You can't stay here."

"No." *Of course not.*

"Do you have an uncle, an aunt. Anyone who can come and get you?"

No.

"No."

"Then I'll take you back to the home tomorrow. Okay?"

"Okay." What else was he supposed to say? Bentheim's presence was practically paralyzing Till.

"Why did you run away, Till? Was it so bad?"

Yes.

"I didn't like it."

"Why not?"

"It . . . it was okay. But then . . ."

He broke off. But Bentheim wasn't about to let it rest. "What then?"

"Something happened." Till's voice was barely perceptible. "I don't want to talk about it."

He heard Bentheim stand up, saw the black form loom in front of him. "Tomorrow I'll take you back."

Till nodded. He knew that Max's father couldn't see his head, but he didn't have the strength to answer anymore.

"Okay?"

Okay, he wanted to say, but something else came out of his mouth. "My brother hanged himself."

He heard Bentheim draw a sharp breath.

"He was in the home, too, on the floor above mine. I . . . he was my brother. I loved him."

"Did you see it?" The man's voice had grown quiet.

"I found him. He did it sitting down. On the heating pipe." Unopposed, the images Till had blocked out for so long came back to him. He saw the door to Armin's room in front of him, saw his hands push on it, saw himself stagger into the room with wavering steps, his line of sight rising and falling as if he were on the ocean—until it fell on a form lying on the floor in front of the heating pipes. It was a form that Till knew well but had never seen like this—his brother, his head lowered to his chest, his arms on the floor, the backs of his hands on the linoleum, palms up.

"That's why you ran away."

"I told them they needed to look after him. But they didn't."

Till looked up and was shocked to see that Bentheim had moved over to the door of the shed. His face was no longer in darkness but was lit almost imperceptibly by the pale glow of the night. Till half expected to see the rippling motions under his skin the swirling, gelatinous eyes. But instead, he saw Bentheim's face shimmering in the dark just as it was when they'd met: thin-skinned, pale, elongated, delicately cut.

"So, there's nobody to look after you."

Till could see Bentheim's eyes turned in his direction. "I'll get by," he said.

The man in front of him was silent. He seemed to be thinking. Then his voice broke the darkness again. "Maybe I shouldn't take you back first thing tomorrow."

Till hesitated. *Why . . . not?*

"No need to rush things. Right?"

Till could hear his heart beating.

"There's a room right next to Max's that no one uses. Did he show it to you?"

Till's heart was no longer beating in his chest; it was beating in his throat.

"Maybe you could spend a few days there, to start with."

Now it was fear that crept over Till, fear that he was mistaken, fear that Bentheim would take back what he had just said.

"We'll have to see what we can do, but to start with, I mean, would that be okay with you, Till?"

"Yes," Till heard himself shout. "Yes." He jumped up. Threw himself at the man at the door. "You mean I can live here for a while? In the room next to Max?"

"You two get along, don't you?"

"Yes! Of course we do!"

"Then let's give it a try. I'll talk to the authorities. Maybe we'll come up with a solution by the end of summer vacation, something better than just sending you back where you came from."

Till was having trouble catching his breath. He could stay?

"Sleep now; we'll set up the room for you tomorrow."

And with that, Bentheim left him alone.

Almost as if floating, Till staggered to the air mattress, pulled the blanket over him, and stared into the darkness of the shed.

He was staying here, with Max and Lisa and . . .

It was as if a distant voice wanted to add another name.

. . . and Bentheim.

For a fraction of a second, Till saw Bentheim turn to the mirror and study the waves that were racing across his body under his skin. His eyes dancing up and down in their sockets before—and here, the night's words and events merged into an inextricable mass— the shimmering eyes settled on Till's face and the man, in a voice almost a whisper, said to him: *You can stay here, kid. Here with us, if you want.*

11

TODAY

"Did you tell Mom about it?"

"No way!" Claire leans back in the armchair Lisa has offered her. "But I have to talk to someone; I can't get it out of my head."

"Obviously, I mean, I can understand that." Lisa refills her sister's cup from the teapot. Claire is visiting Lisa in her apartment, and they have made themselves comfortable by the picture window in the sitting area.

"This afternoon, in the hospital, he . . . Konstantin is . . . he won't admit it, but the accident has hit him pretty hard."

"What do the doctors say?"

"Not much. He should rest, but of course he doesn't want to rest; he's dead set on some case . . ." Claire doesn't finish the sentence.

Lisa looks at her without speaking.

"He asked me to marry him," Claire suddenly bursts out.

Lisa smiles. "And?"

But Claire doesn't feel like smiling. She makes a steeple with her hands over her nose and looks past them at her sister. "I didn't answer." She sees her sister nod.

"Talk about timing," Claire continues, "after what happened at the boxing match. I never would have thought I could be so reckless. It . . . I really don't know how it happened."

"What are you going to do now?"

Claire falls silent. She has no idea.

"Do you *want* to marry Konstantin?"

"No." She paused. "No. And now, after what went on with Frederik, definitely not. It's just . . ."

"What?"

"You know, Konstantin was always—is always—I have a good feeling when I'm around him. It's like I don't have to be afraid of anything if I know he's there, there for me. And when I think splitting up, it's as if the fear . . . as if nothing would be there to protect me from it. I know it's an unexplainable fear, maybe an irrational fear, but it's still real to me. You know what I mean?" Claire looks at her sister, hiding nothing. "When I think of us breaking up, it's like the fear would reach out to grab me, would overpower me."

Lisa listens to her in silence.

"I don't know. Is that love?" Claire sighs, then continues. "But the thought of marrying Konstantin. It feels wrong, somehow. I can't stop thinking about Frederik."

****

"What do you mean, 'what's wrong?'" Claire stands in the doorway to the living room and looks down at Butz, who has taken off his shoes and is lying on the couch. His eyes are sunken hollows—the accident has hit him hard, even' if he tries to downplay it.

"Why don't you tell me how things went for you," she says, exaggeratedly opening her eyes wide.

He waves it off. "I was far too late. I should have just left instead of wasting my time with the doctors."

"What was the problem?" Claire's eyes come to rest on the stubble on his chin.

"It would have cost, what, two million a day if they'd stopped construction for any length of time?" Butz has to chuckle. "I haven't got the slightest idea. I've forgotten the exact figures again. Doesn't matter. They're back at work on the site. And we can't get to the tunnel from the other side, either. We'd have to tear down half an office block." He sits up a little, reaches out for a glass of water he's set down on the table beside the sofa.

It is evening. She has just come home.

"And with you?" He looks at her intently. "I hope the pictures turned out?"

"From the boxing?" *I don't know what to say to you, Konstantin. Frederik has left eight messages on my voice mail.*

"Claire?"

"Hmm?"

Butz sits up on the sofa. "Come here, sit awhile."

She hesitates.

"What's the matter? You're acting like a bird that's fallen out of its nest."

It's crazy. How can she let Frederik put her under pressure like this? But even as Claire is trying hard to be outraged on the inside, she can feel her thoughts of Frederik running riot. Her memory of what happened so suddenly between them in that changing room hounds her, confuses her, intoxicates her.

"Are you expecting someone?" Butz looks at her in surprise.

Claire pulls herself together. "What?"

"The doorbell rang. Are you expecting someone?"

Claire shakes her head. *What? Why?*

"I'll see who it is." Butz stands up from the sofa.

She hadn't heard the doorbell at all. He brushes past her to the front door.

Claire picks up her handbag from the floor and leaves the living room, heading for her room. A shower, then bed. She's dog tired. But she doesn't make it to her room; she recognizes the voice of the man at the front door.

Claire stops in the hallway and turns around.

It's . . .

"Claire!"

She takes a sharp breath.

"Claire?"

"Yeah?"

Butz is calling to her. "Did you order drinks?"

No.

But the voice. It was Frederik's voice she'd heard. *"Claire??"*

She moves. When she reaches the entry hall, she sees him standing on the landing in front of her apartment door. It *is* Frederik. And he's holding two crates of bottles in his hands.

His eyes meet hers and Claire feels as if she'll fall down on the spot. Frederik's eyes are smiling at her. "Did you order the mineral water?"

Butz is looking at her, frowning.

Claire nods. A lump blocking her throat. "Yes!" she blurts. "Exactly. I'll take care of it." She nods at Butz. "I totally forgot. I thought . . . so we wouldn't have to carry it."

"Oh, okay." Butz smiles.

"Follow me." Claire looks at Frederik. "I'll show you where you can put the crates."

Frederik steps past Butz and carries the crates into the hall. Butz turns away and makes his way slowly back to the living room. Claire turns around without making eye contact with Frederik again. She walks down the hall ahead of him, leading him toward the kitchen.

"I've still got the two crates of juice down below," she hears Frederik say at her back, his breath tickling the nape of her neck.

She stops in the middle of the hall and turns around. He towers behind her, his face frank and open, angled above her. And he smiles.

Claire can hear Butz in the living room. She is nearly choking on her excitement. She sees Frederik's face close to hers, feels his lips at her ear, as if an enormous bird were brushing past. Something explodes in her belly.

She backs away, practically runs into the kitchen from the hallway. "Here. Here's good." She opens a small door that leads to a pantry.

Frederik steps past her into the storeroom and drops the crates of water on the floor.

"Why haven't you called?" His voice is husky, breathless. "I can't stand being without you."

Is he crazy?

His hand touches her, seems to want to hold her and caress her at the same time. "I need you, Claire. I want to see you."

Then she's out of the pantry again, Frederik following close behind.

"Are you still going to bring the crates of juice up?" She looks at him levelly.

"Be right back." He leaves the kitchen.

She stands in the bathroom, her eyes scanning her face frantically. She looks tired. She turns her head, pulls her hair together, and reaches for a hairclip.

"The juice in the pantry, too?" Frederik is there again.

"Yes, please." Claire shoots out of the bathroom, sees his back moving down the hallway, the crates in his hands.

As she returns to the kitchen he is just entering the pantry—and she follows him. He turns around, sets the crates down, and touches the waistband of Claire's jeans with his right hand. She pulls the door of the pantry closed behind her, her breath coming hot from her throat. In one movement, he opens her jeans and slides them over her hips. Then his left arm is around her waist. Claire can feel herself flying. For a moment, she has the impression that her senses are getting confused. She sees him inclining his head, feels his hair against her cheek. She holds tight to his shoulders, his neck, and she can feel the muscles tensing under his skin. She hears very clearly the click of her belt buckle as it taps against the wall. Then she lowers herself onto him.

****

She pushes her head out from behind the shower curtain and listens for a moment. Butz must have gone into his study; she can't hear him at all.

She lets the hot water stream over her.

She is standing under the shower; Frederik left the pantry ten minutes earlier. It took only moments, the whole thing.

The second time! Thinking about what she's done makes her dizzy. She can't explain it. How could she lose control of herself like that?

Hot steam fills the air behind the shower curtain. She lathers herself with shower gel, rinses. Then she turns off the water and grabs her bath towel from the rail. She throws it around herself and steps out of the shower.

He was like a man possessed—by *her*. But they barely know each other. They'd seen each other for the first time when she was taking the pictures of him at the fight. The thrill of victory, the exhilaration. Maybe it was the way she was taking pictures of him that spurred him on—she could understand that. It was just something that came over them in the changing room. A moment of madness—that can happen.

But today? He really must have done his homework, found her address. He had to come up with the story about the crates of drinks.

And then, in the pantry, she could actually feel how he burned to be near her.

Claire rubs dry the hair tumbling halfway down her back. She can't deny that the minutes in the pantry shook her to the core. Frederik was unstoppable, and more powerful—many times more powerful—than any man she has ever known. As much as she hates to admit it, it was an encounter with an intensity that she has never felt with Konstantin.

It wasn't just that Frederik was hell-bent on having her. His passion—wherever the impulse had come from—had swept her up and carried her along with him.

Claire is unable to suppress a smile. She must have really turned his head at the boxing match. As crazy as it might sound, she can understand it in a certain way. The same thing had happened to her.

She ties her hair, still damp, into a thick knot on the back of her head and slips into the bathrobe hanging on the door.

Still, when she had taken Frederik's head in her hands just now to look into his eyes, there'd been something in his look.

Thinking it over, Claire pulls open the bathroom door and strolls along the hallway, heading for the kitchen.

There'd been something vulnerable in his eyes. He had stopped, had looked at her; they had looked deep inside each other. And she'd had the feeling that he wanted to say something to her. She had stroked his cheek, hesitant—his lips moved; it was clear he was searching for words.

She'd had the feeling that he wanted to explain something. But what was there to explain?

She opens the refrigerator in the kitchen, takes out a mineral water, and drinks deeply, straight from the bottle.

What had he been trying to explain?

Claire puts the bottle back, closes the door of the fridge.

The apartment is almost deathly still. But Konstantin must be in his study. Mustn't he?

Suddenly, a completely new thought strikes her. Had Konstantin noticed something? She hadn't seen him again—not since he'd opened the door for Frederik. She'd been convinced he was in his study, working.

Claire tilts her head slightly to one side. Not a sound.

Of course he noticed something! But it had only taken minutes.

She creeps along the hallway cautiously, heading for the living room, which connects to Butz's study.

The door to his room is closed. Nothing unusual about that. Butz is always careful to close the door behind him when he's inside.

Claire moves past the couch silently and goes to the door. Not a sound from inside. She spins around—suddenly struck by the thought that he could be standing behind her. But there's no one there. Just the living room, quiet.

Claire turns back to the door to his study. She hasn't been inside for weeks. It's where Butz keeps files from the office, and she knows he doesn't like her going in there.

Slowly, she puts one hand on the door handle, presses down on it. There's a slight creaking of the latch but no response from inside.

"Konstantin?" No answer.

Claire throws the door open and recoils. The room is empty. But the four walls of the small study, normally bare and white, are now almost completely covered with notes, cuttings, pictures, forms, sketches, and documents. Interview records, minutes of meetings, site plans, transcripts. And photographs, everywhere. Dozens—hundreds—of photographs.

Claire moves over to the opposite wall and leans forward to take a better look at the photos, which she has never seen before.

She quickly realizes that the pictures on the walls are from two different cases. Pictures of a woman's dead body lying in a parking lot—the shopping center, the cars, detail shots of her injuries, the evidence around her—and pictures of a woman lit up by a car's headlights, lying in a pit on a construction site at night, an electric drill, her T-shirt. There is an image of Butz himself bending over the woman, looking deep into her eyes and holding her hand.

Claire scans his desk, which has been shoved back against the wall, below the photos. Files, court records, notes—at a glance she realizes the documents are connected not only to the two cases involving the dead women but also to other crime scenes and locations that seem similar to where the women were found.

The whole study looks to Claire like a kind of shrine—a memorial to the two dead women.

They must have become some sort of obsession for Butz. He'd started talking about it while he was still in hospital. Claire sighs.

And without being able to say why, the question that has been gnawing at her subconsciously the whole time comes back: *What was it that Frederik had wanted to tell her?*

Suddenly, she feels cool pressure on the back of her neck. The hairs on her neck rise; her heart falters and her body stiffens. Goose bumps suddenly rise on her skin like a rash. She wants to turn around, but the hand on her neck pushes her forward, forcing her down over the desk. She wants to scream, but it's as though her throat is paralyzed. The glossy photos buckle and bend under the palms of her hands.

And at the same time, she feels the bathrobe being pushed up and over her raised, naked buttocks.

12

"Please!"

The voice sounds muffled, but still it drowns out the whispering of the forms that are in the room with Till. It seems to penetrate the walls.

"Can you hear me?"

Till's eyes scan the wall, which is no more than ten feet from him. Black. Windowless. Shining in the darkness.

A man steps into his field of vision and Till turns his eyes upward.

An involuntary shudder runs through his body. At the same moment, his sides start to burn, as if someone is running a flame along them.

"Everything okay?" The man winks at him. He has no knobs on his head, and there are no tattoos crawling out from under his collar, no metal dangling from his face.

"Help me up, Felix," Till chokes out.

But the man in front of him lifts an index finger to his lips.

"What?" Till tries to raise his arms but the pain throws a black shadow across his eyes. When he can see clearly again, Felix is bending down to him.

Felix places a hand behind his ear, as if to hear better, and turns to the others, who are milling around under the woman suspended on the hooks. "Everyone be quiet," he hisses.

Till holds his breath; the figures fall silent. The only sound is the shuffling of their feet on the concrete floor.

And . . .

A metallic clacking. The sound is jerky, agitated, as if stumbling along.

A *ticking.*

Felix opens his eyes sharply. Till can see them shining through the darkness. "Six minutes to go," he hears Felix whisper. Six minutes.

"Yes?" Till's breathing turns flat.

"Yes." Felix grins down at him and nods his head.

"Six minutes of *what*?!" Till explodes.

"You," says Felix, cutting off Till's shout like he's wielding a razor. "*You've* got six minutes to go."

Till's torso folds forward. He can't move his arms, can't move his legs—but he can sit up.

The blanket slides down his body and he is looking at his abdomen. His eyes cloud over, the sounds drag and drag; it's like he's hearing them gurgling from a drain in the distance.

But he knows what he is looking at. It is a throbbing, racing, flickering. A rippling motion coursing through his body. Burrowing, breaking him down, disfiguring him.

And suddenly, Till knows what Felix has in store for him.

****

It's like a black screen bursting open, a flood of red jelly erupting from behind it. Then Till is there again.

He stares at the concrete ceiling overhead. Hears the chattering of voices. Felix's face moves into his field of vision.

With a jolt, Till sits upright.

Felix opens his eyes wide and takes a step back. "Till? What is it? Is it starting?"

Till looks down over the length of his body. He is naked. The blanket has slipped off onto the floor.

Waves are rippling across his body.

"What do you think, Till? Like it?"

Only now does Till see the coarse thread zigzagging through his skin, his flesh. That explains the burning in his legs and arms . . . The twine stitches his legs together. His forearms are sewn to his hips, his upper arms to his chest. Whenever he moves, his entire body lights up with pain, as if someone has plugged him into the mains. But the feeling of constriction—and the urge to burst out of the corset they have stitched together for him from his own skin— is also growing unbearable.

"We sterilized everything, Till. Really." Felix opens his mouth wide like Kermit the Frog, but no laugh comes out. He steps forward quickly and grasps Till's hand, which is hanging uselessly from the forearm sewn to his thigh. Felix shakes the hand.

"See? There's still feeling in it." He flinches, feigning shock. "Isn't there?"

Till screams. The power seems to emerge straight from his spine. Then he pulls his right arm away from his side, hard. At first, it holds—he feels his flesh stretching—and an ice-cold fury washes over him. A sharp jolt—the tear seems to slice him right through the middle. He feels his own blood, hot, streaming down the side of his body.

"Bravo!" Felix claps his hands and Till sees the dark figures crowding around him in the room.

"He got free," says Felix loudly, turning like a master of ceremonies to the nocturnal creatures around him. "Bravo, Till; I knew you had it in you!"

But Till can hear Felix's voice only softly, as if muffled, heard through a veil. Everything happens in what feels like slow motion. It's like he's weighed down, outside the real world. He tenses his left arm, jerks the elbow down. The suture splits and blood pours down his side. He throws himself back onto the mattress, pulls his stitched-together legs up to his stomach—screams—and rips them apart. For a second, he thinks he's losing consciousness. The pain is so fierce, so real, so physical; it is as if a mountain is crashing down on top of him. Then his feet are swinging freely through the air. He rolls off the mattress, sees the figures around him fall back. Staggering, dripping, howling, he straightens up next to the bed.

Till screams unintelligibly. It is a scream to keep unconsciousness at bay, even as he feels the blood flowing out of him. He dimly sees the man with the extended mouth step up beside him and ram a needle into his thigh—a slight prick only just perceptible over the wall of pain surrounding him.

"A drop of *epinephrine*, Till. That's what you wanted, wasn't it?" Felix's bottom lip is curled over his teeth.

The needle hits Till's thigh a second time. He feels the pressure as the hormone is pumped into his body.

****

"You conned your way into my confidence, Till. That's why I brought you here!" Felix's voice cut through the basement room they were standing in. "You sneaked into my company, and you never told me what you *truly* wanted. I trusted you. I asked you to take care of Max; I showed you what we were working on. 'That's very interesting, great, fantastic'—those were your very words. You deceived me, and you tried to flatter me . . . you were not *straight* with me, Till. I thought you were smarter than Max. I thought I could rely on you, but you never showed me your true face!"

"Felix!" A gurgling scream comes from behind the wall, as if water is being sprayed into the mouth of whomever they have hidden back there.

A blow strikes the wall.

Till's body is burning. The epinephrine courses through his arteries.

"What do you want to do? You want to help him?" Felix has noticed how Till has turned his attention to the wall. "Don't you think you've got enough to worry about?! Do you really think you can take care of him, too?"

"Get me out of here!"

Felix's eyes glitter. "Three minutes, Till—you've got three minutes left," he says, and throws a bundle of clothes at Till: Till's own. "Plenty of time to get dressed."

Till scrambles into his pants and shirt, stuffs his feet into his shoes, ignoring the laces. Felix doesn't take his eyes off him.

"You're already on your feet, Till. So, what's it going to be?"

TWELVE YEARS AGO

For most of the first two weeks Till spent with the Bentheims, Lisa stayed out of his way. Because she had met him before Max had, she initially felt that there was a special, secret bond between them. But she soon came to realize that Max, who hardly left his new friend alone for a minute, had staked his claim on all of Till's attention. In the mornings as the house slowly came to life, he stormed into Till's room, still in his pajamas, and together they went down to the breakfast table. Then—even before Lisa had finished eating— the boys ran into the garden, ready to tackle the day's adventures head-on. Usually the two boys returned only briefly for lunch, then disappeared for the entire afternoon, even into the evening. Sometimes a whole day would go by without Lisa so much as catching sight of either one of them.

Nevertheless, she was happy Max had finally found a real friend. She loved her brother more than anyone else in the world, but in the last year he'd become increasingly solitary and brooding. She could almost see him blossoming under Till's influence, could see how much he loved the presence of the level-headed, reserved boy and luxuriated in the feeling of having found in Till

someone he could trust unreservedly. Within a few days, the withdrawn, difficult Max of the previous year had once again become
the happy, high-spirited youngster he had been before. Before . . .
meaning back in a time that Lisa could only vaguely remember
now, before her father and Max had begun to clash almost every
day.

Lisa couldn't remember exactly when Max had begun to with-
draw into himself. But what she did know was that the more Max
shut himself away, the more relentlessly her father hounded him.
Lisa was far from reproaching her father for that, though, not even
silently. She had always been too fascinated by the man, whose tall,
dark figure was, for her, the very epitome of power and mystery.
But there was something threatening about him, as well. He was
a being far beyond her meager powers to control but the mastery
of which hovered hazily in front of her, like a goal she might reach
when she was a little older. Not just physically older, but also more
knowledgeable, more able to understand those things she didn't
yet comprehend. An age when her thoughts would no longer get
so jumbled, when her ideas would not come so thick and fast, her
courage not desert her so rapidly.

Lisa sat up in bed and listened. It seemed like she had been
hearing Max and Till running back and forth in front of her door
for hours—ever since dinner. But finally her mother had called up
that it was bedtime and that was that. If they were not quiet up
there this instant, she would go and get their father. Even though
they all knew she was hardly likely to carry through on her threat,
there was always the possibility that she really would bring their
father from where he was working in the guesthouse. And that
would mean their father, disturbed from his work, coming into the
house in a mood that did not bode well. So peace had gradually settled over the wing of the house where the children's four bedrooms
were located: Lisa's room, Max's room, Till's new room, and the

big room where the two younger sisters had already been asleep for nearly two hours.

Lisa reached for the remote control lying on her nightstand and shut off the stereo playing softly on top of her dresser. She swung out of her bed and padded carefully to the door. When she opened it, the hallway lay quiet and dark before her. All of the rooms' doors were closed. Lisa stepped out, closed the door behind her, and tiptoed toward the room directly opposite her own. In front of the door, she stopped and listened again. Not a sound from inside. Should she knock? But then she decided to just push down the door handle carefully.

When Lisa entered the room, she saw Till sitting up in bed in the dark. She stopped and stood by the door.

"You already asleep?" *Dumb question,* she thought.

"No." He leaned forward and clicked on the lamp on his bedside table. A soft light spread through the room. Till was wearing one of Max's striped pajama tops and it was clear to Lisa that her visit had taken him by surprise.

"Can I sit for a while?"

Till hesitated. "Your mom sounded pretty mad."

Lisa wasn't particularly worried about that. When her mother threatened Max with something, it rarely applied to her. And certainly not when it was just about getting some peace and quiet in the house.

Without asking for further permission, she sat down on the edge of Till's bed. "You've been pretty tight lately, you and Max."

Till looked at her, weighing her words. He seemed to be wondering what she wanted from him.

"Hmm." It sounded noncommittal.

"Max is happy to have you here with us."

Till smiled, rather helplessly. The praise clearly made him uncomfortable. "You came in here to tell me that?"

"Am I bugging you? Should I go?"

He smiled. "No, it was nice of you."

She could tell he felt obliged to encourage her to stay—but he really didn't need to. "I wanted to talk to you about Max," she said.

"What about him?"

She tried to find the right words. Till leaned against the wall at the head of his bed and waited.

"It's not just Max, exactly," she finally said. "It's . . . the two of you, you know?" She looked up and their eyes met. "Since you've been here, you've been hanging around together and . . . no one knows what you've actually been up to the whole time."

Till grinned a little.

"I mean, that's not bad," Lisa continued. "Max never used to tell me everything anyway, but . . . I mean . . . he's never been like this before. I haven't got any idea what he does all day." She was silent for a moment before adding, softly, "I love my brother, you know—"

"I can tell," Till interrupted. "You should just talk to him. We don't do so much . . . mostly just play. He shows me his things. I could only dream about that stuff in the home . . ."

"Yes, sure, but . . . that's not it . . . you're planning something," she said, digging deeper. "I can see that. And I know Max. He's really excited—and when I ask him why, he never gives me a straight answer."

Till looked at her. "So, now you want to find out from me what we do all day."

"Why not?" She returned his gaze, defiant. "You know you can trust me. When you told me you'd run away from the home, when we were in the kitchen, I only told Max and didn't breathe a word about it to my parents."

Till looked down at his blanket and seemed to think about this.

"I'm not asking you to give away any secrets or anything," she said to reassure him. "I just wanted to hear . . . you know, Max can be kind of reckless sometimes. My mom always used to tell me that I should look out for him, even though he's older. Sometimes Max just loses . . . all sense of proportion—that's how Mom puts it. He heads off down the wrong track and then there's no stopping him. Like last year, he was crazy about chess. Everybody had to play chess with him all the time. He could hardly think about anything else; he was totally obsessed with it. Then he stopped caring about chess and all he talked about was track and field. The records, the tournaments, the athletes . . . he got completely hung up on all that. And now, of course, I'm wondering: What is it this time? What's he got in his head now? With the other things, he'd usually answer if I asked, but this time . . ."

Till looked at her. *He had such beautiful, pale eyes,* Lisa thought. Now that her mother had had Till's hair trimmed at the kids' hairdresser, you could see just what an open and honest face he had. His eyes could suddenly glance in your direction or skim cautiously over you and away again—or shine flatly, as if his gaze had turned inward.

"I'd like to help you," he said, "but Max asked me not to talk to anyone about it."

"So it's true," she squealed. "You're up to something and you're deliberately keeping it secret!"

Till leaned forward and laughed lightly. "Don't worry, Lisa, it's nothing dangerous, really. Max will tell you everything as soon as it's ready. And I can tell you this much: everything's okay with him. There's no need to get wound up."

"But if anything happens, you'll tell me, right? Promise me that?" She looked entreatingly at Till. He returned her gaze, frowning slightly.

"What do you mean?"

"Nothing special, just . . . Well, if something happens, we can talk about it."

"Without Max finding out anything?"

The question hung in the air like a wrong note. Lisa felt a breath of air sweep across her skin and give her goose bumps. Had she given herself away?

"Is that stupid?" she asked, uncertain how to rescue the situation.

"Max is my friend," said Till, quietly. "I don't want to do anything behind his back."

She nodded. "'Course not . . ." She was ashamed. He was right, but she really hadn't meant anything bad.

"Why don't you talk to him yourself?" Till asked a second time, obviously making an effort to figure out what was going on once and for all.

"It's like I said. He won't give me a straight answer."

"What is it you're worried about?"

"Just stuff . . ."

"'Just stuff'? What's that supposed to mean?"

Till frowned—and Lisa realized that now he really wanted to know. And that she was on the verge of losing the trust that he had accorded her from the very beginning. *Best to own up and face the music,* she decided. "It's my dad. He asked me to talk to you."

"Your father?" Till literally jumped. "He asked you to talk to me about Max?" His face was flushed bright red.

Lisa nodded. "It's nothing bad. He just wants . . . he wants to understand Max better. They hardly ever talk anymore . . ."

"And you come in here and act like you want to talk to me about Max—but your dad's really behind this?" Till screwed up his face.

"Yes . . ." She stared down at the blanket, upset. "Now I've told you. Are you going to tell my dad about it?"

"My God!" Till punched the blanket. "What's the matter with you? Of course not!"

"But . . ." She was confused. "Then you're going behind his back, too."

"Your father? That's completely different. I'm not friends with him."

"But you are with me," Lisa heard herself saying softly—and looked up into Till's eyes.

He smiled. "Yeah, 'course." He said it like he was saying it to one of his buddies. "Don't worry about Max," he added. "I'll take care of him."

She nodded. And suddenly she had the feeling that Till wasn't just saying it, but that it was actually true: he would take care of her brother. Till would make sure that nothing happened to Max, her brother who got into trouble so easily. And when that was clear to her, she was not only infinitely grateful to Till, she suddenly saw in him more than just a boy that she liked to look at. He suddenly seemed to her to be more grown up than her brother, more grown up than any of the boys in her class, with whom she had little in common. It was a feeling of affection that rose vaguely in her, a feeling she had never experienced before, that didn't fit in, that confused her. But at the same time, it was a feeling that excited her more than perhaps anything else she'd experienced in the eleven years of her life so far.

TWELVE YEARS AGO

"Come on, do it!"

Max waved impatiently—and with a little annoyance. From where he was standing, Till was really making a hash of things. Max was in the hallway; from there, the stairs led up to the top floor. At the foot of the stairway crouched Till, looking back at him wide-eyed. Max could see through two doorways into the kitchen down on the first floor, where his mother was talking with Rebecca. He could hear the muffled voices of the two women. They were talking about the buffet that had been set up that morning in preparation for the party the following day.

Till scurried down the hallway toward Max. "Couldn't we just ask?" he whispered, looking at Max doubtfully.

Ask! Of course they couldn't *ask*! The answer would be that they were not allowed to look at them. Better not to ask in the first place. That way, at least, they weren't doing something they'd been told expressly *not* to do. Or rather, been expressly told *again* not to do. Because Max's mother had, in fact, expressly forbidden the children to look at his father's books. But that was a long time ago and Max had been a lot younger then. So, maybe the ban didn't apply anymore, right? Instead of replying, Max pulled Till by the arm in the direction of the living room. They had to hurry. His mother wouldn't be discussing dinner with Rebecca too much longer. And after that, she would probably go and sit in the living room to call someone or read the newspaper.

Max stepped silently through the wide sliding doors into the living room and made his way firmly toward the bookshelf next to the fireplace. He knew that on the top shelf stood the various editions of his father's books. He grabbed hold of the armchair as he passed and tried to pick it up. The chair was heavy, but Till helped him, and a moment later they had it maneuvered in front of the bookshelf. Max nodded to Till; it was his job to position himself on the armchair and give Max a boost.

Max planted his bare foot into Till's cupped hands and felt Till sink deeper into the upholstery. Till straightened up, and Max slid up the front of the bookshelf. He pushed against the spines of a few books that he would have to pull out again later—otherwise, it would be pretty obvious that someone had touched the bookshelf—then he placed his other foot on one of the shelves and held on tight.

"Give me the bag," he hissed to Till.

Till fished the linen bag out of the sleeve of his pajamas and handed it up. Max held one corner of the bag with the open end down between his teeth and reached into the compartment where his father's books were lined up. There were paperbacks, hardback editions, various translations, volumes of stories, anthologies, new editions, deluxe editions—but Max took no notice. What mattered to him was throwing at least a few of the volumes into the bag as fast as he possibly could. Then they could look at them in his room, undisturbed.

Max hastily filled the holes left in the row by the volumes he had taken out, removing several books from the second shelf and using them to fill the gaps. That section of the bookcase was not in any particular order in any case and no one would notice that he'd helped himself to a few of the books. *I should have done this ages ago,* he thought.

Ever since Till had told Max about the strange text that his father had read aloud during the night two weeks earlier, Till and they had begun secretly observing Max's father—when he joined them for meals at the table, when he left the house in the morning to go to his desk, and now and then when he came to the house at midday to talk with Max's mother. Max had also tried—cautiously—to sound out his mother on the subject of his father, or at least to turn the discussion around to him, asking her how and where exactly they had met. But all he could get out of his mother were superficialities. And the harder he tried, the clearer it became that there was actually only one way to learn more. To actually find out something more definite about his father, he had to read the man's books.

"Here!"

He let the bag of books drop onto the armchair next to Till's feet. Then he stepped back into Till's interlaced fingers and slid back down the shelf.

****

Max did not understand most of what he read that night. He knew he would have been better off taking a little more time with the text, that he ought to have begun with just one of the books and hidden the others for a few days under his shirts or between the games in the cupboard. But he couldn't shake the fear that Jenna, who cleaned for them, or his mother might discover them. So, he decided they could use that night to get a broad overview and return the books to the shelf the next day. This, however, resulted in Max hastily opening one after the other, beginning to read, and then—before he could even get into the story—clapping the book closed again to start on the next. This flightiness may also have been rooted in his fear that he might come across things in one of the books that he would rather not see at all.

The story in the first book he picked up seemed to be set in a spaceship traversing the universe, centuries in the future—the story, as Max read in the blurb on the book flap, dealt with "time paradoxes." He noted this with interest, but it also made him a little uneasy because he suspected he would *believe* he could understand the story, but that he wouldn't *really* understand it—that he'd be missing something crucial but wouldn't know what it was.

He put the book aside and reached for one bound in black cloth. By tilting the book a little in the light, however, the title *Thirst* and his father's name could be seen. Skimming through the pages revealed that this was a novel assembled from diary entries, extracts from other books, newspaper articles, and transcripts. Max understood that it told the story of a young girl stricken by a certain compulsion that her parents, in their helplessness and desperation, took as proof of her possession by . . . the *devil*. It didn't take long before the parents saw themselves forced to entrust their daughter to the care of a priest. Max's father had set the events in eighteenth-century rural Prussia and, in passages that filled several chapters, narrated in minute detail how church emissaries attempted, through spiritual discipline, to cope with the girl's increasingly vehement and all-consuming desire. Max focused especially on those parts of the book told in the girl's own voice, and it slowly began to dawn on him exactly what kind of compulsion they were talking about . . .

"That's a vampire book, man. Haven't you ever heard of Dracula?"

Till, who had been concentrating on his own book and was lying on the bed next to Max, had looked over Max's shoulder out of curiosity and read a few lines from the volume that Max was reading.

Max glanced at Till. Of course he knew who Dracula was. There were vampires of all shapes and sizes: cartoon characters, Muppets, and in every conceivable manifestation in movies. He'd never had any interest in the topic; for him, vampires were something for his little sister Claire. But what had confronted him on the pages he just scanned had absolutely nothing to do with the vampires he was familiar with. This story had nothing to do with coffins, castles, candlelight, or fangs. This was a tale about an inner power at once strange and overwhelming. A *compulsion*, his father had written, an *impulse* that literally enslaved the girl in the book. A compulsion that grew from the core of her being and at the same time subjugated that being. A compulsion that made the girl so alarmingly desirable that it plunged the priest entrusted with her care into serious moral danger. Max had not fully understood what this compulsion of hers was really about. He sensed he was still too young to do so.

Till, in the meantime, had turned back to his own book, so Max tossed the vampire story aside and reached for another book. The only thing on the dust cover was an enormous mountain rising up from a sandy plain. The book was called *The Great Ancients*, and as Max skimmed the first lines, he felt as if he had been plunged into a cold and windy night, transported to that expanse below the mountain. A plain on which he was all alone, and where his loneliness took on something immeasurable, a loneliness the depth of which would be felt by a human alone in a universe where everyone else existed only in his imagination. The only human, but not the only *being*, mind you. In the infinite depths of the night that surrounded him, they lurked—the great ancients of the title—beings whose form, aims, and origins would be forever beyond his comprehension unless they helped him by *transforming* themselves for him. But hardly had Max begun to understand this transformation before he also began to fear that he could lose himself in the process.

"If I try to follow this transforming . . . isn't it possible that I could get lost?" he whispered to Till, who only reluctantly let himself be distracted from his book.

Till took the book out of his hand. "Here," he said and held up another one. "Why don't you try this one?" Then he turned back to the pages in front of him.

Max looked at the book that Till had passed him. *Tides,* it was called, and on the cover he could see a sandy beach and a wave rolling in. It was an image of uncommon beauty, which Max—overtired and overstimulated from the rushed reading of the past few hours—could only stare at, lost in thought. Suddenly, he saw in the picture, through the water, a shimmer that on closer inspection turned out to be a school of fish, which in turn formed the outline of a female body. The outline of a woman drifting on her back, just under the surface of the water. She was naked, and her long hair flowed around her face and body; her eyes were open, so the briny seawater, it seemed, would flow into them, dissipating her, breaking her apart. But this dispersing, this dissolving, was only an impression created by the intermingling of the bodies of many, many individual fish.

Max jerked the book open in the middle—as if to forcibly free himself from the strangely flowing image on the cover—and stared at the words. He had already read the first sentence, then the second and third, before he was consciously aware of what it was that he was reading, what kind of incident his father had depicted in short, clear sentences. It was an incident that Max himself could never have come up with. He never knew such a thing was even physically possible. But his father's description distended, in a sense, his spirit, opening it into regions of the imaginable that, until now, had been kept hidden from him. Into regions of unease, sleeplessness, fear; regions he suddenly realized had already trickled inside him—as though the few sentences he had read cracked open a *fissure* into his head. A fissure that allowed new imaginings, new traumas, and new distortions to creep into his head like black and toxic maggots, a gap he wanted to close up. Deep inside him something like a shrill alarm was growing louder and louder. To plug the gap, he gobbled down sentence after sentence, faster and faster, not realizing that his father's words, which had battered this chink in his armor in the first place, would never ever be able to seal it again.

"Max!"

Till had taken hold of him by the shoulder. "MAX!" He tore the book away from Max, clapped it shut, and threw it on the floor. "You okay?"

Max sank onto his side and looked up at Till. He felt the veins pulsing at his temples, his eyes burning in their sockets. His mouth was dry. He nodded. *Yes, yes.* But he didn't say a word.

"What was that about? The book, I mean." Till grinned. "You suddenly got so quiet."

It was the horror, something in Max said, but he didn't trust himself to say it out loud.

"No idea," he croaked. "I . . . you can read it yourself . . . sometime." Suddenly, he felt immensely tired.

****

Replacing the books on the shelf where they belonged the next day wasn't difficult. There was no sign of Max's father, which meant he had worked late in the guesthouse and had also spent the night there, which happened occasionally. And Max's mother had no time to devote to the boys because of the reception that evening, so all they had to do was wait for a convenient moment. When the coast was clear, they quickly backed the armchair up against the bookshelf in the living room and Max slid the books in front of the ones he had used the evening before to fill the gaps. The bookshelf was deep, and when he heard the books fall out of sight in the gap behind the row of books, he was glad that he had decided to put them back today. Although he had fallen asleep quickly the night before, he was certain that wouldn't have been the case if Till hadn't been lying next to him reading.

"It was a strange story," said Till, who was sitting on a soccer ball and explaining what he had read the previous evening as he rolled slightly backward and forward. "But I was sucked into it right from the start."

He was sitting in front of a rusted swing set—a ladder, a pair of rings, and a swing—in the garden not far from the house. Max was sitting on the swing in front of Till.

"It was about a writer of mystery, horror, and fantasy novels," Till continued, "who loses himself, in a way, in the last story he writes."

Max swung back and forth a little on the swing.

"Okay, in order to write the story, this author has to bury himself in it," said Till. "And the more he buries himself in it, the more real it seems to him. More believable, more true. But at the same time, the author progressively loses touch with the *real* reality, *the reality he lives in*, you know what I mean? It's like he's practically sucked out of real reality into the book's reality."

Max planted his foot on the ground to stop swinging. "So? Was it any good?"

Till's eyes lit up. "Yeah, it was great. Mostly because you could really imagine it happening. Because while I was reading it, I basically found the same thing happening to me. The deeper I went into the story, the more the reality around me shifted into the background. Your room, you in your bed, everything around me was moving away. In a way, I was drifting away into the world that your dad was describing—and that's what I wanted to do, too. Every time I got distracted from it, I was sorry I had. It was like a dream, except you could decide for yourself when and if you wanted to keep on dreaming."

"And also that you yourself weren't the main figure in the dream, right? In my dreams, it's always me who goes through everything."

"Yeah, that's right . . ." Till looked down at the trampled grass between his feet.

"And what was the story that the author was writing about? Was that in the book, too?"

"It was about a guy who suddenly gets the idea that an old friend of his . . . your dad builds this up carefully and when I say it like this it sounds crazy, but he really took his time with it . . . so this guy, the main character—who doesn't really know yet what he's supposed to do with his life—suddenly, he gets it into his head that his oldest friend . . . that the things they go through together, that there's something weird going on there."

Max screwed up his face.

"No, I mean really basic things . . . it starts with him, the main guy, wondering how his friend always seems to know exactly what's going on with him. For instance, when the main guy wants to meet up with someone else he knows, some other friend, then suddenly the first friend comes by, even though there's no way he can know that the main guy is meeting someone else at that time, right there. Then it turns out that the other friend had spoken to the first friend on the phone and told him about the meeting, so it seems there's a completely normal explanation for the way he suddenly knows when and where they're meeting. But then other things happen and the guy that the story's about, he begins to think about this more and more. Like how is it possible that his friend always knows what he knows or can do just the right thing every single time? Until finally he begins to suspect that his friend can *read* his thoughts, the main guy's thoughts . . . but at the same time, the guy's completely normal, like I said, someone who wouldn't usually believe in any kind of hocus-pocus or sixth sense or anything like that. In fact, that's just it, that's what's bugging him so much. He's actually totally convinced that ghosts, telepaths, magicians, that none of those things are real or ever were real, right?"

Max nods slowly.

"I mean, when we read a book or see a film," Till continued, "then we're able to imagine that pretty much anything can happen. But when we're *not* reading a book and *not* watching a film, and just living our lives, meeting people and stuff, then we think that anybody who *seriously* believes in ghosts or magicians must be some kind of freak or nut job, right? That's how it is for me, anyway."

"Me, too," Max murmured.

"I know, right? And that's exactly what the main guy in the book thinks. Of course those things don't exist! But why is he experiencing the strangest things only with this friend? Why does his computer conk out just when he sits down to write about what he's going through with this friend? Why can't he ever reach his friend when he wants to call him but his friend always reaches him? How is that possible? He even talks about it with a girl he knows, because he can't get it out of his head. But she just makes fun of him. She's like, what's he thinking? That his friend is some kind of wizard? What supernatural powers is he supposed to have, exactly? So then the main guy begins to think about it: Could there maybe be something like . . . he doesn't know what . . . like waves within or below the reality we normally see, which *average*-sensitive human beings can't perceive but which *this friend* can, maybe completely unaware that he's doing it at all? Could *this* be what's giving him the extra information that means he can do all this amazing stuff? But it doesn't matter how much the guy thinks about it; it doesn't really get him anywhere. Because everything that he experiences with his friend happens in a kind of gray zone. The main guy's never able to prove that his friend must have found out what he knows in some kind of special way. Every time he tries to figure it out, his thoughts get all tangled up and he can't ask the decisive question. Then his friend manages to dodge him, and a few hours later he's alone again, wondering how it could have happened again, and still not understanding how his friend does all this."

"Hmmm." Max kept swinging.

"Yeah," continued Till. "And the more the main guy thinks about it, the more he's convinced that there can actually only be two possible explanations: Either everything he experiences with this friend—for some weird reason he can't figure out—just *seems* magical to him. I mean, what he goes through is actually completely normal in reality, and it's only in his own *mind* that it takes on this air of mystery. Or there really are things in the world that can't be explained with known natural laws."

Max had been listening attentively to Till, but now there was doubt in his eyes.

"That's about it so far for the story that the author's writing, okay?" said Till, returning his look.

Max nodded and swung back and forth peacefully on the swing.

"And now it happens," said Till, going on with his report. "While the author is writing the story, the story becomes increasingly real. And at the same time, normal reality—meaning his life as an author, the day-to-day life he lives—becomes blurrier and harder to hang onto.

"And the weird thing is, at the exact moment he begins to write the story, he gets it into his head that what's happening to the guy in the story is happening in exactly the same way with him and one of his own friends! Before, he'd never thought that something like that could really happen, but now he gets the feeling that he's experiencing strange things with this one friend. And he begins to ask himself whether he'll only be able to make sense of these strange events if he believes that his friend is somehow more sensitive—or more *magically gifted*—than everybody else in his life."

"So, this is the change he goes through?" Max asked, casting a glance at Till. "The guy who's writing the book, I mean."

"Yeah, that's exactly it. And, of course, he wonders if he wouldn't be better off if he stopped writing the book. Because if he's going to be honest with himself, he has to tell himself that there's no way he can seriously believe in these sorts of things. But then he thinks about it again and wonders if maybe what's going on with him—that the reality in his story seems to be overtaking the reality of his life, you could say—if this change might be *because* of the book! As if the story that he's creating in his mind and writing down has some kind of special power . . . which, of course, is super interesting to him."

"What kind of special power?"

Till looked at Max and seemed to be thinking it over.

"Come on!"

"Yeah, okay." Till was searching for the right words. "I think it has to do with the idea that particular concepts or texts or thoughts can affect somebody . . ."

"What do you mean, *affect*?"

"Well, the author believes that while he's writing the story, it's *changing* him."

"That the act of writing his story is changing him?" Max bit down on his bottom lip.

"Uh-huh." Till rolled around on his ball.

They were silent for a while.

"How does it go?" Till finally said, picking up the thread again. "'When you gaze into the abyss, the abyss also gazes into you,' right?

The book also talks about that, and it's the same idea: that stories aren't just objects—well, they're not that anyway, but . . . they're not just, like *dead* things, but more something like living beings, which once they're planted in your head . . . they can change things in there. And when it comes to living beings, there's nice ones and cute ones—but there's also nasty and dangerous ones."

Max stared at Till. "Then *that* is what's happening to my dad! He's writing a story that's changing him! And that's why he's becoming more and more like a stranger! *He's changing.* All because he's working on a story like the one you just said, a story that's affecting him!"

Till sighed. "Hold on. What I said was what happened in the book I was reading. Now you're saying it's happening to your dad in *reality*?"

"It could be! He's definitely changing! And I don't know why. I mean, he's still living the same life. He still goes out to the guesthouse and writes. The only thing that's happening is that he's continuing to work on his book. You just said it yourself. Some texts, concepts, thoughts . . . they can change you. Even more with the kind of books and stories that he has to completely *bury* himself in while he's writing them, because he's the author. He has to really see it in front of him; he has to picture it. And this makes him . . ." Max hesitated, but then said it anyway: ". . . in a way, this makes him a prisoner of his story, you know what I mean? At least, that's how I see it!" He swung back and forth, considering.

But Till wasn't yet convinced. "You think that's going to happen in real life? That a story that your father thinks up changes reality and changes him? Isn't it the other way around?! He lives his life and he uses that to shape his story to be how he wants it to be? So, the reality of his life makes a difference to his made-up world—*but not the other way around.* The made-up world doesn't affect reality!"

Max jumped down from the swing. "No!" He rounded on Till. "No way! *Of course* it works the other way around. The book I read last night, what did it say in there? That was also just words, a story that he'd made up! But the fear that it made me feel—that was real! I didn't just *imagine* I was scared! It came out of the book, jumped on me, and got inside me! The *fear*, you know? The fear that the horror that was slumbering away, coiled up inside the book, that it could overpower me the next time I go down the stairs into the basement in the dark by myself. He's the one putting a form on it. My father gives the horror a form by pouring it into his stories! And that's how he lets it out into the world! He digs it out of its hole and throws it out into the world, and if you're unlucky it jumps into your face!"

Sweat pearled on his forehead, and his hands were trembling.

TWELVE YEARS AGO

Till liked Rebecca. Max had told him that she'd been with his family for as long as he could remember. Rebecca was a trained chef who not only cooked but also took care of the shopping and, because she didn't mind doing it, the laundry. The only thing she didn't do was the cleaning. That was the responsibility of Jenna, who, like Rebecca, had her own room in one wing of the villa.

Till grinned at Max, who sat across from him at the kitchen table. Each of them had a large blue-and-white bowl and was digging into a blend of custard and cookies. "Good stuff?" he asked.

Max looked up for a second, grinned, and nodded.

Rebecca had no time to look after them. She was standing at the kitchen counter feverishly adding the final touches to the appetizers. Max's mother had come into the kitchen a few minutes before to check that everything was on track. Now they were just waiting on the tinkling of the bell and Rebecca would start serving.

Max and Till had already eaten but had come to the kitchen to sample the evening's dessert. All day, the kitchen had been a scene of frantic activity and excitement as Rebecca—assisted by Jenna and her daughter—prepared the various courses for the evening's

131

dinner. Once the guests had begun to arrive, the hubbub of voices slowly growing louder in the front part of the house could be heard as far back as the kitchen.

Till preferred to sit with Max behind the scenes in the kitchen, where the women were bustling around getting everything ready and had no time to chew them out when they helped themselves to tasty tidbits from the various pots.

Max threw his spoon into the bowl and gave Till a nod. "Wanna take off?" He seemed to have had enough of the kitchen for today.

Till wolfed down the last of his custard and jumped down from the stool he'd been sitting on. Without saying good-bye to Rebecca, they sauntered out of the kitchen toward the stairway, heading for the children's rooms upstairs. As they entered the hallway, where the stairs climbed to the floor above, Till saw Max's father standing at the front door looking out—it seemed more guests were just arriving. Till had the sudden impression that Bentheim's cheeks were a little hollower than usual and that his skull was sunken at the temples. He was wearing an expensively cut, dark-gray suit and turned his pale face in the direction of the two boys.

"Okay?" His eyes moved over Max and then stopped on Till.

"Xavier. How lovely to be here again!" chimed a woman's voice simultaneously. She must have come up to the front door just then, though out of Till's sight. Till noticed how Max's father's attention veered away as he turned to the new arrivals outside. He took a step back to allow them into the house, then bent down to the woman in a fleeting embrace and grasped the hand of the man accompanying her. For a moment, Till was able to watch him from the side, no longer intimidated now that Bentheim's eyes were off him. He was able to observe how Max's father switched to playing the host, how he welcomed his guests with an affected affability, a mixture of pleasure and irony and a touch of aloofness. An inborn gentility suffused his greeting, but as Till watched him he thought he could see that, more than anything, Bentheim was playing a role. He had to concentrate and didn't leave any gesture, word, or eye movement to chance. He seemed rather to be keeping constant vigil over himself.

Till turned around. Max had been standing next to him, but now Till saw that he had stepped into a niche in the hall that led to a small guest toilet.

"Don't feel like saying hi to them," Max mumbled with a nod toward the couple who had just arrived, as Till slipped in beside him, out of sight of the guests. Till poked out his head a little and saw Jenna moving back and forth between the kitchen and the dining room, adding final touches to the table. At the same time, he could see Max's mother, dressed in a simple iridescent turquoise evening gown, greeting the two new arrivals in the living room. Till stepped completely out of the niche, setting course for the stairway, when Max touched his arm.

"Look." He was pointing toward the living room.

Till followed his gaze and saw Julia walking with the woman who had just arrived, the pair heading slowly into the rear section of the spacious living room, while Bentheim and the man turned to the door that led from the living room into the side wing of the house. In addition to Rebecca's and Jenna's rooms, that wing contained a few rarely used rooms and the music room, which housed the grand piano. And—as the boys couldn't help but notice—several workers had been hard at work in there the whole day.

Max cast a glance at Till, and Till knew what he meant: What had the workers been working on in the music room all that time? They waited until Bentheim and his guest had vanished through the doorway, then set off.

The corridor that connected all the rooms in the wing and ended at the music room was deserted by the time the boys reached it. All they could hear was an unfamiliar sound coming from the music room. The closer they got, the louder the sound grew. The first thing Till thought of was the rustling of a wedding dress, a purring, clapping, scratching, scraping, ringing.

Till stopped in his tracks, as if some force was stopping him from going any farther. But Max, a step ahead, turned around. "Come on," he whispered, "they won't even notice us."

He scuttled the last few steps to the music room door and laid one hand carefully on the wood. The door stood ajar a fraction of an inch. The scraping and rustling coming from inside the room could be heard clearly now: a chattering, a hoarse screeching and cooing, scratching and pounding, clattering and tearing.

Max stood in front, his face pressed to the gap. Till looked over the shoulder of his friend but was unable to see into the room. Till had laid one hand on his back and could feel Max's breath coming in short, sharp bursts, his body softly vibrating, his ribs palpable through his shirt.

Max suddenly turned around and his face looked oddly askew. The eye he'd had pressed to the gap almost looked a little swollen, and partly closed.

"Anything to see?" Till's voice was no more than a breath as he whispered directly into Max's ear. Max stepped back and made room for Till, who edged forward very gradually. The pounding and screeching grew louder. He could actually feel the fierce movements that filled the room, could feel that living things were flying around wildly, the pounding of wings stirring the air, beaks snapping at beaks, claws catching, feathers brushing feathers.

They've transformed themselves, Till thought. Those are birds. Max's father has turned into a bird. A raptor as big as a man, a beast built for killing—it would rip you to pieces on sight.

His heart seemed to want to leap out of his mouth and his guts were twisted into a knot. Then he had his eye to the gap in the door and was peering inside. Because someone was passing inside the door he couldn't make out very much immediately—but in the next moment, he saw that something like a grid of bars had been set up in the room. That must have been what the workers had spent the whole day building! They had been erecting a plain, cubic grid of bars—a *cage*—in the room. And the flapping and screeching they could hear was coming from inside this cage!

Now Till could also see the flailing feathers, pointed claws, and savage beaks. The creatures seemed to have been drugged, making the brilliant colors of their feathers appear even more dazzling than usual. Parrots. Six or eight—maybe even twelve of them—penned inside the steel bars that filled half the room. In their cage, the birds attacked each other with such viciousness and ferocity that they ripped out each other's feathers, even biting small chunks of flesh from the bodies of the other birds.

Till's gaze fell on one of the animals that no longer seemed able to defend itself from the onslaught of the others. It was screeching, its eyes opened wide, wings beating, looking almost like a man in a feathered costume spreading his arms wide, baring his chest, and trying to hold on with red claws. But the other parrots, as if sensing its weakness, dived at this one bird over and over, burying their beaks deep into their victim's flesh, white where the feathers had been torn from its breast, clawing out the last few feathers, ripping up the soft skin. The desperate animal would not be able to withstand the assault much longer; death already seemed to have crept into its eyes, its pupils twitching back and forth, looking now at its attackers, now down at its own body, now through the bars at the men standing around the cage. And also at Bentheim, who—tall and gangling—was just then tipping a bottle of sparkling wine and filling the glasses of the new guest and another, much smaller, man—someone Till had never seen before. Just then, with the fierce fury of a creature bent on killing, the largest of the parrots plunged onto the injured bird. The force of the impact flung the victim against the bars of the cage with a loud clank and its claws lost their grip on the bar it had been perched on. Its wings beat feebly and helplessly, and the tiny, colorful, wrinkled eyelids slipped down over its small black eyes, the beak gaped open—and the animal fell to the floor of the cage.

The other birds seemed to rest for a moment, and only the men standing around the cage could be heard, exchanging a few words. Till looked at Bentheim's face, which looked somehow lit up, as if hot from the animal blood spilled in his house, warmed by the ferocity of the birds that had slaughtered one of their own.

Simultaneously, though, it was as if Till had been immersed in ice water, for he saw that the last guest, the one Bentheim had led to the room minutes before, was looking right at him—through the narrow slit Till had been watching from. It was a gaze that drove into Till's eye like a red-hot needle—then the door smacked against his forehead, slammed shut from inside. Till staggered back and only now did he remember that Max was standing behind him. For a moment the boys looked at each other, and then Till took him by the arm and pulled him away. He had the spontaneous impression that what they had seen had not only horrified Max but had also reached directly into his personality and twisted and deformed it like a chunk of putty.

They had no business being there; they shouldn't be disturbing Max's father and his guests, Till was thinking as they stumbled back along the hallway to the main section of the house. But Max was whispering the same words over and over to himself: "They belong together and my father is one of them. They belong together and my father is one of them . . ."

And for the first time, Till had the feeling that Max might be right.

16

You're already on your feet. So, what's it going to be?

The words seem to follow her into the tunnel.

Anni presses one hand over her mouth and stumbles on. The reek of blood in the room had become unbearable. Behind her, she can hear Felix raving—and every sound he spews out chases her, presses her deeper into that passage. Away from the basement room where the screaming of the man behind the wall had nearly driven her crazy. Away from the woman dangling on hooks from the ceiling, who should have been taken down long ago, who must have long since lost herself in the feeling of suspension, lost herself in the ecstasy that the pain brought on. Away from the young man they'd stitched together.

Anni pushes away from the walls of the passage she has stumbled into and hurries on. The rustling of her steps, the sound of her hand scraping over the wall, the buzzing of the lamps hung at regular intervals—slowly, all of this begins to drown out the shrill sounds she can still hear coming from the basement. The farther she gets away from there, the more her overstimulated senses begin to calm.

The nausea and disquiet that only minutes before were nearly driving her crazy, slowly start to drain out of her system. She turns into a smaller tunnel that branches off the main one, and speeds her steps. Soon she'll be back at the exit, back in the open air, on the surface—out of this confusion of passages, tunnels, and shafts that sometimes seem to her like the bowels of some animal slumbering under the city.

She stops, catches her breath.

Silence.

Somewhat slower now, she moves on. Lost in her thoughts, she listens to the sound of her steps reverberating from the curved walls of the tunnel.

A rustling, whispering, rasping . . .

Crunch, scrape, pitter-patter . . .

It hits her like a hammer.

It is not the sound of her steps!

Anni abruptly stops moving.

Silence.

Suddenly, she is certain that as soon as she moves the sound will start up again. The rustling, rasping, scraping that *is following her footsteps like a shadow.*

As if she had turned herself into a dog, slinking along the tunnel on *four* legs.

But she is no four-legged animal—two other legs are moving, legs that have *matched their gait to hers*! Steps touching down mere fractions of a second after her own!

Anni doesn't dare to turn around.

She plunges on. Her breath feels frozen in her throat; her legs move as if by themselves—and *it* moves behind her like a shadow . . .

Stumbling along in panic, blind as a wind-up toy, she slams into a projecting section of the wall and pain shoots through her ribs and chin.

She stops, her arms wrapped tightly around her body. The steps behind her stop.

She knows that if she turns around now, she will see it—her shadow, her companion, the pursuer whose attention she has drawn in the dim tunnel.

She doesn't risk it.

Her head fills with a roaring noise. And all at once, she sees clearly just how infinitely astray she has gone. A turn she took in the wrong direction, a mistake that goes back beyond the moment she slipped into this tunnel, back even beyond the moment she went into the basement with the others. It is a wrong turn that reaches so far back that, at some point since, she has lost her way in her own mind—a mistake now beyond correction.

And in that moment, something lunges at her from behind, burying her.

TODAY

Is it *Frederik*—is he still in the apartment after all?

Claire doesn't dare say his name.

Because if it's Butz, how could he . . . ?

Her thoughts churn in confusion. Had he noticed something—is this his way of punishing her?

She feels the hand of the man who has crept up on her, grabbed her by the neck, and pushed her forward over the desk—then his other hand slides between her bare thighs, forcing its way up . . .

She tears herself free. Spins around to face him.

It's Butz.

She can see that he is firmly in the grasp of his own arousal.

What the hell are you doing? she wants to scream at him. But does he know something . . . or not?

His head is tilted forward. His hands push her robe open, push her back onto the desk.

Without wanting to, a gasp escapes her—she realizes it sounds like a moan, knows there's no stopping him now.

His hands glide up her arms, stretching them upward over her head . . .

Claire turns her head to the side. She feels tears seeping from the corners of her eyes, but not another sound escapes her. Why doesn't she just tell him everything? Right here, right now!

She has to push him off her—but she can't. She loved him once. He's always been there for her. She has to tell him . . . but not now. She closes her eyes.

Konstantin is always a good lover. Perhaps a little on the awkward side, but passionate, honest, and caring.

She knows him better than anyone does. She can see that his body is practically smoking in its desire for her. She can see it in his eyes and his body almost screams it out loud. She knows that her body, her breasts, her hair, her thighs, and her belly drive him out of his mind. Every touch of her skin spurs him on. The excitement that has him in its grip is rising to the limits of what's bearable . . . rising so high that the fire she has ignited in him threatens to spread back to her again.

"I can't."

Her face crumples then. She senses his gaze on her and she turns her head and opens her eyes. He is looking at her, stunned, frozen in midmovement. He wipes at her tear-soaked cheeks with a thumb. Claire rolls to one side, across the desk—only too aware of her own nakedness. Only too aware how the sight of her is like a knife in his heart. She bends down and picks up the robe.

Butz stands in front of her—as still as stone.

She can't help him.

Without another word, she slips out of the room.

✳✳✳✳

"Are you sure?"

"Absolutely."

Butz looks the officer in the eye. The officer returns his look calmly—finally grins. "What? That's not so hard to understand!"

Butz looks down at the laboratory bench where the portable electric drill is lying. He knows the forensics department well. Even as a young officer, years ago, the place held a certain fascination for him. A block of buildings opposite the police complex in Tempelhof, bristling with high-tech forensics gear. Forensics: a science in its own right, and this was the playground for the force's eggheads and whiz kids—police-force nerds.

"It could really only have been a man. He tore open the trailer with his bare hands," says the forensics technician, with a nod to a few crime-scene photos lying on the bench.

"He took the drill from the trailer."

The technician nods. "The rain washed away any prints, but I assume he already had the victim—the woman—there with him."

"And the injury to her stomach? How was that done?"

The technician turns serious again. "She would have been lying on the ground already."

Butz looks at him.

The forensics technician picks up the heavy industrial drill from the table—the bit protrudes a good sixteen inches—and holds it in front of him with two hands. "He must have positioned himself in front of her," he says, bending lower at the knees. "Then he rammed it"—he drops onto his haunches and lets his arms fall in a hard, determined downward motion—"straight into her solar plexus, allowing him to put the full weight of his body behind the blow."

Butz inhales sharply.

"But he didn't just use it to stab her," the officer continues. He is still squatting, his arms outstretched. He looks up at Butz. "He switched the thing on."

"Ugh!" In spite of himself, Butz jerks the back of his left hand to his mouth.

The officer straightens up and lays the heavy drill back on the table. For a moment, the two men stand side by side, unnerved, trying to come to grips with the images running through their heads.

Why did you force yourself on Claire like that in the study? Butz's head is whispering to him. *You could see she wasn't interested!* He tries in vain to escape the memory. She'd been standing in front of his desk, in her bathrobe . . . he knew she would be naked underneath. He couldn't stop himself; he pulled up the robe, revealing her bare skin beneath, still slightly moist from the shower. He took her by the neck and held her tight, pushed her down on the desk, for a moment unable to hold himself back even though he could sense she didn't want it like that . . . For a moment it was as if he was enslaved by the sight of her, as if he'd been taken over by the desire to touch her, to feel her in his grasp . . . until, almost violently, she'd had to wrench herself away from him.

"And the woman in the parking lot?" says Butz, forcing himself to push aside his thoughts of the night before.

"No murder weapon."

"Her face. That's . . . it's . . ."

The officer nods, pensive. "Her injuries must have been inflicted by hand."

By hand . . .

"We sent you the paperwork on similar cases," he continues. "But it's true that the two women, the one from the construction site and the woman in the parking lot . . . basically, they don't compare with any other cases we have on file . . ."

The technician turns back to the documentation lying on the bench and picks up a few photographs processed by the forensics branch. They show the knees and the palms of the victims' hands. The scraped skin is clear to see.

"Apparently, they tried to get away."

"On their knees?"

"The woman on the construction site must have crawled a few hundred yards like that."

The officer indicates a pair of high-heeled shoes in a transparent plastic bag on the bench. "The heel is broken off—those are the shoes from the woman in the parking lot. She seems to have tried to get away as well. And here"—he holds up a shot of a bloody handprint for Butz to see—"she stumbled several times, but she always managed to get back up and keep going . . ."

"Any sign of rape?"

"Mr. Butz?" a voice interrupts the two men.

Butz turns around. A young assistant approaches him, carrying a large cardboard tube under his arm.

"No," Butz hears the technician say. "No, nothing like that."

"What is it?" Butz is looking at the assistant.

"The layouts from the planning authority are there. I've brought them along."

"Okay, good." Butz casts a glance at the forensics specialist. "Can we look at them here?"

"Of course." The officer pushes a few machines aside on the bench to make some space, and the assistant takes a large sheet of paper out of the cardboard tube.

"Here." He spreads the plan out on the bench.

At first, all Butz sees are gray areas; fine, black lines; and tiny labels.

"This is the building site on Invalidenstrasse." The assistant runs his finger over an area that Butz now recognizes as the street where he stopped his car. "This shows the system of sewers under the street. And these are the water inlets and drains from the houses along the street."

Butz props his arms on the bench and concentrates on the plan. "Okay."

"This here is a tunnel . . . it's old, from the industrial boom, 1905 or 1910," the assistant explains. "It runs along the back of the

site . . . but there, where you saw the shaft in the embankment"—
his hand indicates a conspicuously blank part of the map—"there's
nothing marked."

Butz keeps his eyes down. He hadn't been imagining it! He'd
damn near died in the fucking thing!

****

It stinks.

The crunching of steps echoes off the compact, curving walls
of the tunnel. A narrow pathway close to the wall ensures their feet
stay dry. In the center of the tunnel, where the floor angles down to
the middle from both sides, a brown stream of sewage rolls along.

"You should try walking along here when it hasn't been raining
for days beforehand." The man from the utilities laughs. "Without
a breathing unit, it's basically impossible."

Butz takes a handkerchief out of his pants pocket and holds it
over his nose. The smell is strong enough for him as it is. He regrets
not putting on the protective suit the man had offered him. As soon
as he's out of here, the first thing he's going to do is shower . . .

"Hey—whaddaya know?!" The utilities man in front of him is
pointing the beam from his flashlight straight ahead. Butz looks
past him. In the beam of light cutting weakly through the stuffy air
of the tunnel, he can see that a number of stones have been broken
out of the tunnel wall. They block the pathway, and some have
rolled into the putrid stream in the middle.

Butz pushes past the man and walks the few yards to the
stones. In the hazy light of the tunnel lamps he can dimly make
out a gap broken into the wall by the removal of the clinker bricks.
The flashlight beam swings into the gap.

The opening is a good three feet high and about the same
across. Inside, a crude shaft dug into the earth leads away from

the gap. There are no cables, no lamps, and no kind of structural support at all.

"Who'd do somethin' like this?" The man next to Butz takes a cell phone out of his protective overalls. "This has to be secured immediately—the whole wall could come down!"

Butz turns his gaze into the shaft where the light from the flashlight disappears. He knows from the plans that they are less than three hundred yards from where he was buried. But he doesn't even think about crawling into the shaft again.

"Did you get an ID on her?" Butz keeps his ear to his telephone as he hurries along the tunnel. The utility worker has remained at the demolished section to wait for the emergency team.

"Not much we could do," comes the voice of Butz's assistant. "Either the killer robbed her or somebody took her wallet and phone while she was lying in that pit."

"What about the missing persons reports?"

"We're checking them—nothing yet."

"And the woman from the parking lot?"

The phone crackles.

"What?"

Not a great connection.

"The woman from the parking lot! Did she have any ID? Have you been through her things?"

"Hold on," says his assistant. Butz hears only his own steps, and then the other man is on again. "Fehrenberg already took care of that . . ."

"Really?" Fehrenberg was the detective who had originally been assigned to the murder in the parking lot. But Butz had found out only that morning that Fehrenberg had left two days earlier for a three-week holiday with his family. "Okay . . . I need you to get the details of the victim and . . ."

"Fehrenberg's on holiday."

"And what about his sub?" Butz feels himself growing impatient. "Get whoever's filling in for him on the horn and—" But he doesn't need to finish.

"Of course, Mr. Butz," his assistant hurriedly reassures him. "I'll call you back."

TODAY

The wood splinters as the officer's heavy boots crash into the door. Butz and his colleague had been trying for ten minutes to get the door open, pushing buttons on the huge, smudged doorbell panel, shouting, and hammering on the door. No one answered.

The door swings inward and slams against the wall. For a moment, in the dim, narrow corridor on the other side, Butz thinks he sees a figure running away. He takes a step back, tips his head, and looks up at the massive facade. How many floors is that? Twenty? Thirty?

The postwar apartment block stands on the edge of Hohenschönhausen and, at first glance, nothing distinguishes it from the mountains of similar buildings all around—but it is different from the other towers in one key point: this colossus is empty. Nearly six hundred apartments where no one lives. At least not officially. Of course, the police are aware that, now and then, people do set up house in the enormous building. Until today, though, Butz has not had the dubious pleasure of needing to enter the place.

"You want to wait in the car?" he says, looking over at his colleague. Definitely the best option, or chances are they'd come out afterward and find their nice police BMW a smoldering wreck.

"No problem." The officer turns away.

Butz turns back to the building.

"Hello?"

No answer.

He moves inside the main door.

A distant crackling and rustling, as if the whole building is breathing, if not actually alive.

"I'm coming in!"

The woman from the parking lot was registered as still living with her parents. From them, Fehrenberg found out where their daughter had been living the last six weeks of her life.

Butz walks as far as the elevators and presses a button. The light blinks on. But then he changes his mind and turns back to the stairs. The last thing he wants is to find himself stuck in a pre-nineteen-eighty-nine elevator shaft.

Cautiously, he starts to make his way up the stairs. The steps are bare concrete, and decades of grime and dust have gathered in the corners.

As far as Butz knows, Fehrenberg didn't even pay a visit to this place. Should he try to find the apartment where the girl had been living?

He stops. He can hear footsteps, someone running away.

"Hello?"

Butz leans out over the railing in the middle of the stairwell and looks up. He thinks it's a shadow, as if a cloud were passing in front of the sun—then he jerks his head back. The rush of displaced air hits him in the face. Something flies past him with a hiss and slams into the floor a few yards below with a loud crash. Through the metal bars of the railing, he looks at the smashed remains of a cheap built-in cupboard at the bottom of the stairwell.

His heart pounds.

"Are you crazy?!" He storms up the steps two at a time. They want to pelt him with furniture? Like they're under siege in some kind of castle?

Second floor.

Butz quickly glances down the hallway that leads off from the stairwell. Doors, doors, doors. Most of them open, some closed. The hallway floor is bare cement. It smells like piss.

Higher.

Third floor. The same.

Butz holds his breath. He has a stitch in his side from running up so fast. The rustling and crackling seems louder.

Another floor.

Again, the hallway and doors. But this level doesn't smell quite as putrid as the others.

Butz bends down and picks up an old newspaper from the floor, throws it behind him into the stairwell. The fluttering sound recedes as it falls.

He freezes, doesn't move a muscle.

Then he hears it. A kind of whispering.

Then he's running down the hallway. Past the first open door. The apartments are still partly fitted out with old East German furniture.

Now he hears it clearly. The quick patter of running feet.

He races on—pauses.

The sound of running abruptly stops!

It has to be behind him, in one of the apartments he's already passed.

Butz spins around. There's no one in the corridor behind him.

He runs back a few steps to the last apartment, storms inside.

"Don't!" The scream seems to drive in under his skin.

There! A skinny figure slips around the corner, disappears behind a door that leads deeper into the apartment. Butz follows. As he crosses the threshold, he sees him out of the corner of his eye: a young guy, maybe twenty, probably younger, pressing himself to the wall behind the door—he slips past Butz and out the door he's just come in through.

Butz whirls around; his hand brushes the young guy's arm, but he doesn't manage to get hold of him.

He's running. In front of him, he sees the young guy's thin sports shoes bounding over the cement floor, the shirt flapping around his emaciated body.

Butz leaps. He throws himself to one side to avoid landing on the kid with all his weight. They hit the floor hard. Butz feels the wind get knocked out of him.

But he holds on tightly to the thin body of the boy who'd run; he sees dark eyes staring back at him in fear.

****

The colors on the photo are washed out, the figures unclear—but the young woman is still easy to recognize. She holds one hand over her eyes, shielding them from the sunlight most likely, and laughs for the camera.

"We all loved her." The scrawny boy lowers the phone again.

He and Butz are sitting on the floor, their backs to the wall.

"She never said what was going on, not exactly—something about her stepdad at home . . . whatever, she liked living here more," the young man continues. "We left her to herself. But everyone still knew her."

He stuffs the old phone back in the pocket of his jeans and looks at Butz. "Did you find anything out, about what happened?"

Butz pulls his legs up and rests his forearms across his knees. "Just dead ends so far." He doesn't even look at the kid. "But there was a second body—the day before yesterday. And from what we have, there are similarities with Nadja's case." Now he looks to the side. The young guy's head is hanging and he's doodling in the dust on the floor with his finger.

"While we're fishing around in the dark, somebody's going around the city chasing girls to death . . ."

"'Chasing' ? What do you mean by 'chasing'?" The young man looks at him.

"The injuries point toward Nadja being . . . it looks like she was hunted down. She and the second victim, both of them. Hunted down and murdered."

The young man seems to be mulling over Butz's words.

"Were you close to her?"

"It's like I said. All of us wanted to be her friend, but Nadja kept everyone at a distance."

"Didn't she say anything? Anything that stood out? What did she do all day?" The young guy continues scratching in the dust on the floor. "Hmm?" Butz nudges him lightly with his elbow.

"Yeah, okay, you're right," says the young guy, not looking up. "Seems she'd been meeting up with some bod mods lately . . ."

"Some what?"

"Bod mods—like body modification . . ."

"Tattoos, stuff like that?" Butz has a rough idea.

"Tats. Also implants, scarification. All kinds of shit."

"That's who she'd been meeting lately?"

"I asked her if she'd take me along. She told me that they got pretty extreme—I figured maybe it'd be exciting—but she didn't want to."

"Take you along?"

The boy nods.

"Take you along where? Did she say that? Where she met up with them?"

The kid lets his head gyrate slightly.

"Hmm?"

"No, nothin'."

"Really? Nothing?"

In the half-dark, Butz can see the young man's eyes shimmering. The evening is creeping in slowly.

"She said it was in the city—that they'd hook up in the city."

"Which city?" Butz hears the young man sigh. "In Berlin?"

"Not in Berlin. I mean, yeah, sure, but . . ." The young man's voice trails off.

"But . . . ?" Butz gives him another friendly nudge in the side— he almost believes he can feel the young man's ribs with his elbow.

"Oh, come on, you already know," he hears the kid quietly say.

"What?"

"That's what she said."

"*What* did she say?" Butz can feel his muscles cramping impatiently. But what was he supposed to do? Beat it out of him?

"That she'd meet them in the hidden city."

"In the *hidden* city?"

"Uh-huh."

Butz's palms grow moist. This isn't the first time he's heard of it: the hidden city. But up to now, he'd written it off as a rumor, no more.

"Isn't that just a story? I mean, that it even exists . . ."

The young man beside him has let his head sink again. Butz watches as the kid lifts one hand to his nose, blows into his fingers, and wipes his hand on his pants.

"Chased to death." The boy's voice sounds husky and quiet, as if through a veil. "They really chased her to death."

Butz lays one arm carefully around the boy's shoulders. *Yeah, that's what it looks like.*

TWELVE YEARS AGO

Till poked at his cornflakes. He was watching Bentheim in his peripheral vision. Till had become adept at observing Max's father without looking at him directly. He seemed slightly paler than usual. His thin hands plucked repeatedly at a napkin that lay beside his plate; he clattered his coffee cup on the saucer and ran his fingers through his hair. Till had fallen asleep very late the night before, but he guessed the sounds from the guests down on the ground floor could be heard in his room until much later.

Till glanced over at Max and saw that he, too, was watching his father. When Max met Till's eye, Till turned his attention back to Bentheim. He looked much as he always did, perhaps a little hollowed out, a little nervous; but in his casual suit, freshly pressed shirt, and thin, burgundy tie, he looked as if the only thing bothering him was his work, which also brought in a lot of money. Only when you looked closer, thought Till, when you didn't let his gaze intimidate you into turning away, when you looked him in the eye a little longer instead and realized just how big his pupils were, how gray the whites of his eyes had become, how deep the lines creasing his eye sockets were . . . only then could you begin to suspect that there might be more to what tormented the man than just professional preoccupations. That it may have been fears one could normally leave behind just by growing out of child-hood—gnawing, grating fears that must fill him with a disquiet that maybe, sometimes, he believed he was no match for. It was a disquiet, an agitation that he had to struggle with unremittingly, that made him—the word came to Till unbidden—*dangerous*. Because anyone plagued so much by their inner demons was not only unpredictable but would also go to great lengths to finally find some peace, some protection from the attacks he felt himself exposed to.

"You want to talk about it?" Till heard him say, and he raised his head with a jerk. But Bentheim had addressed Max, not Till.

Max gripped his cornflakes spoon tightly and shook his head.

Bentheim looked briefly at Till. "You were standing at the door. Felix saw you."

"Yes. We didn't know you didn't want us there." Till's heart pounded.

Bentheim scrutinized him. Then he turned back to Max. "Is that why you've been staring at me the whole time?"

Max looked over helplessly at his mother. She smiled back, but said nothing.

Bentheim set the coffee cup he'd been holding back on the saucer and leaned forward a little in Max's direction. "Listen, Max, it was nothing bad. It was just a game. Maybe you didn't like it, but I also didn't want you to watch it. I met up with a few friends and we did it. And I will not justify the things I do to my twelve-year-old son."

Max had lowered his head. He nodded. His hand was still wrapped around the spoon in his bowl. Lisa and her sisters sat at their places in silence, as if hoping that the threatening cloud suddenly looming in the room would drift on as quickly as it came.

"Max just got a fright," said Julia, looking at her husband. "That's understandable." She placed her hand on Bentheim's arm.

Till noted how the sharp edges of his face were suddenly softened. But he wasn't finished. "Have you given any more thought to what we talked about before?"

Max glanced quickly at Till.

"There's no need to look over at your friend. You have to answer me yourself. Have you thought about how we're supposed to proceed?"

"But you said I had till the end of summer vacation," Max blurted, and Till could hear how upset he was because he was sure the grace period he'd been given would be cut short.

"That's right, you did," said Julia, cutting in again. She turned to Max. "But that doesn't mean you can't still talk about it in the meantime."

"And have you gotten any further?" Xavier asked. "Have you already made a choice? Have you even thought about it or—I don't know—talked it over with Till? He doesn't seem to have his head quite so high in the clouds."

Max looked over at Till again, as if he hoped Till would find something to say in reply.

"Now he's looking at him again," Till heard Bentheim say to his wife.

"Have you talked about it?" He was looking at Till now. "It seems my son isn't able to tell me anything about it."

"Yes, we have!" Max burst out before Till could reply. "But I'm still thinking. You said I had time . . ."

He broke off. *Until the end of summer vacation*, Till thought. *Until the end of summer vacation.*

Bentheim stood up. "'Until the end of summer vacation.' That's what you wanted to say, right? Say it three more times and the deadline might shift by itself." He wiped his mouth with his napkin, then threw it on the table. "Coming?"

Julia stood up.

"Till? You and Max clear the table. It's Rebecca's day off."

Till nodded to Bentheim. *Sure, happy to obey.* As long as he obeyed, everything would go smoothly, he thought—and at the same time, deep inside, he had to add: *But what happens when I can't obey, because what you want me to do is too hard?*

Lisa and her sisters jumped up and ran out of the room.

"I've got your ticket in my handbag," said Julia, before leaving the room with Bentheim.

Max stared at Till. They were the only ones still sitting at their places at the table. They were silent for a moment while they listened to Max's parents getting ready to leave in the entrance hall.

"He chews me out but you can't do a thing wrong," Max whispered, and his eyes were huge.

"Get off it!" said Till. But he had noticed it, too. When Bentheim looked at him, his eyes were milder; when he turned his attention to Max, he eyebrows knitted together, his pupils seemed to become more penetrating. "You mean much more to him, that's all it is."

Max slowly stood up. There was something burning in his eyes. "I don't know what it is they're up to. But he's one of them," he said, leaning over and whispering into Till's ear. "Watch out, Till. They're after you. That's why he took you in."

It was as if a hot stone had dropped into Till's stomach. He pulled away from Max with a sudden jerk. *What?* But Max just looked at him sadly. There was no hidden hate in his eyes, no calculation, nothing shifty. Only the weariness and strain that always seemed to be there. It was something that made Max seem older than he really was, that weighed down on him and took the flashes of joy, so rare these days, and suffocated them.

Till slapped Max on his chest with the back of his open hand. "Don't talk crap!" But he, too, kept his voice low . . . and felt his heart pulsing in his throat like a jellyfish.

****

"He's locked it up, Max. There's no way he'd leave his workroom open!"

Max turned around to Till, who was trotting behind him through the garden, and held a closed fist in his direction. Till stopped. "Are you going to break a window?" Max opened his fist, and a key appeared in his hand.

Till hissed air through his teeth.

"It hangs in the broom closet next to the kitchen," said Max airily and he started off again. "It must fit the glass door that opens onto the terrace." He was so happy to have stumbled onto the key that his stomach seemed to make a little hop. "How long will it take them to get to the airport? Two hours there and back? So we've got a bit of time."

At the end of the lawn, beyond the hedge, the guesthouse beckoned. Max gave Till a jab in the ribs and broke into a jog. "But that doesn't mean you gotta drag your feet!"

The key slid into the lock effortlessly. Max turned it twice and shoved the glass door wide open. His father's office lay before them, bright and tidy. His desk in the middle, the shelves along the walls, the heater, the parquet floor. At the same time, Max felt himself go weak at the knees. There was no way his father would find out they'd been there. But what if he did? He pushed the thought firmly aside. They didn't want to steal anything or break anything. They just wanted to poke around a little. That couldn't be so bad.

The old computer monitor standing in the middle of the desk caught his eye.

"We can't switch that on!" breathed Till behind him. "He'd notice."

Max nodded. Till was right, of course. He stepped up to the desk and swept his eyes over the papers strewn across it. Notes, diagrams, sketches, half-written pages. His father's material for his new book, all composed in the tiny handwriting that Max couldn't read. He laid one hand on the armrest of the huge swivel chair with the high back that stood in front of the desk. For a moment, he thought he could smell the presence of his father—every day for years, the man had spent hours and hours in that chair.

In fact, the entire room seemed to have absorbed his father's spirit. Even though the room was flooded with light and well ventilated, the years of Bentheim's mental concentration seemed to have eaten its way into the plaster, the walls, and the parquet flooring, like an endlessly repeating wave.

"There are steps going down over here," he heard Till call. He looked around—the room behind him was empty. Max stepped back from the desk and looked in the direction that his friend's voice had come from. He saw him standing in the hall, which was accessible through a door from the office.

"Have you ever been down there?" Till pointed at a steep, narrow stairway that led down from the hall.

Max shook his head and went over to him. Till turned on the light switch at the upper landing. The old-fashioned switch clacked and a yellow glow lit the stairwell and the concrete steps leading down.

Max stood next to Till and looked down. All they could see at the bottom of the steps was the concrete floor of the basement. Suddenly, Max felt a push from behind and was so surprised that he jerked his arms up in front of his face to protect it from the terrible impact—then he felt Till holding his arm tightly. For a moment, it seemed to Max as if he was floating over the abyss. Then he heard Till laughing and, in a cold sweat, he dug his fingers into his friend's arm and sagged awkwardly against the wall.

"D'you really think I'd push you down there?"

Max could see how much Till was enjoying himself. He pushed himself away from the wall and whacked Till on the back of his head with the palm of his hand. But Till just ducked his head quickly and didn't give it another thought; he'd already begun bounding down the steps to the basement.

Max hurried after him. At the bottom, they found themselves staring into a dark corridor with the same musty smell and dirty plaster as the stairs. Till flicked a light switch at the entrance to the corridor and they stepped inside. Several wooden doors opened off the corridor, and as none of the wooden doors were locked, they were able to look in every room. All but one were empty.

The basement room directly underneath the study was furnished. Large antique paintings decorated the walls: a landscape in Roman style depicted a lonely monk lingering among ruins, while in the shadow of a willow, a group of young men attended to an undressed young woman, plying her with food and wine while two ladies-in-waiting swung her back and forth on a rope swing. And an extravagantly conceived painting of a battle, with soldiers massing in the background and riding at one another with drawn swords and raised lances, while in the foreground their commanders, magnificently decorated and looking serious, huddled over a map depicting the valley before them, where the battle was taking place. They were the kinds of paintings Till had seen only once before, when he visited a museum with school. Now here they were, hanging on heavy fabric wallpaper with a beige-pink pattern that gave the whole room a cozy hue.

Apart from the paintings, there were two beautiful pieces of antique furniture in the room: an armchair upholstered in the same material covering the walls and a small table with a silver lamp. Nothing else. A fireplace dominated the wall opposite the door, which was the only way into the windowless room.

Max leaned over the table. On top of it lay a wine-red file, tied with a leather band. Without thinking, he untied the band and opened the file. Till looked over his shoulder.

In the dim light of the room, which seemed like some kind of oasis from earlier days, like a study from the nineteenth century, the photographs in the file seemed at first glance to be images from a fantasy world, with ragged monsters and hairy creatures locked away behind bars. But on closer inspection, Max saw that the monsters were normal animals housed in long rows of cages. Goats. Sheep. Dogs. Birds. Monkeys. He set the topmost photos to one side. Behind those, more black-and-white pictures appeared: a leopard, various small rodents, a hedgehog; most of the animals were sleeping or unconscious, lying on a small divan or on an operating table. Among them was a cat, its legs stretched out in four different directions, its white-furred belly turned up, head to one side, eyes closed. A dog in the same position. Now and then, a man wearing a white apron could also be seen in the images, standing at the operating table and examining an animal. Or he was squatting in front of a cage, looking down at one of them, a rabbit or a fox, half hidden in shadow, that looked like it was pressing itself back into the farthest corner of the cage, the legs pulled in and belly pressed to the floor, a glaze of submission or fear in its eyes. The man wore *pince nez* and an old-fashioned beard that covered only his cheeks and chin, which made Max think of photographs of his ancestors, pictures of his great grandparents that his mother had shown him one time.

Suddenly, he flinched. Till had grabbed him by the arm.

"What . . . ?"

As Max's eyes met Till's, he fell silent. Till had his right forefinger pressed to his lips and his eyes glinted. Then Max heard it, too. A clatter, a rapping sound—no, footsteps! Someone was coming down the stairs!

His eyes flew to the door. It was wide open! And there was nothing they could hide themselves behind.

"What now?" The words flew from his mouth like tiny birds, little more than a breath, but it seemed to him that the whole basement reverberated with them.

Till quickly nodded toward the doorway. Make a run for it? There was no time for that! But before Max could pull together a single clear thought, Till had already grabbed him and pulled him behind the open door.

Max pressed himself to the wall and he found one eye was close to the gap between the top and bottom hinges of the door. He could look through the gap into the flat illumination of the corridor. There was no one there! But he could still hear the steps!

Max turned to Till with a terrified look. Who was making the footsteps? And in the same moment, a thought came to him that was so ridiculous and crazy that it shook him to the core. A ghost? Some invisible spirit sweeping down the stairs and terrifying them with its footsteps as it did so? Of course, it knew they were down here and it wanted to have some fun at their expense.

Max pressed his face to the gap again and looked out, ready to spot some creature of indefinite form, a miasma, a fog . . .

Suddenly, it was clear to him that the footsteps they were hearing weren't coming from the stairs. But just as this realization hit him, the footsteps stopped. Max held his breath. "Where are they coming from?" he whispered—and only then noticed that he was holding tightly to Till's arm.

Till nodded toward the wall. From the room next door! But there were no stairs there!

A rattling sound—a bang. Scraping and creaking, as if a door were being pushed open, then the rattling again. More steps, now more distinct and closer to them, clacked sharply. They weren't the steps of a ghost or a man—they were hearing the steps of a *woman*!

And just then, Max saw her. She was wearing a striped summer dress and her hair was loose and flowed over her shoulders. She was slightly shorter than his mother, and younger, too, and there was something springy in the way she moved—she looked as though she would have rather been skipping along. She was already reaching for the handrail of the stairs, and Max saw her petite hand, a gold ring flashing on her little finger. Then her feet entered his field of vision. She was wearing plain, black pumps, the heels not especially high. The heels looked almost like funnels running down to a tiny point, and where they hit the concrete steps they made the sharp clacking sound. A little ankle chain—and that was all Max saw before she disappeared from view. He heard the basement door at the top of the stairs open and close, then, more distantly, her footsteps crossing the ground floor of the guesthouse, then the front door opening—then silence.

They held their position behind the door for a few minutes. Was anyone else coming? But everything stayed quiet.

"Let's take a look," Till finally said, extricating himself from their hiding spot.

Max nodded and followed him into the corridor. A faint trace of fresh perfume still hung in the air over the earthy smell of the basement. It was a scent that could only have come from the young woman and had the effect of replacing the surprise and terror that had gripped Max with another feeling, a sense of anxiety, of promise, of deep anticipation. It was something he had felt a few times already in his life, and which he did not know how to evaluate . . . but he knew it only hit him when a girl was involved.

Till stood in the middle of the room that the woman had come out of. It looked exactly the same as it had just a short time before: a dusty, unused basement room with no windows.

"Did she just materialize in here, or what?!"

Max grinned back at him. "Maybe she beamed in?"

He turned to the wood paneling that covered the walls of the room. Till checked the floor and the ceiling. But no kind of hatch or anything similar was visible. So they started knocking on the walls.

It took them only a few minutes to find it: a door they hadn't noticed the first time they'd glanced around the room. Despite lacking a doorknob or handle, you could see it in the paneling once you knew exactly where to look. The hinges, too, had been installed as invisibly as possible in the wood cladding the walls, with small slats glued over them. Till tried to jam his fingertips into the narrow gap that marked the outline of the door, but it was far too narrow.

Max took out a small pocketknife he'd received at Easter. He folded out the blade and slipped it into the gap. He was about to try using it as a lever when Till stopped him. "It could snap off."

"Don't we wanna see what's back there?" Max gave Till a look and couldn't stifle a smile at the "well, duh!" face Till put on.

"Try it with the corkscrew," said Till, and he took the knife out of Max's hand, folded away the blade, and eased out the small corkscrew on the knife. "Okay, it'll leave a little hole, but we can plug that up with dirt later."

He leaned against the paneling and, roughly where a door handle should have been, pressed the tip of the corkscrew against the wood and twisted it forcefully two, three times into the board.

Then he let the knife go and nodded to Max. "You want to pull it?"

Max grabbed the knife. As first, he was afraid the corkscrew would pull out of the wood, but then he felt the door slowly begin to move. With a hefty jerk, he swung it open.

A dark, narrow opening appeared on the other side. The hazy light from the bulb hanging in the room behind them sliced a bright triangle into the space. The cavity was no bigger than a broom closet. It was significantly narrower than Max had expected, closed in on one side by a brick wall and on the other three by wooden walls only provisionally covered with wallpaper.

Max stepped inside and thumped at the boards on the narrow wall straight ahead. They sounded hollow.

"There's another space back there," he said.

But Till was kneeling on the floor, where a steel plate was set into the concrete. He banged at the plate with his fist. The sound was muffled and reverberated.

Max gave him a nudge. "Careful," he hissed. "The ones down below'll hear us."

Till smiled and repeated the words, "*'The ones down below'* . . ."

But it made sense, of course. The woman must have come from down there. Till grabbed hold of the iron ring that was attached to the plate and pulled hard. He managed to heave it up a little, and then there was a clack and a latch or lock prevented him from pulling the plate any higher. Max positioned himself next to Till and grasped the ring as well. But it was instantly clear to them: they could pull all they liked, but no amount of pulling—and no toy pocketknife—was going to shift that plate.

TWELVE YEARS AGO

Julia sat on a chair in the boys' wear section of the department store and waited. Till had taken a mountain of clothes and disappeared into the changing room to try them on. Claire and Betty had gone with Jenna to the toy section to look around until Till was finished. After Julia had driven Xavier to the airport—he had a meeting in Munich all day and had flown down with Felix—she had returned home and looked for Till and Max in the garden. She'd found them lying on the grass near the guesthouse, deep in conversation. For a long time, Julia had been planning to get a few clothes for Till; she insisted that now was the time to finally take care of it, even though Max had protested that today of all days was not good.

Julia gazed around the boys' wear section. While she was waiting for Till to emerge from the changing room, it occurred to her, for the first time, just how much she had taken the boy into her heart. She liked the way he looked at her, how he spoke, how he thought for a moment before he said something. And she was also pleased by the way he got on with her own children, Max especially. But hadn't they been a little hasty, taking him in like that?

They hardly knew him. Could she be certain that he wouldn't upset the fragile harmony of her family, a balance that Julia had worked hard for years to maintain. As far as she could judge, there hadn't been any sign of anything like that so far, but then he'd only been with them a couple of weeks . . .

Julia noticed a mother shopping with her son. What had come over Xavier, making such a far-reaching decision so lightly? Of course, Xavier had asked her from the start what she thought of the idea of Till staying with them. She hadn't said no. She'd thought she could support the idea. But she also hadn't exactly pushed Xavier on the issue. No, Xavier *wanted* this; he had wanted to take the boy in. But why? This was the question that had been going through Julia's head lately, but she hadn't yet come up with a clear answer for it.

Asking Xavier this question directly seemed to her somehow inappropriate. She could imagine his reaction only too well: Why did he want to take in the boy? Should he have taken him back to the children's home instead? The boy was a good kid; he got on with Max; he needed a home. *Of course we had to take him in,* Xavier would have answered, *at least for the time being.* But it was clear to Julia that the longer Till stayed with them, the harder it would be to send him away. It was already close to impossible; Max would never forgive them.

She leaned back on the chair and put the bags holding the shirts, T-shirts, and socks they'd already bought on the floor beside her. Now she was sitting there, and Till, whom she hardly knew, would come racing out of the changing room to show her whether the jeans fit or not. *Like a son,* she thought. But that wasn't it. What kind of people were his parents? He'd been born in Berlin, that much they'd managed to find out, but everything else was a mystery. Xavier had taken it on himself to deal with the red tape—Xavier, who was otherwise so meticulously careful not to waste a minute of his valuable work time . . .

Julia took a tissue out of her bag and dabbed at her nose. Xavier . . . what had happened at Felix's place, that sudden nosebleed? True, he'd regained his composure, at least to some extent, quickly enough. But at the moment he had seemed totally distraught. The only thing that really seemed to matter to him was whether the other guests had noticed anything! She had been worried that he was sick, and all he could think about was the others? When she had asked him if he was okay, he had just snarled incomprehensibly and then suddenly recovered enough to share a few witticisms with Felix about what had happened. She hadn't been able to get a sensible word out of him about the entire episode.

"Mrs. Bentheim?"

Julia looked up. Till was standing in front of her. His long, thin legs were in a pair of jeans, and he wore a long-sleeved T-shirt that looked like the one he'd had on when she'd driven him here. Over his arm, he carried a blue-and-white Windbreaker. Julia smiled. He looked very nice.

"How's this? All right?"

She stood up and ran her hand through his hair. What was he supposed to call her? Mrs. Bentheim? That was no good. Mom? No way. Julia? What would the other children think of that? Auntie Julia? Hmm . . .

"Great. Now all we need are some shoes, right?"

Till grinned. "Can I get some sneakers? Everyone's wearing them."

"Only a pair of decent ones!" Julia set off in the direction of the shoe department—and was acutely aware of the way the boy trotted along next to her. So trusting, mindful, and affectionate; it melted her heart.

✷✷✷✷

"You *talk*?!" Lisa stopped the forkful of spaghetti halfway to her mouth and glared at her brother. "You can try that one on Mom if you like, but not on me!"

Max chewed his noodles. They were sitting on stools in the kitchen eating the spaghetti Rebecca had cooked for them.

Max finally swallowed. "When Till gets back, you can ask him," he said.

Lisa threw the fork back onto her plate. "Yeah, right. And before I do, you'll grab him and tell him what he's supposed to say!"

Max was chewing again, his eyes on his plate. But Lisa wanted a straight answer, right now. "The other night, I asked Till what you two do all day, but he dodged me. Did you tell him he shouldn't tell me anything about it?"

Max shook his head, and she had the impression that he'd bent a little lower over his plate.

"Max?"

He looked up. Even though Max was a little older, Lisa had never had the feeling that he was superior to her. Sure, he was stronger and even faster, but Max was flighty; he was easy to impress, she knew, and she also knew she could scare him half to death if she wanted. If she so much as told him she'd heard a sound in the night, she could see how uneasy it made him. But Max could never scare her. Lisa instinctively knew that she would always keep a cooler head than her brother.

"I mean it. Tell me. So far I've left you both in peace, but you can't keep a secret forever."

Max looked at her wide-eyed. "So, what is it you want to know?" There was a touch of impatience in his voice.

"I want to know what you and Till spend all your time doing. You're cooking something up!"

Max leaned back. "Yeah, and as soon as I've told you what we do all day, you run to Dad and blab to him."

"Oh, please!" Lisa didn't have to think about her reply. It came to her spontaneously, which, she thought, was why it also sounded so convincing.

"Why do you really wanna know, Lissi? Don't you have enough on your plate with your girlfriends? Just leave us alone," said Max, but Lisa could tell his resistance was starting to falter already.

"I think Till's really nice," she said, jabbing at her cooling spaghetti. "But what should I tell Mom when she asks if we should let him stay?" She raised her eyes casually. Bull's-eye. Max looked at her, aghast.

"You don't think Mom and Dad'll send him away?"

Lisa could feel how unsettled her brother had become. "I don't know," she said, which was true. "What was it Dad said to him? He could stay for the time being, then they'd have to see. That doesn't mean he can stay forever."

"I can't imagine what it'd be like not having him here anymore. Can you?"

Lisa rolled her head on her shoulders. It could have been a nod, but she could just as well have been shaking her head. She knew she was doing exactly what she must to get Max where she wanted him.

"We were out back, in Dad's workroom," she heard him say, his voice hesitant.

Lisa breathed out. "What the heck for?"

"We wanted to have a look."

"Without Dad's permission?" She had just managed to trick her brother into telling her what she wanted to know, and now she was wondering if that had been such a good idea.

Max nodded. He looked around, but Rebecca was no longer in the kitchen. "He's got a woman down there."

Lisa froze. *What?*

Max's gaze was fixed on her, as if to check the impact of his words.

"A woman?" *What sort of woman?*

"We went in and poked around, then Till found some stairs going down to the basement. And we saw her down there. She was young . . ."—it seemed to Lisa that Max's voice had grown slightly hoarse—". . . and pretty."

"What was she doing down there?"

Max looked past her to the window. "No idea." Then his eyes came back to Lisa's face. "I don't know what Dad does with her. But she didn't notice us at all. I got the feeling she felt right at home."

. . . what Dad does with her . . . The words drove into Lisa like needles. "Does Mom know about it?"

Max shrugged. He pushed the plate away. "Did she ever say anything about it to you?"

"That Dad has another woman down in the guesthouse? Are you crazy?" Lisa felt her mind racing, her thoughts getting tangled up. She loved her father more than anything and she knew he was extremely proud of her. The two of them got on so much better than he and Max did, which was part of the reason he'd asked her to talk to Till about Max. But now she'd discovered that the two boys had been down in his workroom in the garden and that they'd seen a woman there. Shouldn't she tell her father that . . . before it was too late? Before Max had dug a hole for himself so deep he might never be able to climb out again? But what would her father do to Max then? And what about her mother? Shouldn't she tell her? Even though Lisa couldn't keep a clear head about it all, she knew that what Max had just confided in her was something that threatened her, too.

"Maybe the woman works with Dad," Lisa blurted. She looked at Max.

But he just raised his eyebrows. "Yeah, maybe." Then he propped his elbows on the table and bored his fists into his cheeks. His look was calm, as if he had come to terms with it all already. "And? You gonna tell Dad we were in his workroom?"

"No, of course not, I already told you," Lisa defended herself. But she knew it would be difficult, and she also knew that she, Max, and Till were perhaps still too young to deal with things like this alone.

"Really?" Max smiled. "Guess I'll just have to wait and see." He lowered his arms and stood up. "But listen up. If Dad sends Till away because you didn't keep your trap shut, then . . ." He seemed to have to think about it for a moment before going on. ". . . I'll chop the heads off your Barbies."

He grinned at her. And it was as if someone had switched on the light. Lisa laughed and jumped up. She loved him; she loved her Max. She went around the table and threw her arms around her brother. She may have felt older, but she was more than half a head shorter.

"I don't think Mom and Dad are going to send Till away," she said. "Mom told me yesterday that Dad had enrolled him in our school."

Max beamed at her. "And? Are you happy?"

None of your business, something in her cried out. "Why shouldn't I be?" she said, dodging her brother's question and letting go of him. She had been relieved to hear that Till was able to stay with them—*infinitely relieved?* She didn't know exactly what it was, but when she found out that Till wouldn't be leaving them anytime soon, she'd felt as if she'd fallen into an enormous cloud of cotton wool.

TWELVE YEARS AGO

Till was just about to slip under the blankets when there was a knock at the bedroom door.

"Yes?"

The door opened a little and Max's mother looked in at him through the gap.

"Xavier is reading Max a good-night story. Do you want to listen in?"

Till already had the blanket in his hand, but he let it drop and ran to the door. "Super."

This had never happened before. Until now, if anyone had read them a story, it had been Julia. Till suspected that Bentheim was doing it tonight because he'd been traveling during the day and was happy to be home again with his family. And they didn't want to exclude Till, so they asked him to join in, too. The very idea of saying "No thanks" was out of the question. Apart from Julia, he couldn't remember anyone ever having read to him at bedtime.

"Bengt had just turned twelve when it first occurred to him that he could make his life a lot easier if he took certain sentences that he used all the time and replaced them with simple numbers,"

Bentheim read aloud once Till had curled up on the comfy arm-chair in Max's room and pulled a blanket over himself. Max was lying in his bed, the blanket pulled up to his chin, his hands behind his head. His father had taken his place on the chair in front of the desk, and Julia stood in the doorway, half out of the room, as if preparing to leave again.

Bentheim continued: "'Let's say I want the salt when we're eating dinner,' Bengt said to his mother, 'just as one example. Up to now, I've always said: "May I please have the salt?" Right?'

"His mother nodded. *Where was the boy going with this?*

"'Okay,' Bengt smiled. 'Well, from now on, I'm just going to say "4" instead. "4" means "May I please have the salt?" Understood?'

"Bengt's mother gave Bengt's father a long look. But Bengt's father had long since stopped listening when his son started talking. He had the newspaper lying next to his plate and completely ignored the fact that his wife was looking at him. She heard Bengt say '4'—and looked at him.

"Her son gave her a big smile. His eyes moved to the salt shaker that was standing close to his mother and he nodded significantly. She almost had the impression that he was forming the words silently with his lips—'The salt, Mom, the salt!'—but there were no words actually spoken.

"She sighed, reached for the salt shaker, and pushed it across the table to him.

"'9,' said Bengt, shaking a few grains of salt onto the soft-boiled egg in the eggcup in front of him. He was obviously very pleased with himself that everything had gone so well with '4.'

"'And that means "Thank you," I suppose,' said his mother, looking at him.

"'1.'

"She could almost see him laughing inwardly.

"'"1" is "yes," right?' Now his mother was grinning, too.

"'1.'

"'77,' replied his mother.

"Bengt's spoon stopped halfway to his mouth.

"'77?'

"'Means "Okay."'

"'2. "Okay" 12 "20."'

"'No. "Okay" is "20"?'

"'1.'"

Xavier paused and looked over to Max, who hadn't taken his eyes off him the whole time. "Everything okay?"

Max looked across at Till. "1."

Bentheim nodded and also turned his attention to Till. "Do you want me to go on, or would you rather I read something else?"

"Don't stop, Dad, keep reading," Max said before Till could answer. "You've never read me any of your own stories before. I want to hear the whole thing."

Bentheim smiled and it seemed to Till that his son's reply pleased him. Max's father turned back to the book. "From that day on, Bengt was . . ."

"'Bengt' . . . what kind of name is that?" Max had pulled his hands out from behind his head and propped himself up on his elbows.

"Swedish, I think." His father frowned.

"Okay." Max sank back onto his mattress. "Sorry."

"From that day on, Bengt was not to be stopped," Bentheim continued. "He began systematically taking every sentence and combination of words that he commonly used and replacing them with numbers. When he played with his cars and imagined that the open-top racing car overtook the Jeep, all he said was '454' to himself and knew that he had saved himself a lot of words. When he thought about whether he wanted to read a book or play soccer, he said to himself '2008' and knew what it meant. But most important of all, for the stories he dreamed up as he lay in bed before he fell asleep, he came with up with a huge collection of numerical abbreviations to get through the beginnings of the stories, which were always the same, as fast as possible, to get to the parts where the stories became more exciting. Otherwise, it would take hours for his imagination to get that far. A boy loses his way in the woods? '97.' The boy stumbles across a house deep in the woods? '112.' A poor woman lives in the house with her daughter? '217.' The girl falls in love with the boy? '242.' She *doesn't* fall in love with the boy? '243.' Not *at first?* '244.' And so on. In this way, all he had to do was say to himself '97 112 218—'"

"'218'?" Again, Max chimed in, interrupting the story.

"Yes, '218': It wasn't a poor *woman* living in the house with her daughter; it was a poor *man* with his daughter."

Max glanced over at Till.

But Till had his eyes fixed on Bentheim.

Max's father had his eyes back on the pages of the book in front of him and went on reading. "'218 244' and that was all he needed to know that the boy had lost his way in the woods, stumbled across a remote house where a poor man lived with his daughter, who didn't fall in love with the boy at first. *At first*, mind you. And he could go on assembling his story this way: '411 739 9030 9966,' and in the twinkling of an eye, the story included a gang of thieves who caused the girl's father no end of worry, a fight between the boy and the leader of the thieves, and the first of a series of setbacks."

Till saw Max pull the blanket up a little higher to free his feet.

"This was when Bengt was twelve years old," Bentheim continued. "When he turned thirty . . ."

"Dad?"

Bentheim stopped reading and looked up. Max had propped himself up in bed and was looking at him. "Dad, I don't understand any of it. Do we have to read this?"

Till recoiled inwardly. Why didn't Max just listen? What was there not to understand?

"What don't you understand, then, Max?" Bentheim asked, and Till had the feeling that he was making a real effort to seem so composed, despite the calm in his voice.

"Why Bengt comes up with these numbers, what that's supposed to . . . I don't understand what it's all about. I thought we'd read . . . maybe a pirate story . . . didn't you say something about a pirate story the other day?" Max's voice trailed off a little, as if his courage had suddenly abandoned him.

Bentheim wiped a hand across his eyebrows. "But now we've started this."

"Yeah, okay. But what's the deal with all the numbers?"

"Don't you want to find out how it turns out?"

Max laid his head back down on his pillow. "So, how does it turn out?"

You have to let him finish reading if you want to know! Till screamed inside, but to his surprise, Bentheim clapped the book closed—with his index finger wedged between the pages he'd been reading from—and leaned forward. "The boy keeps on doing what he's doing with the numbers," he explained, "replacing more words and sentences with numbers. Soon he's replacing whole paragraphs, then chapters and entire plotlines. He summarizes the most complicated trains of thought with a single number. Naturally, this requires tremendous concentration and enormous brainpower, but Bengt is so smart that he manages to keep it all straight. He studies every possible science, absorbs their outcomes and conclusions, labels them with a number, then turns to the next discipline, so that by the time he's an adult he can manage all the knowledge of the world with a few numbers. By then, though, it's been years since anyone has understood a word he's said. It's all just an endless series of numbers. But that doesn't mean that what Bengt says is nonsense. When someone goes to the trouble of writing down the series of numbers and manages to get Bengt to explain what each individual number signifies, then he is able to comprehend clearly what Bengt means. But doing that takes several months, while all Bengt says is '8000677 784529 775344219.'"

Max stared at his father. "Ah."

"Yes." Till saw Bentheim looking fixedly at his son. All the sharpness had gone out of his eyes and in its place was a loving look, a concerned look, a look that Till had always longed for, always wished would come to rest on him. "A couple of times at the start, Bengt had gone to the trouble of translating his number-sentences for other people, but pretty soon that starts to take too long for him, and then he stops talking to other people altogether and only talks to himself. He's convinced that one day in the far-off future, the human race will be advanced enough to comprehend his number-sentences—even if no one is capable of doing so today."

A little color had returned to Max's face. "And?" he asked. "Do things turn out the way he imagined they would?"

Bentheim smiled. "Almost. In fact, it takes two hundred years. For two hundred years, Bengt's writings lie in a cellar and molder away. Bengt has been completely forgotten, and even when he was alive, everyone had stopped taking any notice of him: he was just a number-spouting crackpot. But two hundred years later, his writings are rediscovered, and the rest of the race, in the meantime, is advanced enough to understand what he has written."

He paused.

Max's eyes sprang open. "That's it?"

Bentheim laughed. "Well . . . the $64,000 question, of course, is what Bengt had written, isn't it?"

Max took a breath and Till noticed that the interest that his father had kindled in him for a moment had already begun to fade again. "Yeah," he said, but it sounded more like a question.

"The people read Bengt's writings and they discover that it makes sense. Two hundred years earlier, he had already predicted all the things they had only recently discovered. Everything he had written down had come to pass."

Bentheim looked to the door, where Julia was still standing.

"Bengt had been faster—but in the end, everyone else had made it to the same point that he had reached first. Basically, his speed—which he had achieved thanks only to his special language—had been of no benefit to him at all. More than anything else, Bengt had only been one thing: staggeringly lonely."

Bentheim looked at Max, whose head was now sunk deep in his soft pillow. "And that was the end of my story."

Till could see Max's big eyes looking at his father from the pillow.

Bentheim stood up. "We'll read another one tomorrow, eh? Maybe you'll like another one better."

Max nodded. "But I liked this one," he murmured softly. Then he suddenly started and sat up. "Why did you want to read us *this particular* story?"

Bentheim looked at Till for a moment, as if he wanted to say something to him, but then changed his mind and turned back to Max. "I was thinking about what we were talking about just recently, that you should give some thought to what you want to make out of your life. Maybe I was a little strict. I'm sorry. So I wanted to read you the story of Bengt. I'm not an ogre, you know."

Max nodded.

"You shouldn't go thinking that I want to turn you into a Bengt." Now Bentheim's voice, too, had become very soft.

"So, I don't have to think about anything, then?" The hope in Max's voice was plain.

Bentheim laughed. "That's not what I said! You *do* have to think about it. I just wanted to show you that I really do know exactly how hard it all is. But what happened with Bengt in the story is extreme. That doesn't mean anything like that's going to happen to you just because you spend a little time preparing yourself for the future."

Max sat up, confused. "I don't get it. You just said it yourself: Bengt was faster than all the others; he left them all behind—but where did it get him? He was just hopelessly lonely."

Bentheim sighed. "Max, my boy, I read you a story to broaden your perspective. And now you're trying to tell me that it was too much for you?"

Till saw Max's eyebrows draw down steeply toward his nose, forming a sharp *V*. "What am I supposed to do now? What's going on? Was that all just a trap? Did you want to test how close I'd stick to what you said—but what you really want is for me to resist?"

What the heck's he talking about? thought Till, who was feeling more and more out of place the longer he sat there. If he hadn't felt that he should stand by Max, he would have made his escape much sooner. From the corner of his eye, he noticed that Julia had already abandoned her place by the door.

"I can't stop you thinking what you want to think, Max." Bentheim's voice remained calm, but it was also clear from his tone that he believed that what he was saying was extremely important.

"Then why read me such a stupid story, Dad? What are you trying to tell me with that?"

Till saw how Bentheim's hands tensed around the book he was still holding, how the flesh between his knuckles turned white. "I want the best for you, Max, and part of that is teaching you how to use your own head."

"Yeah, right!" Max had jumped up and was standing on his mattress, his head now at the same level as his father's. "The best for me? You just want one thing, Dad: to be with that woman in your workshop!"

Hardly had he blurted the words when a leaden silence seemed to settle over the house. Bentheim took a step back, as if Max had rammed him in the chest with great force.

Simultaneously, Till spun around and was at the door in two big steps. Max's mother was standing in the hallway. Her face looked as if an underlying asymmetry had crept into it. One hand was laid across her breast; the other hung limply at her side.

Till slipped past her into his room and slammed the door behind him. *He said it, he said it, he said it!* kept hammering in his head. Bentheim would throw him out; they'd been in his basement; it was all over.

Till jumped into bed, buried his head under the pillow, and pulled the blanket up so it covered him completely. He felt as if a shrieking saw was slicing through steel inside him. Until it suddenly occurred to him that he wasn't just imagining the shrill noise—it was actually filling the house. It was Max screaming; but the sound he was making no longer seemed to have anything in common with the voice Till knew as Max's.

TODAY

The hall is spacious, the ceiling high and vaulted. Below the ceiling, dust motes dance in rays of sunlight streaming diagonally down through barred windows on two sides. The walls and ceiling are clinker brick, roughly plastered in white. It smells like sweat, and when the trams rattle by overhead, the entire structure rumbles.

Claire has simply pulled open the iron door that led into the front room of the hall. No front desk, no receptionist—just a few Turkish teenagers who had grinned when she saw them.

She has asked them where Mr. Barkar is training, and the youths have pointed her toward the door that leads into the main hall. When Claire enters the hall, she sees him immediately. He is standing in a raised ring beneath the streaming rays of sunlight; his upper body bare; his long legs in loose jogging pants; his hands taped. She quickly ducks behind one of the pillars supporting the ceiling before he looks in her direction.

"What the hell, Fred?" she hears the unusually husky voice of the man with the blunt head, who is standing in front of Frederik in the ring, say. "You know how it works better than anyone. Lubajew was a tough one—and you snapped him like a twig. But it makes no difference. What's the use of all those wins to look back on if you lose your next fight?"

Claire pushes her head out a little until she could see the ring.

"I got it, Ulli, come on, let's keep going." Frederik has begun springing lightly on his legs. The man in front of him—a white-haired older man with a dramatically broken nose—raises his hands, which have something like small mats attached to them. With the right, he touches Frederik on the head, almost fondly, then pulls the hand back and raises both pads up in front of him. Like Frederik, he falls into the bobbing, weaving movements of a boxer.

Tack, tack, tackatack . . . Frederik lands light punches on the pads, which the old man moves around in front of his face. Tacktacktacktack—now, like two pistons, his fists circle lower down, turning around each other. One of the pads gets through and hits him on the head again, making him change his rhythm and punch high again.

Half a dozen men are standing around outside the ring. Some of them have their arms propped on the edge of the canvas; others watch from farther back. All eyes are on Frederik. Their T-shirts and sweatshirts are emblazoned with "Team Barkar," and beneath that is the logo: a dog with a huge head and tiny hindquarters, red-rimmed eyes above a snarling mouth, razor-sharp teeth bared threateningly.

For nearly an hour, Claire stands behind the pillar and follows the training session. Whenever anyone goes past, she just smiles—and no one takes further notice of her.

As the rays of sunlight through the barred windows slowly lose their intensity, she realizes the training session is coming to an end. The only ones still in the hall are Frederik and the trainer. They clamber out of the ring through the ropes, jump to the floor, and head toward the exit, passing the pillar she is standing behind.

"Frederik?"

She doesn't miss the way he starts. Both men turn to face her. Frederik's eyes gleam. The trainer frowns.

"'S'okay, Ulli," Frederik murmurs to the smaller man. "I'll be right behind you."

Ulli rocks his blunt head up and down, then turns and leaves the hall. Frederik moves toward her. She sees him open his mouth, sees that he wants to say something. But Claire doesn't want to hear a word of it. It's almost like she's flying. She feels her lips pressing hotly against his mouth. She closes her eyes, feels his arms encircling her, holding her. She gives herself over to him, completely.

Her head lolls back on her neck; his nearness intoxicates her; her whole body seems to unfold.

It's like a cut or a stab, then, when his head suddenly jerks back. Her eyes open as if she's waking from a dream. His face rises above her, large and clear; his dark eyes are fixed on her—but she sees instantly that something has happened. It's as if something has bitten into him and is tormenting him.

Shocked, she lets him go.

His face is tense, his cheekbones standing out.

"What is it, Frederik?" She doesn't dare touch him. "Why didn't you call me?" She hadn't seen him since he'd tracked her down to her apartment. "If it's because of Butz . . ."

His head pulls back between his shoulders and a look of pain crosses his face, as if she has slapped him.

"Claire"—he raises his hand, the palm in her direction—"we can't see each other." His head sways, as if something inside him is trying to get out.

Can't see each other?

Claire's mouth goes dry. *What . . . what's happened . . . how can he . . . ?*

"I can't tell you why . . ." His eyes meet hers again. "It's better . . . for everybody . . ."

"Not for me, Frederik!" Her voice nearly cracks as she speaks. But she isn't angry. Just shocked to the core.

"I can't do that." Now she is close to him again, standing on tiptoes, and her body—which seems very small to her whenever she's near him—leans against him, her arms wrapping around his back, her face close to his. She feels how her lips are driving him wild; then she lays her head on his chest, and her hand strokes his throat. "I can't lose you now, I . . ." *I've . . . how can I say it . . . isn't it clear to you?*

She leans her head back and looks at him. The hardness that had just been inscribed on his face has dissolved. His eyes look down on her as if the sight of her alone is enough to sate them.

"It was the last time we met, Claire. At your apartment, in the pantry, I . . . I . . ." Frederik lowers his voice a little, grasps her hand, his eyes look as if they want to swallow her whole. "Claire, I love you, but I—we—can't see each other anymore, I can't . . ." He throws himself back in his seat.

They have found a small restaurant located diagonally opposite from the training hall. The waitress had greeted Frederik brightly and found a quiet table for them in a corner by a window.

"If it's Butz"—her mind is racing, thoughts jumbling—"I'm sorry, we should never have done it this way; it has to change, Frederik. I know. I . . . I'll talk to him. I'll do it today; it won't be easy, but . . . He'll understand. He has to understand!"

Frederik's face is in half-shadow. She can hardly see him, but she can't shake the feeling that his look is pure stone.

"I don't get it, Frederik." Confused, Claire reaches for his hand. "I don't see why we can't see each other again, not if you say you love me." *I've fallen in love with you, Frederik. It's . . . why can't things be simple?* "We can't just throw it all away . . ."

"Yes . . . no."

Claire nervously rubs her forehead with one hand. In every fiber of her body, she knows she can't allow herself to let go, that she would never forgive herself if she doesn't try to hold on to him now.

"Talk to me, Frederik." She looks at him, wants to lie naked beside him in bed, to caress him, to make it unnecessary for him to search for words. To drive away his thoughts with this urge, this impulse she wants to draw out of his body—that body she already knows much better than he does, a body she can rely on, not torn apart by doubt or by dithering, but a body that desires her. She knows this—because she desires him.

"I . . . after the fight, in the changing room . . ."

"Yes?" Claire falters. *What?*

". . . when I picked you up from the floor . . ."

"Yes?"

"They told me I should do it, Claire."

They told me I should do it, Claire. She doesn't understand. *They told me . . . ?*

"They . . . who?"

He gestures dismissively.

They told him he should do it. Claire hears herself repeating the sentence to herself, but she can't grasp what it means.

"My trainer, Claire. And a man I'd never seen before."

"What did they say?"

"That I should do it."

"Should do what?"

"Get to know you."

Claire shakes her head.

"They knew that you'd be there for the photos. You'd put in a request with the press agency. They told me to be nice to you, to build up a connection with you. They said it would help me with my next fight."

Claire still doesn't get it.

"I was weak, Claire. I thought maybe I'd never make it without their help. Boxing isn't always simple. Being good's not enough. You have to get the right fights. You need friends, Claire—and they said they wanted to be my friends. They showed me a photo of you—and I thought: *No problem, I'll be nice to her.*"

It wasn't *her*, then, who'd turned his head.

"And then when you were alone with me in the changing room, it was just the rush after I got the KO, and I gave in to it."

Her belly is ice.

"I didn't think it through. But when I went looking for you in the apartment, in the pantry—suddenly, everything was different, Claire. Suddenly, you weren't just the pretty girl that I was supposed to be nice to. It was like I could see clearly, suddenly. Just like that. I fell in love with you there, Claire. Suddenly, everything was wrong. I'd lied to you. I was in another man's apartment. I'd . . ." His voice trailed off.

But now, thought Claire, *is everything still just make-believe?* She sees the sheen of his face through the half-dark.

". . . I went along with it. I never should have done that."

She leans forward, sweeps her loose hair back behind her ear. "Why, Frederik?" Her voice is firm. "Why did they want you to do that?"

"I don't know."

Is he still being dishonest with her?

"Why, Frederik? What do you think?"

He says nothing. They can hear the murmur of low conversations at the other tables.

"I think it has to do with the man you live with."

"With Konstantin."

"He's with the police, isn't he?"

Two murders. Two dead women.

"I think they want to get to him."

****

"You can't leave Butz," he'd said, as she lay in his arms. "They . . ."

"Who are they, Frederik?"

But he just went on speaking, not answering her: ". . . if they find out that I told you about them . . . that that's why you left Butz . . ."

Claire turns to the wall. Konstantin is lying beside her and she senses that he's awake.

Frederik hadn't finished his sentence. She'd hammered him, but he'd dodged every shot she took. But there was no doubt at all: if they—whoever "they" were—found out that he'd told her about them, they'd be after Frederik. And even if she left Butz, it would put Frederik in danger.

She feels Konstantin's hand push up the T-shirt she is wearing as pajamas. He had come into their room, had lain down beside her—she hadn't found the nerve to ask him to let her sleep alone. The passion running through him practically crackled, seemed to fill the room.

She has already fended him off once, in the study. But that isn't what's bothering her most. She can sleep with him; she's always been fond of him, and yes, perhaps, was even once in love with him—there was a time she'd believed that. But what torments her now is that she still likes him and respects him, and at the same time has to do this to him: keep from him that the only reason she's sleeping with him is because she's afraid for someone else. He doesn't deserved to be treated like this. And Claire doesn't know what she's supposed to do. His movements confuse her; the urge in him is growing, consuming him.

She suppresses a moan when he rolls her over onto her back and straightens up next to her. He's almost got her T-shirt off, her nakedness fuels him, urges him on, opens him up like a barely healed wound.

His lips move down to her and she slips her hands around the back of his neck, her lips brushing his ear. Some inkling of what is going on in her head seems to infuse the relentlessness of his lovemaking.

It seems to her that Butz, in a certain way, is saturated with her. Soaked with the smoothness of her skin, the curve of her breasts, the scent of her hair, her shining eyes, the movements she makes as she gives herself over to him, the sound of her breathing . . .

He shudders, a jolt runs through him, and he rolls onto his back, holding her tightly in his arms so that she ends up lying on top of him.

She has to open her eyes—and he is looking at her.

She can't say anything. But she feels her face stretching into a smile, a smile that shows her teeth, a smile—as she knows only too well—that he's never been able to resist.

"Well," he breathes.

"Well." His arms around her tighten their grip and their naked, sweating bodies press together.

She lays her head on his chest. Her hair flows over his body; her hands drift across his skin.

And suddenly, Claire knows that she may not have the power to protect Frederik.

TODAY

"Down in the South, in Rudow . . ."

"That's the one. There was a tunnel just like it."

"Built by the Americans."

"The Cold War was at its peak."

Butz and the official from the city administration accompanying him are approaching a small brick building standing on the edge of a neglected park. They are not far from the tram interchange in Gesundbrunnen, in the city's north, where Moabit and its increasingly Turkish neighborhoods approach the border to Prenzlauer Berg.

"And the Soviets never discovered the tunnel here?" Butz waits a step back while the official unlocks the steel door.

"Doesn't look like it. But it was pretty extravagant, the way they did it back then," says the official, giving Butz a grin. "Just because of the snow. That was a major problem. They had to stop it melting up on the surface. That would have been a dead giveaway that there was a tunnel underneath. So when it snowed in winter, they had to cool it down, which was expensive . . . not to mention that the technology to do something like that properly was only really fully developed in the seventies."

The man pulls open the steel door. Behind it a black, iron stairway spirals down into the floor of the small building.

The scrawny kid whom Butz had tackled back at the housing project didn't know about this. But Butz had kept after him until the young man had finally cracked and taken him to see a few other denizens of the place. Among them were two women who had been friends of the dead woman in the parking lot. Butz had to show them some pictures from the crime scene, but then they reluctantly coughed up the information he wanted: Nadja had told them about her get-togethers in the hidden city and had mentioned the small brick building in the park. That's where Nadja and her bod-mod friends apparently climbed down into the city's underground, they told him. At least that's what she'd indicated to them. And in one aspect, at least, this information actually fit into the whole picture very nicely. The brick building was barely a ten-minute stroll from the parking lot where Nadja's body had been found.

"Were there any more of these eavesdropping tunnels in Berlin back then?" Butz and the official are climbing down the iron stairs, which clang underfoot. "Apart from this one and the one in Rudow, I mean."

Butz hears the man in front of him laugh. "Who knows?! The more we poke around under the city, the more relics we turn up."

The official had explained to Butz that the tunnel they were descending into had been used by the Americans during the Cold War to reach the eastern part of the city unnoticed, passing underneath the sector border between East and West Berlin. The only reason for doing so was to access the telephone cables that connected East Berlin and Moscow, and tap into them. Just like the CIA had done in the fifties in the Rudow tunnel.

"But this tunnel here, they didn't even have to dig." The official stops and looks momentarily at Butz, the headlamp on his helmet now switched on. "This tunnel here is much older than the one in

Rudow. It goes back to the forties." He points at the walls, and as Butz turns his head he can see them too: signs, painted directly onto the walls of the tunnel, the letters in Gothic script—"exit," "bunker," "clinic."

"The anti-spy agency in the East had no idea the tunnel even existed. The plans stayed in the West after the war, which meant the Americans could use the existing pipes and tunnels easily to get into the other half of Berlin underground. Without anyone finding out about it, let alone any agencies in the East."

"And what was it originally?"

"This tunnel?"

Butz nods.

"It was part of the so-called Gesamtbauplan Reichshauptstadt— Hitler's vision, an overall plan for the capital of his empire. Megalomania, all of it."

"Germania."

"Is that what it was called back then?" The official narrows his eyes. "Or did they make that name up later on?" He dismisses it. "Whatever. In any case, the tunnel was part of the transport system, the big East-West Axis. The plan was to lay massive railway tracks all the way to Russia, what they called the broad-gauge railway. Trains as big as ships that Hitler wanted to use to cart huge quantities of goods from the region beyond the Urals back to Germany. Of course, it was all madness; almost nothing went beyond the planning stage. But they did make a start with some things, even back then. They dug up cemeteries, cleared apartments, did some stress tests on the ground to see if it was actually able to carry the weight of such crazy constructions . . . and they started digging a few of these tunnels. Even today not all of them have been opened up."

Butz looks past the official into the black tube, piercing its way into the underground ahead of them. For a moment, he feels that he can see where the tunnel was meant to lead, how Berlin was supposed to be connected to the immeasurable steppes of Russia, how the massive, two-story trains would roll along on their broad-gauge rails to Moscow and beyond.

He pulls himself back to the here and now. "Would it be possible for anyone to get in here?"

"Of course." The official knocks the key in his hand, causing it to ring. "Oh, sure, there's that lock back there. But the key passes through many hands . . ." He sets off down the tunnel again. "We did install a new system not long ago—up there!" Without stopping, he points to a small surveillance camera attached high up on the tunnel wall.

"And it's functioning?"

"As far as I know."

"Can I see the footage?"

"Make up your mind." The official stops and looks doubtfully at Butz. "You want to look at pictures or go down the tunnel?"

****

As it turns out, there is a plan for the tunnel, but the man from the city administration wasn't lying when he said the details were incomplete. "The entire system of tunnels, passages, and ducts has never been systematically opened up. Just figuring out all of the access points . . . the damage done by the bombing raids during the war—the damage underground, too—makes it far too dangerous even to find all the ways in . . ."

As they head down the tunnel, moving east, they pass a number of steel doors that are not marked on the plans.

To Butz's surprise, however, the images from the surveillance cameras have been stored online by the security authorities responsible, and the worker guiding him is able to access them with his phone.

"The days before March 16, when Nadja's body was found," Butz asked him. "If we could take a look at those first . . ."

Almost nothing is recognizable in the first images flickering across the screen on the official's phone. Signal noise. The tunnel.

The official fast-forwards the recording.

Suddenly, the light from a lamp attached to the wall in the distance is interrupted a number of times.

Butz takes the cell phone out of the official's hand and freezes the recording. Plays it. Rewinds.

Those are people passing between the lamp and the camera! Butz looks at the few seconds of footage more closely. At a conservative estimate, there are between eight and twelve people. They are wearing dark clothes and hooded sweatshirts—the hoods pulled firmly over their heads.

Butz lets the recording play again. He begins to differentiate between the shadows, stopping the replay at various points to look at different frames. In one frame, he can clearly make out a hand, visible below the end of a sleeve. A tattoo marks the back of the hand down to the fingernails. In another frame, Butz thinks he can see one of the hooded figures turning slightly as he passes the camera, giving Butz a glimpse under the hood; the hard face of a young man is vaguely visible, his cheek threaded through with a metallic chain.

Did they take her with them? Did they set her loose down there and then hunt her down?

He plays the sequence several times and tries to work out whether any of the people he can see are not there by choice. If one of them is being held by the arm or threatened. But nothing points to that.

Did she go willingly, not suspecting what lay ahead?

The images begin to flicker before Butz's eyes. The friendly camaraderie with which the official had accompanied him at first has been replaced by irritable impatience; the man can't understand why Butz doesn't just go through the material back at the office.

"Yeah, sure, no, sorry." Butz hands the phone back to him. He stares into the blackness of the passage, where the hooded visitors had been marching east. He still can't drag himself away, can't bring himself to turn and leave . . .

A new thought suddenly flashes in his mind. What if it was the other way around? What if she hadn't been dragged along as prey to be turned loose and hunted down? What if they all came down here together, just to poke around a bit . . . and *stumbled across* something? Stumbled across something *that had hunted them*? Stumbled across something they had fled from. Something that had caught Nadja?!

Butz lowers his head. He has no proof, but he feels in his gut that it would explain everything. The hoodies go into the tunnel together; Nadja is one of them—maybe they like the atmosphere, the strange mood that hangs in the air down here. Then everything suddenly crashes down on them. They are attacked and Nadja is injured—they flee—carry Nadja out of the tunnel and back up to the surface.

But it's too late. Nadja's injuries are too serious. She's probably already dead. The others leave her behind in the parking lot, afraid they'll be in trouble for breaking into the tunnel.

But what? Or better yet, who? Who had scared them away like that?

Who or what did they unearth down here?

TWELVE YEARS AGO

"I've never, ever done that—and I didn't do it just now."

Julia saw her husband as a black silhouette, standing in front of the bright living room window. The light reflected from his gaunt cheek, his short, parted hair.

So, he hadn't hit Max.

"He just started screaming." Bentheim took a step toward her. "I think he was suddenly afraid that I might do something to him."

Julia's eyes drifted past Bentheim to the night-cloaked garden. She was sitting in a wicker chair next to a table, out on the small stone terrace in front of the living room. Her legs were shaking and her whole body felt numb.

"Julia, I . . . can I talk to you for a minute?" Bentheim stood at the table and looked down at her.

What woman? The question kept resounding in her head.

"In case you're upset about what Max said . . . Julia?"

She looked up to him.

"There's nothing you need to be upset about."

"What woman, Xavier?"

"She works for Felix."

"Why was she down there?"

Xavier propped the fingertips of his right hand on the glass tabletop. "It has to do with what I'm working on for Felix."

"What business did she have in the guesthouse?"

"I can't tell you that."

She felt as if a long, thin, infinitely sharp blade was slowly slicing through her belly.

"Why not?"

"It's too early, Julia. It's not that simple . . ."

"What isn't that simple? That Felix is supplying you with women? That you meet up with them here, on my parents' property?" Julia forced herself to suppress even the slightest quaver in her voice but was aware of how flat and thin her voice was, how short of breath she sounded.

Xavier pulled a chair over and sat down beside her. He laid one hand on her arm—for a moment it felt to her like his hand was the body of a large spider with five bare legs.

"There's nothing going on between me and that woman. You have to believe me. She was here to pick something up. A manuscript. Maybe it's overdoing things, but I don't trust sending what I'm writing through the normal mail. She delivered it to Felix. Okay?"

Why is he asking me if it's okay? To Julia, it sounded as if he was asking her if this version of things was acceptable to her.

"A courier?" She pulled her arm away . . . but would rather have slapped him in the face. "Don't lie to me."

But the spider crawled back; Xavier laid his hand on her arm once again. "You have to trust me, Julia. I can't tell you everything just yet; it's too early. But it's got nothing to do with our family."

And what if that's true?

"It's the work for Felix," Xavier continued. "What he's planning is madness; it's preposterous. But it's also incredibly fascinating. I've never been part of a project like this. It's . . ."—she notices how he averts his eyes—". . . a once-in-a-lifetime opportunity. I can't just let it slip away."

He fixes his gaze on her face again. "It scares me, Julia. Felix demands everything from me. Every idea I've ever had, every trick I've ever learned, every moment of my time, every conceivable thought. He sucks it all up, like a sponge. He wants everything, and he has a place for everything in his system. And he needs it— I'm not just saying this—he really needs it. Because what he's planning is so overblown, so immense, so disturbing."

Xavier stopped to draw breath. She had never heard him speak like this before. She felt the pressure of his hand increasing.

"He takes the things I give him and modifies them, Julia." Xavier's voice had suddenly turned raw and husky. "My writing, my words are living things, but he doesn't give a damn about that. He amputates a leg here, an ear there; he reattaches the leg above the eye, sews the ear to the sole of the foot. When I get it back again, my creation has been turned into a monster. But you know what the worst part is? That I can see the intention in what he does! He's guided by a different concept of beauty. I know it's hard to understand, but when I see with his eyes, then I can see the beauty in the creatures he makes out of my creations. And that is exactly what he wants to achieve. He forces me to see my own creations through his eyes. He makes me rewrite the text. Once, twice, ten times, three thousand times. Until the words have completely lost all their meaning. Until the characters I've dreamed up have become empty, soulless things—things from hell that would scare the shit out of you. But it's not like you stop caring about them. It's not like he kills them and leaves the corpses lying by the side of the road! He takes them and reworks them. He warps the relationships between them. He takes a well-balanced group, an ensemble that warmed my heart just to look at, and turns it into a clan that chills me to the bone . . .

because I can still see in them the traits I gave them. He takes the life I injected into them and turns it into a mask of horror. Then he forces me to look at them and to see that only now are they truly beautiful. Beautiful, but a ghastly kind of beauty that has nothing to do anymore with the harmony and charm that fascinated me in the first place. And then he wants to know if I, too, wouldn't rather see how much more wonderful this ghastly beauty is, how much nobler, how much prouder than the pretty faces and kitsch I'd started with."

Julia feels how Xavier's hand has grown cold . . . as if the blood has drained from it at the thought of Felix.

"He's planning something with my writings, or with what he's transformed them into, Julia. Even if I could never have imagined thinking like him at first—now I've come to understand what he means. I see what he sees . . ." He leans forward, and his breath streams over her face. ". . . *I want what he wants.*"

****

It seemed to Till that he had just fallen asleep when he felt someone touching his blanket. He opened his eyes. Beside the bed stood Max. He was wearing his light-blue pajamas and was bent over Till, one hand laid on the blanket.

"You asleep?" he whispered.

Till should shook his head. He was too rattled to say anything.

"Can I sit here for a bit?"

"Sure." Till took the blanket and scooted over a little toward the wall. When Max sat down on the mattress, it barely sank an inch. *He's so light,* thought Till. *He'd better watch out or he might suddenly blow away.* Till shook himself. *What time is it?*

Max folded his legs onto the mattress and wrapped his arms around his knees.

"Wouldn't you be better off in your own room? If he sees you here, you'll get in trouble again."

Max laid his chin on the top of his knees.

"So, what did he say?"

But Max just shook his head.

After Till had run to his room and heard Max screaming, he'd thought feverishly about what he should do. *Should I go back to Max and attack his father? Out of the question. It had nothing to do with me,* Till had tried to tell himself. *Fathers and sons had always fought—it's just that I have never known what it's like.* But he could not stop thinking that the *real* reason he'd stayed out of it was because he was afraid that if he got involved, he'd have to leave the house.

"So, what happened?" he tried again. "Didn't he say anything?"

Max tilted his head down so that his chin was on his chest and his forehead on his knees. Till heard him snuffling heavily through his nose.

"Did you tell him we were in the guesthouse together?" He sensed more than saw that Max was shaking his head.

"Did you say you were alone?"

Max suddenly swung around to Till. "My father doesn't have a woman down there. It's something different." He swallowed and just breathed out the final words. "Much worse."

Much worse. What could be worse? thought Till. But at the same time, deep down, he knew Max was right. It was worse. Much worse.

"I don't know exactly what it is, Till. But earlier, when you were out of my room again and I was in there alone with him— that's when I sensed it."

Till looked at Max. He seemed a little thinner than usual, his close-cropped hair sticking out on his head, the wrists that extended from the sleeves of his pajamas looked to Till like they were made of straw . . . as if he could snap them simply by pressing hard.

"He didn't touch me. But he was really mad. You could practically smell it. I've never ever seen him so angry. He didn't want us to see her. The woman down there, I mean. He never thought I'd go poking around in his world. He thought he was safe and all-powerful, but suddenly he realized that I'd disobeyed him. It didn't scare him, though. It just made him mad. So mad that what he wanted most was to . . ."

Max broke off, his eyes fixed on Till.

Till didn't make a sound. It was as if he could physically feel the storm raging inside Max, as if Max's agitation, scorn, and confusion might leap across to him.

". . . what he wanted most was to grab hold of me and throw me through the wall."

Till noticed that he'd started breathing faster.

Max's voice had grown quieter now, almost a whisper, his head turned toward Till, his arms still wrapped around his drawn-up knees. "He's a killer, Till. That's what it is. My father kills women. That's why she was down there. He buries them under the house. He kills them. He wrings their necks; he rips their heads off. Nothing's too terrible for him. There's no boundaries, no mercy, no stop sign. All he knows is one thing: his will. Maybe he's a slave to it himself. He can't stop—once it's got hold of him, it just drags him along with it. He murders the women, then buries them in the cellar beneath the basement." The whispering voice evaporated in the darkness.

"Maybe that's why he asked you to stay with us, Till. Because he wants to kill you. Does anyone know you're here? Are you registered anywhere? He thinks you belong to him; he thinks he can do whatever he wants with you."

NO, thought Till. *NO, that's not true.*

"We have to watch our backs, before it's too late," Max murmured. "You know? We can't just wait till he's ready with his plan. We have to look after ourselves."

"I . . . do you really think . . . Max, that with the women, I don't think . . . that's . . . it's crazy. It's not right . . . I . . . I can't see that at all." Till had rolled onto his back and was staring at the ceiling.

Max seemed to be letting the things he'd just said run through his mind one more time.

"The parrots? The woman in the basement? I'm telling you, he's changed," he finally said. "Maybe it's because of that book he's writing. I don't know why things are the way they are, but something's going on with him. You should've seen him; you should've seen his face. When he stared at me, it almost seemed like something was bubbling under his skin. Something's going on with him, Till. And when I look at my mom, I know she's thinking the same thing."

TWELVE YEARS AGO

Three days later, Till found himself wondering for the first time whether Max might actually be right.

He pressed back into the corner of the green-tiled tunnel, the hood of his new fleece jacket pulled up, his hands buried in the pockets over his stomach, his heart beating like a jackhammer trying to gnaw its way out through his ribs. His eyes were fixed straight ahead and didn't dare move. It was quiet in the tunnel. Only far in the distance could he make out individual voices, an announcement over loudspeakers, steps, running. There was no one anywhere near Till anymore and it had grown cool in the passage. But he was not alone. A low growl could be heard, then silence, then came a gurgle, a snarl, the smacking of chops.

The dog was standing barely two steps in front of Till. It was a little larger than he was, and half-starved, the sinews standing out under its fur. Its eyes were like the heads of nails—metallic, dead, and glinting. The eyes were fixed on Till and the dog reacted to every move the boy made by intensifying its raw growl. The bitter, putrid breath streaming from the animal's mouth wafted over Till's face, clogging his nose, throat, and eyes. But the worst thing about the beast was its teeth, which looked like they'd been sharpened with a whetstone, and jutted more than an inch from the bottom jaw, sharp as needles at the tip, dirty white protruding from gray-pink gums, the mongrel flashing them with every twitch of its flews.

Till and Max had waited three days for the opportunity to find out more about Bentheim. But finally, their patience was rewarded. At breakfast they had overheard Max's father tell his wife that he would be going into the city that afternoon and—knowing that he normally took the train when he went into the city alone—they decided that Till should follow him unobtrusively. After lunch, Till had explained to Julia—they'd agreed that he should call her "Julia"—that he wanted to make the most of the nice weather and ride out to the lake. Lisa had been invited to a birthday party that day, so the question of whether he'd take her along with him didn't come up. And Max had said that he wanted to spend the whole day just reading; he couldn't think of anything nicer than that.

So, Till had pedaled off alone as planned. But to the train station, not the lake.

On the platform, he looked for a spot where he would have a good view of the parking lot in front of the station. After an hour, his confidence had begun to wane. The possibility that Bentheim might drive to a different station hadn't occurred to them. Or maybe he'd changed his mind and driven directly to the city instead?

Alert, Till quickly ducked his head behind the information board where he'd taken up position. The Jaguar had finally pulled into the lot below. Till waited, holding his breath. If he was unlucky, Bentheim would simply walk down the platform. Then Till would suddenly find himself face-to-face with him! But it was too risky to look out from behind the board now. He could only wait. From his hiding spot he could see the sign displaying information about arriving trains; the next train was headed for Ahrensfelde. If Bentheim wanted to go into the city, he would have to take that train. Till knew he'd need to have luck on his side. He couldn't see whether Bentheim really boarded the train. He had to get on at the same time, ideally in the next carriage. If Bentheim was too far away, Till could easily lose sight of him. But if they got into the same carriage, it would be practically impossible for Bentheim *not* to see him.

The minutes slogged by like footsore soldiers. When the train eventually pulled in, Till's palms were sweating. He waited until the train had come to a stop and the doors had opened. Then he zipped across. Not too fast, but briskly. That would have to be the moment when Bentheim himself would be focused on stepping over the gap between platform and train, the moment when he wouldn't be paying too much attention to what was going on around him. Just before he jumped aboard the train, Till chanced a glance to the side. The platform was empty. Had he lost him?

Then came the high-pitched warning signal, and the doors closed with a rattle. A jolt, and they were off. Till concealed himself behind a group of tourists. After they'd been rolling for a few seconds, Till pushed his way forward and looked past the group, through the window into the carriage in front of the one he was in. It was only half-full. Most of the seats were taken and a few people were standing. Bentheim? No sign. Till approached the window for a better look, scanned the seats one by one. The man was not in the carriage.

They pulled into the next station. Westkreuz. The train had hardly stopped moving when Till jumped out of the carriage, hustled along the platform, and jumped into the one he'd just been checking. Whistle, jolt, rolling. Till hurried through the carriage to the front. Halfway there, he suddenly jumped down out of sight, hiding behind the side wall of the seats running along the carriage lengthways. Bentheim was in the next carriage, just a few yards on the other side of the window!

Till let himself slide down to the floor and pressed his back against the wall he'd taken shelter behind. When he looked up, he saw a woman sitting in a seat opposite looking at him in astonishment. He smiled. Okay, sitting on the floor wasn't exactly how you were supposed to ride in a train. But it could have been worse. She should mind her own business.

Charlottenburg. Savignyplatz. Zoo. Tiergarten. Bellevue. Central. Friedrichstrasse. Before every stop, Till peeked out to see if Bentheim was making any signs of disembarking. But he simply kept standing there, a newspaper in front of his face, leaning against a pole, just riding along. Until they reached Alexanderplatz. When the train hit the broad curve on the approach to the Fernsehturm, Till saw Bentheim stuff the newspaper into the pocket of his raincoat and move toward the door. The train pulled into the station and Till jumped up. No way could he go out through the door directly next to the one Bentheim would use. They'd practically collide! Till hurried down to the end of the carriage and got there at just the right moment to press the green-lit button to open the door. The sliding doors opened with a hiss. Till stepped out.

The platform was bustling. People were standing shoulder to shoulder. Till slipped between them. He was smaller than most of them and would therefore not be seen easily from a distance. But he also had no idea which stairs Bentheim would use. Then he saw him. Max's father had taken the down escalator directly in front of the door he had exited through. A press of people had formed at the head of the escalator. Till pushed his way between the passengers, making his way to the stairs. The escalator was on his right and he hurried to the stone stairway descending between the up and down escalators. There, too, passengers were pushing past one another.

But he made himself as small as he could and was able to pass between them inconspicuously.

Reaching the bottom of the stairs, he lost his orientation for a moment. Passages led off in every direction. A tangle of stairs, platforms, intersections, corridors, overpasses, and halls. At least eighty different trains—underground lines, streetcars, and long-distance—used the station as a hub. It was as if the hall that Till had arrived in when he came down the steps was located precisely in the heart of this tangle, and the designers had attached great importance to having direct access from there to every single one of the God-knew-how-many platforms there were—regardless of how convoluted, skewed, or complicated the route might be. A multidimensional labyrinth linking various levels with each other, a maze of crisscrossing people movers, elevators, escalators, and tunnels. It was a puzzle in which one could choose not only the directions but also the speeds, a knot whose complexity stood in stark contrast to the startling emptiness of the public square above, a confusion of possibilities from a time when the surface of Alexanderplatz, too, was a beating heart of streetcars, houses, corners, and alleys—and not a wasteland dominated by an absurd tower. Now the square above was a vacant plain where it seemed a whole city would fit—a wound ripped open by war and never healed over. But down here, the people still rushed around like ants in a nest, bustling through corridors and halls that stemmed from prewar times.

Till spun around. In the various arms of the monster in which he had found himself, the steps and voices of the people reverberated, the grating and grinding of the trains and the rap-rap-rap of the stairs blended together to form a whirring, buzzing din.

Then Till saw him again. Bentheim. At an entrance to a tunnel that led out of the hall.

Till ran. He collided with a woman and very nearly knocked her off her stiletto heels—and he raced on. Into the tunnel that Bentheim had disappeared down. After a few yards, the tunnel opened into a second hall, which was not as central as the other one but made up for that by being filled with the rancid stink of the countless fast-food joints that had put down roots there and which seemed to exude steam, fumes, and grease directly into the air. Bentheim was already heading down another set of steps, into a passageway that dove yet another level deeper into the Berlin Underground.

Till followed. When he reached the passage, he saw Bentheim turning a corner a good thirty yards ahead. Till sprinted after him. He reached the corner—and came to a sudden stop, as if someone had pulled the plug on the moving walkway he'd been running along.

The passage in front of him was empty.

Till could see along the entire length of the green-tiled corridor, stretching a good hundred yards before him. The pedestrian tunnel inclined slightly downward at first but went up higher at the other end, so that Till could see only the feet and lower legs of some people just then turning into the corridor at the other end. But when he lay down on the floor, he could see them from head to toe—and Bentheim was not among them.

Till stood up again and ran down the passage, passing a Chinese fast-food stall that seemed to be hiding here, away from all the other fast-food joints in the last hall. He ran around the next corner, beyond which the corridor forked. Choosing fast, Till sprinted into the left fork, but just a few yards down it opened out onto a platform, and Bentheim was nowhere to be seen. Back to the fork and into the other tunnel. This one ended at a set of stairs heading up to street level, where Till could see daylight. That made no sense. If Bentheim had wanted to get outside, he wouldn't have wandered down through this labyrinth first. Still, he raced up the steps. At the top, a cool wind swept across the open square. The Fernsehturm towered into the clouds like a mast. But there was no sign of Bentheim. So Till turned and headed down the steps again, and hurried back to the passage where he'd lost Bentheim.

The man couldn't just evaporate into thin air!

Till made his way slowly along the tunnel he'd last seen Bentheim turning into. Almost a hundred yards long, maybe fifteen feet across. Posters glued to the walls on both sides at regular intervals. Could he have missed a door somewhere? But why would Bentheim disappear through a door down here?

Ten minutes later, he was back where he'd first turned into the corridor. No doors. No tunnels branching off. No trapdoors underfoot. Perhaps a hatch overhead, a ladder leading up that Bentheim climbed? Crazy. But Till had scanned the ceiling, nevertheless. It was plastered and smooth. White. Dirty. And no sign of a hatch. Had he simply allowed Bentheim to outpace him? Even though Till couldn't entirely rule it out, he thought it was unlikely. No, there was only one possibility, one that had been haunting his thoughts since he'd stepped into the passage.

He strolled past the Chinese restaurant as casually as he could. The place was set directly against the wall, perhaps twenty feet of frontage, not even six feet deep. The outside wall on the right was solid, and there was an entry door on the left. The front was glazed from one side to the other. Behind the glass, Till could see the Chinese proprietor at the stove, wielding several large cast-iron pots. Woks? Till wasn't sure. Anyone wanting to eat would have to do so outside, standing at a board mounted below the glass front. As Till sidled past, there was only one customer there, bending over a bowl and slurping down the contents.

Till cast a glance into the customer's bowl. Dark-brown lumps swam in a glistening orange sauce. The board the man had set his bowl on was sticky and stained. Behind the stove, where the cook was stirring in his pots, spread a layer of brownish, dried grease— all the way to a door set into the rear wall.

Till knew the instant he saw it that had to be the door where Max's father had disappeared. But what was he supposed to do? Order soup and ask if he could poke around back there, too?

He spent the next two hours hanging around nearby. Once the customer had left, he took up a position behind the end wall, where the cook couldn't see him but from where Till could keep an eye on the door at the other end. Not so close that he was getting in the way of guests wanting to order something inside, but also not so far that he would draw attention by loitering in the middle of the passageway.

The minutes plodded by painfully. *What did the cook do when he had to go to the toilet?* Till wondered. Probably the door in the back wall opened into a toilet and Till had somehow simply lost sight of Bentheim earlier. Till was starving, too. But ordering something from the fast-food place was out of the question. The sweet smell wafting from inside had seeped so deeply into the tissues of his nose that he would have paid *not* to eat anything that the cook was frying up back there. Slowly, the passageway grew quieter. The walls still vibrated at regular intervals whenever a train pulled into one of the surrounding platforms. But the trains were less and less full. Entire minutes passed with no one entering the tunnel, but then a dozen or more people from a newly arrived train would suddenly wander by.

Till was already starting to wonder if it wasn't about time he headed home, when a different smell suddenly overlaid that coming from the Chinese place. Till raised his head to look toward the door—and found himself staring straight into the dead eyes of a dog.

The dog was certainly scrawny, but it was still at least as big as he was. And its mouth stank of rotten meat. It felt to Till as if his nerves were being stretched to the breaking point. He'd never particularly liked dogs, but this thing was downright repulsive. When Till had shied away from it, the dog had begun to growl and now it was pulling back the soft flaps of its muzzle and baring its teeth.

I've gotta get away from here. But as soon as I move, he'll bite me. He'll rip my arm open, or maybe even bite me in the stomach. If I run, he'll be at my throat in two strides. Sweat ran down Till's back. *Dogs can smell if you're afraid. It makes them suspicious.*

A scream rose from his throat. He couldn't have stopped it if he'd wanted to. He simply screamed—and saw the mongrel's sinews tense, saw it brace its back legs against the concrete floor, stretch the front paws forward, and hurl its scrawny body—which seemed to have turned into a single, tensed muscle—straight at Till. Till jerked one arm up, incapable of running, unable to think, as if he could already feel the beast's filthy, stinking teeth at his throat . . .

"Chao! Come!"

A howl, an impact, fur and legs against his chest, a muzzle sliding past Till's arm, saliva smeared on his pullover. One paw dug into his stomach, then the creature spun around, shoved away from him, and loped back to the fast-food joint, where the side door was now open. The claws scrabbled over the cement floor; the animal made a sound almost like the whinnying of a horse and ran toward the Chinese man, who—with a backpack on his back and a friendly wave to Till—had just stepped through the door.

Till remained sitting on the floor. His legs were numb, his T-shirt soaked with sweat, and his face rigid with panic. Returning the cook's wave was impossible. His limbs refused to obey. He couldn't even smile. But that seemed not to trouble the cook, who apparently hadn't noticed that his dog had almost attacked Till; he had no reason to think he ought to apologize. He simply slammed the side door of his shop, locked it twice, looked briefly at the dog, which seemed to have forgotten about Till completely, and without further ado marched down the tunnel, heading in the direction of the hall that held the other food stalls.

Till let a few minutes pass. The sounds in the background had melded into a far-off hum. The hum of the city.

Slowly, he stood up. He went to the little restaurant and peered through the grimy glass. It was dark inside. Till could make out the outline of the door in the back wall. It was closed. There was a gap under the glass where the cook passed through the food he prepared all day, and a board had been attached horizontally in front of that. But the gap was definitely too small to squeeze through. Till glanced up at the ceiling of the shack. It was continuous and looked solid. Till shook himself. This close to the place, the smell was even worse. In the same moment, he realized that the sickly sweet stink of garbage—now that nothing was actually being cooked—wasn't coming from the shop itself but from a trash bag that hung in a frame directly beside the shop. This was where the few customers who'd eaten had thrown away their disposable bowls. Till stepped over to the plastic trash bag, which was only closed with a loose-fitting metal lid that formed part of the frame. The bag hung loosely underneath; no more than the bottom quarter was full.

Till narrowed his eyes. And suddenly he saw it. A gradual dragging motion, exceedingly slow—but when he watched carefully, it was unmistakable. The thin, blue plastic of the trash bag was wafting lightly back and forth. It swelled up, then collapsed again, the loose folds billowing and moving, and then Till could hear, very quietly, the contents of the bag sliding back and forth with the motion. A sticky swishing sound, interrupted now and then by a creak whenever the steel cover holding the bag onto the ring slipped out of place.

Till couldn't get that mongrel out of his system. The endless waiting around. The stink that was becoming increasingly unbearable. But this was his only chance. If he didn't manage to raise that cover now, he would have to leave here with nothing at all to show for all his effort.

He exhaled forcefully, forcing the air out of his lungs, tensed the muscles in his arms and throat, stepped up to the bin, took a deep breath—and threw back the lid.

A warm reek rose to meet him. Till quickly buried his mouth and nose in the crook of his arm and cautiously peeked over the rim and into the plastic sack. He could hear the slimy swishing and grating sounds clearly—and could now also see where they were coming from. Worms. Worms as big as fingers. They oozed over each other, white, blind, gorging themselves on the leftovers in the sack. Hundreds, maybe thousands, as if drunk on the stink they were wallowing in.

For a moment, Till felt like he would collapse headfirst into the spawning mass, but then his dizziness gave way to another sensation. The burning feeling of recognition. Because down there, among the whitish bodies of the worms, he saw something green, something blue, something yellow shimmer through. Brilliant colors, or they would have been if they hadn't been dulled by worm excrement. The colors of feathers—the colors of wings—the colors of two dead parrots lying among the scraps and dregs of food.

****

As soon as his father's Jaguar had rolled away, Max—instead of lying down and reading a book—had made his way, unseen, back to the guesthouse in the garden.

He just couldn't get it out of his head. Of course, his father had hammered into him that he had no business being down there. But Bentheim hadn't considered the key hanging in the broom closet.

Minutes later, Max was standing down in the room with the door concealed in the paneling. He pulled it open with the corkscrew, then turned his attention to the wooden planks he'd noticed the last time, when he'd discovered the hatch in the floor with Till.

He knocked against the wood, heard the dull reverberation from the hollow space that had to be back there. His hands slid across the wood-chip wallpaper carelessly pasted over the wooden boards. With a quick swing, he gouged the corkscrew across the paper. Rough planks showed through on the other side.

Max scratched away a large area of wallpaper. Instead of each board being nailed flush up against the next, the planks had a half-inch gap in between. He shook at the boards and was able to bend them a little but not break them free. He lay on his back and pushed against the planks with the soles of his shoes. He managed to bend them a little farther, but still not enough to break through. He pulled his legs back and slammed his feet against the boards with all the force he could muster. There was a crack. He kicked again, kicked as if in a frenzy now, flushed with the need to see whatever was in the room on the other side.

WHAM—the soles of his shoes smashed against the boards. WHAM WHAM—and the first plank broke through. Max turned around, kneeled in front of the wall, and pulled at the broken board. A sharp pain exploded in his index finger, a wave of heat rolling up his arm and spreading through his body. He jerked his hand back and looked at his finger. For a moment, he'd thought that something had bitten him. But then he saw that it was just a splinter. Carefully, he pulled the fine sliver of wood out from under his skin. The wound bled a little. He licked off the blood and sucked at the sore spot. But he had to hurry. It wouldn't be long before his mother started wondering where he was.

Max pulled the T-shirt he was wearing over his head and wrapped it around his still-bleeding hand. Then he started pulling at the broken plank again. Now that his hand was protected, he yanked at the board twice as hard. With a crack, the board broke free. He took the broken piece and wedged it between two more boards, leaned against it. More than enough leverage—the next plank broke through the middle. He took out his lever and set to work on the next board. Within a few minutes, he managed to break through all of them. Then he lay on his back again and kicked his feet like a jackhammer against the smashed boards. They cracked and split. He cut his legs open on the planks, and his pants caught on the splintered wood. His bare back was scraped raw on the concrete floor. But he didn't care. Gasping for breath, he paused, straightened up again, and peered into the niche he'd opened.

The room was bigger than Max had expected. A low shaft, stuffed to the ceiling with boxes.

Just as he finally managed to break through, something suddenly occurred to Max that he'd shut out completely as he was smashing open the hole: there was absolutely no way to patch up the shattered planks again, no way to erase the traces of his break-in! Even if the paneling concealed the damage, once his father pushed open the hidden door he'd see that someone had smashed through the planks!

Max climbed through the opening he'd made almost as if he didn't want to acknowledge this thought. He'd deny everything. The woman had been here. She must have come out of the hatch in the floor. How could his father know there wasn't someone else who'd come up through the same hatch and ripped open the planks?

Shivering in the damp air of the low passage, Max looked around. A meager gleam of light came from behind one of the boxes at the far end. Max scrambled to the box down there and shoved it aside; a matte sheen fell over the room from a light well overhead.

Impatiently, Max ripped open the box he'd pushed from under the light well. Inside were small tin cans and an old-fashioned device that reminded him of a hand-operated film projector on which his mother had once shown him the wobbly images that her great-grandfather had recorded of his family a hundred years before. Right here, on this piece of land he'd bought at the beginning of the last century.

Minutes later, a cone of light sliced through the room. Max pushed the empty carton back under the light well with his foot, so that he could better see the image cast on the opposite wall by the projector. Max could make out a man, not so old, wearing a goatee and an outdated suit. Depending how fast Max turned the handle on the projector, the man moved like either an overcharged robot or a sleepy doll. It didn't take him long to find the right rhythm, but the man's movements remained jerky and oddly stilted. Still, there was no doubt it was the same man who Max and Till had seen in the photos they'd discovered in the other basement room. *But who was the woman?* Max wondered as he watched. At first, the goateed man was alone in a kind of laboratory, but a woman entered the room shortly thereafter. She wore a sweeping, high-buttoned dress that reached all the way to the floor. Her hair was bundled into an enormous bun on the back of her head, and her feet were clad in dainty shoes. She nodded briefly to the man, then sat down on a chair with a high back and soft armrests.

Spellbound, Max stared at the black-and-white film, the contrast of which was reduced by the irregular surface he was projecting it on. The man seemed to be speaking to the woman, raising his hand repeatedly to underscore his words. It was impossible to know what he was saying; the projector was not equipped for sound. The woman kept her dark eyes fixed on the man, but had let her head sink back against the back of the chair. The man turned briefly to a long, tiled table that stretched the entire length of the rear wall of the room, picked something up, then moved slowly in the woman's direction. He was holding something in his hand. A needle? A hearing aid? A lamp?

Max swallowed. But he didn't stop turning the handle. The projector beside him hummed evenly, the light slightly flickering.

The man bent over the woman. Her head was back as far as it could go, her eyes were closed, and her chest rose and fell slowly and heavily. Now the body of the man moved between the woman and the camera, blocking any view of her.

As he stood leaning over her, the man glanced repeatedly at the young woman's face, and Max could see the man in profile. Tension was etched into the lines of his face. Suddenly, the man no longer looked like some oddball from a hundred years before. It seemed to Max now as if he could see the man's face clearly in all its expressive power, as if the human being under all the heavy layers of an actor's makeup had suddenly appeared, as if fashion and guise fell away and before him, Max could see a man who was completely focused on his task.

Then the man—the small, pointy, black device still in his hand—took a step back and the woman was once again fully visible. At first glance, her pose seemed unchanged; one sleeve of her dress had been pushed up. But then it seemed to Max that her breathing began to slow down and her head turned even farther to the side. The man's gaze was fixed on her face. He was watching her reactions and his expression was serious. Max saw his lips moving and even thought he could read there the word he was saying. He seemed to be uttering her name. Katharina? She nodded flatly, her head moving just a fraction.

Relief flooded over the man's face; he took her hand, laid it on her bare arm, then stepped back and, at the tiled table, began cleaning the instrument he'd just been using.

Because he had his back to the chair where the woman was sitting, for a moment he did not see was happening to her. Her movements must have been completely silent, or the man would certainly have turned around immediately.

Instead, only Max saw what happened. First, her head rolled forward again. She raised the eyelids that had slipped down over her eyes; the effort of doing so seemed tremendous. Her face looked slack, almost as if she was sleeping, her posture reminiscent of a marionette whose strings had been cut. She had the look of someone who had been hypnotized, as if she was no longer in control of her own senses, as if she had been taken over by some outside power. With heavy, fluid movements, she began to raise her arms, the hands hanging limply but the arms themselves straight. And then, without warning, she stood up. Max didn't see how she had shifted her weight, but suddenly she was on her feet, almost as if she'd been ejected from the armchair, her eyelids still heavy, her face waxen. Max held his breath. Everything about the woman—her stance that made him think instinctively of a marionette, of something soulless, her face that seemed hidden away under a layer of wax, her strangely unwilled movements—reminded him hazily of nightmares he'd had, of feverish terrors, of scary, long-forgotten movies he'd maybe seen or imagined as a small child. But more than all these vague associations, what he was looking at in the rectangle of light in front of him was a stifling, unsettling reality. A reality that almost sucked up everything he thought he remembered, that slipped down over those memories and impressions and seemed almost to bind all the vague imaginings together. Max was certain: if, in the future, he ever tried to remember

those impressions he'd once had, the image he was looking at now—
that was searing into him like a dazzling lightning bolt—would force
its way to the front. It was the image of a woman, profoundly ill,
whose sickness seemed to be eating into her like a blind, soulless,
inexorable thing.

Although she may have felt nothing, the changes that her body
was being subjected to and the transformation taking place in her
left their traces on her face. It was still her face, the face of the
woman who had sat down in the armchair a few minutes earlier.
But her pretty features, to which Max had at first been instinctively
drawn, now seemed to him like a husk, flaking off, revealing something else underneath, something like a reinterpretation of those
features. It was a transformation, taking everything fine, everything worth loving, everything open, sensitive, respectable, and
turning it into something withdrawn, closed, waxen, blind, numb.

At that moment, the man must have heard her, because he
wheeled around and a glass bowl he was holding slipped out of his
hands when he saw her standing behind him. He seemed to call her
name—but he couldn't reach her like that anymore. As if distressed
at the sight of the woman, he backed away, reaching behind him
with his hands, propping himself against the lab table.

Just then, a loud chattering noise sounded next to Max. He
jumped as if scalded, let go of the handle, and turned to the side.
He heard a frantic whipping sound. The rectangle of light dissolved
into a diffuse shimmer. The take-up reel was still turning and the
end of the roll of film, which had just been pulled through the projector, was slapping unpleasantly against the metal of the machine
with every revolution.

Then everything fell silent. Max had stopped the spinning reel.
And the gleam of light died.

TWELVE YEARS AGO

"I don't know *what* it is, Till, but it isn't my father."

They were riding bicycles with no particular destination in mind. Grunewald Lake was already behind them and they were heading in the direction of Glienicke.

Max started pedaling harder, and Till rode along next to him. Till was still using Lisa's bicycle, even though it had only three gears and was really too small for him. But he could still keep up.

Max had insisted they go riding. It was clear to Till that Max had no special destination in mind, and that he just wanted the chance to speak to Till in private. Not in his room, not in Till's room, and not in the garden, but away from the property, where Max's father had once again made his way down to the guesthouse after breakfast.

After they had been riding for a while through Grunewald, Max stopped and got off his bike. Till followed him down from the bike path into the forest, where Max finally let his bicycle drop among the leaves and sat down on a fallen tree. He took a small, black-bound book out of his backpack and handed it to Till. Till already knew that Max had been back to the basement, and Max didn't need to tell him that he had discovered the book down there. Till peeled off the rubber band that was holding it closed and carefully opened the cover. It was a small, high-quality notebook; the pages were not just glued but properly bound, even though the book was not printed. Instead, it consisted of graph pages written on in a fine, compact, and easily readable hand. Till flipped to the first page.

"March 1947, Haiti," it read.

He looked at Max, who was sitting with his hands on his knees, staring off into the woods.

Till looked back at the book. "'Katharina unchanged,'" he read. "'Would it have been better not to bring her here? The weather is already unbearably hot. She hardly speaks and when she does the words she says are spoken unclearly—I almost want to say sloppily—and I often cannot understand her. But she is impatient; she never repeats herself. When I ask what she has said, she turns away. The heat doesn't seem to make any difference to her. The moment I step from the shade into the sunlight, I feel like a lobster thrown alive into a pot of boiling water. But Katharina sits on our terrace in the sun with her head leaned back, as if she is drinking in the radiation. Even when her body is covered with sweat, she makes no move to avoid it. I have spoken with Dr. Gerrit, who tells me it cannot harm her as long as she protects her head from the sun.'"

Till looked up. "Katharina? Who's that?"

"The same woman who's in the laboratory in the film." Max went on staring fixedly straight ahead. "There were ten or twenty of these diaries in the box with the films. I've skimmed through a few of them. It's pretty much all about her. Katharina."

Till looked back at the book and went on reading. "Gerrit. Is he the right man? She has been in his care for two months with no perceptible improvement. On the contrary. It almost seems as if her condition is deteriorating, if not from hour to hour, then at least from week to week. How can I describe it? She seems dull, lethargic. (I should never have let things come this far!) Without a will of her own. Sometimes the feeling comes over me that Katharina, my beloved wife, has already slipped free of the body that lies there baking in the sun."

Till lifted the book so that Max could see the page. Apparently, in an attack of fury and despair, the writer had taken a pencil and scratched it hard across the page, a manifestation of his inability to maintain his self-control, a scrawl as if from a child, an outburst that showed that he no longer had the strength to compel the feelings and fears washing over him to take on a readable, comprehensible form.

Max nodded. Till turned the page. The next two pages, too, were covered with heavy, black lines. He leafed farther.

"March 23. At the café in the city today. Met an American who owns a plantation close to Cap-Haïtien where with some success he grows coffee and sugar cane. Housten is his name. He says his natives are saying preposterous things about Katharina. He mainly has people from Africa working for him. They have been living one or two generations in the Caribbean, but brought their legends, crude notions, and rudimentary religion from their homeland with them. Housten says they have observed Gerrit treating Katharina these last weeks. They believe the Swiss doctor is to blame for her condition. He, Housten, said he tried to tell the workers that she was sick and that she was there in the hope that the climate would be beneficial to her health. But Housten said his people did not want to hear it. They even have a word for her. A word from their language, from Kimbundu, but which word exactly he did not know."

Till flipped ahead in the book.

"March 29. Finally tracked down Gerrit. Spoke to him regarding the rumors Housten had told me about. The doctor laughed. Claimed not to know why the Africans considered him to be some kind of sorcerer. Said, to them a medicine man is a medicine man, regardless of what form of medicine he practices—be it the remedies of Europe or the magical rituals of voodoo. As to Katharina's condition, he was unable to give me much hope. It seems true that the climate is advantageous for her health, but that only applies to the bodily aspect, so to speak. She is absolutely 'fit,' was his word (and for a moment I had to think that perhaps the natives had in some way struck upon a nugget of truth. What does he do with my wife in the hours I hand her over to him for therapy?), but his impression is that, when it comes to her spirit, she is moving further and further away from us."

Till lowered the book and looked at Max. "Am I meant to read the whole book?"

Max swung one leg over the tree trunk he was sitting on, so that he ended up straddling it. "The man who wrote that is named Otto Kern. I found that out from one of the other books, where he'd written his name in the front. He's the same man who we saw in the animal photos we found in the basement."

Till clapped the book closed and handed it to Max. "Aha."

"And he's the same man who's in the film I told you about. The man who does something to his wife in the lab."

Till didn't say a word.

"I've only brought along this one diary," Max continued. "But in another one from the box, one from 1958, he writes about how he came back to Berlin."

Till narrowed his eyes. The summer heat was slowly beginning to find its way through the green roof of leaves. "Should we head down to the lake for a swim?" he asked.

Max unzipped his backpack and slipped the diary back inside. "You know what happened in '58?"

"The same thing that happened to his wife happened to him," Till blurted.

Max threw the backpack to the ground. "Exactly! And he kept a record . . ." He lowered his voice a little. ". . . he kept a record of how he was changing."

Till nodded. Crazy. Changed. But Max was already speaking again.

"It happened slowly, he wrote. It's hard to understand, according to him." Max's gaze moved beyond Till, into the forest, where the angled rays of sunlight were filled with dancing pollen. "He writes page after page about how healthy he feels, how powerful, as if all of his energy has been combined together. He sounded totally euphoric . . ."

"Euphoric." Sometimes Max used words that Till didn't really understand.

"Happy, ecstatic. Like he was ready for anything. Not exactly himself, though, that should be clear. But then he started to hit low points, seemed beaten, complained that the things he valued and that were important to him had been lost."

"What do you mean?" Till could hardly follow what Max was saying.

Max shook his head thoughtfully. "That he would never be able to be uncertain again?" He cast a glance at Till. "That seems to have been pretty important. No more hesitation, no more pondering, no doubting. But he didn't really seem to be particularly happy anymore, either. He wrote about how he suddenly wondered what love was. How so many feelings and sensations that he could still remember had once been obvious to him now suddenly seemed like things that he only knew from other people, but which no longer had any connection to himself."

"For instance?"

"The most basic things. Stopping in a landscape and discovering that it was beautiful . . . that was one example he gave. Or mourning. Mourning a swatted fly. Or sympathy—sympathy for

Katharina, who seemed to be losing herself more and more in her muddled state. Patience, tolerance, scruples—all completely normal emotions that suddenly seemed incomprehensible to him, like something foreign, something artificial, in the way or just plain ridiculous. And instead, other emotions, which had previously played more of a background role for him, suddenly seemed incredibly important."

Till did his best to follow his friend's account. "Greed. Lust. Action," he heard Max say. "Kern writes that it was almost a kind of frenzy. No more thinking, no more weighing alternatives, no more understanding. Just doing."

"Doing what?"

"Didn't matter. The main thing was to get going, to act, to carry out, to just *do*."

Till thought this over.

"He wrote that he no longer had any feeling for beauty. Or for justice. The difference between truth and lies became blurred. There was no longer any sense of him standing apart from the world—in place of that, he was overwhelmed by the certainty that he was actually part of the world, part of its motion and its development. As if the world went on inside him, so to speak, in the same way that it goes on in a tree standing in a field. In a sense, the sense of separation from the world around him that he'd attained up to then was cut down to zero, and he was more or less pulled into the world—like an animal unable to separate itself from its basic instincts."

Madness.

"At the same time, he sensed that he was more fanatical than an animal—that a fanatical force ran through his blood, and that was something that only human beings know. Animals always come back down to earth, he wrote. All they did was fulfill their needs. But that wasn't enough for him anymore. He'd been taken over by some kind of obsession. Insatiable, invincible, uncontrollable."

"And it was like that from the beginning? What set off the change? Didn't he write anything about that?"

Max shook his head. "All he wrote was that it began very slowly. I've skipped over entries from 1958, '59, and '60. At the start, in the first days, he thought it was just some kind of nausea that would soon pass. He only gradually became aware of just how deep the change went. He only slowly began to suspect, he said, what was coming, began to realize that something irresistible was happening, that it was a race against time, you could say, for him to get his emotions and his fears down on paper . . ."

Max broke off. "It must've been pretty rough," he continued, after a while.

Till was leaning back, his arms propped against the tree trunk at his back.

Max wiped his nose on his sleeve. "You'd have to have seen his handwriting. Not here, not in this diary from 1947, but later, after it got started in him. When he describes how he doesn't know why he feels ill; in 1958, the handwriting is still completely sharp, and the lines run across the paper like they're written with a ruler. But then . . . the individual letters get thinner and thinner, and longer and longer . . ." Max's eyes grew wider. "Sometimes words find their way into his sentences . . . and it's not just that I've never heard them before, it's that they *don't exist*. And then his words kind of stagger across the paper, like he's not in control of himself when he's writing them, but when you look at the sentences, you can understand them; it's just the spelling that's all over the place. And other times the sentences really look like they're correct, but the words have been put together in such a way that they don't make any sense. Then there are moments when it's crystal clear to him that something incomprehensible is going on with him, and where you can see plainly what kind of agony he's going through. And you can see he regrets not doing anything earlier to stop it, but also that the part of him that's actually able to regret anything is getting smaller and smaller! Pushed out more and more by the other part, the new and forceful part! So he had the feeling that he had to hurry, because the ability even to experience what was happening to him was getting weaker by the day . . ."

Till stood up, which meant he had to look down at Max, who was still sitting. "But you don't have to be afraid just because of that, Max," he said gently. "The guy must've been dead for a hundred years."

"A bit more than thirty, actually."

"Well, it's enough."

Max looked up. "Yeah, Otto Kern is dead. But what's bugging me isn't Otto Kern."

"But . . . ?"

When Max answered him, it seemed to Till that an icy chill crept under his T-shirt. "Seems to me that the changes Kern talks about are exactly the same as what's going on with my dad."

"You mean he's going through the same thing? He's living through the same changes?"

Max slipped down from the tree trunk onto the ground and leaned back against the wood. He did not answer Till's question.

****

A truck passed them and the blast of wind as it passed nearly pushed Till into Max's bike. The long blast on the horn—the driver's way of telling them to stop taking up half the road—died away. They rode on.

When they reached the bridge that separated Greater Wannsee from Little Wannsee, Max steered his bike over to the curb, stopped, and held on tightly to the railing on the bridge without getting off his bike. He looked out over the water, his head buzzing. Now that he had told Till what he had discovered, he saw for the first time just how seamlessly everything fit together.

He pushed away from the railing again and rode off. He heard Till pedaling behind him. When they were once again side-by-side, Max looked over at Till. "When I think that I have to ride home later and that I'll be sitting across from him at the table this evening . . ."

The more he thought about it, the more unbearable the thought became. That wasn't his father. It was some physically modified beast.

They turned onto the shoreline road that followed alongside the Wannsee. Max braked and hopped off the saddle, straddling the bike between his legs. Till also stopped.

"Let's run away, Till," he said—and it seemed almost like the words were out of his mouth before he'd thought about it. "We'll manage it if we do it together. You already did it once. I can't stand what's going on at home anymore." Max felt himself break into a sweat just at the thought of being home again. "It's like there's a kind of smell hanging over the place, and the smell is making me sick, you know?" He realized he was looking almost pleadingly at Till and pulled himself together. He'd never convince Till like that. He couldn't ask him. He had to *inspire* him.

"I've got an account that my parents set up for me when I was little." The words were pouring out now. "There's gotta be a pile of money in there—okay, maybe not so much, but a few thousand for sure. I can get that; we could live on that—"

"It won't work," Till interrupted, his face serious and sad. "Max, it won't work. That I found all of you, that . . . that can't happen twice, no way. And we won't manage it on our own. We could survive for a few days in the forest, but what then? What happens when they catch us? They'll find out who we are fast enough, and then it's back to Brakenfelde—for me—and you'll be sent home again."

"NO!" screamed Max, but instantly brought his voice under control again. There were houses close by and a woman was already looking at them over her front hedge. "No." His mind was racing. If he didn't manage to convince Till, he'd have to sleep at home again tonight. His face flushed hot and cold as thoughts raced wildly through his head. With all his might, he drove himself on, searching for the right words, the words he needed to finally bring Till over to his side! "Till . . . we . . . it's not impossible. We'll take the money, okay? And get on a train . . . that's it, they won't check on us on a train, right? We get on and head south. It stays warmer longer in the south . . ."

A great idea occurred to him. "The house in Italy! We've got a house in Tuscany! We can get in there. I know how to get in; we just have to get down there. There's food in the house, and heat. And if anyone asks? I know the people there. I'm the son of the owners, nothing can happen to us. And by the time my parents have tracked us down, we're sure to have come up with something!" He was staring at Till. That was it; that was THE solution! It could—it *had to*—work!

Till's eyes settled on him. His face seemed somehow haggard, and Max could see how hard this was for him.

"Max, I'm sorry . . . I know that in some way it's not right . . . it's your family . . . you want to get away . . . and I'm the one saying it won't work . . . but . . . you know, it really won't work. Even if we get by down there for a few weeks. What then?"

"Then we look for work. If we dodge things a bit, we'll pass for fourteen. They don't worry so much about that kind of thing in Italy. I'm sure there'll be work there."

Till's face screwed up as if he was thinking of something that Max didn't know about.

"Just stop," he heard Till say . . . and deep inside, he had an inkling that Till might be right. That it couldn't really work out, finding work down there . . . but there had to be a way, there had to . . .

"Did you ever think that you might be wrong? Okay, maybe you and your dad don't get along, but maybe that's the same for lots of people? That maybe the best thing to do would be to keep your head down for a few weeks or months or whatever, even years, till you don't need him anymore?"

That was it; that was the voice of reason that Max had always hated, recommending the hard way, the way of trouble and privation. And who could guarantee him that failure wasn't lying in wait for him at the end of that road, too? But Max also realized that he had lost the battle, that he hadn't managed to convince Till. Not because Till was mean—nothing like that. No, it was because Till was fundamentally right. Because there was no other way. He had to go back. He had to go home.

And suddenly he grew dizzy. It was like a massive wave rolling toward him and swallowing him up. Max reeled and heard the bicycle between his legs crash onto the street, and then he saw himself moving to the side of the road, heard Till behind him, muffled and dim, shouting something. The next moment, Max was kneeling on the curb, supporting himself with his arms, his head hanging from his shoulders—and the wave came up from deep in his stomach, filling his mouth with a soft, warm, lumpy fluid. The bitterness penetrated his nose, his eyes, then flooded out between his lips. The stink of it nearly took his breath away—and he vomited into the gutter. His guts clenched again and again as surge after surge of half-digested muck forced its way out of his body. Until he felt Till holding him tightly from behind just at the moment when his arms gave way, and he came within an inch of pitching face first into the puddle of puke.

"Sometimes the trains still ran. Then they could hear a rumbling in the distance, a jolting and rattling that slowly came closer. The beams

that supported the walls and the ceiling began to vibrate and the sand drizzled through between them. Then they pressed themselves into a corner and threw their arms over their heads to protect themselves from the falling grit. As the train drew closer, the entire room began to shake. They could hear the shriek of the steel wheels scraping over the rails, the rumble of the axles lumbering along the malformed tracks. When the train finally roared past, every single wheel that slammed in and out of the gap between two sections of track was a small earthquake. The walls seemed to buckle, the noise to fill the room.

"When that happened, Laila pressed close to her father until he took one arm and placed it down around her shoulders and pulled her close to him, as if to protect her from the rattle and rumble and roar that rushed past so close above them. Only when the last carriage had passed their room would he let her go again. But Laila still lay pressed against him for some minutes, as if she wanted to be sure to be close to him, in case the steel monster came back. But, in fact, they were actually very well protected in their room. Because there were no windows, no doors. No air shafts, no gaps, no hatches. Every opening had been sealed by Laila's father when they took refuge in there. He had nailed the boards he'd brought with him across the front of the door where they'd slipped inside. And over the windows he screwed the steel shutters so tightly closed that there was no way to open them anymore."

"'I'm hungry, Papa,'—that was what had set everything in motion, the second day after their escape to the room. Throughout the first day, Laila had sworn to herself that she wouldn't bother her father with it— but on the second day, she couldn't hold out any longer. At the start, it was a biting feeling, as if her stomach had begun to feed on itself. Then the feeling dulled, but the pain and the deprivation spread through her body like a fever. She felt as if she hardly had the strength even to open her mouth.

"'I'm hungry'—she had spoken very softly, almost as if she hadn't wanted him to hear her. But she was still certain that he had, even if he had not answered at first.

"Veit had known that it must come to this point soon. He would never have believed that Laila could hold out so long. When he heard her humming away to herself, heard her say she was hungry, just a whisper, he knew the time had come that would make everything leading up to this moment an adventure—and what lay ahead the true horror.

"Because there was nothing to eat. There was no food stored in the room, just the beams, the steel shutters, the sand. The door he had nailed shut and the clothes they were wearing. It was hot in the room and when the trains rolled past—with the dust that trickled from the cracks, the shrieking of the wheels, the heat still blasting against the walls from outside—the air grew musty and stale. But there was nothing to eat. And they couldn't leave the room. Veit knew that. He and Laila had been lucky even to make it this far. But outside, they were waiting. Thousands, hundreds of thousands. And they would be on them instantly. They wouldn't hesitate, not for a second.

"Veit felt Laila curl a little closer against him. He looked down at his daughter's small face. At her fine features, her translucent skin, her eyelids now closed. She had fallen asleep. Carefully, he lifted her and laid her down on the floor. Then he crawled to the other end of the room and stood up.

"'I'm hungry, Papa.'

"There was only one way.

"He pulled at the shirt he was wearing, tugging it out of the waistband of his pants. Beneath it was the blade in its leather sheath. He pulled it out. The knife glinted in the dust-filled space. He laid the steel against his forearm. The blade cooled his burning skin. Then Veit took the one handkerchief he still possessed out of his pocket, twisted it to a cord, and stuffed it between his teeth. Arm or leg—those were his choices.

"As the knife sliced into his forearm, he nearly passed out. The blood poured from the cut and streamed over his hand. He heard the *air gurgling in his throat, sank back against the beams of the wall, and braced himself with both feet against the floor.*

"She kept on sleeping. He could see her small body lying by the opposite wall.

"Veit pulled the knife toward him, watched it as it slid through the flesh of his arm below the elbow. He tilted it upward slightly and the flesh came free. The raw mass that appeared underneath seemed to throb. He let the blade fall, pushed himself across the floor with his feet, propped his back against the beams. As he lost consciousness, he held the sliced off piece between thumb and index finger to stop it from falling into the dirt."

"That doesn't work. He . . . he wouldn't do it . . . And most important, how was he supposed to cook the meat he'd cut off? Idiot! A room with no way in or out, no windows, no door."

"All I hear is the next train rattling past, all I see is the sand trickling down between the beams."

"But he can't cook the meat!"

"So . . . raw, then?"

"That's . . . I mean, that goes too far! They wouldn't . . ."

"Don't let yourself get distracted! If they cook it or not, that's beside the point. What matters is that he bandages his wound. That she wakes up and he says he's found something to eat. It doesn't go too far; it's going exactly the right way. Listen, you don't want to disgust yourself? You've had enough? Then I'll tell you how it goes from here: *'Two weeks have passed. Veit lay . . .'*—sure he lay, because he can't stand up anymore—so: *'He lay on the floor. He was practically down to a _torso_.'*"

"NO. I don't want to hear it."

"But I can see him—I see Veit in front of me, in the room made of beams—and here comes another train. It rumbles past. And Veit slices. Laila wakes up."

"But then . . ."

"Nothing then, goddamnit. I don't want to hear that! What are you afraid of? You don't want to write something like that? What's the danger? Is it going to warp your spirit, your head, your mind, or your soul if you string these words together like this? What gets bent out of shape? You have to go down this path—this is *your way*! So, Veit is lying on the dusty floor, a torso, I can see him looking up at Laila. He's cut off another piece, but this time, she—you can see it in her eyes—she has *realized*. *"I can't do it, Papa!"* Can't you just hear her? I can hear her. I see her right in front of me. *"Please, Papa, I can't . . ." but he holds out the piece of flesh in front of her. She has to retch. "I don't want to, it's nothing; I'm not hungry!" He stares at her. "Eat!"*"

"Are you sure?"

"He yells at her: "You have to eat, Laila. You can't let me . . . I can't . . . it can't be that it was all for nothing!" She trembles. They haven't been out of the room in two weeks. He sinks his teeth into the last piece he's sliced off. "Look! You can!" The blood streams out between his teeth . . .' Too far? You think so? It's not too far at all. It's only just begun! The descent."

"He's chewing on his own flesh . . ."

"It doesn't go far enough. You're afraid of climbing down that far with your words? What a gutless piece of shit you turned out to be! The words are just the facade, the foyer, the front garden. It's not about the words at all! *It's about the act!*"

TWELVE YEARS AGO

Julia returned to the living room. She had just walked the last of the guests to the front door. Xavier sat on the sofa across the room from the fireplace. He glanced up as she entered the room, then looked back at the fire.

He looked tired. The party seemed to have been a real strain on him.

"Everything okay?" Julia sat down in the armchair beside the sofa, which was also turned toward the fireplace.

Xavier smiled. "I think I've drunk a little too much wine."

"Do you want an Alka-Seltzer?"

He shook his head. "No, I'm fine."

Julia sipped at the glass she still held in her hand. She hesitated . . . and then broached the topic that had been playing on her mind for days.

"The other day, at Felix's place . . ."—Xavier didn't take his eyes off the fire—"I haven't been able to stop thinking about it . . . 'he's got me over a barrel,' I think those were the words you used."

Xavier still had his face directed at the fireplace, but Julia had the feeling that he was no longer lost in thought, that now he was making an effort to keep looking straight ahead.

"What did you mean by that, Xavier? Felix has you 'over a barrel'? In what way?"

The fire crackled in the fireplace. Xavier had his head propped on one hand. "He's my publisher, Julia," she heard him say quietly. "I could, of course, go to another publisher, but I *am* with him. He determines when and how my books are published." Now he turned and faced her directly. "You know what that means. All my work . . . Felix is the one who makes all the decisions about it. But why do you ask? Isn't that clear?"

She looked him in the eye. Wasn't that clear? Of course . . . what else could he have meant? But still, his words did not reassure her in the slightest—try as she might to persuade herself otherwise.

A heavy silence settled over them. Julia had said good night to Jenna and Rebecca hours before. It had to be after two in the morning. Now she, too, felt the stress of the day weighing on her. She saw Xavier sink sideways onto the sofa until he was lying flat, his legs pulled up. The lines of his angular face seemed a little softer than usual, the reflection of the flames dancing in his eyes.

Julia spontaneously wondered if he had been like Max when he was a boy. Or more easygoing? Serious, but not so glum—*maybe like Till*, she thought, and felt a pang in her heart.

She was well aware that Xavier seemed to be observing Till, and that the favor he showed the boy was something that Xavier had always withheld from his own son. Julia knew that Max had his weaknesses, that even at his young age he gave the impression of being unstable; he was torn between a runaway ambition that vented its rage in his wishes and visions, and talents that were not up to achieving these things. But she loved her son dearly. She knew that Max tried hard, that he struggled not to let himself be brought down by his own eccentric imaginings. And that he longed to be loved by his father. But she also knew that was something that Max and Xavier had to sort out for themselves. She could not force her husband to love a son who was clearly foreign to him in some way, and perhaps always would be.

A few years before, when all this had become clear to her for the first time, she had tried to talk to Xavier about it, and had realized just how much he, too, was suffering from the situation. It was as if he had tried to command himself to love the boy but couldn't manage to do so. But to ask him directly what he thought about Max . . . that was one thing Julia had never dared to do. She was too afraid of hearing something she would never be able to forget. When Max was very small, still a baby—barely able to walk, let alone speak— Xavier had spent hour after hour with the boy. But not lovingly, not oblivious to the world around him, as Julia might have expected from a father; instead, it was as though he was testing himself, struggling with himself. As if he was trying desperately to find the depth of feeling he assumed a father had to show for his son. Later, he gave up trying. He and Max had increasingly less to do with each other—and the feeling came over Julia that, in those first hours he spent with Max, Xavier might have come to the decision that he would be unable to build a deep relationship with the boy. At the same time, Xavier's way with Lisa, Claire, and Betty seemed to Julia to be steeped in a natural, pleasant, reassuring warmth. Something she had always wished for—in vain—for Xavier and Max.

"How have things been going with the birds lately?" she said, trying again to start a conversation, although she knew it was late and maybe the best thing to do would be simply to go to bed.

"The boys were just outside the door . . . they probably shouldn't have seen what was going on," she heard Xavier say from the sofa.

Of course not, thought Julia. She had been against it from the start, but Xavier had said that a few of the guests he'd invited that evening would appreciate it if he staged a parrot fight. When Xavier had told her about it for the first time, Julia had instantly been certain that it would be brutal, bloody, and horrible. But Xavier had insisted. He had said she wouldn't hear a sound, and that he simply had to do it. And now? Did he regret it? Again, Julia recollected what she had heard the other night in the hallway. Max's shout that there was a woman down in his father's workroom. What woman? Was she really a courier there to collect a manuscript, as Xavier had told her? But Julia couldn't bring herself to raise the issue again.

"Did you use the bird fight for your book?" she asked instead, and saw her husband nod, his eyes still closed. A nod that signified nothing.

"Sometimes I have the feeling that I do everything wrong." He opened his eyes. "As if I have to take certain risks to get just far enough out—"

"Out? Out to where?" she interrupted.

"Out of the familiar? Into the new. The free." He fell silent for a moment, as if to give her the opportunity to respond, but she just waited. "But then," he said, picking up the thread where she had interrupted him, "it can happen that I completely lose sight of what I actually wanted to achieve. And nothing remains except for the fact that I took the risk."

Julia exhaled. *What was he talking about?*

"Do you know what I mean?" He looked at her.

"What kind of risk are you talking about?"

"The parrot fight, for example . . . I wanted to offer the guests something they'd never seen before. I'd heard that such things were done. It seemed like a great idea and it did work. The two or three friends of Felix who I wanted to show it to, they were deeply impressed. And yet, for a moment, I could no longer see why I even did it. For a moment, all I saw was those poor, feathered beasts hacking at each other, and right there . . .

how can I put it . . . all of the energy that had been driving me, that had got me to the point where I actually staged the fight, all that energy was suddenly gone—and there was nothing left except the horrible slaughter of those animals, really beautiful animals, but injected half out of their minds with God-knows-what-sort-of chemicals."

How could he ever have believed that this fight would be anything but degenerate slaughter? But just as Julia was about to say exactly that, Xavier sat up. His legs seemed to pull him down onto the floor, his face looked gray and tired, his eyes watery. He nodded to her and left the room without saying another word.

****

Lisa looked at the cards in the hand. The seven? Then he would have to draw two, and she would probably win. Again. Lisa loved playing Mau Mau, but she hesitated now when it came to laying the card that was exactly the right one to play in that situation. She sat in the chair she had pushed up close to Max's bed. They were already on their fourth hand. Max was sick. It had been two days already. He'd thrown up a few times and was running a fever. He ate poorly, felt weak—Lisa could see it when she looked at him—and his skin looked more greenish yellow than flesh colored. Dr. Trimborn had been to visit yesterday and had mumbled something about rest; her brother was probably suffering from exhaustion. The doctor had given him a calcium shot and Max had turned even paler than usual. Since getting the injection, all he'd done was lie in bed.

Lisa felt sorry for him. Max had never been particularly robust, but she had also never seen him really sick. She played an insignificant two and held the seven in her hand. Maybe it would be better if she let him win; he was weak enough as it was, after all.

"Mau." Max looked at her, his eyes bright and one card left in his hand. Lisa looked at the discard pile. Clubs. Wrong suit. She drew a card.

"Mau Mau!" Max slapped down his last card energetically onto the discard pile. "Two all. Wanna go again?" But before she could answer, he sank back onto his mattress. As if the excitement of winning had already cost him too much energy.

"Don't you think you'd rather sleep for a bit?" she asked, and gathered up the cards. We can play again later. Maybe Till can play with us, too."

He stayed lying down and just looked at her out of his large, dark eyes. Finally, he nodded. "Wake me up in an hour?"

Lisa stood up. "See you in a bit."

She lay the pack of cards on the night table and quietly exited the room, pulling the door closed behind her.

Out in the hallway, she hesitated. Ever since Max had gotten sick, she hadn't seen much of Till. The door to his room was closed now, too. But she knew he was in there. Making up her mind, she went to the door and opened it. Till was lying on his bed, a book in his hand. He looked up.

"I was just in with Max," she said. "He's sleeping now."

Till slid his legs off the bed and sat up. "How's he doing?"

Lisa crossed to the desk that her mother had had set up in Till's room and sat down. "Nothing new."

Till dog-eared the page he was on—Lisa shuddered, but chose not to say anything—and laid the book on the bed.

"The doctor doesn't know what's wrong with him." She kept her eyes on Till. He'd been spending days on end with Max, but when she asked what they did all that time, she couldn't get a straight answer. Lisa decided to go on the attack. "Max is my brother. I've known him all my life," she said, and heard her own voice, a bright, clear, girl's voice, the kind of voice—it seemed to her—that she would love to hear if she were a boy, "but I've never seen him like this. Do you know when this started? When he started to get so weak and unfriendly and withdrawn?"

Till glanced up at her, but his eyes didn't have the openness that Lisa was used to from him. These eyes reminded her of the first time she had seen him, in the front garden, before anyone knew that he'd run away.

"Nope," he replied.

"Since you came," she said, knowing this would unsettle him. But Lisa wanted to find out what was going on with her brother. Maybe it really had something to do with Till's arrival, even if she couldn't imagine exactly what.

Till's look was still a little guarded, but the puzzlement in his eyes was genuine. "Are you saying *I'm* to blame for him being sick?"

"Are you?"

He seemed unable to easily answer no, because instead of simply rejecting the suggestion, Till let his head hang again.

Now! thought Lisa, and she stood up and sat next to him on the bed. "Sorry, Till, I don't mean to offend you. Maybe it's just a coincidence that Max has been sick since you came, but it certainly stands out."

Pause. Silence. From downstairs came the sound of Rebecca gathering cutlery.

"I didn't do anything," Till murmured. "We were just riding around on the bikes. Max was showing me what there is around here."

Lisa looked down at her toes.

"I don't know what it is," said Till.

She looked at him. He sighed, and suddenly his voice grew quiet and calm. "I can't tell you any more than that, Lisa. Max would . . . I promised him I wouldn't talk about it with anyone . . . it's . . . he's really taken it to heart."

"What do you mean?" She sensed herself getting nervous. So it was true that Max and Till were up to something. She knew it! Lisa tried to keep her voice low and cooing, at a pitch she knew other boys always reacted to because they stopped what they were doing, swallowed, and grinned self-consciously. "I won't tell him that you told me . . ."

But Till shook his head.

"Do you want to make him sicker?" Indignation crept into her voice. Max trusted Till, but not her? "Max isn't as strong as you. I can understand him not saying anything to Dad. But what about Mom?" She noticed that a vein was standing out on Till's temple, and thought she could almost see the blood inside. "Can't you even tell me why you don't trust us?"

Till mumbled something that she didn't catch.

"What?"

He looked at her. Helpless, but keeping his mouth shut.

Lisa stood up again and went back to the desk. "So, is this your idea of fair? After my parents took you in? First, you and my brother get mixed up in something that's made him really sick, and then you won't even say what you know about it?!"

Summing up the situation like that, Lisa shuddered more than ever at the enormity of it all. But another thought, another sensation, also went through her mind: that despite everything, she did not feel she was wrong about Till. Even though she'd only known him a few weeks, she was sure that Till was all right. There was no denying that she trusted him—even if that didn't seem at all justified at the moment. She asked herself whether there might be a good reason for him to hold his tongue. Whether it might actually be *right* for him not to say a word, even if it *seemed* he might be endangering Max's health by doing so.

TWELVE YEARS AGO

As Max awoke with a start, *he* was standing in front of him. A black shadow, looming high. The sky outside the window was still blue, dark blue, but everything else—the trees beyond the window, the table in the room, and the man standing at his bedside—was black. Max felt immeasurably small and defenseless, like a snail pulled out of its shell. He felt himself break out in a sweat, but his skin was cold as ice.

"Are you feeling a little better?" he heard his father ask, and the voice was gentle, warm, endlessly familiar. Max pushed his feet into the mattress and shoved himself up against the wall.

"Yeah, I'm okay," he heard himself say, his voice a little shaky but clear. *Stay away from me,* he screamed inside as he saw his father bending forward—then the lamp on his bedside table came on. The pale, gaunt face appeared in the light it shed. Bentheim sat in the chair that Lisa had been sitting in earlier. In his hands he held a small tray with a deep bowl on it.

"Your mom said I should bring you a little broth," he explained, and set the tray down on Max's legs. "Is it okay like this? Or do you want to come down and sit at the table?"

Max reached for the tray and held on to it tightly. Although he wanted desperately to avoid being alone with his father, the thought of pulling on a robe and going downstairs terrified him—instead of legs he felt like he had two lumps of rubber attached to his hips.

"No, it's okay . . ." He reached for the spoon. His father stayed in the chair. "You don't need to stay. I can take care of it," Max said.

But his father seemed unwilling to leave again so soon.

"You know, I've been wondering if I haven't been a little too strict lately," he said, and looked at Max. "That's partly because of the book. It isn't coming on like I want, and it makes me irritable . . ." He nodded and looked at Max as if to see how he reacted.

Max spooned soup into his mouth. There was nothing to say to that.

"I'm sorry if I've done anything wrong, Max," he heard his father continue. And again Max wanted to hear that scream inside him—*Leave me alone!*—but this time it didn't really come out right. It was as if the all-too-familiar voice of his father, sitting there next to him and bending forward slightly, was trying to soothe away all Max's caution.

"Did anything else happen? . . . I mean . . . we're all wondering why you're feeling so poorly, my boy." His blue eyes came to rest on Max's. Could he see something lurking back behind those pupils? He couldn't let himself be lured out onto thin ice. He had to watch out. WATCH OUT!

The strain of balancing the tray with the soup on his knees, the tension that came from the presence of his father, the inner voice that was nearly driving him crazy, the effort of not letting any of that show—it was all nearly too much for Max. He felt his knees starting to shake . . . just don't spill any of the soup . . . he couldn't let anything show . . .

"Even Trimborn doesn't really know what's going on with you. He says it's exhaustion . . . but from what? . . . in the middle of summer vacation." Spotlight eyes trained directly on his face. Max swallowed—and coughed. His armpits were sweating and he felt the fever rising. "That's why I'm wondering if something has maybe happened in the last few days."

"No." Short and sharp.

"Are you keeping something from me, Max?" Was there a threatening undertone there, or was it just the concern of a father for his son?

"No. Why should I?" Max drew a sharp breath. Was he back to whimpering and shying away?

"It's okay," he heard his father say, relenting, "I just wanted to say that you can trust me, Max. I'm your father. If you can't trust me, then who?"

Max let the spoon drop into the soup and pushed the plate away. "Can you take the tray? I've had enough."

His father leaned forward and looked into the bowl. "But you haven't eaten anything."

"Dad, please, take it away," said Max, thinking he would just hurl the tray and plate to one side with his legs if his father didn't take them away in the next second.

But Bentheim reached for the tray and lifted it off Max's legs. "If this goes on, the doctor said we'll have to take you to the hospital. Do you understand?" His voice was now more insistent. "The doctor doesn't know what's going on. And your mother is really worried."

"Sure, Dad. It's . . . what can I say . . . I don't know what's going on either . . . but . . . I think my temperature's gone up again; I don't feel good at all."

He saw the pained look in his father's eyes. "Is that true?"

Max forced himself to smile. "Nooo . . . it's okay . . . I was just kidding. I'm starting to feel better; tomorrow I'll be a hundred percent again. Really." But the chatter in his head was saying: *If he doesn't go now, I'll scream.*

"Could you put the light off again? I'd better sleep for a bit." Max closed his eyes and felt a cool hand pressed against his forehead, testing his fever. Max blinked and saw his father bending down, giving him a light kiss on the cheek.

"Poor little Max, what's going on with you?" he heard his father murmur—then he closed his eyes again so as not to have to answer. Everything in him longed to be able to throw his arms around his father's neck and finally leave behind all the worry and confusion and darkness that had been settling over him in recent days and weeks, but he forced himself to keep his arms underneath the blanket. Because if there was one thing he was certain of, it was that his father was faking it.

Then he fell asleep and didn't notice his father turning off the light, going to the door, and leaving the room.

✳✳✳✳

What he saw was a shadow. As high as a man, black, lurching. Till's hands seemed to be growing into the balcony rail. A second shadow appeared. And a third, then a fourth. They were moving directly toward him, reeling between the thin tree trunks of the small patch of woods on the neighboring property, rustling through the fallen leaves with heavy steps, as if they were unable to lift their feet properly. Till felt like he was encased in a block of transparent resin. His limbs no longer obeyed his commands; only his eyes continued to function, absorbing what he was seeing, taking in images his brain could no longer process. He was reduced to merely watching, mesmerized by what was happening, overwhelmed by the incomprehensibility of it all.

The first shadows emerged from the woods and approached the seven-foot-high wire-mesh fence that separated the Bentheims' property from the neighboring lot. Silvery light washed over them, but they had their heads lowered and Till could see only their hair—or rather, what was left of their hair, and the scalp underneath, strangely roughened and scabbed . . .

Spellbound, Till watched as the creatures surged against the fence; it stopped them for the moment, but their legs were still making the walking motion, like the legs of wind-up toys.

More and more of them emerged from the woods. The stiff substance that seemed to have engulfed Till began to chill. It froze him, his skin stiffened with the cold—but he couldn't take his eyes off the fence, where still more of the figures were massing. The wooden uprights supporting the fence were already creaking, although they were strongly built and firmly anchored into the ground. Till knew with absolute certainty that the posts wouldn't hold up against the onslaught much longer. Already, two, three, five rows of the things were pushing against the fence. There was a crack, as if a shot had been fired, and one of the uprights splintered—then the next one snapped and sixty feet of fence sagged to the ground.

The figures that were up against the fence went down with it, but the ones pushing from behind kept their footing and stepped on and over the ones in front. Till saw their dirt-encrusted shoes stomp on the heads of those lying on the ground. Then they were lurching across the Bentheims' lawn, closer now, their heads still hanging, lit by the moonlight. A swarm of filthy black beings, silent, their feet brushing over the grass as they moved, seemingly unstoppable in their advance—and heading straight for the house. They were already moving under the balcony Till was standing on. He heard them career against the shutters attached to the walls below, heard the windows groan under the strain, heard calloused hands grasping at the posts that bore the weight of the balcony. And felt the block of icy resin clutch him even tighter.

Then the window below shattered, pressed in by the horde, and the resin block enclosing Till shattered simultaneously. Finally, he was free, the numbness he'd fallen into now shredded and gone. Till spun around, knowing more than seeing that the first of the creatures already had to be climbing the posts, clambering up to the room where Max was still asleep. He hurled himself through the balcony door to his friend's bedroom, wanting to wake him up, warn him, rip him out of the coma-like slumber he must have been in—if not, why hadn't he heard what was going on around them? Even as he rushed to the bed, he wanted to call Max's name, but it was as if his throat was sealed shut. No matter how hard he tried, no sound made it out of his mouth.

This can't be—this isn't possible—he had to shout a warning! Till threw his arms back and, gathering up all the strength he had, thrust out his chest, trying to break through the leaden blanket that seemed to have wrapped itself around his throat. He knew it was only through an effort of will that he could break through this inexplicable bluntness. He bolstered himself up and, pushing from deep in his belly, he blasted out all the air he had inside, out through his throat, up through his windpipe, out with the yell that must finally wake Max before it was too late: "MAAAXXX!" Till heard himself bawl, and felt relief coursing through him at his success, that he'd taken control of himself, that he'd been the one to choose whether he would yell or not—and in the same moment felt everything suddenly start to distort and buckle.

The sound of rustling started to fade, and he sensed himself slipping out of the grim dreamworld he'd found himself in, no longer running toward Max's bed, but—still wound up from the dream-scream he'd let out—now lying instead on his own mattress, the bedding disheveled. But at least he was no longer in a dark room at night. Instead, he was in one filled with morning light, a gorgeous summer day, and there were no lurching, faceless hordes lurking by the door to the terrace. Like rainwater from a leaf, the anxiety, the fear, the creeping sensation, all of it dripped away. He'd been dreaming. Everything was okay.

Till threw back the quilt, suddenly feeling smothered by the weight of the feathers, and jumped out of bed, wanting to tell Max about his dream. But the block of ice around him in his dream, so recently burst apart, suddenly seemed to freeze around him again.

Max's bed was empty.

Max hadn't been out of bed for eight days. The evening before, he had asked if Till would sleep in his room with him. Till hadn't exactly understood why, but it was clear that Max needed his help. His proximity. His presence. So Till had said yes, moved his mattress into Max's room, and set up camp for the night—something he liked doing anyway. And he promised Max that he'd wake him up if anything unusual happened during the night.

But then he'd gone and fallen into the deepest of sleeps.

He's already up! What's so bad about that? He's probably already downstairs . . . he must be feeling better. That's great! Till heard the voice in his head, heard him say the words to himself, but they were not reassuring; they couldn't shake off the icy grip that surrounded him, even as he raced out of the room.

"Max!"

Nothing. Till ran to the bathroom. The door was unlocked and he shoved it open. Empty.

"MAX?!"

Back into the hall, to Lisa's room. The door was open, the room empty. Till pelted down the stairs. "MAX!!" He wouldn't have cared now if he suddenly found everyone standing around him. All he felt was blind, naked panic.

He arrived at the bottom of the stairs, in the entrance hall. "Hello?" There was no one in sight. Rebecca, Jenna, the girls—no one. He ran to the kitchen. Everything was tidied, wiped down, and in order—but there was no one there. Out of the kitchen—a moment of confusion—then into the living room, empty, the corridor that led down to the music room . . . "Helllooo??"

"What's the *matter?*"

The words hit him like a fist. The door at the end of the corridor flew open. Lisa.

"Why are you screaming like that?"

Till was so happy to see her that he didn't stop running. He sprinted all the way to her and grabbed her hand.

"Where is everyone . . . I fell asleep, and . . ."

He noticed how serious she looked. "Max took a turn for the worse. Mom's taken him to the hospital."

Till was still smiling.

"He threw up again. Dad didn't want to wait any longer, so he called the doctor this morning, really early. And the doctor said that Max was . . ." She had to pause for a moment to think ". . . dehydrated."

Now the smile vanished from Till's face. All he could think about was that he'd fallen asleep; he hadn't watched out for Max.

"Mom drove him there." She looked at Till. "You want something for breakfast?" Her voice was low and gloomy.

She's talking like there's a body in the house, Till thought, and the icy hand gripping his stomach moved up to his throat.

They were once again sitting at the same high table, the one they'd sat at the day Till came to the Bentheims' for the very first time. The silence in the empty house around them weighed heavily on Till. His concern for Max filled him. He'd grabbed the bag of muesli, splashed a bit of milk over the flakes, and was spooning the stuff into his mouth. Lisa sat opposite, watching him while he ate.

What was she doing in the music room? he thought absently—but he said something else. "Which hospital did they take him to?"

"The Ben Franklin Clinic, or whatever they call it these days," Lisa answered. "The big one in Steglitz."

Till stuffed another spoonful of muesli between his teeth and spoke with his mouth full. "You want to come along? I'm going to go down there."

Lisa looked at him wide-eyed, as if to say, *Are you out of your mind?*

"He . . . there were some pretty crazy things that Max had in his head," Till continued, swallowing. He had to take her into his confidence; he couldn't wait any longer. He saw that he had her attention, saw her small, pretty face become tense. "It's about your dad, you know?" Till blurted, and his face turned red. How could he ever explain it to her? She'd think it was *him*, not Max, who'd thought it all up. "He thinks your dad's been changing." Lisa rumpled her forehead. "I tried to talk him out of it, but Max was so stuck on the idea; he got it so fixed in his head; he thought it explained everything that seemed strange to him."

"*What* did he get stuck in his head?" She kept her eyes fixed on Till.

"That's . . . kind of hard to explain . . ."

Lisa looked perplexed.

"He's so on edge," Till mumbled. Maybe it wasn't such a good idea to tell her about it. Till leaned forward, suddenly intensely aware of a brand-new danger. "But you have to promise me never to tell anyone!" He took hold of her arm and squeezed. "Lisa? You gotta swear. Okay?"

Swear . . . he nearly laughed. But whatever. She couldn't tell a soul, not under any circumstances, not her mother, but most of all—and Till grew weak at the mere thought of it—not her father . . .

"You can't tell anyone. They won't leave Max in peace again, ever. They might put him away in a home! He wouldn't make it through that!" He could see that the more he said, the more he was losing Lisa. "We have to help him, you and me. Not your parents; they can't help him. He's afraid of your dad, and the fear goes down deep inside him. You can't get it out so easily."

"We can't do that by ourselves," he heard Lisa say. "What's wrong with you? Do you think I'm just going to keep quiet and watch my brother go down the drain?!" Her voice grew shrill and Till realized that the responsibility he was placing on her shoulders was too much for her to carry.

"Listen, Lisa," he said, letting go of her arm—he saw that her skin was completely white where he'd been holding her—"it's not about how sick it all sounds, all the things that are weighing on Max. It's about him being scared. Okay? He's scared of your dad. If Max found out that you told your dad what he was scared of . . ."

"Max doesn't need to find out."

"No!" Till jumped up angrily from his chair. "That's not it! Your father took me in. I owe you all so much, but . . ." He hesitated for a moment. Could he trust her? But then the words came out of Till's mouth by themselves. He couldn't have stopped them if he'd tried. ". . . But there are a few things that are pretty weird." Till felt like a drowning man, clutching at driftwood in a heavy sea. But the beams he was trying to grasp were the right words. "There's only one way we can help Max. We have to show him that he can trust us and that he's not at his dad's mercy. That there's someone on his side, standing by him. Whatever happens."

He was asking a lot of her. He was asking her to trust him more than her own father. Was it pointless? Was he being *stupid*, even, to take her into his confidence like this? Wasn't he asking her to do what he himself was unable to do: to keep it all to herself and not get anyone else involved?

"What are you going to do now?" She looked at him.

"I'm going to ride to the hospital. I have to see him. He asked me to watch out for him last night, but I fell asleep."

Till saw a trace of sympathy in her eyes.

"Okay."

"What?" Could he trust his ears?

"I said 'okay,'" Lisa repeated. "I'll wait till you get back and tell me how he's doing."

It seemed to Till that he was surfacing from a great depth. "Okay. And if your mom asks, just tell her I've gone to see Max. That would be okay."

TWELVE YEARS AGO

When Julia entered the room, her son was lying on his side and staring out the window.

"Max!" She set the bags she was carrying on the floor and went to him. He rolled onto his back. His pale-skinned face seemed a little more sunken than usual. He hadn't had a haircut for ages, and his hair hung down over his forehead. A smile spread across his face.

"Mom."

Julia sat on the edge of the bed and took her son's hand in hers. He rolled over and lay his head on her lap. She swept the hair off his forehead and stroked his head. Max's hair still felt as soft as a small child's.

Julia's gaze wandered to the window that Max had been staring out of. The room was on the top floor of one of the two towers. The window took up almost the entire wall. Looking out, she could see the Teltow Canal and parts of the concrete anatomy of the hospital complex. Open expanses, squares, different levels: a massive construction from the sixties, at one time the largest and most modern hospital in Europe—today weather-beaten, aging, almost shabby.

She looked back to her son. "I brought a bunch of stuff for you."

He didn't move at all.

"Max?"

Max slid off her lap again, stretched out, and sank back against the big, white pillow at the head of the bed. Metal rods, rails, pulleys. His hospital bed looked like he could fly out the window with it if he just pulled the right lever.

Julia stood up and fetched the bags she'd put down at the door. Before driving to the hospital, she'd spent two hours cooking in the kitchen with Rebecca. She sat down again on the chair beside Max's bed, pulled over the night table, cleared off the top, and began to set out the things she'd brought. A small bowl full of clear, hot chicken soup, a tiny portion of ravioli filled with ricotta cheese and spinach, some goulash with half a dumpling, a chicken drumstick fresh from the oven . . . she'd prepared everything she knew that Max loved the most.

Julia pushed the bags to one side and looked at her son, who was watching her wide-eyed. There was no need to talk about it. Julia knew that he knew: the main reason he was here was that he hadn't eaten in days. At home, they had tried to put him on an intravenous drip to give him the electrolytes he needed. But Max had pulled the drip out of his arm again the moment he was alone. Trimborn had asked Julia if they should restrain him, then he wouldn't be able to pull the drip out of his arm anymore. Shocked, Julia had refused. But she knew it was only a matter of time. The doctor looking after Max here in the hospital had made things perfectly clear: today was the last day he could accept the responsibility of not ordering the boy to be force-fed. She had to manage it today; Max must eat something. Otherwise, she'd be forced to ask the doctor to take care of it.

"You're not hungry, are you?" Her eyes met her son's. He shook his head.

"I brought your favorite food."

Nodding.

"I cooked it all myself."

"Yeah."

"You haven't eaten anything in days, Max; it's not possible that you're not hungry."

His eyes looked away from her face, back to the window.

"Max, if you don't eat something today . . . I spoke to the doctors . . . it can't go on like this."

She had tried everything. She'd threatened, begged, tried to convince him with words, asked Xavier to talk to him. She had even sent Lisa to talk some sense into her brother. Julia had promised him gifts; she'd confiscated the things she knew he loved and announced that he'd get them back only when he started eating again. But none of it worked.

Then she had started going to the doctors. Had her boy turned anorexic all of a sudden? She had heard that the condition used to be mainly restricted to girls but that it was no longer uncommon for boys to suddenly develop eating disorders. But what the experts could not give her—even after speaking with Max—was a clear reason *why* Max had stopped eating, although one psychiatrist had raised the possibility that Max might be suffering some sort of psychotic disorder. That maybe Max thought—even though he'd never said as much—that his meals were poisoned. Until now, she hadn't ventured to ask him about the possibility.

"Are you afraid the food could be poisoned?" Her voice was low now, not much more than a whisper.

Max stared at her. Bright-red flecks appeared on his cheeks.

"Listen, Max, I don't believe you'd ever think anything like that. That I . . . that I would be able to do something to you . . . but . . . if you don't eat today, then I have to ask the doctors to take care of it so you don't do yourself any permanent harm. Your body is getting weak. You're damaging it."

She suddenly felt her eyes welling up. Quickly, she turned away and wiped her eyes with the back of her hand, then turned back to her boy. She wouldn't get anywhere if she started bawling now.

She took his hand. "Is that what you want?"

Max had opened his mouth a little. He was breathing in short, sharp gulps, not deep into his belly, but fast and shallow.

"They'll tie you to the bed so you don't pull out the drip." Julia felt unbearable images fill her mind, flashes in which she saw her son being restrained—but she forced them out of her head. The doctors had told her that Max would be under sedation. *Sure,* she'd whispered to herself, *when you connect the drip. But if you force-feed him? Then you can't put him under . . .*

"They'll have to push a tube down into your stomach, my Max"—It was as if every word she said to her son sliced her own heart open. "That's like . . . I mean . . . you can imagine what that's like . . . but it doesn't have to go that far . . ."

The tears were rolling over her cheeks now, but she didn't wipe them away again; it didn't make any difference anymore, she had to get through to him, to get him back to her, to get things back to how they were before—they'd loved each other so much . . . When had it happened, when had she lost him?

"You only need to swallow a few spoons of the chicken soup, my Max . . . or whatever you like . . . I've packed the bags full. There's candy and chips and sausages and cake . . . whatever you can think of. And if that's no good, I'll go and get you something else."

She saw Max's eyes, too, brimming with tears, overflowing, his little face endlessly sad, disappointed, as if he were wandering around in some pitch-black world of hurt and heartache, desperately searching for a way out, calling, but nobody could hear him, nobody could help him, nobody could rescue him because he did not see the hand reached out toward him. He did not see it because something was blocking his view; something was eating away at him from the inside, but what it was nobody knew.

"Can't you tell me what you're thinking, Max? What you want? Shall we take a trip, go somewhere far away, just us? Is that it?" Suddenly Julia found courage, because she thought she saw his face brighten a little, as if a single ray of sunlight had fallen across it.

"For how long?" he asked.

"I don't know, a few days. A week. How would that be?"

"And after?"

"Then we'd go home again."

And just like that, the sunbeam was gone. As if snipped off with scissors. And Max's face once again looked so lonely, so abandoned, baffled, sad, and helpless.

"What . . . do you think we should stay away longer?"

It came out of his chest like a desperate groan: "Ahhh . . . it doesn't matter. However long we stay away, we'll always come back in the end."

Really go away? Forever? Of course not.

"What would become of Lisa and the little ones?" *And your dad?* she thought, but kept it to herself because something told her that perhaps Xavier was in some way responsible for the way Max was behaving. She wasn't blaming her husband at all. It was Max who'd gotten himself so worked up. But the state Max had worked himself into, maybe that had something to do with Xavier . . . with what she herself had seen in him, that there was something about him lately, something there since not so long ago, something that was not transparent to her . . .

"We can't go away forever, Max." Julia wiped her eyes again. If that's what he wanted, if he'd thought even for a moment that that might be possible, then it made no sense to keep on trying to get through to him. It was beyond her power to do so.

"Max, I can't do any more," she said, and her voice was now a little firmer. She had to think of her other three children. "I don't know what more I'm supposed to do."

But he had already turned away again, his eyes on the window behind her.

"If I go now, I'll have to let the doctor know."

Her words just rolled off.

But she didn't leave the room immediately. She stayed sitting there. Until her son—exhausted as he was—had fallen asleep. Then Julia stood up, packed up the bags again, stowed them in the corner—*maybe he'll rethink things*—and went off to find the doctor.

****

"It was the smell . . . much stronger than here . . . nearly makes you numb . . . the smell of the disinfectant . . . it was like this smell was waiting to ambush me when I opened the door at the end of the stairs. And that's where it was, Till, back there. Everything was white. The beds, the sheets, the lab coats, the walls, the lights." Max's voice sank to a whisper. "It was the ward, Till. Behind the door was the ward. A room as big as a football field, as big as the whole hospital, but there weren't any single rooms there; oh no, the beds were just separated by movable partitions. And the air was full of different voices and shouts and whining and moaning. Instruments were rattling, forceps, styluses, levers, screws . . . and there was a sound in the distance, a grating, grinding, gasping sound. And it was hot. Really, really hot, as if the air were blowing out of an oven straight into the low hall that seemed to go on forever."

Max lay on his hospital bed on two pillows lying one on top of the other. Till had pulled up a chair and sat down beside him. At first, they'd just exchanged a few words, but Till quickly realized that Max was very upset. And that was when Max had started to talk.

About the feeding tube they'd put in him, about how his mother had stayed with him the whole time, then taken him back to his room afterward and gone off to talk to the doctors again.

"I closed my eyes to sleep a little, and suddenly I heard the door squeak. And when I opened my eyes, he was already standing in the room."

"Who?"

"No idea. A man. He was wearing a doctor's coat and when he saw that I was awake, he excused himself very quickly. He probably got the room number mixed up."

"Uh-huh."

"Yeah. And then he went out. But you know what?"

"What?"

"I'd seen him before. But not here in the hospital." Max's voice lowered again. "It was at our house, at the parrot fight." His eyes were on fire. "He was one of the guests in the music room."

Till propped himself on one elbow on the bed. "Seriously?"

Max nodded, openmouthed. "So, I stood up and followed him, but so that he didn't notice me following him. Along the hallway, down the stairs, just behind him the whole time, all the way to the ward."

Max tried to sit up a little, but then gave up the attempt and just went on with his story. "I didn't really think about it. I just followed him into the ward and looked around a bit inside. But the farther I went, the more it occurred to me that the coats on the nurses weren't as spotless as I'd thought at the start, and that maybe the floor could stand being mopped, too. And I had the feeling that behind the smell of the disinfectant I could pick up another smell that was hidden underneath. It was a smell I wasn't too sure if I could place, but it tasted like copper."

Max's face lay palely on the white pillow. "Then I saw him again, the doctor who'd been in my room. I'd lost sight of him for a moment. He was weaving between the moveable walls. I went after him and I came to a section where . . . I don't know . . . where somehow the clear distinction between passageways and places for patients was gone. There were tons of beds, Till. Hundreds, I'd say. And there were men, old guys, women, kids, pregnant women . . . I saw a man and a woman lying together in one bed, and on another bed the cover wasn't white anymore but looked like it had a gray crust. Kids were running around wildly in groups between the beds and a surgeon came toward me dressed in the green outfit they wear in operating theaters. His eyes were circled in bright red in their sockets and his face almost looked like it was drawn on. I mean, his eyes were focused, right, but any softness seemed like it had been sucked out of his face, you know what I mean? There was nothing sensitive left, *nothing human*, I had to think, because what he'd been through, what he'd experienced, it all seemed to be too extreme, too raw, and too crappy. It seemed like it had destroyed all the human sensitivity inside him. He had nothing left to feel sympathy with."

Max looked at Till, and it seemed to Till that Max's vulnerable eyes were literally burning in their watery sockets.

"The sensitivity that . . ." Max hunted for the words. ". . . that you need to be able to warm to the tiny capacities of humans—tiny compared to the capacities of nature."

What?

Till's head was spinning. He thought he had a vague idea of what Max was saying, but before he could get in a question, Max was already forging ahead with his report, gesticulating breathlessly with his hands, his head jerking back and forth, his eyes fixed on Till.

"Then the surgeon went past and I went on quickly, like I was glued to the coat of the doctor I was following, but also dazed by all the impressions that were pouring into me. The patients down there weren't so bad off, I thought. Hardly anyone screaming, hardly any complaints about pain, and no one lay in his bed with his eyes rolled up. But it was still as if something like a curse was hanging over the place. I couldn't explain it any other way . . . something suppressed and subliminal, something that maybe not even the patients in the ward were aware of. But still, it was something that hit me with force and real fury. It seemed to be telling me to get out of there as fast as I could . . . *Before you get infected,* I told myself, before it gets you, before it takes root in you—and you can't get away again—and you need the doctors down there, too!"

Max sank back on his bed, breathing deeply, strained by his account, by the memory of what he'd experienced. But he soon gathered his strength again. "For a moment, I thought I should talk to one of the patients in the beds. I'd already gone over to one of the beds and had touched the shoulder of one of the women—but she turned around and I saw her vacant eyes, the empty face of a person who seemed to have given up on herself—and I knew they wouldn't hear me. No one down there would have heard me, Till. No one would have cared; it wouldn't even have occurred to anyone there that something like help even existed. Because everyone rotting away down there has forgotten that there's something more than the dullness they're filled with." His voice rasped out of his throat. Something besides the confusion and the restlessness filling their heads, something besides the disgust they have to bottle up artificially just to protect them from themselves."

Speechless, Till could only listen. A thousand questions occurred to him, but Max was unstoppable.

"We were wrong, Till," he continued, his words an unceasing stream. "What I saw down there . . . my father . . . he isn't alone . . . it's . . . the people there were completely changed." Max's eyes flicked around the room. "The diary, the pictures . . . the papers we found down in the basement?"

What about them?

"I thought the man in the old films . . . I thought he'd *injected* her with something, but he didn't, Till. He *examined* her!"

He's not well, Till thought. *Max is not well.*

"Down there, in the ward . . . at the start, it was okay, but the deeper I went and the more I lost myself down there"—Max had instinctively grasped Till's hand—". . . they've got people laid out down there who can only make hissing noises, who look like their skin has dissolved. They look all bloated, their bodies, they're like . . . jellyfish, all soft, like their bones must be porous; all they can do is lie there . . ." His hand clawed into Till's arm. "They're not human anymore, Till. They're just shells; something else has *implanted* itself inside them and hollowed them out. It's taken them over, gotten inside them, and sucked them dry."

A thought jangled in Till's head: *What will they do to him when they find out what he's thinking?* But he said nothing and instead just looked down at the shining face of his friend.

"I don't know what kind of beings they are, Till," Max stammered, "but they've sucked out the people down there and taken over their empty shells. When you look into their eyes, that's when you can see it best. At first, you think it's just an inflammation of the cornea, but then you figure out that it's like a membrane they've pushed up behind their pupils. And if you look at it long enough, you can see this membrane pull back out of the way for a second . . . and then it's looking at you, Till. *A creature has taken these people over.*" He had to draw breath. "It's not a disease and not some virus. It's a *hollowing*. They're not themselves anymore, those people. They're *inhabited*." He nodded toward the water glass standing on his bedside table. Till handed it to him. Max emptied it in a few swallows. But he was too weak to put it back himself. Till took it from him.

"I don't know how many there are," Max finally said, "but I'm sure the number's growing." And suddenly he had tears in his eyes. "He's not my dad anymore, Till." He looked in anguish at Till. "They've kept it a secret up to now, but they're already everywhere. How old were the photos? The film? At least a hundred years! It's an invasion and it's been going on for decades, you know? My father was on to them. He'd been collecting material about it. And then they got him, too. He's not *him* anymore; now he's one of *them*."

Till stared at Max. *One of them, one of them, one of them.* The phrase reverberated in Till's head.

"That's why he took you in with us, Till. They want you next."

"But why me?" Till blurted. "Why not you?"

Max let his arms fall on the blanket. "Look at me. I'm . . ." His breath hissed between his teeth, as if he didn't want to say it. But then he pulled himself together. "I'm too weak," he whispered, "They can't get far with me."

Get far . . . but where to? Till thought. But when he looked at Max, he lost the nerve to ask. "I have to see it," he said. "The ward."

Max nodded and lay down on his side so he could look out the window. "No, sure," he said. "Go and see for yourself. They're so wrapped up in themselves, they won't do anything to you." But then he looked up at Till again, his face frightened. "But you'll come straight back to me afterward, right?" His eyes were large and shining. "Before they take me back to the room where they give me the shots . . ." His body suddenly began to shiver. "Mom'll be there, too, but . . . but she doesn't know what's going on. And when I tell her what I've seen . . . she doesn't wanna know."

Till raised his hand for Max to high-five, and Max's hand felt small and feverish against his.

"Or should I stay here for now?" Till asked, his voice soft. "Here with you."

"No, it's okay," Max murmured. "Be quick. And tell me what you see."

"Where exactly? Which stairs?"

"Down the corridor, the last door on the right, then just keep going down . . ." Max's voice trailed off.

Till looked down at him for a moment, then stood up and left the room. As he closed the door behind himself, he had the feeling that he could hear, back in the room, his friend's body shaken, wracked, Max trying with all his might to overcome the shivering, the turmoil, the tears.

A dog.

But snatching a dog away from a passerby?

And wild dogs? No such thing . . .

A cat? Too small . . .

A bird?

An ant?

Go with a dog!

. . .

I already got one from the animal shelter.

They wanted to force a dachshund onto me. But I didn't want a dachshund. I wanted a real dog, a big dog, with glossy fur and bright eyes.

Hey, you, you panting? You want some more water?

What a magnificent creature! It's as though he's already mine.

How much longer do I want to wait?

Won't I become more attached to him the longer he's with me?

Yes. And isn't that exactly what I need?

(Are you strong enough, if you truly love him?)

Yes!

You insidious, stunted little goblin!

I AM STRONG ENOUGH!

Come here, big fella, lay your snout here on my knee.

There's a good boy. You're a good guy.

(The trust he has in me.)

Well, then. It's time.

We can't just wait and wait and scribble this journal full.

Now is the time to act!

Come on, mutt. Your master's just going to fetch something and then we'll head out to the woods.

(I need a tarp, too . . . I can't go riding through the night in soiled clothes. And a shovel? Is he supposed to just lie there under the trees?)

Oh, forget it!

I don't need anything. Not even a knife. I can just break his neck.

TODAY

"That's our rat man." Felix's eyes glisten. "At first, it was ants and locusts he was into. Crawling over him. One day, I said to him, 'Why not give it a shot with rats?'"

Till stares at the wall. He can still hear the man screaming back there.

"We shut some up in a kind of wire-mesh cage, but it's so thin they can chew their way through." Felix nods—and Till sees it in front of him. The bare paw at the end of the furry leg, the needle-like claws sticking out through the fine mesh of the pen. Above the paw, the animal's teeth gnaw at the mesh. Its nose jerks up and down; the little teeth vibrate, nip, nibble, and bite at the wire, which is already growing brittle, flimsy, thin—until it splits with a fine, bright cracking sound at the spot the rat has been gnawing on. Flushed with success, the creature presses its little paw through the larger opening and sets its teeth on the next wire.

"They're already covering the floor," whispers Felix, beside him. "They're crawling over each other, stretching their noses, and pressing against his feet with their claws."

Till wheezes. "He's had enough. Why won't you let him out?"

But Felix seems not to have heard Till at all. "They're stretching up, reaching for the leg of his pants; one of them's already begun to crawl up inside. Others are climbing up his leg on the outside. He's spinning around and ripping them off and throwing them at the wall. He's stomping on the ground, kicking them away . . . but there are more and more of them. And he knows exactly when he will have lost: the moment they manage to nip a little wound in him. As soon as they've smelled his blood and figured out that *he* is what they're after. Food. And they realize they can eat him. They can chew on him, nibble him away, gorge themselves so full on his meat that they're as big and heavy as cats." He stares at Till. "And you know why?"

"Why . . . what?"

"Why we do this."

"No." *No!*

"To test him, Till. To see . . . to see what he's made of." Felix's face stretches, as if he's about to laugh. "*What he's made of,*" he repeats, but silently, his lips forming the words, but no sound coming out.

"For God's sake," Till says, his voice low and hoarse, "let me out of here, Felix."

Till's skin burns from the wounds he's ripped open; his nerves are singed and frayed by the rat man's screams from behind the wall.

"*They* wanted it this way. They said it would be so nice," whispers Felix, nodding over at the figures with the scarifications, piercings, and bulges under the skin, now huddling together under the woman suspended from the ceiling. "They wanted you to be injected with the stuff; it causes the muscles to contract at regular intervals. Those aren't grubs moving under your skin, Till. The ripples come from your muscles puckering—it will fade away soon enough . . ."

Till has stretched his arms out in front of him and is staring at them. His head is buzzing.

"And the stitches," he hears Felix say. "Those are also part of it."

Also part of it . . .

"They make it that much *nicer*—" but Felix is interrupted by a howl from the rat man behind the wall.

In agony, Till turns to face Felix—and sees him point to a vertical bar mounted on the wall.

"There's the handle! It's just a wooden wall, Till. It's not down to me to let the rat man out—*you can do it yourself.*"

Till's eyes fix on Felix's. What the hell is this? What's he trying to prove?!

Felix's tongue flicked across his bottom lip. "But let me make things crystal clear for you, Till. Trust me. There are two minutes to go. Wait them out, and the man lives, even if he's screaming now."

"Or?"

"Or don't wait, pull the wall back—and you'll kill him. You'll rip the cage open, and that's all that's protecting him from being overrun by so many rodents that he won't be able to defend himself."

A new scream splits the air. Till can't understand the words. It sounds like the man behind the wall is being cooked alive.

Till's hand is shaking.

"One more minute . . ."

"And he'll be dead," Till bellows. "Is that it? Then I've waited too long! You're trying to drive me crazy. You want me to wait even though I can hear him screaming. You want me to wait till it's too late—to consciously wait, consciously fuck it up, and miss my chance at saving him when he's screaming for help!"

"If that's what you think." Felix runs his fingers through his hair. "I've told you what I think."

"I can hear you out there," shouts the voice behind the wall. "Are you mad? They're . . ."

The voice distorts. In his mind's eye, Till can see the rats beginning to feast on the rat man. He can see him bend down to his pants, where one of the rodents is crawling up his leg. The pain shoots through his body; he rips at the seam of his pants and it tears apart. He stares at his skin where the rat is digging at him, the claws buried in his flesh, the bare nose already pushed under the skin.

"Trust me, Till." Felix indicates the watch on his wrist. "Just a few more seconds."

"You want me to trust you? After you brought me here, after what's been going on down here? After you *what? Modified me?*"

Felix's eyes gleam. "Exactly that, my friend. *That* is the challenge!"

Till's nerves are jangling. The screams cover his thoughts like syrup; he can't think straight. But he pulls himself together and with a spring he's at the wall, the rat man screaming back there . . .

"Think it over, Till!"

He turns around. Felix is standing in the middle of the room. "Why should I prove you *can't* trust me? You know I still need you! So I ask you! Why should I do it?"

"How should I know? Maybe you want to prove I can let myself get sucked in by you one more time! How am I supposed to know what your sick mind is thinking?" Till is beside himself.

"You know me well enough, Till. Have I ever done anything that didn't make sense?"

No.

"So. What could be in it for me? You listen to me, you wait . . . then you open the door and it's too late; they've already chewed off his face. Now, what would I get out of that, Till? Wouldn't I lose you forever by doing that? But let's say you wait and open the door when I tell you—and he's alive! Don't you think I want to show you how right you are to trust me?! How you can save a life—when you listen to me?"

"But he's dying. He's dying! Isn't *now* the last chance to save him?! And if I ignore the screams, all I'm doing is letting you drag me down into an injustice again?!"

Felix smiles . . . and it drowns out the screaming. "Till, Till . . . what can I say?—it comes down to exactly *that*: the poor bastard's life depends on your trust in me! So, what's it to be? What . . ."

But Till has his hands pressed to his ears to shut out the shrieking and the madness. It's no use, though. He sees Felix's lips moving and all he can do is hear through his hands the words that Felix is hissing.

"What's it going to be, Till? Listen to your head—or your gut?"

That's it? That's what it comes down to for him?

"Still dithering . . . still mulling it over?"

Till practically *feels* the rat man falling to the floor, sees the rats leaping onto him, scuttling onto his back, in his hair, scratching at his forehead. And he hears a seemingly endless noise, a cracked cry that spills from the man's mouth. It's as if he no longer needs to draw breath; the cry of terror simply pours out of him—while the animals dig deeper and deeper inside.

"Isn't that deciding, too, Till—if you hesitate—isn't that decid-ing against your gut?" Felix yells at him. "Time's running out, Till, while you hesitate! It's running out for you, and it's running out for him! Think about it: your dithering could cost him his life!"

But if I open the door—you said so—I'll kill him just by doing that! Till feels how his head is going this way and that, feels himself shivering with indecision, hesitation, wavering, feels it tearing at him—while his heart just stumbles along . . .

He sees Felix throw his hands in the air.

"Now!" Felix shouts. Till spins around; he's already grabbed the handle on the wall. He jerks at it, and the wooden wall rattles back on its rollers—and he stares into the room laid bare behind.

"He's not the one we're testing, Till!" he hears Felix scream behind him. *"You are!"*

And Till jumps. He doesn't turn back to Felix. He jumps into the hole revealed behind the wooden wall. Down into a bare room with high, unplastered brick walls.

He stares at the floor in disbelief.

The machine emits a scream that grabs hold of Till like a pair of tongs.

Before he can even think about what he's doing, Till raises his leg high and slams the heel of his shoe into the machine. Plastic cracks, a high-pitched howl, crunching—then silence.

Till exhales. The sweat on his forehead is cold as ice.

There was no man back there screaming. It was just a *recording*.

Neon lamps, mounted on the ceiling, are buzzing. Till looks down at his arms, which he'd hardly been able to see in the basement gloom. Here in the neon light, he sees the damage for what it is: the stitches they'd used to attach his arms to his torso, and the seam that had joined his legs . . . it had felt to him as if a sewing machine had stitched—very nearly welded—his skin together. But now he can see that the blood is only oozing from a few places, not much more than stains on his shirt and pants. Two points on each arm, three on his legs. That's it. That's all they had done.

He wheels around, confused by how abruptly he's been dragged out of the nightmare he was in.

"FELIX!" He looks back to the room from where he jumped down into the hole with the tape recorder. The floor of the basement is some three feet higher than the floor he's now standing on—and below that is an opening that twists down into darkness. Half-blinded by the neon light, Till can barely see back into the dim room. "FELIX!"

No answer. With one stride, Till is at the low wall, which rises to his waist. He lays his elbows on the floor of the basement room and stares into the darkness. The room is empty. The only one still there is the woman dangling on hooks from the ceiling!

The figures that had been crowding under her . . . all of them are gone. There's no sign of Felix. They must have abandoned the room just as Till jumped into the pit.

Pushing off with his feet, he hauls himself up to the higher floor, rolls over, and stands up.

Is that what it was all about for Felix? To con him, to see him hesitate, vacillate . . .

What's it going to be, Till? Listen to your head—or your gut?

Till glances toward the woman suspended from the hooks. Her body rotates slowly in the hot air. He sees her head, lolling all the way back on her neck, sees her eyelids slightly open. The nape of her neck—it must be overstrained . . . he goes to her, holds her head in his hands, wanting to support it, to prevent it from becoming any more kinked . . .

"Can you hear me?!"

. . . but in the same moment he feels how heavy her head is, lying in his hands, and he feels the give in her neck, the complete lack of muscular tension, and it is plain to him that they have left her hanging for too long . . . she is no longer hanging from the ceiling in ecstasy or rapture, but as a corpse, a cadaver, a body without a soul.

And then all hell breaks loose.

It is a roar, as if a dam has burst, a scratching, scraping, squeaking flood. Horrified, Till releases the head he's holding, hears the crack of the gristle in the neck as the heavy skull sags. He spins around and sees them pouring up from the hole in the floor, up from the pit he'd revealed behind the wooden wall. A torrent of small, furry bodies, a flood of rats rising so fast that they start pouring over the threshold of the bricked-in hole—three feet high—in seconds.

Their claws are already scrabbling on the cement floor. They are not running; they are being forced forward by the masses pushing from behind. Till sees their noses stretching, their hairless tails waving and weaving, smells the stink of carrion rising from the living wave washing toward him. And almost keeling over with the shock, he presses against the cement wall behind him.

Felix's words ring in his ear: *He's not the one we're testing. You are.*

Testing? What are they testing? What he's made of? In a blinding flash, the truth hits him: *Doesn't this have to be what they're testing—whether he, too, is changing?*

TODAY

"Where?"

"Over here!"

Claire holds tightly on to her camera case and sprints across the road. On the other side is her colleague, who was just waving to her.

The street is like a canyon, both sides lined with tall buildings. A voice blares: "MOVE CLEAR OF THE SIDEWALK. PLEASE CLEAR THE SIDEWALK." A police van blocks the roadway. A loudspeaker is mounted on its roof.

Claire ignores the announcement. Her colleague lifts the red-and-white barrier tape. Claire bends low, and she's through. The high-rise inhabitants pour from the main entrance.

"Come on!" Claire's colleague nods toward an inconspicuous side entrance.

"Go ahead. I'll be right behind you!" Claire reaches for the camera that is hanging around her neck.

The faces of the residents: an old woman with her hand pressed to her cheek, a fat guy in sweatpants.

"What's going on?" Claire asks, stopping a young woman carrying a small child. The woman's eyes dart to Claire.

"What?"

"What's going on? Why have the cops cordoned off the building?"

"I don't know. Excuse me . . ." The woman pushes past Claire, but then turns back. "On the eighteenth floor. It had to be up on the eighteenth floor," she says, and hurries on.

The call came in as Claire was speaking to her photo editor about her Berlin crime scenes series. Just after eight in the morning, a reporter driving along Leipziger Strasse had noticed a commotion at the high-rise. He had climbed out of his car and spoken to a resident in front of the building. No one knew what was going on, but screams had been heard coming from a high floor. The police had been alerted and Claire, too, was quickly on her way. By car, Leipziger Strasse was barely five minutes from the editorial office. Maybe she'd get a few good shots for her Berlin book.

Her colleague is well ahead of her, out of sight, as Claire pushes open the glass door of the side entrance. It leads into a low lobby. To her left, people push to exit the front door. The air is filled with voices, shouts, the noise of many feet, the banging of doors.

"Hey, you can't come in here!" A police officer hurries in her direction. "Ma'am?"

In two steps, Claire reaches the stairwell door and pulls it open. She hears herself panting as she leaps up the stairs.

"Stop!"

The officer also runs into the stairwell, a few steps behind her.

Claire races upward. The stairway is packed with people coming down. One glassy-eyed man is still in his robe, his wife beside him, her hair unkempt; a pensioner wearing a small hat; two women in Muslim garb. Claire pushes her way through them, heading up. Behind her, the shouts of the officer fade into the con-fusion of voices. Third floor, fourth . . . Claire gasps for air. A teenager leading a younger kid by the hand jostles her as they fly down the stairs. Claire swings the camera bag to her other shoulder and pushes on.

On the eighth floor, she steps out of the stairwell into the main hallway. Tenants crowd in front of the elevator. No chance of using that. She has a stitch burning a hole in her side. She pulls out her phone. Should she try to reach her colleague?

"Clear the sidewalk . . ." The muted announcement over the loudspeaker below penetrates the thin walls of the building.

Claire battles her way up the stairs again. Fifteenth floor . . . six-teenth . . . seventeenth. The way up to the eighteenth floor, though, is blocked by police tape. Should she ignore it and climb under?

Claire throws open a door into the corridor on the seventeenth floor. If they intercept her now, she's got nothing.

She sees three young women standing at the window. They are decked out in party gear, even though it's much too early in the day to be dressed like that: hair piled high, tight sleeveless dresses, high heels. One is wearing fishnets, garters flashing through the slit in her skirt when she moves.

An apartment door opens and a family with two children emerges. Claire raises the camera to her eye—through the lens, the three women at the window look even more exotic. The eyes of the one wearing fishnets lock on to Claire's lens. Her skin glitters as if sprayed with gold dust. Claire clicks the shutter, takes a step to one side. The woman's eyes follow her. What a contrast to the shabby corridor! Claire turns the camera, framing vertically. The woman's black hair shines, her tight skirt no more than halfway down her thigh. She turns around to face Claire fully, the slit in the side of her skirt opening wider.

"Hey! What are you doing?"

She has a face like a Hindu princess. Claire crouches. The woman comes toward her, her high heels exaggerating her swaying gait to the edge of absurdity.

Click.

The eye makeup, full lips, the fury on her face. Claire lowers the camera. "What?"

"No photos!"

The Hindu princess's small hand reaches out toward Claire. Her fingernails are long and silvery. Claire can smell the awake-all-night on her, the buzz, the temptation . . . and suddenly jumps at a loud bang behind her.

She spins around.

The stairwell door flies open. Two more women come through. A blonde who looks like Barbarella, the other woman wearing a tight bodysuit that looks like aluminum foil. With a quick movement, Claire flips open her camera's display and holds it at hip level, still able to see the image on the small screen. The new arrivals ignore her completely. They shout something in French to their girlfriends at the window.

Just then, on the display, Claire sees another woman—more a girl—come in through the door—and feels a lump forming in her throat . . .

Click. Click, click.

Japanese, Claire thinks. One of the women is already pushing past Claire, moving to throw a blanket around the shoulders of the Japanese girl.

Claire looks at the camera display. The girl's porcelain-colored skin is sheathed in a thin layer of plastic wrap. The transparent film clings tightly to her shaved body, encircling her flawless stomach, encasing her thighs, wrapping her breasts. The forms and curves of her body appear almost artificial, straining against the plastic. She is shrink-wrapped as if for instant consumption.

The diminutive girl's eyes turn in Claire's direction. Click.

Her hand reaches out and covers the lens.

Claire looks up from the display, her eyes meeting the shining black eyes of the girl.

"No, please . . . ," she hears.

The blanket closes around the girl's body.

TWELVE YEARS AGO

Pain exploded in Till's wrist. For a moment, he saw yellow rings converging from the edge of his field of vision into a single point. Cold sweat beaded on his face. He wedged his sore hand under his left armpit. Then he turned, slid down the steel door to the floor, and let his head fall back. His skull hit the door with a dull thud.

Everything had gone smoothly enough at first. After leaving Max's hospital room, Till walked along the corridor and opened the last door on the right. On the other side was a spiraling stairwell he'd followed to the bottom landing. There was only one door—in place of a handle or a knob was a horizontal crossbar, a panic lock, that Till promptly pushed. The door swung wide, but there was no neon-lit ward on the other side. Instead, another corridor appeared, the walls at one time white but now scratched and graying.

Till took one curious step into the corridor, momentarily losing his concentration. Only when the door clacked shut behind him did he whip around in fright.

The door!

The blank surface of the door filled the doorframe, leaving no gaps. There was no handle, no knob, and on this side, no panic lock. A seamless steel surface. Till threw himself against it, realizing as he did how pointless it was: he hadn't pulled the door open when he came through a minute before. He had pushed it; the door would need to be pulled open if he wanted to get back to the stairs.

But *how*? How could he pull open a door that had nothing to hold on to?

He scratched desperately with his fingernails at the tiny cracks between the door and frame, but they were far too small to get a finger into.

"Hey!"

His voice cracked. "HEY!"

He took a step back.

All he could hear was a low, dull huuuummmmmmm as if from massive generators.

No voices. No answer. Not a sound.

In desperation, he balled his right hand into a fist and slammed it as hard as he could against the door. Pain rose between his eyes.

Breathing heavily, he sat down and leaned against the door, staring down the corridor.

Had he broken his hand? Till carefully curled his fingers. He could still move them.

He looked down the corridor, which turned a corner about ten yards away.

Till pulled himself together.

The corridor had to lead somewhere. The main thing was to stay calm.

Till set off at a trot. Around the corner, the corridor ended at a ramp big enough to drive a semi on. To Till's right, the ramp sloped gradually downward, deeper into the bowels of the hospital. To his left, it gently rose.

Till turned left and walked up the ramp, and a few moments later found himself confronted by a massive steel roller-shutter that sealed off an entrance.

He kicked the steel door angrily. A clanging wave rolled through the metal slats. But there was no bar, no handle, no electronics to raise it.

Till leaned forward and pressed his mouth to the tiny spaces between the slats. "Heeelllllloooooo?!"

But all he heard was that dull thrumming from below, somewhere behind him: Huuuummmmmmmm . . .

Something about the ramp caught his eye. Even in the dim light, Till saw that the road surface was immaculate. Pale-gray, virtually pristine concrete. No tire marks, no oil, no grime.

He squatted down and ran his finger over the concrete. A little dusty, but otherwise clean. Was he in a part of the enormous complex that had never been put into operation?

Till straightened up again and looked back down the ramp, descending darkly into the subsurface of the building like a throat.

It looked like some kind of subterranean radiology ward. Innumerable connectors were mounted on the walls, and in the corridors stood discarded hospital furniture with half-rusted equipment and browning packages piled on top.

Till walked down the slope, passing rooms lit by narrow skylights. Stairs off the slope led even farther downward. Signposted corridors seemingly led to other buildings and massive concrete halls could have held entire companies of soldiers being nursed back to health. But whenever Till left the ramp, whichever way he went, he ran up against giant security gates he couldn't budge, try as he might. He even found a kind of control room set up down there, although all that was left were the most rudimentary of indicators.

Till vaguely recalled hearing about facilities like these around West Berlin, back in the days of the Wall, intended to give some protection to the Berliners in case of a Soviet blockade renewal. Supposedly, the storerooms, with blankets and canned food for hundreds of thousands of people, as well as underground fuel and gas reservoirs, could keep the city going for weeks if the Russians cut off fresh supplies from West Germany. Till wondered if he had stumbled onto one of them, a cross between a hospital ward and an air-raid shelter built to withstand an atom bomb dropped right on top of Kurfürstendamm.

The deeper he wandered into the bowels of the hospital complex, the more slowly he went. If the first concrete rooms were straight from a seventies science-fiction film, the writing he now saw on the walls looked more like remnants from World War II. Arrows pointed to a radiology ward, a fuel depot, a warehouse. Levels D, E, and F were indicated, and the concrete was no longer light gray but the color of anthracite, with a dirty greenish cast. The floor was no longer dusty, but damp. Till had no interest in finding out what was concealed in the moldering, black piles in the corners.

Finally, he stopped completely. The low thrumming sound he'd noticed earlier was now a booming roar, a prodigious rumbling noise. It was evenly formed, as if an expressway tunnel ran eight floors beneath his feet, with hundreds of semis—each on its eighteen wheels, the bellow of their V-8s gurgling up through the pipes—looking for an ear to hear them. Till abruptly drew a breath. For a moment, he'd been so focused on listening that he had forgotten to breathe. He realized how musty, ferrous, and damp the air tasted, and suddenly he felt that if he went any deeper into the foundations of the building, he might never find his way back to the surface. Like a diver who comes to his senses before the raptures of the deep drag him down forever, Till turned around and ran back up the first set of stairs he came across.

Aluminum housings, vibrating machine covers, pipes, and illuminated signs. He was no longer surrounded by wartime technology. This looked like a typical boiler room.

Till had wandered through the underground maze for nearly two hours before finally stumbling on the boiler room at the top of a stairway.

He made his way between the machines. Square ducts made of sheet metal, at least three feet wide, crisscrossed the ceiling. Along the wall above a heating unit, a duct ran a short distance horizontally before turning ninety degrees and going straight up.

Till looked at the duct more closely. Its sheet-metal plates were held together with screws. He laid one hand against the steel. It was cool—likely the system for cooling and ventilation.

After ten minutes of searching, Till discovered an iron bar beside the base of a heating unit, apparently left by a worker. He went back to the duct and wedged the flat end of the bar between two overlapping brackets, then leaned on it with all his weight. The sheet metal twisted up and cold air spewed out of the opening. Till pushed the bar in farther and heaved. With a loud shriek, the carefully mated plates moved apart. A rivet popped out and clanged against the cladding of the ventilation unit.

Till rammed the bar between the brackets again. Despite the ice-cold wind blowing over him, he was sweating. With a howl, the already-damaged sheet metal bent even more, and the gap became a large triangle big enough to crawl through. Till threw the bar aside, jumped up on top of the ventilation unit, and stuck his head through the gap and into the ventilation duct.

The icy wind billowed around his head, swirling his hair. It was dark; the only light came in through the gap he'd torn in the cladding.

Till stretched his arms above his head to make himself as thin as possible and used his feet to push himself up, forcing himself into the gap. The bent steel plate tore a triangular piece out of his T-shirt and scraped skin from his shoulder. He was inside.

He crawled through the duct on all fours. A few yards past the hole he had crawled in through, the duct abruptly turned upward. Till gazed up into the hole. In the meager light, he could see no fan blocking his path. But there were also no handgrips, let alone any sign of a ladder. The duct was built for distributing fresh air, not for crawling around inside. There was no other way: he had to try to chimney up the shaft, using his feet and back as a wedge to move himself up.

The steel was freezing. With the cool air continuing to stream over him, Till's skin turned ice-cold within minutes.

He tensed his leg muscles. The rubber soles of his sneakers gave him good grip against the metal wall. His back slid easily over the finely polished steel. Till pulled his right foot up a short way, then his left. He pushed, and moved his body up to the same level. The next step, the next, the next. Just don't look down, he told himself. First, he knew he hadn't climbed very high and didn't need the discouragement. And second, he was afraid he might fall back down. He had to focus on keeping up the pressure holding him on the walls of the duct. The muscles in his calves and stomach burned, and his injured shoulder pulsed with pain where the raw wound pressed against the chilly steel.

Right foot up. Then left. Hands pressed back against the duct wall. Slide the back upward, over the steel. Another step. *Keep going!*

He leaned his head back and peered up into the yawning black hole of the duct rising above him.

His hands, pressed against the walls of the duct on left and right, were throbbing. His throat was a hard knot; the icy air never stopped streaming over him.

Till forgot time for a moment. One more step . . . one more step . . . until suddenly he felt a sharp edge against the back of his neck.

At the same time, the soles of his shoes lost their grip—and the pressure keeping him wedged in the shaft lessened. He started to slip. Instantly, he pushed off with his feet, twisted himself around, and threw his arms into the darkness, grasping for a handhold. Instead of the smooth steel wall, his hands banged onto the floor of a horizontal duct branching off the vertical one he was in. His stomach and chest slammed against the wall of the vertical shaft as his fingers scrabbled helplessly at the floor of the horizontal duct.

Pain again clouded his vision when a raised duct edge cut into his fingertips. But it was a moment of traction—he wasn't slipping anymore. Desperately, with all of his strength, Till pulled himself up with his fingertips until he got one knee into the branching duct.

Gasping for breath in the icy air, Till lay on his back in the horizontal ventilation shaft. The film of sweat covering him made him feel like he was bathed in ice cubes. His fingertips throbbed; his shoulder was tingling. But he made it.

He rolled onto his stomach, laid his chin against the steel, and stared down the tunnel ahead of him. Far ahead, he could make out a shimmer of light.

Till pushed himself up onto his hands and knees and began to crawl—shaking, strength failing, chilled to the bone.

****

"Excuse me? Can I get an espresso, please? A double? Yes? Thanks."

Why's she got that look on her face?

(I don't want to think about the dog!)

Why would I? It isn't necessary. It doesn't get you anywhere. It's not about reflection, or wallowing in the memories—or slashing your wrists with them.

It's about the doing!

Doing, doing, doing . . .

Doing what?

The next dog? The next cat? The next flea?

"Thank you. Sugar? Uh, sure . . ."

Does she have to bend over like that, so I can see down her top?

"I'll take some of that water, too, thanks."

Mmmm . . . I love espresso when it's well made. When was the last time I was in here? A year ago? Two, perhaps?

You have to break her arm.

Whose?

The woman back there? Her arm?

(No, the waitress's!)

The waitress's?

But I get it. I get the idea . . . how . . . how do I do it? Twist it over backward? No, that just dislocates . . . smash it over the knee—the bone in the forearm . . . no, no . . .

Do you want to go that far down?

"Everything's fine, thanks."

(Just rip her top open, set 'em free!)

No, that's not what it's about! Should the dog have lost its life for nothing? You're still at the beginning.

B r e a k   h e r   a r m!

But until she gets off work . . .

"Sorry?"

"Excuse me?"

Her breasts. That valley in between . . . exposed.

Excuse me, I . . . no . . . no, never mind."

She's laughing! She thinks I'm funny. She likes me!

"No, really, it's okay, I just need to take care of a couple of things, then I'll come back . . . what?"

She gets off in a minute and then she's done for the day?

What is that perfume she's wearing?

"Okay, then, I'll wait. Just a moment . . . here, let me pay my bill . . . so . . . no, keep it. No, absolutely not, I . . . I like how happy it makes you. Can't I at least give you a little tip?"

And tear open your blouse later?

"Sure, no problem—happy to wait—I'll go out on the street and wait for you out there, okay?"

How old is she? Twenty? Twenty-three? I should just take her home, take her clothes off . . .

That is not your path!

Stop prattling like a schoolboy! She's not your girlfriend. You need to break her arm!

That is the path you've chosen!

TWELVE YEARS AGO

Lisa opens the large cupboard in the dining room and takes out seven plates.

"A gray crust?" she asks, looking over at Till, who sets the cutlery on the table. "What's so weird about that? It's a hospital, Till. Maybe the patient injured himself, they disinfected the wound with something, and the nurse hadn't gotten around to changing the sheets."

She went to the table and set out the plates.

"It wasn't just a gray crust on a sheet." Till slid one of the chairs back from the table and sat down. "It was the atmosphere down there, Max said. He'd never seen anything like it."

Lisa's mother had brought both boys home in the afternoon. Lisa tried to wheedle out of them what had happened in the hospital, but nobody was up for answering her questions. All she could work out from Till was that Max wanted to get out of the place as fast as he could. So he started eating again.

She went back to the cupboard and sorted glasses. "Being in the hospital's never very nice," she said, taking four glasses in one hand, three in the other, and returned to the table. She looked at Till. He had lowered his head and was staring at the tablecloth.

"I looked around, but I couldn't find it. The ward that Max told me about," he said.

"Is that why you were so filthy?" said Lisa, eyeing him.

Till nodded. "I went down into the basement, and I got locked in . . ."

"Yeah?"

He waved dismissively. "Well . . . I got out again . . ."

"Oh, come on, tell me!" Lisa sat down opposite Till and laid both arms on the table, palms up, pleadingly.

"I think I did some damage in there . . . ," said Till, and low-ered his voice to a whisper, ". . . but I was so happy when I got outside again."

"What did you damage?"

"It was a . . . I'm not sure what it was exactly . . . some kind of grate," he said, and drew a breath. "But it wasn't so bad. An air vent, something like that . . ."

"You broke it . . . ?"

"I kicked it out." Now he was grinning a little. "Don't ask me how I ended up behind it . . ."

"Huh." Lisa looked at him. "But you didn't see any sign of the ward that Max told you about?"

Till shook his head.

"I told you!" she nearly shouted, and jumped up so impetuously that her chair nearly tipped over. "Max got himself into something. And instead of facing up to it, he runs off to some fantasy world. And you're encouraging him!"

"Really? You think he's just talking rubbish?"

Lisa hesitated. Was she really sure it wasn't true? "I mean, maybe they do have a ward down there that's not open to the public," she said, relenting. "But what's so special about that? And what's wrong with my dad taking him to *this* hospital because he's friends with one of the doctors there . . . wasn't that the right thing to do?"

She watched as Till drew circles on the table with a fork.

"What else were my folks supposed to do?" she sputtered. "Stand by and watch Max starve? They took him to the hospital. That's reasonable. If they *hadn't* done that, and *then* you started thinking you had to do who-knows-what for Max, then okay, I could understand that. But I don't get this." Lisa felt her cheeks going red, and a few strands of hair had worked loose from her hair clip.

"Mom tried everything, Till. Can you imagine how guilty she felt? She's thinking she should have done something to stop it getting so far in the first place. But Max wouldn't let her help him. He's always pigheaded."

"So, we can't help him," said Till, looking up. He was becoming as tense as she was.

"*Yes*, we can help him! We can be there for him, make him think about other things, maybe even make him see how stupid it is to fight against Mom and Dad like he does."

Till pushed out his bottom lip thoughtfully. Lisa felt drawn to him and longed to be on his side, to be able to support him. But she also truly believed that her parents had done everything right.

Of course the doctors sedated Max. Who knows what could have happened? He could have jumped out the window one night. And anyway, it was probably the medication that made him think the ward was real.

"Max has always been crazy," she said. "I love him, but he's unpredictable. Once, he talked me into going on a bike ride with him. We ended up in an area that everyone knows is swampy. I told him we shouldn't ride any farther, but do you think he'd listen to me? He kept on going, straight ahead. I should have turned around on the spot, but I didn't want to leave him alone . . . and I didn't know how to get out of the swamp, either. So I stayed with Max and we rode deeper and deeper *into* the swamp, instead of turning back. The ground got boggier and boggier; the path we were following kept branching and it started to disappear in the mud and grass. When the front wheels on the bikes began to sink in, even Max started to get worried. You know what he said to me?"

Till shook his head.

"He said, 'You were right, Lisa. We shouldn't have ridden in here.' See what I mean? That's what Max is like! He just rides in and then he's sorry he did. And if you're unlucky, you're in there with him."

"But you *did* get out in the end."

"Yes, we did. We got back onto solid ground just before it got dark. Otherwise, we probably would have had to spend the night in there. Maybe we wouldn't have died, but who knows? Who knows?! The point is, we knew it was dangerous. I didn't want to go any farther. Max did. Can you explain that to me? What makes him go on and on like that, deeper into danger? And if he has to do it, why doesn't he do it *alone*?" Her eyes met Till's. "Did you ever think about that? Why he's dragging you into this?"

****

". . . that's right. Yes, that's something we still have to take care of, of course," Max heard his father say.

Have to, have to, have to, have to, have to, have to, have to, have to, have to, have to, have to—Max felt the fury taking hold of him.

Was there anything he hadn't already had to do?! Get into a good high school, take piano lessons, be the fastest swimmer . . .

He was lying on the couch his parents had carried into the dining room so that he could join the family for dinner. He didn't want to stay in bed, but he was too weak to sit at the table.

"We don't *have to* do anything," he muttered angrily, and his voice betrayed how overwhelming his anger was.

The clatter of cutlery at the table stopped abruptly and all eyes turned in his direction. Claire and Betty looked frightened, his mother concerned, Lisa almost a little amused, his father's brows pinched. Only Till continued to look at his plate.

"I can't listen to this anymore, Dad. We don't *have* to do anything except die. That's how it works!"

"Did you tell him that?" said his father, looking at his mother.

"Isn't that how it goes?" Max grumbled. "I get that you *want* me to play piano. But I don't *have* to play it just because you want me to. I can do it, if I want. But I don't *have* to."

"If you don't want to be punished . . . ," his father began, then stopped himself. "You know, to hell with it. I've about had it with all this, too, Max. You don't want to learn an instrument? Fine! Then don't. Whatever. I don't really give a shit!"

Max flinched. He hated it when his father swore.

"It's not just about playing the piano, Dad. As far back as I can remember, you—and Mom, too—you've been telling me I have to do *this*, and this and this and this and this and this and this—"

"Stop it, Max!" his mother yelped, cutting him off, conscious of Max's overexcited state.

"But it's true!" Max picked up the small table that was laid across his legs and set it down on the floor. Lying there in his pajamas! Everyone else at the table was properly dressed, wearing pants and shoes. And he lay there like some bum in his pajamas. Maybe that was the main reason for his anger.

"I don't want to argue with you, Dad. But I don't *have* to learn piano. Nobody *has* do anything. Not Claire or Betty, not Lisa, not Till!"

His father eyed him carefully. Max felt his heart thumping in his throat.

"You think you don't *have* to do anything—that it's all a question of what you *want* to do?" His father's voice had grown very calm. "That's a grave mistake."

"Didn't you decide that you wanted to write books?" Max snapped.

"No, I did not. I simply did it. That is something else."

"You could have decided not to."

"That never occurred to me," his father said, genuinely wanting to convince Max. "I wrote, and I gave what I wrote to others to read. First, my mother thought they were good, then my friends did, too. Then I started to sell them, first to small magazines, then to major ones. I wouldn't be a writer if I just *wanted* to write— without actually doing it. Don't waste time thinking about what you *want* to do, boy. Go ahead and *do it.*"

Max stared at the woolen blanket that lay across his legs. What was his father talking about? What was this?

His father went on: "What I hear you saying, Max, is 'I have to know what I want.' You think you have to? I think you don't have to know anything of the sort!"

Max looked up and saw his father rising as he continued speaking. "Right? Do you agree with me? Or do you want to throw in yet another objection? Do you want to make your sisters' heads spin even more than they already are! Don't you think it's enough that one of you is lying on the couch because he's too weak to sit at the table?"

"I'm not like you," Max whispered, his voice as firm as he could make it—but it sounded brittle, husky, hoarse.

"If all you do is what you *want* to do, you'll just end up going around in circles," his father barked at him. "You'll never escape from listening to your own *will*. In your mind, every decision could be wrong. If you're not sure if you should go down this road or that, you're already going down the wrong one!"

Max glanced over at his mother. Was she just going to listen to this?

"Xavier, leave him along. He's not well," Max heard her say, as if his looking at her was the spur she needed to say something.

"And isn't that the best sign that I'm right?" his father retorted, his voice clear and almost intimidating. "He is so twisted up in his own doubt that he doesn't even know if he should *eat!*" He turned around to the table and looked at his wife. But when she didn't respond and instead seemed to be searching helplessly for words, he turned back to his son. "Don't you feel how your uncertainty is gnawing at you, how it has already started eating away the healthy body your mother and I gave you? Isn't that doubt something that comes from *you*, Max? Your personality, your ego, whatever you want to call it? The will you're so proud of? Is it your *will*, Max, that's telling you to starve yourself?"

He gestured with an open hand to his wife and other children. "Take a look at them, Max, your family, a wonderful bloodline. And then there's you. That's what it's all about for you. You yourself. Your will. But what is that? Who are you, apart from the fact that we gave birth to you, Max? Max? Oh no! Forget the name; I chose that for you! Think of yourself using a different word, not 'Max'—which you got from us—think of yourself as 'I.' This 'I,' this soul, staring back at you from the mirror. That's you: nameless, helpless, vulnerable. And you know what that 'I' is? I'll tell you: it's the pollutant, the toxic contaminant injected into an organism whose development up to that point had been no less than an outstanding success. *You* are the pollutant, boy—and you want to know why? *Because you only do what you want to, and not what you have to!*"

Max swung around and was sitting on the edge of the couch. He felt his legs shaking. His arms lay in his lap; his feet touched the ground a few steps away from his father's shoes. His face was burning.

He knew that Till was still looking down at his plate, and that Till was on his side—but what about the others? How were they supposed to know if his father was right or wrong? How was he supposed to know? One thought pounded in his head: *I'm not going to let you stomp on me.* Defiance blazed inside him. *Even if you're right . . . I am me, and one day* you'll *be old, and* you'll *be the one who's rickety and lying in a bed, and I'll be dressed and standing there!* But simultaneously, another thought sparked in a back corner of his mind: *Perhaps his father, on his deathbed, wouldn't want to have him at his bedside at all? He certainly wouldn't want to spend his last few minutes on earth with a toxic contaminant . . .*

And Max lowered his head, because he didn't know how to redeem his shame.

"I'm sorry, Max," he heard his father's voice, "but it doesn't make sense if I don't tell you honestly what I think of the ideas that I know you take such pride in. Or one day you'll come to me and accuse me of not warning you!"

Till heard the light slap of Max's bare feet on the stone tiles in the hallway and up the stairs to the first floor.

Everything in him was screaming to go after his friend. He had seen how Max had been shivering, how he tried to stand up to his father's power, and how, finally, with his head down, he had stormed out of the room. But to simply get up and leave the table? Till knew that Julia expected the children to ask permission if they wanted to leave the table before the meal was finished. Could he really be the first to speak, to ask, "May I be excused?"

"Till?"

He looked up. But Bentheim was already looking at his wife again. "I'd like to have a brief word with Till. We'll be out in the conservatory."

Julia stood up. "Of course . . ."

Bentheim glanced at Lisa. "Help your mother clear the table for Rebecca. She can take care of it tomorrow." Then he laid one hand on Till's shoulder. "Coming?"

Till looked at the man's long, pale face, now friendly and pleasant, and wondered for a moment if the fury with which Bentheim had attacked Max had come from a different person altogether.

The conservatory was connected directly to the spacious living room, which was in turn connected to the dining room by a wide archway. The Art Nouveau–style extension was enclosed by windows on three sides and was filled with exotic Mediterranean plants. An iron table with a marble top stood in the middle of the room. Till knew that Max's father was especially fond of the conservatory; he had often seen him tending to the miniature orange trees, the palms, and the oleander.

"Sit down," Bentheim said, pointing a thin hand at one of the high-backed, cast-iron chairs arranged around the table. Till hastily sat, his feet barely brushing the conservatory floor. Bentheim sat across the table from him.

They sat in silence for some seconds, then Bentheim said, "You're probably thinking I was too strict with Max." His blue eyes gazed at Till, his voice gentle, his mouth curved in a smile.

Till shoved his hands under his thighs, palms up. Was there anything to what Max had told him about Bentheim in the hospital?

"In the last twelve years, I've tried everything I know to deal with Max," Bentheim continued, "and I'm sure you'll realize what I mean once you've got to know him a little better. I know you're good friends, and if I was your age, I'd also hate someone who talked to my friend like I just did to Max." He leaned back and crossed his legs. "But one day, you will understand that I had to act the way I did. I'm not saying that Max could become particularly dangerous or degenerate, it's just . . ." He broke off again, searching for the right words. ". . . to put it bluntly, he is just not up to the demands."

Max's father's eyes shifted momentarily to the living room. He seemed to be checking to see if someone was there, perhaps listening to them. Then his eyes moved back to Till's face, as if to assess the effect of his words. "Do you follow what I'm saying?"

"Yes." *No. Demands . . . what demands?*

"Good." Bentheim leaned forward. "Listen, Till, I know you want to go to Max and commiserate with him a little, so I'll keep it short. I've always liked you. I don't know you very well, but the little I've seen of you so far pleases me. You're young but you've got both feet firmly on the ground, as they say. Your ambition doesn't get in the way of your judgment. You look people right in the eye. You can be charming when you want to be, but you're not vain. You seem fairly capable of rigorous thought. When you speak, what you say has real substance." His eyes rested thoughtfully on the boy's face.

Till looked at him in confusion. Praise like this . . . was unknown to him. He was a little dizzy and feared falling off the chair.

"I'm not trying to give you a big ego, Till," Bentheim continued. "That's the last thing I want to do. But to be honest, I'm really not too concerned that that could happen. I've told you what I think of you because I hope that you won't disappoint me in the future."

Till felt uneasy. After the compliments Bentheim had just paid him, letting the man down was about the last thing in the world he wanted.

"You've heard how Max is doing," said Bentheim. "Pretty miserably, to be frank. It's obvious that he can't look after himself, and that's been the case since before he had to go to hospital. That's why I wanted to talk to you, Till. If Max doesn't manage it, I need to be sure I can rely on you."

"What am I supposed to do?" Till said, worried he wouldn't be equal to whatever task Max's father had in mind for him.

"I need you to be there for him. Understand? You have to be there for him when he needs help."

Till felt as if Bentheim's crystal-clear gaze was boring right through him. He had no idea what he was supposed to say.

"Will you?"

"Yeah, sure. I'm there for him, Mr. Bentheim. Whenever he needs me."

Bentheim sighed and let himself sink back in his chair. And he smiled. "That's good, my boy. You might think that I'm overdoing it and that Max can look after himself quite well. And even if not, then *I'm* here to pick up after him—not you. On some level, that's true . . . but . . . I'm happy to know that you're there to back me up. That you are keeping an eye on him, too."

Stop picking on him so much, Till thought. *Max is all right; you just don't know him.*

But Bentheim was already standing up. "If there's ever anything going on, then come talk to me, okay?"

"Sure," said Till, and smiled. But the palms of his hands were cold.

Had he just become part of a conspiracy? Till and Bentheim against Max? Whose side was he on? Was he with the man who had taken him into his family—or with the best friend he'd ever had?

Despondent, Till dropped his gaze and listened to Max's father leaving the conservatory.

Bentheim had stood by him in his hour of greatest need. But did that justify going behind Max's back? For Till, it was out of the question.

34

TWELVE YEARS AGO

When Till finally came upstairs, Max was standing at the bathroom sink with his toothbrush in his mouth. White foam ran down over his chin. He spat in the sink, threw the toothbrush on the glass shelf, then caught water from the tap in his cupped hands and splashed his face clean. When he looked up, Till's eyes met his in the mirror.

"He's a jerk," said Till. "I don't care what he says. I didn't listen to any of it."

Max braced his hands on the side of the basin, the water still running. "Maybe he's right. Who knows."

But Till dismissed it. "Forget it. It's sick. Don't take any notice." He stopped and thought for a moment. "Before, back in the home, you wouldn't believe the stuff I heard. Not the teachers, it was mainly the guys in the older classes. If I'd taken all their crap seriously, I'd probably never have gotten over it!"

Max turned off the water, reached for a towel, and dried his face. Till could see how upset he still was.

"He's said stuff like that before, but up till now he always held back." Max hung the towel back on the hook and glanced at Till.

"He'd stomp all over you, but there was a limit. He's never, ever gone as far as he went just now." His face seemed translucent and tense. "And Mom used to step in, but not today. It just didn't stop. I mean, what was he trying to do? What does he want *me* to do? I always used to think, okay, fine, he wants me to be or act like he thinks I should. He wants to bring me up the right way and get me straightened out. But today? What he did today wouldn't straighten anyone out. Something like that just kills you."

I can't argue with that, thought Till.

Max stepped toward him, keeping his voice low. "I wondered where it came from. The hate . . . okay, he's pretty much mad at me because I've let him down. But for him to throw it back in my face like that? That's sick, isn't it? It never used to be like this."

Max leaned in a little closer to Till's ear. "That's not my father, Till. It's like I told you. I know my dad, but whoever was standing in front of me in the dining room . . . *it wasn't him*."

"What do you mean, it wasn't him?" Till wasn't sure if he'd heard Max right. "Who was it then? He looks like your father; he sleeps next to your mom in their bedroom—"

"Did *you* understand what he was saying?" said Max, interrupting him.

Till shook his head. "Yeah, you're right. Which is why I'm saying: don't pay attention to it. Your dad is wound up pretty tight at the moment. Maybe he's sick?"

"See!" Max cut in. "Sick! That's what I mean. He's sick. Sick in the head, in his brain, I don't know what the connection is, exactly. But if something in your brain gets shifted or warped or changed . . . don't you think it's possible it could turn you into another person? What you like or don't like, what's important to you, the things that make you *you*, all of that is set in the brain. If something in there gets screwed up, your character and your personality change, too. And that's exactly what's happened to my dad. I can't explain it any other way."

That doesn't sound too far-fetched, thought Till.

"And if you change even more," Max went on, "then . . . well . . ."
—he seemed to be fighting what he wanted to say—". . . then sooner
or later, you're not a human being anymore, are you? Doesn't that
make sense?"

"You think so?" Till looked at him, unconvinced.

Max hesitated, but a subconscious conviction seemed to over-
take him. "He's not a human being anymore," he whispered, "not
anymore."

Not a human being anymore. "So, what is he?"

"What is he, what is he . . . ?" said Max, aping Till. "If you'd
found the ward in the hospital, you'd know what I'm talking
about!" His eyes stared at Till, and the red around the rims
seemed to have seeped into the whites. His eyes looked sunken
in their sockets and his temples seemed to bulge. His voice was
reduced to no more than a whisper, but the words jabbed Till like
needles. "I already told you. They've hollowed him out and taken
his place."

For a moment, Till felt like he was suffocating in the bathroom
and wanted to open the window. But then he forced himself to let
Max's words bounce off him, and to smile. "Man, have you looked
in the mirror lately? If anyone around here looks like a zombie, it's
you."

Max's eyes stayed on Till's face for a moment, and then he had
to grin, too. "Shit," he whispered, and stepped past Till and out of
the bathroom.

****

When Till entered Max's room, his friend had already thrown himself onto the bed and buried his face in the pillow. Till shut the
door behind him, pulled a chair up next to the bed, and sat down.

For a while, neither said a word. Finally, Max rolled onto his back. A little color seemed to have come back into his face.

"I don't know what they've turned him into," he said, his voice husky. "I always loved him, you know?" His eyes sought out Till's but drifted away to stare into space again when he saw that he had Till's attention. "I mean, sure, my dad was always kind of weird. Other fathers took their sons to the swimming pool or the stadium or played football with them, right? Not my dad. We never really did that much together." His eyes focused on Till's face again. "Mostly, we talked. I used to try to find out more about him: what he liked, what he didn't, what was important to him, and what wasn't. He used to talk to me about writing. He said there was a world of imagination and make-believe and that you could only enter it by reading stories—or by thinking up your own. I was fascinated by that, of course. When he talked about it, I could sense how he forgot everything else around him, and how all that mattered to him was teaching me all the things that he had learned about that world. But . . ." Max let his arms drop onto the blanket. ". . . later on, I realized that I didn't really understand most of what he told me."

Till slid off his chair and lay across the foot of the bed, stretching out on his back, gazing at the ceiling.

"But I still loved him, maybe *because* he was different from the other fathers." Max's voice was low. The room was dark, indirectly lit only by the lights in the garden. "Somewhere along the way, he stopped telling me about his work and the things that he was thinking about. I don't know why. At first, I thought maybe it was my fault, like maybe I'd let him down and he didn't want to teach me all about writing anymore. Maybe because he'd lost hope that I could ever do it."

Max folded his arms behind his head. Lying down, Till turned his head to the side to see Max. "But then I realized that it wasn't my fault," Max continued. "He always got angry really fast and didn't seem to listen to me at all anymore when I tried to say something. It wasn't just a change in what he thought of me, Till. *He* had changed."

Max pressed his chin onto his chest to look toward Till at the foot of the bed. "Nothing on the outside changed. His face and his body didn't change, but everything else got messed up!" He sat up straight on the bed. "Don't you see how he's paying so much attention to *you*? Why do you think he's doing that? He's planning something, Till; I know he is." Max jammed his feet into the mattress and pushed his back up against the wall. "I know he's my father, but he's not human anymore. And I'm not going to let a monster ruin me!"

Till realized that Max had already made up his mind.

"I'll do it, Till. I'll do it."

Do what? thought Till, but didn't dare to put the question to Max. Instead, his gaze wandered back to the ceiling. Since Max had started speaking, Till had felt as if someone was tightening a noose around his neck. Maybe Max was weak, tired, shocked, whatever. But Till also knew that he couldn't take what Max said lightly. Till had seen the bird fight, had heard Bentheim reading, and had practically seen him disappear in the tunnel at the train station. Something was going on with Max's father—something that Max could feel, too, but which they were simply at a loss to explain. But it was dangerous—and it was more dangerous for Max than for him, Till knew.

"Tonight really did it for me," he heard Max murmur. "I have to set my dad free from the monster that's taken him over." Shocked, Till turned his head and saw Max's bright eyes trained on him. "I'm going to do it, Till—as soon as I'm strong enough to do it. I'm going to kill him."

And he seemed positively radiant about the decision he'd made.

****

And now? Wait till the waitress comes out? But what to say to her . . . "Ah, there you are . . ." Where would that lead?

No, no, no . . .

Forget the waitress. Down this way instead, the shops are still open . . . Friedrichstrasse is just ahead . . . still so packed . . .

Slowly . . . not so fast . . . this is the best spot . . . this is where they all walk . . . don't forget to smile.

Her! She's good! . . . No . . . she isn't alone . . . that's . . . how many? Four? Impossible . . . she has to be by herself . . . but who walks around here by themselves? All with some guy, or with their girlfriends . . . or with a dog. Not good either . . . it'll be quieter down below Gendarmenmarkt . . . and north of Linden . . . but here . . . this is where it's best—and if I just stop? At the corner? Impossible . . . her! She's . . . hot.

Okay . . .

Heading north . . . good . . . go ahead and make that phone call . . . it won't take long . . . then I can get a little closer . . . she moves well! Do they do that on purpose? That swaying with their hips? Or is it a natural gift, so you stay stuck like glue, so you're drawn in, and practically sucked onto them . . .

Look at that! It isn't just the hips in motion—look at that ass—but it's not jiggling; it's undulating—almost imperceptible . . . careful . . . I'm too close . . . my moment will come soon enough.

Okay . . . phone call's over—now's . . .

Ah . . . in the Galeries Lafayette . . . still want to shop a little? Fine.

Can you hold the door open for me?

Bang! Now we've looked at each other!

Pretty. Oh, no doubt about that. No cold beauty, this one—just the way I like it! Did you see her hands, at least the one she held the door open with? Lightly tanned. And she looks after them. But her

*nails, no nail polish! Or maybe a transparent varnish? A small hand . . .
I wonder what it looks like when she . . .*

*She's tied her hair back in a ponytail. If she took off the hairband,
her hair would drape over her shoulders . . .*

Shit. Now she's stopped.

There. She looked.

She saw me following her!

And now?

Okay—keep going . . . just keep going . . . but now she knows.

Ha-ha! It's like you can hear her heart start to beat.

*Sure, reach for your phone . . . no messages . . . good girl, put it
away again.*

*Are you looking at belts? Do you need a belt? That's why you came
in here, isn't it?*

*No problem. I've got time, haven't I? See? I'm looking at watches—
but you know I don't give a damn about the watches, don't you? You
know I'm zeroing in on you, don't you?*

*Don't you want to look over my way one more time? No? Don't
worry . . . you don't need to turn your back on me . . . see, I don't look
at you the whole time, either.*

But I'm in your head—can you feel *that?*

Do you feel my hand, the way I move it over your belly . . .

*Now she takes another look. Her face completely different—suddenly
she knows; she knows I'm not letting her out of my sight! Hasn't her expression changed—almost as if she doesn't want anyone to see how much she
enjoys it—enjoys it, that I'm on her scent . . . that I've picked up her trail . . .*

*So, you're not buying the belt? Should I? For you . . . I could wrap
it around your waist—afterward—if you let me . . . and? Can't make
up your mind?*

Look, I'll show you how it works.

*Are you looking in my direction? Are you watching where I go?
Yes?*

Yeesss—that's nice—how my eyes catch yours and yours mine. Look at what I'm doing:

"Can I help you?"

Most important for the sales assistant when it comes to serving customers: don't leave the customer waiting.

"I'd like to look at this one."

Are you watching?

Yes, you've stopped. That's good.

We exchange glances again—I could drown in your gaze . . . your eyes are like caramel sugar—like something you put off and put off and put off eating until you can't stand it anymore—and you throw yourself on it . . . and it yields . . .

"And this here—could you show me this one, too?"

*Gorgeous! Green. It would complement your eyes, no doubt. Now I don't have to look in your direction at all anymore—*I know *you're not moving from that spot, that* you *can't* move *from that spot, that you are far too curious, far too stimulated by the way we looked at each other.*

Or not?

"No, it's fine, I . . . just need a moment to think it over . . ."

There she is.

Yes, you smile. Exciting, isn't it?

Now she runs her hand through her hair. Show me—yes—get it out—get that hairband out—let it fall free, shake it over your face—I see your eyes through your hair—good—uncover them—that's very good!

She's the right one.

"Sorry?" *I nearly forgot about the saleswoman.* "Lovely—I'll take this one. Cash, thank you."

Even the box is elegant . . . the necklace is perfect . . . it will feel cool against your skin—but you'll still be getting warm.

"How much?"

One thousand, seven hundred, and fifty-eight. Okay.

"Receipt? Yes, of course, please."

One thousand, seven hundred, and fifty-eight euros? Fine. What does it matter?

Look at her standing there, looking like a schoolgirl. She's doesn't know what she's supposed to do.

"No, I'll take it as is. Thank you."

You're nervous, aren't you? It suits you. Don't worry; I'm nervous, too.

I'm coming toward you. Are you thinking what I'm thinking? That I've got the necklace in my pocket? Turn your eyes away, okay? So I can see your neck? Beautiful! Everything about you is beautiful.

We've never been this close, have we? What's that in your eyes . . . a smile? Yes. You don't need to be timid around me. Just like that . . . play with me.

TODAY

"Nah!"

The woman must be pushing seventy. She's small, and her voice sounds like she's had a pack-a-day habit for many years.

"It wasn't the garbage chute. That's outside, back down the hallway behind you! It was in the dumbwaiter. In the kitchen at my place!"

Claire leans against the wall outside the door. "You've actually got a dumbwaiter?" She smiles. She likes the old lady.

"Yeah, you don't normally see 'em in the high-rise projects, I know. But we've got one. At the start, the plan was to use it to get meals up to the old folks on the top floors. That never really took off . . . but they'd already put the thing in." The woman grins. "You wanna see it?"

"May I?" Claire smiles.

She is still standing in the hallway. The Japanese girl and her friends have disappeared down the stairs and the family with the kids is still waiting for the elevator. The old lady appeared alone at her apartment door and—with her hands on her hips and her no-one-fucks-with-me look—immediately caught Claire's eye.

"I got no idea why that went all the way to them up top," Claire hears her saying as she follows her into the apartment. "I heard the dumbwaiter rumbling and all I knew was: no way you're goin' to open that up just now." The woman takes a step to one side. "After you."

Claire looks past her into the small, blue-and-white tiled kitchen. The built-in cupboards and kitchen furniture look like they've been there for forty years: worn-out and battered, but scrubbed and clean. Beside the refrigerator is a hatch set into the wall, its two doors opening one up, one down.

"Can I open it?" says Claire, looking at the old woman.

"You'll have to call it up first."

Claire steps over to the hatch and touches an off-white plastic button with an Up arrow on it, mounted on the wall on one side of the hatch. The button lights up.

"So, what happened next?" Claire turns back to the woman, who screws up her face.

"It gets pretty loud up there—but they really outdid themselves today. I got no idea what they were up to . . . I thought the ceiling'd fall down any second."

They hear a clicking sound.

"Now it's there," says the old woman with a nod toward the dumbwaiter.

Claire pushes the upper half of the hatch upward and the bottom half slides down at the same time. Inside she sees a plain, empty box about three feet by three feet square.

"Hmm," says Claire, eyeing the opening doubtfully. "Ever tried sitting in there?"

"Ha-ha!" cackles the old woman. "That shaft goes straight down a good two hundred feet. If that cable broke . . ."

"Do you mind if I give it a try?" asks Claire, chewing on her bottom lip. She turns back to the woman, who only shrugs.

"Be my guest. Then what?"

Claire thinks for a moment. "Then I'll ride up to the apartment."

"And how do you plan on doing that?" The old woman looks at her curiously. "It's not like an elevator where you can push a button for the floor you want!"

Claire nods. That's right. The dumbwaiter doesn't contain any buttons inside . . . it's not built for people to ride in, after all. The button *beside* it, however, catches her eye. Apart from the button with the Up arrow, there are two more: one with a G and one with a B.

"Once you're in there, all I can do is send you to the ground floor or down to the basement," she hears the old woman saying.

Claire doesn't have to think about it long. "Down to the basement." She sits on the edge of the dumbwaiter, pulls her legs up, swings them around, and squeezes inside. She feels it sag under her weight.

When the dumbwaiter stops in the basement with a jolt, Claire pushes open the doors from inside. She hadn't been mistaken: there is no one in the room in front of her. She had clearly heard the confusion of voices as she rolled past the ground floor.

Claire eases out of the box. On the left, beside the elevator hatch, is a panel of push buttons, one for each floor of the building. She memorizes where the 18 button is and squeezes back into the dumbwaiter.

But it doesn't work: unless the doors are closed, the button doesn't do anything when Claire reaches around the corner of the wall and pushes it. From inside she pulls the outside doors closed, braces herself against the back wall of the box, and slams both feet into the top half of the hatch as hard as she can. The wood breaks out of its frame with a sharp crack. Claire pokes her head out and can see the panel of buttons. All of them are lit . . . did kicking the hatch mess up the electronics?

She cautiously presses number 18—the floor the cops have sealed off.

With a jerk, the elevator starts to rise. Claire quickly pulls her arm back inside to avoid it being crushed against the wall of the shaft by the rising elevator.

The dumbwaiter stops at the eighteenth floor and Claire opens the outer hatch doors a crack.

Highly polished steel cupboards, ceramic and glass countertops, chrome surfaces. This isn't a kitchen . . . it's a high-tech gourmet temple.

The room is empty, but through the open door to the hallway she can see two men in uniform, their backs to her.

Claire silently pushes the dumbwaiter doors completely open and swings out of the box. She quickly moves over to the kitchen window, out of sight of the two men. She turns the handle and carefully pulls the window open.

More than two hundred feet below, Claire can see pedestrians on Leipziger Strasse, where traffic has again started to move. She lifts her gaze. The building is L-shaped, and from the open window she looks across and can see another window of the same apartment. But the reflections on the glass obstruct her view; all she can make out are several people in the room on the other side.

"Hello?" The voice sounds friendly but curious.

Claire turns around. Smiles. "Okay." She knows that nothing is actually okay but doesn't wait for a response from the young officer who has entered the kitchen, and instead marches resolutely past him and out of the room. The two men in the hallway have left.

No one stops her.

Most of the officers seem to have gathered in the living room, which opens out onto a balcony. Claire turns in the other direction, away from the officers, heading deeper into the apartment.

The place has been completely renovated. No trace remains here of the seventies charm one floor below. The window offers an outstanding view over Leipziger Strasse and the patchwork grid of the city. The apartment walls have been painted in vibrant colors: bright green, yellow, and orange—vivid candy colors more reminiscent of brilliantly colored plasticware than of brickwork and plaster. But most strikingly, most of the interior walls have been knocked out, turning the apartments on the floor into a single, enormous loft.

Nearly thirty champagne bottles in a corner catch Claire's eye, and the remains of sushi and other delicacies are strewn across the elegant sideboards and tables. A high-end stereo system seems to have been set up for a party, with speaker wires feeding out to every room. On the floor in one room lies a skimpy pair of red and silver underwear. Clearly, the tenants threw a wild party. Claire's camera clicks away. Behind one door is a bathroom completely lined with mirrored tiles. The endless reflections shatter the bathroom's interior into countless fragments. Claire adjusts her shooting angle—and hears steps behind her.

Without turning around, she steps into the bathroom, closes the door, and turns the lock. Not moving a muscle, she listens to the footsteps move past.

Her eyes sweep the room: a luxury bathroom with two hand basins, an octagonal tub, and a shower with no fewer than forty water jets. On the glass shelves under the two enormous mirrors crowd makeup containers of every size and shape, as if twenty party girls decided to fix their faces at the same time.

Claire puts her camera to her eye and clicks away. Through a window, she sees the next high-rise block on Leipziger Strasse. She pulls up the image on the camera's display. The contrast between the high-tech luxury of the bathroom and the minimalist design of the apartment block beyond the window is striking.

She blinks. *What's that?* In the image, she can see a thin, flat, black object lying on the towels on a raffia shelf beside the window.

Claire raises her eyes, looks at the shelf, and takes a step. A cell phone, with the display facing up. Without touching it, Claire looks closer at the phone. She knows this type. Carefully, she presses the button that turns off the screensaver.

A virtual viewfinder appears on the small screen. Claire touches it with the nail of her index finger.

The phone is switched to silent. A video starts to play.

It is the apartment. But not brimming with police, and not in daytime. Instead, the clip shows the apartment at the height of a party.

The smile of a girl in heavy makeup. The corner of Claire's mouth twitches—she knows the face. It's one of the glam girls she saw in the hallway.

The young woman's eyes light up—then her cherry-red lips form a kiss over the lens. The next moment, she grabs the phone away from the person holding it. The image lurches around and bounces down the hallway, into the living room.

There must be fifty, sixty people. Every one of them dancing.

The camera pans across the dancers. Claire sees someone climb onto a table in the background. The Japanese girl! But dressed now. She crosses her arms across her belly, takes hold of the hem of her top, and peels it up and over her body in one smooth movement. She tosses the top into the mass of dancers and turns her naked back to the camera. The people dancing have raised their arms in the air, clapping in rhythm to music that Claire can't hear.

The camera swings to a young man with short hair standing in front of the table, holding a roll of plastic wrap. The Japanese girl has her head thrown back and seems to understand what the young man has in mind. She takes her hands away from her bobbing breasts. The phone jerks down, comes up again, stabilizes. The guy has peeled back one end of the plastic wrap and presses it to the Japanese girl's body. She crooks her arm against it, holding it in place, and starts to turn in a circle. Her naked skin is compressed under the sheer plastic. Claire sees hands reaching out of the crowd, fingertips gliding over taut plastic-wrapped skin, caressing the girl's fluid torso.

Now the Japanese girl has her hands over her head. Her shaven armpits seem polished. The plastic wrap is holding by itself and wraps around her more and more. Someone inserts a finger into the elastic of the girl's skirt and begins to pull at it. She shimmies her hips and the waistband slips a little lower, revealing her lower back. She spins around again and more hands reach up for the skirt. She continues to dance, finding a common rhythm with the hands, and with every revolution, the skirt slips a little farther down—until, with a tug, it drops off completely. Her tongue caresses her lips, and her dark eyes seem to gleam. It's as if she knows just how much control she has over her audience with her nakedness.

Then something goes through the crowd, a kind of collective jolt.

Heads turn. The camera swings away, then back to the Japanese girl. But the fluidity of her movements has vanished. She has her shoulders pulled up, arms crossed over her breasts—and she jumps down from the table.

Simultaneously, a second jolt seems to run through the crowd. A confused face wipes past the camera. Then the image is bouncing over the floor—legs, shoes, the ceramic tile floor. For a second, Claire sees the face of the girl holding the camera. She seems distraught, alarmed, breathless. The shoulders of another woman, the door opening into the kitchen, the confused face of two guests in suits, hurrying down the hallway toward the camera.

The dumbwaiter doors are open. The camera whirls around. A neck, hair lacquered into spikes, the bulky back of a man . . . he spins around—his eyes, they . . . where are his pupils?! His eyes are just white!

Claire stares at the display. *All white!*

She gazes at the grotesque face in disbelief until she realizes that the image has frozen. The recording has come to an end, stopped exactly at the moment when the man turned his attention upward, causing his pupils to disappear momentarily under his eyelids. That's why she can't see them!

Claire's head jerks up. *What?*

"Open the door *immediately*!" a voice barks, followed by an ear-splitting crack.

Claire swings around, her heart in her mouth, her hands pressed against the ice-cold mirror-tiles at her back.

The splintering wood hits her body, her face. Then the lock breaks out of the door, which flies open and smashes against the doorstop screwed into the floor behind it.

Two officers from the special unit, dressed head-to-toe in black, force their way into the bathroom. Their guns level at her, their eyes unwavering behind the slits in their protective masks.

✳✳✳✳

"ARE YOU INSANE?!"

The police officer grips her camera in his hand.

Claire tries not to let it show, but she is seriously intimidated by the very real outrage of the powerfully built, Kevlar-clad officer.

They had literally dragged her out of the bathroom.

"Are you freelance or with a paper?" The officer pulls off his balaclava, revealing close-cropped gray hair underneath.

"Freelance."

Didn't make sense to drag the paper into this. Entering the scene of a crime without authorization was not something her editor would have sanctioned in any case. Of course, if the pictures are any good, she'll sure take them . . .

Claire sees the officer press a button on the camera, displaying her pictures.

Shit! Does he want to delete them?

"What are you doing?" says Claire, frowning. "You can't even see anything on them . . ."

"You had no right," says the officer, his voice like a razor blade, "*no right* even coming in here!"

"Chief!"

He pauses, turns around.

In the same moment, she hears it.

A rumbling sound, like rubble pouring down a construction site chute.

"CHIEF!"

The officer flinches. "WHAT?" Without another glance at Claire, he strides off with the camera, heading in the direction of the shout.

Then everything happens very fast.

Claire looks up at the gawky young policeman still standing next to her. Could he simply let her go, maybe?

RATTATAT RATTATATATAT.

Claire freezes.

The young officer's eyes widen.

Shots.

Blood rushes to her head. She hears it roaring in her ears. Suddenly, her whole body feels on fire. Sounds reach her as if through water. Claire can hear muffled shouts, screams, then bellowing from the front room of the apartment.

The rumbling noise again, the same as moments before, but louder. A clattering and clanking, a loud bang.

Claire thinks she feels the building shudder.

Then the young officer runs, and Claire follows him.

Out!

Out of the apartment, out of the building.

People are running from rooms out into the hallway. "In the garbage chute!" someone beside her says. "Now they're in the garbage chute!" As if in slow motion, Claire turns her head and sees the wide-open mouth of a woman, who seems to be screaming at the top of her voice—but Claire hears only the faintest sound.

In the garbage chute . . .

The digital camera is gone, but she still has the Leica—Claire feels her fingers wrap around the small camera—and she has the presence of mind to raise the viewfinder to her eye.

Heads, arms, hair—the low ceiling—a face bumps into the lens, a face in pain.

What is that?

Claire wipes at the lens. Her finger comes away sticky.

It's just one drop of blood, but it has smeared the entire lens.

She pushes her way out through the apartment door. People are in a crush in the hall. Simultaneously, noises like a herd of animals being flattened by a tank emerge from the garbage chute.

And a jingling sound . . .

No, a *ringing*!

Claire's presses her mobile phone to her ear; she's soaked with sweat.

"Hello?"

"Claire?"

"Yes?"

It's Frederik.

"Claire?"

What's wrong with him?

"Claire, they've got me . . ."

Claire sees officers trying to block off the opening to the garbage chute.

Her head is spinning.

"I love you, Claire."

What's that supposed to mean . . . *they've got me?*

She is about to say *I love you, too,* but there is a click and the line goes dead.

36

TODAY

Butz props his feet on his desk in the spacious open-plan office that he shares with four other detectives in Keithstrasse. Over the toes of his shoes, he sees a woman approaching, the new detective on the team.

She eyes him archly, her short, blonde hair bouncing as she walks.

"Yes?" Butz presses the handset of the cordless phone tighter against his ear. "No, Fehrenberg, F-E-H-R- . . ."

He makes an effort to understand the broken German of the receptionist on the phone.

Butz has spent the entire morning trying to get Fehrenberg—the first detective assigned to investigate the murder of Nadja, the girl in the parking lot—on the line. But Fehrenberg was on holiday and his phone was switched off, so Butz asked the human resources department to track the detective down. Nothing is as simple as it sounds. First, the person who could help him was not at his desk. Then, it had turned out Fehrenberg hadn't left an address for the hotel. Finally, he found out that the detective had left an emergency contact number: his mother's. Butz spoke to her and she told him that her son had flown to the Canary Islands. She even gave him the name of the hotel where he was staying.

"Oh . . . yes . . . all right. Thank you." Butz clicks off the call and lowers the handset. No luck: they have never heard the name "Fehrenberg" at the hotel his mother mentioned.

Annoyed, he taps in another phone number, Fehrenberg's mother again.

Beeeep.

Butz swings his legs off the desk and sits up straight in his chair.

Beeeep.

His mind wanders. Of course, he can pester Fehrenberg's mother again. But it's not as though she's suddenly going to come up with the name of a different hotel.

Beeeep.

And why not? Because she had already said something that surprised Butz. He remembered Fehrenberg's words exactly: "I'm going with my girlfriend and the kid." But his mother had told Butz something different: her son had not gone on holiday with his family—he'd flown alone.

Beeeep.

When Butz had questioned her about it, she told him that her son had split up with his girlfriend about a week before he left.

Beeeep.

Butz finally throws the handset onto his desk.

Shit.

Fehrenberg had had three weeks to investigate Nadja's case. What did he find out? Butz needs the information—every conversation, every detail—but he can't even reach the man.

He scans the room. Past the blonde detective—who has stopped to talk to a colleague, Manfred—to the desk in the corner. How long have he and Fehrenberg been working here together? Six years? Eight? Butz can see him in his mind's eye: Volker Fehrenberg. Bulky body bent over the desk, telephone gripped in one huge mitt, his eyes directed somewhere beyond the potted plants, out to Keithstrasse.

Butz stands. He takes a step in the direction of Manfred and the new woman.

"I was gonna go down and grab a bite to eat," he says, and grins. "Want to come along, Manfred?"

"Yeah, sure," his colleague sighs. "Why not?"

The new detective purses her lips. "Now?"

"It's all right," the other man says, placating her, and gets up from his desk.

"Let's go." Butz lays one hand on Manfred's shoulder and they head toward the door. True, the man didn't have the best case clear-up rate, but he was okay, and didn't rock the boat. "Where should we take her?" says Butz, grinning. "Turkish, Lebanese, Thai, Chinese . . . ?"

Joking around, they step out into the hallway, their new colleague trailing behind.

Butz's phone rings back at his desk. He takes his hand out of the side pocket of his jacket.

"Shit." He tilts his head to one side and stops. "You want to go ahead?"

Manfred clicks his tongue and nods. The blonde detective seems less-than-pleasantly surprised. But Butz has already turned away and is hurrying back to his desk. He picks up the phone.

"Butz here."

All he hears is a dial tone. Calling the phone on his desk means pressing two buttons on his mobile. He doesn't even need to take it out of his pocket.

Butz glances casually back to the door. The other two have disappeared down the hallway. He is alone in the office.

Butz hangs up and turns around.

Fehrenberg's desk. He's there in two seconds.

Imitation wood, a mobile file cabinet, phone, computer. A few Post-its, phone numbers on the desk pad, scribbles on the desk diary.

Butz pulls open the top drawer of the file cabinet.

Empty.

It's *empty*.

He tugs at the next drawer. Locked.

He hauls the cabinet out from under the desk and tips it forward. No rustling, no clattering, no rattling, nothing.

The thing's been cleaned out!

Butz pushes the filing cabinet back under the desk and turns on Fehrenberg's computer. The fan whirrs to life. While the computer boots up, he pulls open the drawer built into the desk.

Pens. Loose paper. A few forms. Nothing with Fehrenberg's writing on it.

The computer beeps. Butz switches on the monitor, scans the desktop screen.

Storing documents locally isn't permitted. Everything has to be saved to the network; that's been the rule for at least ten years.

But Fehrenberg's network file is totally empty. And there's nothing on the local hard drive, either.

Butz clicks feverishly through the directories.

In the calendar? No appointments.

Addresses in the email client? Not one.

Wastepaper basket? Empty.

BRRRRIIIIIING!

Butz feels as though his blood is foaming in his veins.

The phone on his desk. He's got it in two steps.

"Butz speaking!"

"You called me again?"

Fehrenberg's mother. She must have seen his number on her display.

"Yes, thanks for calling back. It's about your son again. I called the hotel you told me about . . . but, well, he isn't registered there, Mrs. Fehrenberg."

The line buzzes.

"What . . . ?" Butz hears her voice wavering. "What do you mean, he isn't there?" But before he can answer, she goes on: "Where else could he be? Where is he? He can't be . . . he can't be gone." Her voice has become shaky.

One thought pounds through Butz's head: *The whole damn computer is blank.*

But another thought follows so hard on the heels of the first that he fails to answer the woman on the phone: *How is it possible that no one noticed anything?!* That Fehrenberg erasing everything—cleaning out everything—caught no one's attention?

"Still on the phone?"

Butz spins around to the door. It's Manfred, who should be down getting something to eat with the new detective.

"I thought you'd be right behind us, Konstantin."

What's he doing back up here and not down flirting with their new colleague? Butz wonders. *Did* you *know what was going on with Fehrenberg?* he wants to ask him . . .

"Hello? Are you still there?" he hears Fehrenberg's mother whisper into the phone . . .

Butz's eyes meet Manfred's.

"What's up? You coming or not?" The other man grins. But to Butz, the smile is as cold as stone.

Fehrenberg—*and who else?*

That's what goes through Butz's mind when he sees his colleague's icy, mirthless grin.

Who else is in on this?

Suddenly, it feels fifteen degrees colder in the room.

****

"How many yards?"

"Six hundred and fifty, Mr. Butz. The last six hundred and fifty yards are piped."

"'Piped'?"

"Yep. The riverbed's been built over and the water is channeled through pipes instead."

"All the way to the Spree?"

"Uh-huh. Until 2006, the outlet came out back there, under the Theater am Schiffbauerdamm. These days it's over here . . ."

Butz turns away from the water district worker and looks to his assistant, who is with the forensics specialists, leaning over the body they'd pulled out of the Spree an hour earlier.

"Eisler," his assistant calls to him, rising. "Anni Eisler." He is holding a small, red purse.

Butz looks over to a police officer standing off to one side. "Where's the person who found her?"

"There was no one here." The officer scratches under his hat distractedly and takes a step toward Butz. "The call came through and someone . . . it was a man, Mr. Butz; we know that much. The call was made on a prepaid—"

"So, by the time you got here, the guy was gone."

"He said he saw something caught on the grating." The officer points toward the opposite side of the river to a gap in the Spree's cement-reinforced bank.

Butz looks at his assistant, who still holds the purse. "Where's she registered?"

"Stuttgart." The assistant skims his notes. "She still had her ID on her. We've already spoken with a roommate down there. Seems Ms. Eisler was just visiting Berlin for a few days. Said she wanted to see the city."

"A tourist." Butz sighs. That doesn't simplify things.

The man from the water district suddenly cuts in: "Actually, up above the bunker, where the Panke is still open . . . that's the only place she could have fallen in. Or been thrown in . . ."

Butz's assistant frowns. "Do you think the Panke has enough water to wash a body down?"

"Sure, when it rains. And there's been enough of that lately."

"Or she was in one of the drains the Panke flows through at the end," Butz muses. "And she fell—or was thrown—into the stream there. How high are the pipes leading to the Spree? Could you walk upright in there?"

"Eight or ten feet," says the utilities worker, clearing his throat. "It varies. It's not the same over the whole distance, but yeah, you could definitely walk down there."

"Mr. Butz?"

Butz looks over to the forensics pathologist, an elderly man with glasses and a goatee, squatting by the body. He waves Butz over. "She crawled some distance on all fours," the pathologist says, indicating a crawling posture. "Probably between twenty and fifty yards . . ." He raises one arm of the body and turns it so that Butz can see the chafing on the palm of the hand.

Butz squats beside him and nods to a reddish spot on the woman's collarbone, visible at the wide neckline of the T-shirt. "What about that?"

"She's been branded. It's not new. At least two years old, I'd say." The pathologist's glasses mirror the reflection from the surface of the river. "Thousands of women her age have them."

Scraped hands, body modifications, the covered waterway . . . Butz's eye settles on the woman's face. Her staring eyes look like two glass beads.

"Cause of death is most likely strangulation," says the pathologist. Butz cracks his jaw and stands up, propping himself against the shoreline's railing. On the other side of the river, the pubs lined up along the Schiffbauerdamm are brightly lit. Several passersby pause and look in his direction. They could not have missed the gathering of police, technicians, and forensics specialists. Behind the pubs, a crowd is moving toward the Berliner Ensemble, where the evening program will soon start. Butz watches the people climbing out of taxis, greeting friends. Still time to buy a pretzel if they're quick.

But he can think of only one thing: three weeks have passed between the death of Nadja in the parking lot and the death of the woman on the construction site. Anni Eisler's hand injuries are alarmingly similar to those of Nadja and the other woman. But this time, far less than three weeks has passed. Butz feels his shoulders grow heavy.

Since the murder on the construction site, only three *days* have passed.

It's a series, and the spaces in between are getting shorter.

Three weeks.

Three days.

What comes next?

Three hours?

He glances at his watch.

It is 7:42 P.M.

37

TWELVE YEARS AGO

"I don't know when the time will be right," Max said, "but I won't let him and his people breed anymore."

There were only two weeks left of summer vacation. Till had already visited the school he'd be attending and had been introduced to the principal. He had his schoolbooks for seventh grade and had spoken to both Lisa and Max at length about individual teachers and students. Everything was ready. At the same time, it all seemed completely unreal. Because Till knew what Max was planning, and that he would follow through with it.

But the underlying fear that something might happen to Bentheim was not the only thing that alarmed Till when he thought about how long Max had spent brooding over what he would do to his father. Till was also worried about Max: it was clear to Till that if his friend carried through on his threat, he would destroy his own life as well. Could Till just stand by and watch Max ruin his life by raising his hand against his father? But didn't he have a duty to stand by his friend?

The conflict was tearing Till apart. He knew he was the only one whom Max had told. And he also knew that *Max* knew that once Till realized how strong Max's resolve was, he'd be thinking about it day and night. The moment Max would act was drawing nearer. Till woke up some nights, late, and held his breath. Were those footsteps he heard? Had Max left his bed and crept into his parents' bedroom? One afternoon, when Max's parents were away on some errand, Till surprised him in the kitchen looking intently at knives in a drawer. Till overheard Rebecca telling Julia that one of the knives had disappeared and he was there when Julia asked her son if he knew anything about it. Max, with a lack of feeling in his expression that stabbed Till to the heart, replied that no one could expect him to keep track of every single kitchen utensil.

In the morning, when Till caught sight of Bentheim's car, he wondered whether Max might have loosened the wheel nuts in the night. During the day, when Rebecca was cleaning the fireplace, he wondered if Max was planning to set fire to the house. And in the evening, when the old water heater in the bathroom clicked to life, he speculated on whether Max might put his plan into action by tampering with the gas lines.

At every opportunity, Till confronted Max: He couldn't be serious. There had to be other ways. He couldn't throw his own life away. Till tried to convince Max that his father needed help if there really was something the matter with him. That he couldn't do that to his mother. That Lisa and the little ones needed their father. But Till's arguments just bounced off Max. His old vitality had returned, and his frailty, shakiness, and insecurity had almost completely disappeared. Instead, a kind of delusional mania—something far more bitter than his illness—had taken hold of him. It was as if Max were thriving on his decision to turn against his father, and Till found himself wondering with trepidation what might come next.

Till knew Max was convinced that he had the right to do what he planned. And at times, Till even had the feeling that Max was enjoying having taken Till into his confidence . . . as if Max was absolutely certain that Till would never betray him, and knew what agony it must be for Till to keep this damning information to himself.

****

"What's that?" asked Max, taking the cover of the VHS tape out of Till's hand. Till had pushed the tape into the player.

They were sitting on the floor in front of an old TV in a little-used room. Till had stumbled upon the cassette the day before on a shelf while rummaging through the treasures filling the room. There were dusty videos of classic films and trash movies from the seventies and eighties, Hollywood blockbusters of every genre, boxes of series in different formats, tapes that obviously had not been inside their cases in years. Books, old DVDs, CDs, comics, and an entire wall full of picture books, but also innumerable paperback novels, coffee-table books, all kinds of catalogs, and Till had even stumbled across hundreds of programs from theaters and opera houses from all over the world.

"*The Puppet Masters*," he said offhandedly. "Ever seen it?"

Max shook his head and threw the case back on the floor. "Press Play," he said, and nodded to Till, who was rewinding the tape.

Till hit the Stop button. The tape came to a standstill with an audible click. He pushed Play. The image wobbled and the picture was blurry for a moment. Then it stabilized, and they could see two men in a room bent over a crate. Inside the crate were several dark-green balls packed in straw.

Max creased his brow. "What's that supposed to be?"

Till decided not to answer. He wanted to see how Max reacted to the scene. He knew that there was some danger in confronting him with the film, but Till had run out of ideas for how to bring Max to his senses.

"What . . . woahhhh!" Max was still kneeling in front of the screen, but his upper body was now bolt upright. One of the men had taken one of the balls out of the crate and was holding it in his hand. The ball had opened up like the flower of some carnivorous plant and a kind of tentacle was emerging from inside.

Till narrowed his eyes. The audio impressed him almost more than the images he was seeing. There was low crackling sound, like a spider scuttling across a mirror—or three hundred spiders—and it was as if he was not *larger* than the spiders, but in fact *smaller*, and the creatures' hairy legs towered above him like skyscrapers.

The tentacle that had emerged from the ball had slithered under the back of the shirt of one of the men, reappearing at the collar. As if stung by a wasp, the man tried to swat the thing off his back, but he wasn't able to prevent the soft, sensitive, but unyielding tip of the blind limb from drilling into his flesh as if it were made of butter. The bristling crackle of the audio became a moist slipping and slopping. From the twitching face of the man being attacked, the scene cut to a close-up of the tentacle itself, penetrating the back of his neck and sliding deeper. The thing was amazingly agile and moved with such determination and greed that just by watching it you could practically feel how much it reveled in burrowing into its victim.

"AAAHH!" yelped Max—and Till hit Pause. The image froze in place. "What is that?" Max whispered, looking over at Till.

"One of the *Alien* films?" Till shrugged. "I found it on the shelf here yesterday."

Max nodded. As though magnetically attracted, his eyes wandered back to the image frozen on the screen, the close-up of the tentacle penetrating the man's back. The fine hairs on the tentacle shimmered, moist and black. "And why should I watch it?"

Till pressed Play again. "Why not?"

With a slurping sound, the tentacle slid deeper into the man's spine. You could practically hear the thing lunging into his skull. Suddenly, the man—who had long given up any resistance against the creature—arched his back and tensed his muscles. The camera moved around him. His face was suddenly calm. His body looked both strangely skewered and drooping, as if it was no longer his legs holding him upright but the creature that had bored into him. His eyes stared straight ahead and with an almost trancelike movement, he removed his glasses.

Max didn't take his eyes off the screen. "So he can see better now? Is that it? Because that thing is inside him!"

Till nodded. Just then, the second man reentered the frame, his back now also bare and one of the tentacle creatures embedded in him like an oversized scorpion. The film cut to the man's neck, where delicate feelers were starting to emerge from the glistening tentacle and—like a deformed, transparent hand—stretching out toward similar feelers growing from the other man's tentacle.

At the very moment that the feelers touched, the picture sprang back to a wider view. The music, which had been rising to nerve-jangling twittering, transformed into a deep roar that Till could feel all the way down in his belly. The two men, who only moments before had been leaning unsuspectingly over the crate, were now standing back to back, seemingly lost in the touch of the creatures lodged inside them. They looked almost dreamy, as if they had given themselves over completely to the subtle caress of the feelers intertwining at their backs, which had to be deep enough to reach into their brains.

Till paused the video again. Max turned to him slowly, as if under the control of such a scorpion himself.

"So that's what happened to your father, right?" Till looked at his friend, his eyebrows arched. "They've dug a hole in the back of his neck, and now they're pulling his strings like he's a marionette."

Max slumped his shoulder, sat helplessly on the floor. "To put it bluntly . . . ," he said, without looking up.

Till waited.

"You can think of it like in this film or tons of other ways. Like with an octopus arm or a virus . . ." He glanced at Till. "Maybe an alien is passed on when infected people throw up. And if you don't watch out and get one drop in your mouth . . ." He screwed up his face. "Like with the flu, if someone sneezes. In *Body Snatchers*, the people aren't infected; they're re-created from a sort of head of cabbage. There are all kinds of ways."

"And you think this has really happened? For real?" The more Till thought about it, the less he was able to comprehend how Max could seriously think it had actually taken place.

"I've seen them try it myself," Max murmured.

"Seen them try what?"

"Try to attack me."

Both boys were silent for a moment. Suddenly, the film started up again by itself, but Till immediately hit the Stop button.

"When?" He had a bad feeling about this.

"Just the other night," said Max. "I wasn't asleep and I wasn't awake. I was lying in bed. At first, it was just a sound." He paused for a second, thinking. "Not so different from the sound we heard in this film."

"What then?"

"It was strange. At first, I thought I just couldn't sleep. Remember when it was so hot a couple of days ago? I was sweating and sweating. Then I thought I was already sleeping, but in the very next second I knew I couldn't *think* I was sleeping and actually *be* asleep at the same time. And that was so weird that I really woke up, and that's when I saw it."

"What did you see?" Till threw the remote control onto the floor impatiently and turned all his attention to Max. "Why didn't you tell me about this before?"

"I didn't think you'd believe me . . ."

"Who says I don't believe you?!"

"It's true, isn't it?" said Max, rounding on him. "But it wasn't hairy tentacles like in this film. They were more like newts or slugs . . . and not just one, but twenty or thirty, and they were all over my bed. On the sheet, under it, on the blanket, inside the pillow. I was scared and I sat up; they were crawling on my stomach and they were in my hair, too, and under my arms, and one of them had already stuck its feelers inside my ear . . . they were really stuck on in there! When I ripped it out, it stung! You know?" His voice had grown shrill. "I didn't wake you because I knew you'd say they were just slugs, but so *many*? Till, why were there suddenly so *many*? Why did they crawl into my bed?" He glared at Till.

Till's heart was racing. What was going on with Max? Had he gone crazy?

"I jumped out of bed, and you know what they did? They stopped crawling, and they rolled their feelers in and out, but they didn't crawl around anymore. They stayed where they were. I was *this* close to screaming, but I kept it inside. All I wanted to do was get out of my room as fast as I could." Max had knotted his fingers together.

"But then I saw the slugs, or whatever they were . . . I saw them stretch their feelers out in my direction. And they turned their slimy little bodies to follow me. If I went left, then a few seconds later they'd find me and stretch their feelers in my direction again. If I went to the right, it was the same. So I stopped and waited. And they crawled toward me. And I'll tell you . . ."—his eyes gleamed— "they were so fast. Some of them fell off the sheet onto the floor and kept on crawling, straight over my feet. Have you ever had a snail crawl over your skin? Do you know what that feels like? It's wet and sticky. You feel how their bodies undulate as they move forward. At the same time, they still had their feelers stretched out in front of them—and when the first ones were crawling past my knees, the ones behind them were already on my feet!"

Till looked at him in stunned silence. Finally, he managed to croak, "And then?"

Max's body had been growing increasingly tense, almost rigid. But all the tension suddenly fell away. His arm shot through the air, and his fist landed a blow on Till's shoulder. "Nothing!" Max laughed. "What do you think?! Along came the king of the slugs and gulped me down, bones and all. *Sluuurrrp!* But he didn't like the taste of me, so he spat me out again! Or I wouldn't be sitting here telling you about it, would I?"

Till felt his stomach spasm. Max was joking! He fell onto his back with a gasp and wrapped his arms over his ribs. "Jeez, I thought you'd finally lost it!"

"Grrraarrr!" yelled Max, and ran his hand over the back of Till's neck like the tentacle in the movie. Till recoiled but still had to laugh—especially when he saw how happy his thin-skinned reaction made Max.

I really thought he'd lost his grip completely, Till thought. *But Max knows exactly what he's saying . . .*

Max pulled up his feet and sat down cross-legged. He was instantly serious; his laugh disappeared and he stared at the floor. It was like someone had flipped a switch.

Till's own cheeriness suddenly felt like a jacket that had shrunk in the wash. His laughter petered out; before it stopped completely, he already felt cold, dark, and hard on the inside again.

"I don't want to make the same mistake as you, Till," Max said, keeping his head bowed. Till, still standing, could only see the back of his head.

"The things we found in the basement, the parrots, the way he's been acting . . . ? There's no scorpion in his neck, but he's just not himself anymore. Maybe you can't understand it, but it's true."

Till squatted next to Max, who had both hands wrapped around one ankle.

"I don't want to make the same mistake as you," Max repeated, and now their eyes met. "With your brother, you just waited and waited—until it was too late. That won't happen with me."

"What . . . what are you talking about?" Till stammered, confused.

"In Brakenfelde," Max said, glaring at him. "You knew your brother was in trouble. And what did you do? Nothing. Until he hanged himself. I'm not going to wait till it's too late."

Till, shocked, could only look at him. All at once it seemed to Till that Max—whose hands never let go of his ankle—had reached inside him with fists hardened into tongs and was twisting his guts like wire.

TWELVE YEARS AGO

Julia checked the clock. Ten to three. She had ten minutes. She'd dropped off Betty at a birthday party and only now had the time to get into the guesthouse. But it had to be today; Xavier had driven into the city to visit Felix. He had said he would be home at three. And Julia knew him well enough to know that he was always punctual.

She looked around the room, and her gaze came to rest on rows of identical white cardboard cartons filling the compartments of a shelf on the wall. She pulled out one of the boxes, opened it, and saw that it was filled with typed A4 pages.

She had never nosed around in Xavier's office before. But here she was. Seeing Max lying thin and pale on a bed in the hospital had driven her to find out everything she could. She could not shake the feeling that the crisis her son was going through had something to do with Xavier.

Julia pushed the carton back onto the shelf and pulled out the next one. The footer on the topmost page caught her eye.

"Xavier Bentheim—*Berlin Gothic*—Thriller."

Berlin Gothic . . .

She had never heard him mention this title. It had to be the manuscript he was currently working on. On the page, centered and in bold type, was the number 367.

But it wasn't the page number.

It was the *chapter* number.

Chapter 367?

Julia pushed the box back onto the shelf and took a step back to get a better view. The shelf had four narrow units, each with six compartments. In each compartment were three cartons.

Julia did the math: four times six times three.

Seventy-two.

In the carton she had looked at first, the number on top was 309. Around sixty chapters per box . . . sixty times seventy-two . . . made . . . 4,320 . . . *chapters?*

What on earth . . . ?

She leaned down to the last carton in the bottom row and lifted the lid. This one, too, was filled to the brim with sheets of paper. But . . .

Julia lifted out the first page to look at the one underneath . . .

But the second page was like the first, completely covered with *numbers.*

She flicked through the remaining pages in the box. Each page was exactly the same: thirty lines per page, all numbers. No spaces, no paragraphs, no indentation. Page after page, neat blocks of numbers from 1 to 9.

Xavier was writing *numbers?* Julia felt her hands grow moist with sweat.

It's a code, she tried to persuade herself. *Of course!* He had written sentences like he always had. It's just that the individual letters—no doubt using a simple key—had been translated into this code! The story about the boy, the one Xavier had recently read to Max and Till . . . wasn't that about just such a code?

Julia stared at the block of numbers. The spacebar had to be represented by a number, too, which was why you couldn't separate the individual words. The same for the periods and paragraph marks. So these blocks of texts were actually the result of some straightforward process . . . maybe that wasn't so unusual . . .

But why? Why use a code? Because he feared someone could read his text and steal his ideas? No better explanation occurred to her.

It's just that . . . wasn't such excessive caution strange in itself?

No! She nearly flinched at how intensely she reprimanded herself. *It was* not *strange! On the contrary, it was very clever of him!*

Julia glanced at the time again. Four minutes to three. Quickly, she pulled the chair from the desk to the shelves and climbed up on it. She pulled out the first carton, top left, and pushed back the lid.

Under the title page was a bold-type "1" in the middle of the page. Chapter 1. And below the chapter number? Words! No numbers! The carton slipped back into place, and Julia stretched up and fished out the last box from the first compartment.

Her eyes skimmed over the words. The description of a small town, an idyllic Sunday morning . . . sunshine, a spring day . . . Each sentence was so polished it was obvious Xavier had put a lot of effort into the work. It almost seemed to Julia that he had emulated the buzzing of the insects through the sound of the sentences. The hum had spontaneously crept into her head when she started reading his description of the town. The detailed description had been lovingly worked through, zooming in on the houses, the cars, the grass growing in the cracks between the paving stones . . . Julia flipped forward impatiently. The story seemed to be set in the 1950s. She stopped at one particular word: *tekso.*

"Tekso?"

Julia read Xavier's sentence again: "The heavy shower had washed the dust from the air, cooled the pavement, revitalized the plants. Now the sun blazed down on the earth and one could literally see tekso evaporating again."

A typo! Julia brusquely pressed the cover back onto the carton, slotted it back onto the shelf, and jerked out the one below.

Chapter 248.

Her eye roamed across the page.

Engrabe.

Another typo?

Then *peple* a few lines lower.

Julia began glancing around the page at random.

Fetos.

Setimend.

Frantec.

Hasselgert. Munif. Klarison.

The code! It must be the start of the code . . . which later became the rows of numbers!

She noticed that her lips moved as she read the strange words. As if a kind of fog was rising from the strange letter formations, clogging her mind.

"Frotiker broffte droul, dac ige sano kilie mebrache haulick, af makreshte oli truber camt." The sentence almost leaped out at her when she flipped down to the last page in the box.

Nauseated, she pushed the box back and jumped up from the chair. She pulled a carton from the middle of the shelf.

Chapter 2,530.

She saw them on the first page. The numbers. Not complete blocks of numbers like on the pages in the boxes farther down. But it already seemed as if the numbers had invaded the words like a disease.

We04. Su8der. 7pter.

Could it really be a secret code? Or could Xavier have invented a language all his own? Maybe because he thought that the things that mattered to him could only be expressed in a language he had developed especially for that purpose?

Julia looked at the clock again. Five past three. High time she was out of there. Just a quick look first, though, in the basement where Max said he had seen the woman.

****

"Mr. Bentheim?"

They had never spoken about what Till should call him, but he still preferred to address the man formally.

He stood up from the lawn chair he'd been lying on and took a few steps across the grass in the direction of Max's father.

"May I talk with you for a minute?" Maybe it wasn't exactly the right moment, but Till felt he couldn't wait any longer—couldn't carry the weight of what he knew about Max without doing something. Bentheim, somewhat bewildered, looked up as Till approached and stopped in front of him.

"What is it?" It was after three and he'd returned from the city.

"It . . . it's a bit tricky . . ." Till began, because it really was tricky.

"Well, I don't have a great deal of time, Till," Bentheim murmured, and smiled.

"I thought maybe I shouldn't talk to you about it at all," Till started. "But then . . . I can't stop thinking about it." He looked straight ahead, into Bentheim's face, hoping to see a little encouragement. But Bentheim just looked at him attentively.

"A little while ago, when Max and I were down in the basement in the guesthouse . . ." Till noticed Bentheim's eyes widen slightly. "Well, look, I'm sorry . . ." Till waved his arms rather aimlessly.

"Back in the home, if something like that happened to one of us, like if someone suddenly showed up in the basement, there's no way we could have let it just slide. We would've had to find exactly where whoever it was came from."

Bentheim had stuffed his hands into the pockets of his pants and was looking silently down on Till.

"I had to go and check out the room that the woman came out of. Max was already outside," Till lied, because he'd thought about this in advance and there was no way he was going to drag Max into this. "And I discovered a door in the wooden paneling." He paused, braced for a sharp rebuke from Bentheim.

"And?" Bentheim's voice sounded like he was making an effort to sound calm.

"It's about the boxes in the room back there. That's why I wanted to talk to you."

Is he going to bite my head off? Maybe a tentacle's going to zip out of his mouth and choke me to death. The mental image was so ridiculous that Till felt a mischievous look momentarily come into his eyes. At the same time, he was acutely aware that Bentheim had probably never been closer to throwing him out of his house.

To his surprise, Max's father did no more than glance briefly at his watch. "There's a lot of old junk stored in that room, Till. I collected it all for a book at one time—"

"Really?" said Till, interrupting him. "What kind of book? I saw photos of a man in a lab, an animal lab. And there was a kind of diary where the same man seemed to make notes about the health of his wife . . ."

"You seem to have had a very good look around indeed!" Bentheim opened his eyes wide with deliberate exaggeration.

"It was really cool," Till stammered. "What . . . what did the man do with his wife?" He gulped—then decided to go ahead and say it: "Mr. Bentheim, I know it's none of my business, but . . . do you think you could tell me more about it sometime?"

Let's see if he's really a damn alien after all, thought Till, and wouldn't have been too surprised if Bentheim's face suddenly split open and the huge black eyes of some space monster appeared underneath. Instead, Max's father merely stepped over to the chair where Till had waited for him and sat down.

"Like I said, Till, it's material for a book. I wanted to write a series about . . . I don't know if you've ever heard of this . . . a book about the living dead, you know what I mean? That's what I wanted to do. That was the connection to Haiti, the animal tests, the experiment with the virus. It was meant to be a kind of fictional nonfiction book, really, proving that part of the human population was already infected. But also showing that very few people actually know about it. Of course, that was the most important thing: that only a select few were even aware of it! Because—at least, that was the plan with the book—that would be the only way to make it really sound credible." He smiled.

Till sat down next to him at the foot of the chair. His thoughts were scattered, unfocused.

"I wanted to incorporate historical documents into the book," Bentheim continued. "The idea was to use them to demonstrate how, in Nazi Germany back in the forties, scientists did lots of tests on animals, and even on human beings. The documents would *look* like real historical sources, but in reality, I'd mocked them up myself. They were supposed to show that the virus that was created in these experiments found its way via Haiti to the United States after the Second World War. Showing that America was actually infested with zombies—and that they originated in the Nazi laboratories in Berlin in the 1940s."

Till hung on his every word. "The man in the animal lab, he . . . he carried out the experiment?" *A book*—the thought raced through his mind—*just a book!*

"Exactly." Bentheim laughed. "That was the plan. I named him Otto Kern. Kern notices that his wife comes down with some unknown illness and, at the end of the forties, he travels with her to Haiti where he hopes the climate will restore her health. At the same time, of course, he knows that her illness probably comes from his experiments. But when the natives on Haiti see her, they don't believe she's sick. They think she's the victim of some kind of evil magic, and they call her *Nzùmbe*—which later became the word *zombie.*"

"And the film?" Till said, thinking of the one Max had told him about. "There was a film in the boxes as well."

Bentheim grinned—but this time, it occurred to Till to wonder why Bentheim wasn't actually more upset about Till poking around in his basement.

"Like I said, I wanted to put together a nonfiction book," Bentheim answered. "A fiction book that *looked* so much like a work of nonfiction that the readers wondered whether it really happened or whether someone had made it all up. So I wanted the film to appear in a *second* step. To spice up the discussion. If the people who read the book generally agreed that nothing that was in the book corresponded with reality, the old film roll was supposed to turn up in a flea market, which would suddenly get people asking whether the images in the film weren't, in fact, the best proof that what was in the book was the *real* truth after all."

Till noticed Bentheim giving him a sidelong look.

Is he checking if I believe him? "Wow," he breathed. "Wicked."

Bentheim turned and faced him directly. "Indeed! Just setting up the photos for the animal tests . . . we all put in a tremendous amount of work just to produce those. If you're interested, sometime I can show you exactly how I envisioned the book."

Yeah, thought Till, *sure, I'd think that would be really interesting*—but he found himself saying something else: "But . . . why didn't you finish the book when you'd already set it all up so carefully?

Nothing would have pleased him more than to dig deeper into what Max's father had just told him about—but his head wasn't about to do him that favor. Instead, it was telling him that maybe Max *was right*, that maybe it was *wrong* to trust Bentheim, that perhaps he should be very wary of the man.

"Yes!" Bentheim answered so loudly that Till actually winced. "Good question! How is it that I actually lost sight of that project?" A gray shadow suddenly seemed to pass over his face—even if his lips still formed a smile and his eyes were narrowed to friendly slits.

"Was that it?" He abruptly stood up. "Or would you like to know something else?"

Till's hands held tightly to the bottom edge of the lawn chair. *Yes*, something inside him was screaming. *I want to know why you took me in. I want to know why you torment Max so much!* But the courage to ask those questions was beyond him. Instead, he looked at the ground in confusion and held his tongue. When he looked up again, after a moment or two lost in his thoughts, Bentheim was already thirty feet away, striding over the lawn toward the guest-house, head down, shoulders hunched, hands buried in his pockets.

Would he go down into the basement and disappear through the door in the wood panel? Till had waited for Bentheim in the first place because he had hoped, after talking to him, to be able to put Max's crazy suspicions to rest. But now that that they had talked, he began to worry that telling Bentheim that he had found the boxes with the diaries and films had been a big mistake.

Just then, Max's father suddenly stopped and turned around.

"Till?"

Till jumped to his feet.

"Yes?"

"I'd like to show you something? Want to see?"

No! Till took a deep breath. "Right now?"

"Sure, right now. Are you coming?"

****

Julia froze. She'd left the guesthouse and was out of sight, peering through the leaves of a vine-covered, shaded walkway. She could see Till and Xavier barely twenty yards away, standing on the grass. Till stood up from a lawn chair and walked over to Xavier, who was now bending down to him.

"I'm not walking this path alone, Julia. I'm *paving the way* for others to follow." She could hear Xavier's words in her head. In his workroom just now—it was not the first time that she had come across strange sequences of letters and incomprehensibly formed words in her husband's writings. A few weeks earlier, he had left a few pages lying in the living room, and she had asked him about them.

"What I want to say can't be said with conventional words," he had answered. "I have to create a completely new language. It's the only way for me to tap into the region where I first saw it."

He might as well have been speaking Greek. "What do you mean? What kind of region, Xavier?"

"There you go! We're already running in circles." Then he had brushed her cheek with his hand. "What this means to me . . . it doesn't make sense if I try to translate it back into normal words so I can talk to you about it! If I translate it back, then what this means to me just . . . dissolves."

"You mean, you want me to . . . what? Learn a new language?"

"Yes. Something like that, but—it's like I said—it's still very early in the piece. I'm only just starting to use the first scraps of it myself to find my way in this new region. It's—how can I put it— it's a circular process. The expressions work like a kind of flashlight, and I can use them to light up new spaces. And once I've illuminated those new spaces, I know the expressions—the tools, really—that I need to fashion to be able to move further."

Julia was silent for a moment. Finally, she asked him, "And how long is this supposed to go on?"

"I know it sounds absurd, Julia, but . . . I . . . I'm not sure . . . I'm not even sure which way it's heading. How could I be? I would already have to know the endpoint. I would have to have been there already. It can't be changed . . . we just have to trust it."

She looked through the leaves at Xavier and Till. They had started walking together across the grass toward the guesthouse. The guesthouse, where Julia had just stumbled across an old-fashioned room with a fireplace, a room Xavier had never even mentioned to her.

Trust.

After everything that had happened in the last few weeks, could she still trust Xavier?

Something inside her answered clearly: *no*. And Julia knew that voice was right.

TWELVE YEARS AGO

Don't let him suck you in! Till could practically picture Max standing in front of him. *I don't believe it. A book? So why was the stuff hidden away like that in the basement?*

Till marched in silence next to Bentheim. They were headed toward the guesthouse.

Don't let him fool you, Till. My father never just says what happens to be going on in his head—he's always got some specific goal in mind! And you can be 100 percent certain that reaching the goal is in his *interest. But whether it's also in* your *interest is a completely different thing!*

What did Bentheim want to show him?

Inside the guesthouse, Max's father steered him toward the steps leading down to the basement. Moments later, they were standing in the room with the wood paneling, and Bentheim was pulling open the hidden door that Till already knew about. He ignored the kicked-in planks and heaved up the steel hatch in the floor. With the lid open, Till could see that the locking bar mounted underneath it was pushed back. An iron ladder led down into the depths.

Till smelled the distant reek of sewage. Then he heard a hum, as if high-tension electrical cables had been laid down there.

Leaving the ladder behind them, they made their way through a branching system of tunnels and pipes. The farther they got from the Bentheim house, the more unearthly the passage became.

"Mr. Bentheim . . . I . . . you know, I . . . I didn't tell Mrs. Bentheim that I'd be away from the house today," Till said, as he stumbled along.

She might be worried, he wanted to say, but he realized it would sound absurd. Of course Bentheim had already talked it through with his wife. Thinking about how much rock and earth lay between them and the surface took Till's breath away. *Don't let yourself be led off into the forest to be killed like Snow White,* he heard a voice inside him whisper. *And if that's what this is, then at least beg for your life like she did.*

Bentheim seemed to know the route well. He stayed a few steps ahead of Till, but now he stopped and turned around.

"Why are we walking around down here?" asked Till, doggedly. "I'd really like to get back out again."

Bentheim looked at him. "It's not so much about you, my boy." His eyes looked suddenly sad and dull. "I like you, but . . . it's really about Max. He doesn't listen to me anymore . . . and things can't go on like they have been lately."

"I . . . but . . . ," Till stammered, ". . . everything here . . . all I can tell him is that there's nothing down here except empty tunnels and passages."

"Do you want to help Max or not?"

In the flat shine of the tunnel lighting, Bentheim's eyes looked searchingly at Till.

"Yeah, sure . . . I want to help Max," Till whispered. "Max is my friend."

Bentheim nodded. "I have to be able to rely on you. Because I can't on Max. But I have to be able to rely on you, otherwise you can't help either Max or yourself."

Max . . . or yourself?

Somewhere in the distance, he could hear a muffled rattling that reverberated in the tunnel.

"I have to be sure you can bring Max to his senses."

"Is that why you brought me down here?"

"I brought you down here because I want to show you something. I already told you that. So, do you want to come?"

Till lowered his head—and walked past Bentheim. Behind him, he could hear Bentheim's footsteps following.

"You can let yourself be carried along on the current of things unfolding, or you can stand against it."

Max's father squatted beside him and looked him in the face, which was filthy from the gritty air, sweat, and exertion. Till stared back.

It seemed to Till that they had walked another two hours through the tunnels before he first heard the barking. Muffled yapping noises that sounded like they came from inside a sealed container. Then the tunnel opened out into an underground room. A sheet of glass from floor to ceiling divided the room.

They were throwing themselves around excitedly behind the glass. It must have been days since they'd seen a human being. Their eyes were wide open and they jumped at the glass, leaping high. Till could see the pads of their velvety paws. Two mutts. One of them brown and shaggy with a white chest and bushy tail; the other with gray short hair, floppy ears, and soft eyes. They both looked young and playful, but also very scared.

Till, confused, looked at the two dogs, which were jumping over each other, pressing their snouts flat against the glass, and wagging their tails.

He had barely heard Bentheim when he asked Till the question. But now the words were ringing inside Till.

Which one? That was what Bentheim had asked him: *Which one is to be killed?*

Till felt like he was falling back into that terrible time in Brakenfelde, after Armin had died. When he had felt crushed by gloom, deeply shaken by the loneliness he felt in the absence of the one person he'd thought he could rely on.

That's why they had come down here: to pass a death sentence on one of these dogs. When it hit Till, he was overcome with dizziness. He had liked Bentheim. Bentheim had taken him in—had saved him in a way. But now he was asking him this question—Which dog should die?—and the decision was Till's.

"I can't decide that," he murmured, staring at the floor.

"You have to decide it, boy. You have to. Or they'll both die."

Till started to cry. He didn't know what to do. He couldn't say that the shaggy dog should die to save the gray one. But neither could he say that the gray one should be put to death to rescue the shaggy one.

Till crossed his arms over his face and leaned forward against the glass—tormented by the dread that death could strike in that kennel at any moment.

"You can let yourself be carried along on the current of things unfolding, or you can stand against it."

From below his folded arms, he could see Bentheim squatting there beside him, looking up at him.

But Till didn't understand what he meant.

"I don't want to make that decision. I don't want to choose which one has to die," Till snuffled, his chest heaving.

"You want fate to decide which one lives and which one dies? You don't want to make that decision yourself?"

Till looked at Bentheim, his eyes wide. From the corner of his eye, he saw the scruffy ears of the brown dog, its front paws propped on the back of the gray one. "No, I don't want to make that decision."

He saw Bentheim nod. "You don't have to go on torturing yourself. You can simply surrender the responsibility, my boy, be rid of it. Forever."

Till was shaking. If fate were to decide what happened to the two dogs, then at least he wasn't to blame for the death of one or the other.

"Isn't it like an enormous weight has been lifted from your shoulders, Till? The moment you are liberated from making the decision?" Bentheim said.

Yes. Yes, it's like being set free.

"That is what binds us together, Till," Bentheim continued, looking up at him. "Us. The people who were at the parrot fight, the people I work for. Something has become clear to us, something that many others are still blind to."

Can I go back up to the daylight now?

"We see that what humanity calls freedom . . . that it's an illusion, Till."

Till wiped a hand across his eyes.

"It isn't true . . . ," Bentheim continued, ". . . it isn't true that you can choose freely—*it just seems like you can.* When you do something, it's like a stone rolling down a slope. It simply happens. *You* don't decide it. You are just a tiny part of an unbelievably large whole."

The air in the tunnel reeked of sewage. How could the dogs stand it?

"Once you understand that, once you understand that it only *seems* like you decide, when in reality you don't decide anything, then it's like a high, like a celebration. It's like flying. Can you feel it?"

A stone rolling down a slope?

"It is speed, accomplishment, deed. It is power, change, dynamism, form, and movement. It is *being*—and you are part of it!"

Like an entire world made of nothing but putrid concrete tunnels . . .

"There are many of us, Till. I've shown you only the tiniest part—but there's an entire city hidden down here. A hidden city that belongs to us."

Till rubbed his nose dry with the back of his hand. Behind the glass, the two dogs were standing on their hind legs, looking at him. They were still alive, both of them. Max's father wasn't going to have them killed! He was going to take care of them.

And suddenly, Till felt a huge cloud of happiness flow from his belly up into his head. This was no Hades, no abyss, no dead end where he would be left to rot. Max's father wasn't a cruel slaughterer sacrificing his son, sacrificing Till, and burrowing around in the city's underbelly like a rat. He wanted to help. He knew something Till had lacked the vision to see for himself, until now.

Everything would work out, Till sensed, and raised his eyes. He felt a smile starting to form on his face, felt the crust of grime cracking away, his eyes sparkling. Bentheim caught his gaze and returned it.

It was like a dam breaking, as if a wave of fellowship that Till had never known before was lifting him up and carrying him forward. A feeling of being in the right, of belonging to a group and having the world at your feet. All at once, he knew how *everything*—Till didn't know what else to call it—how *everything*—the universe, space with all of its stars and planets—how it was all connected, and that he was a part of this, a fragment of the whole!

Until now, he had seen the world as something shrouded, hidden away behind a veil of insecurity, doubt, guilt, and self-blame. Now, tearing away the veil, he could finally see things as they really were. He no longer stood *apart* from the world. He was a *part* of it.

Suddenly, Till believed he could see, *actually see*, how all creation reached its peak in him, how it swelled within him, raced through space and time with him at the crest. And *wasn't* he at its very apex? Of existence, of space, of everything there was?! The vanguard of this immense being, the being he now understood the universe to be. Acting in full awareness of the rightness of it, of its inevitable unfolding, of the forward march of time!

It's true, Till thought. *What Bentheim says is right!* He didn't have to go on like this, wondering whether he should make up his mind this way or that. *The matter always decides itself, inside me!*

Bentheim turned away from the sheet of glass separating him from the two whimpering dogs and moved on down the passage that had led them to the kennel room, deeper into the city's underground.

Till followed. His mind was swimming with the thoughts and feelings that Max's father's words had liberated in him.

He had only just ceased to stand against the flow of things and begun to swim *with* it, and already it had embraced him. He knew it was an illusion, an error, a misjudgment to think that you had to reach a decision *yourself*. *That* was the mistake that caused all the evil, sorrow, and confusion in the world. All you had to do was listen inside—and it was already done . . . in you, with you, through you! Bentheim was right. And he was letting him be part of this wonderful and overwhelming insight: there was no such thing as freedom—happiness was realizing that!

Till felt as if he was flying along the tunnel with Max's father.

****

"Hello."

"Hello."

I've got the package here in my bag . . .

"May I?"

Could your eyes get any bigger?

"Hold on." *Don't worry, my hands are shaking a little, too . . . but hold completely still . . . such smoothness, so supple . . .*

"Is it too cold? I just want to see for a moment . . ."

Your eyes are laughing!

The little clasp—her skin feels like . . . I can't think clearly when I touch her!

The necklace fits, like it's made for her. I knew it. The green of the stones suits her . . .

"You're not saying anything."

What a lovely smile.

"May I . . . ?"

What do you think I'm going to say next?

Do you still have a moment or two?

"My car's here, in the parking lot . . ." *No need to be afraid. It's Galeries Lafayette. There are always lots of people coming and going, everyone knows that . . .*

". . . I've got a mirror in there. Can I show you the necklace in the mirror?"

Do you feel how it feels? How cool and heavy it lies against your naked skin?

"Yes? Come on then—this way—we'll be very quick . . . I just want you to see it on."

Tchak! The locks pop open.

She is a little afraid now; I can sense it.

"Your car's huge."

I like your voice! It sounds smoky, and when I hear it it's as if your hand is stroking my neck.

"Do you want to try driving it?"

I know we haven't talked about driving—but she knows if she drives, nothing can happen, right?

"Wait, I'll get the door for you."

There you go.

"Here's the key. I'll jump in the passenger side."

She's doing very well.

"So, what do you think?"

How she looks at herself in the rearview mirror!

"Hold on, I'll just climb over the back; then I can see you in the mirror, too."

Has she opened another button on her blouse?

Calm down! . . . Don't let her distract you!

"It's perfect on you—it must be the color of your eyes . . ."

Not with the hand! Show some restraint! Don't be so inept!

"Let's go for a little spin . . ."

Look, in the mirror; watch the way she reacts . . . she can't think of anything but the necklace . . .

Here . . . the feather, it must still be here—yes, like that—so carefully . . . with the tip, just with the soft tip . . . exactly . . . over her throat . . . look at her face—she likes it . . .

Yes, now you can—not with the hand!—with the feather. Can you feel the way it follows the curve? Let the tip wander down her neckline—not with the hand.

"I . . . I think I have to stop."

See the way her knees have opened just the tiniest fraction . . . that is happening completely automatically.

"Here, turn down this side street . . . there's always somewhere to park here . . ."

Stay calm. She knows what she wants to do now . . .

See?

God, she's doing everything right. She pulls over . . . leaves the key in the ignition . . . comes to you in the backseat . . . smiles . . .

She is attuned completely to you; now . . . all you need is to touch her gently on the side . . . she's already turning around, kneeling on the seat . . .

Slowly.

Push her skirt up . . .

Careful.

Look how small her hand is, her finger—the nail has no polish, but has been filed—how it wraps around the elastic at the side of her panties . . .

There. She looks at you; she knows how irresistible she is.

Now the elastic is slipping down over skin . . . she slides the delicate panties out under her skirt . . . over her thighs, the backs of her knees . . .

Don't touch!

She's waiting. See how she's waiting? She plays with her hair, leaves the panties dangling on her legs—she stretches out toward you—she is ready—

But . . .

You . . .

Are . . .

Not . . .

Allowed!

You must do the other!

40

TWELVE YEARS AGO

It hit Till like a bolt of lightning. His brother. Armin. How was it even possible for him to kill himself if one was not free to choose?

Till stumbled through the passageway. In places, the grit trickled down between the bricks of the tunnel wall. Bentheim strode ahead, his jacket billowing in the stale air.

Armin had killed himself. He had chosen that for himself. He had stood before that choice—life or death—and he had settled on death.

So what Bentheim had said couldn't be true.

The memory of his brother touched Till like an ice-cold hand laid on his shoulder.

He didn't want to lie to himself, not in a flush of enthusiasm that his brother would never have been part of. What kind of world was it that Bentheim conjured up if Armin never would have had the chance to be part of it? And what about Max? Till sensed instinctively that Max, too, could never belong. *And if Max couldn't, then neither would he!*

Till stopped in his tracks, as if suddenly jolted back to reality from a dangerous frenzy, and watched Bentheim moving ahead of him through the tunnel, hunched and hobbling. Till suddenly thought the man looked like nothing more than an oversized toad.

"Xavier!"

Xavier!

Like equals. They were one team—one being—weren't they?

Bentheim stopped and turned around, his eyes red from the dusty air, his tall frame sagging, his upright gait distorted into something creeping, buckled, animalistic.

"What was that, just back there?" Till's voice rang out clear and bright in the tunnel.

Bentheim's eyes narrowed a little.

Till beamed like he was still caught up in the euphoria of a few moments before. He could practically smell Bentheim's belief that he was still enraptured. He did not yet realize that Till—perhaps for the first time—could see the man as he truly was: ground down, eaten away, a man who had given up on himself.

"Back there," Till trilled excitedly. "That chamber just back there?"

"Let's keep going, boy," Bentheim murmured. The words crept out like roaches between his lips.

"No. You have to see it," Till blurted. He even moved toward Bentheim, took his hand—icy, moist, and sticky—and led him back. "It's really strange!" He pulled him along. It wasn't more than twenty steps back to the chamber Till had just noticed.

"Is it one of you?" He knew he was acting like the son Bentheim had always wished for, and that was exactly what he needed to control the man.

They walked back a few more steps. Till let go of Bentheim's hand, ran ahead the last few yards, and disappeared into the chamber he'd seen, not much more than a niche, really, with a door ajar. He heard Bentheim call out to him and pressed himself back against the dank, earthen wall. Seconds later, the silhouette of Max's father appeared in the dim light of the doorway.

"Till? Where are you?" Bentheim's voice filled the tiny room.

A question was grinding in Till's head: *How can you do this to him? What if you can still dissuade him from his path?* But even as he thought it, he was slipping past Bentheim, through the door, and out of the chamber. Till spun around and pushed the door closed as hard as he could. He felt it hit Bentheim's back hard and the impact knocked the man completely into the chamber. Till dropped the steel locking bar into its bracket, securing the door in place even as Bentheim's fist slammed against the wood on the other side.

"Till, my boy, what is it?" The voice of Max's father oozed out through the cracks. But Till was already running away.

The dirt flew up as the soles of his sneakers hit the ground. The clang of iron followed him, the groaning of the hinges, the creak of the door, the voice resounding, winding along the earthen passage.

"You can't leave me here!"

There was nothing clear about Till's thoughts anymore. This was something that was unfolding, *right?* He was not master of himself, *right?*

"Help me, Till!" It already sounded like little more than a distant, tiny roar, as if the sounds Till had heard under the hospital had been Bentheim's voice a thousand times over. A sea of voices calling Till, needing him, bursting from throats that could barely breathe, called by people he had locked away, whose only hope was him now, if they had any hope left at all. People who were staring death in the face and imploring him because only he could save them. People who knew they were at his mercy and were fueled by their fear of death.

The earth was once again the realm of the dead. The tunnel was a black hole that Bentheim's voice had brought to life, had given arms that could snatch at him, and Till ran faster and faster, falling against the gritty walls, picking himself up again. He needed to get out of there before it all crashed down on top of him, burying him a thousand yards beneath Berlin, with Bentheim's human, vulnerable, agonized voice in his ear, the voice of the man with whom, for a few minutes, he'd been flying—and who he was now leaving behind in a dusty grave to die.

****

"Hmm?" Till wasn't listening.

"Where were you?" Max propped his arms on the pool edge, pulled his right knee out of the water, and jumped out. It was one of the hottest afternoons of the year.

A voice was whispering in Till's ear. *He's pounding on the door . . . can't you hear it? That sound is his fists hitting the door.*

"Out," he said, and sat on a chair beside the pool.

Max rolled from the pool's patio stone onto the grass. It was so hot he didn't need to dry himself. He reached for the tray holding a carafe of ice water with chunks of lemon and poured some into a tall glass. The ice cubes clinked. "Want some?"

Till shook his head.

"What's up?" Max seemed to know that something had happened.

Till felt the fine layer of dust still clinging to his sweaty face.

He's calling for you, Till. It was such a tiny chamber.

He felt as if the heavy locking bar that he'd swung in front of the door was going right across his chest, robbing him of air.

"What's up? . . . Hey!" Max had stood up and moved a few steps closer to Till. The drops of water on Max's skin glittered in the sun.

Till blinked and squinted. *I locked your father down there.* That's what he had to say. But he couldn't get it out. *It was like he was . . . transformed . . . He was speaking all weird . . . he wasn't himself anymore, Max. You were right all along.* The words ricocheted through his head like bullets.

"Did something happen?" Max, his hands on his thighs, squatted next to Till's chair and looked at him intently.

We have to go down there; we have to get him out, the voice hammered in Till's brain, *but when we open it up, when he comes out, he . . . he'll kill us both.*

He'll rip me to pieces!

He'll transform into that mouth, those jaws, that throat I read about, a crater I'll disappear into.

"He can't get out." It was almost as if it wasn't Till who said the words.

"Who can't get out of where?" Max crinkled up his nose.

Till wavered. He couldn't leave Bentheim there. But he also couldn't let him out. *How could I let things get so out of control? What got into me . . . ?*

In his mind, he saw them in front of him: the two dogs, one gray and one shaggy.

"We have to let them out or they'll starve down there."

Max straightened up. "Jeez, man. Can you try talking in a way I can understand?" He wandered back to the edge of the pool. When he jumped in, the water splashed Till.

We have to let them out! We have to smash the glass or they'll kill them!

Till jumped up. Max swam across the pool underwater. When he surfaced, Till shouted out to him, repeating the words in his head: *"We have to let them out, Max! Now!"*

Max shook water from his hair. He laughed. "Sure thing, Till. 'We have to let them out.'" He pushed off from the edge and glided through the water back to Till, his eyes open wide and imitating Till's voice. "'We have to let them out. We have to let them out . . .'"

"You coming?" Till held out a towel to him.

"Where to?" Max made no move to get out of the water.

"The basement in the workshop. I got the hatch open."

It was just a few words. But it was as if a dense cloud had covered the sun. Max's hair no longer stood jauntily on end; it clung to his face, hung wet and stringy over his eyes. The cheerful tension drained from his body like air from a balloon.

TWELVE YEARS AGO

The heat above had not penetrated down to the tunnels that Till was leading Max through. But the stink of stagnant water, moldering rags, and rotting bodies had grown appreciably worse.

Till held his hand over his nose. The journey into the sewers was different this time: they were not alone. About half an hour after they had descended the iron ladder into the depths, they stumbled across a group of people who had pitched a few tents on a cement platform beside the drain. For a moment, Till wondered if he had lost his way, because he had not noticed the tents with Bentheim. But then he decided to just keep going. It was possible that they had been set up there since.

He's waiting for you, Till. He's lurking behind the door; he's crawled back into the shadows of the chamber. You won't see him at all. You'll think the chamber is empty and you'll want to turn back. That's when he'll jump on you with a tremendous leap, throw you to the ground, and crawl over you to the door. He'll take his son by the hand, slam the door on you, and they'll leave you behind in the chamber! You can still turn back—tell Max you just wanted to show him the canals, that you don't know what happened to his dad . . .

The canal dwellers looked right past them, their glassy eyes focused on some enigmatic point beyond Max and Till. Only at the last second, when the boys were practically past them, did a shudder pass through one of the men. His voice cracking, he called out to them, asked them what they were looking for down here, begging for a little change to help him out. At his feet, on a mat next to their tent, lay a strangely shaped old man and a harried-looking woman. They gave off a strange smell, warm and damp, and hardship filled their eyes. But they didn't seem as enraptured as Till had been at Bentheim's words. More than anything else, they seemed frightened. There was still some spark in their eyes, still some responsiveness in there.

He has nothing to eat in the chamber. Nothing to drink. It will be hot down there, and he will try to drink the water dripping from the walls. He will poison himself; it will just make his thirst a hundred or a thousand times worse. He will cry out for you, Till; he will scream; he will yell his voice bloody; he will be so furious, so desperate, that he will find you even if he has to creep into your dreams . . .

They walked on without taking any further notice of the tent dwellers.

"I was down here with your father," Till said to Max. "He brought me here. He talked about a kind of delusion and about a kind of illusion that you have to wipe away. And about a choice to make between truth and freedom—I didn't really understand what he was saying."

"So, where is he now?" was all Max said.

Maybe everything I experienced . . . maybe it was just a nightmare. Maybe he's not in that filthy crypt at all.

"I took off. I just wanted to get away and I didn't look back. But he wasn't behind me anymore. I didn't hear him anymore."

You slammed the door on him!

Max stopped, his eyes cast down. "He's down here somewhere?" He started to shake.

Yes. Because I had to protect you, me, Lisa . . . Till touched Max's arm gingerly. "I came down here with him. He wanted to show me something. It was about you, Max. I was supposed to help you . . . then . . ."

Max looked up.

"I lost him, Max." *Lost?* "Somewhere down here."

Max didn't seem to understand. His head moved, wobbling almost the way an old woman's head will.

Till was breathing flat and fast. "I can try to find the place I last saw him."

"You still know where that was?"

He'll get me. He'll kill me. And Max, too.

Till's chest grew tight. "The tunnels down here go on forever. It's a huge system. I'm not sure, but . . . your father . . . there's probably a reason he hasn't come home yet." *Because you locked him up. He's sitting down there, screaming, afraid . . . deathly afraid.* "I don't know if anyone would find him down here."

Max stared past Till, into the darkness. "*Where*, Till? Where should we be looking for him?"

Till took him by the arm. "He isn't your father anymore, Max. You said so yourself. He'd changed . . ."

"What's the matter with you, Till?" Max burst out. "WHAT HAVE YOU DONE WITH HIM?"

He's pounding against the door.

Till turned away, kept walking, heard Max's wispy breathing behind him. It was a long way. Maybe he wouldn't be able to find it again. Maybe they'd get themselves lost in this fucking labyrinth. Maybe they should have gone to Julia after all; maybe he'd done everything wrong . . .

It took nearly two hours for Till to reach the passage with the dogs. But when they were standing in front of the glass, the space behind it was empty. No scratching, no muffled barking, no damp noses pressed against the glass.

They've killed them. Both of them.

And there was no pounding against a door in the corridor back there, where it wound its way deeper into the underworld.

They moved down the tunnel. Till didn't look around anymore, didn't hesitate. He practically ran, as if magnetically drawn to the door behind which, he suspected, horror lay in wait.

When they finally reached it, the locking bar was still in place.

Till glanced at Max and his friend seemed to realize that they had reached their goal. Max jumped forward, threw the locking bar up, and jerked open the door.

On the other side lay a black pile. Max began gasping for air, even as Till brushed past him into the room. A biting stink surrounded him: sweat, tears, death.

It was Bentheim. The pile on the floor. His head was thrown back, the middle of his forehead staved in. He must have thrown himself at the door with the uncontrolled fury of a madman. Again and again, hammered at it, ran at it, ramming it with his head, until his voice was broken, his skull shattered.

His eyes were open. They stared beyond Till.

It wasn't your father, he wanted to shout at Max. But no sound escaped his lips.

He bent down, his mouth and nose buried in the crook of his arm to protect them from the biting smell that completely filled the chamber. He pulled up one of the tails of Bentheim's coat and threw it over Bentheim's face. When he looked up, he saw that Max was still standing outside in the passage. Till couldn't see his face. Just one arm, dangling limply. Max's whole body was shivering.

Till moved back outside. Max looked up. His face seemed to have changed.

"You locked him down here, Till?" His voice seemed deeper than usual, more raw.

"He wasn't your father anymore, Max. You should have seen him. I don't exactly what it was, but it had him in its power."

Max might as well have hit Till in the face when he screamed at him: "What do you know about anything?" he exploded. "My father took you in—and you . . . ?"

He broke off. An intense shudder ran through him. He abruptly turned and ran—away from Till, away from the door, away from the black pile lying on the other side.

When Till finally caught up with him, Max was sitting on a low wall. Behind the wall, a side channel fed water into the main tunnel. Max's legs hung down from the wall, his toes reaching the ground only when he stretched them. He had his elbows on his thighs and his hands dangled between his legs, his torso tipped slightly forward.

Till went around him, planted his hands on the wall, and jumped up, spinning as he did so to sit beside Max.

Max didn't move.

In Till's mind, he could still see the body with the caved-in skull. He couldn't erase the thought that Bentheim's eyes were looking at him, but before the image could really take form, it had already blurred again.

"Because of the dogs, Max," Till murmured. "I was supposed to choose one to die. I couldn't understand your dad at all."

A quick sideways glance at Max. His friend's hair was sticking out in all directions, his lower lip jutted forward just a fraction.

"I didn't want to join him. All I wanted was for it to stop, for him to leave me alone."

That's not how it was at all, something was hissing at Till, inside. *He didn't say anything else at all. You just continued on down the passage in silence. You were practically flying, remember? As if you'd gone through some sort of barrier made of air and found yourself in the place he'd been all along. But then you suddenly changed your mind. You didn't want all that anymore; you weren't sure anymore—and you lured him into a trap.*

"I was thinking about the ward." Till's voice was hoarse. "I didn't want to end up there. It wasn't your father, Max; you said so yourself. I haven't got a clue what it was, but it had . . . I felt it so strongly . . . somehow it had me in its power. For a moment, I was in its world, but then, just in time"—his voice was down to a whisper—"I fought back. I didn't want to be one of them, one of the aliens, one of the ones that changes, that aren't human anymore, that can morph themselves . . ."

He fell silent. Max said nothing.

They sat on the wall for a while, listening to the gurgling noises reaching them from deeper in the sewer. Far above, the day's heat must have reached its peak. Till felt heat emanating from the side channel, while cooler air flowed from the main passage.

"It didn't exist."

What? Till breathed out. Where were things supposed to go from here? Only slowly, like marmalade dripping in his mind, did he begin to realize this thing he had done truly meant. Bentheim. Till had . . . he had . . . he didn't dare even to think the word.

"I made it all up." Max's head sunk a little lower.

Till wasn't able to concentrate on what Max was saying beside him. He had . . . killed Bentheim. The word was hardly in his mind, and Till felt himself grow cold inside.

He had killed him.

Killed.

He came close to tumbling off the wall. Killed—the father of Max, sitting here next to him.

"I made it all up, you hear me?"

"I killed him," Till said—he was wide-eyed with fright as he looked at Max, as if he only now grasped the fact. "But he wasn't himself anymore, Max. That wasn't your father." The words were boiling out of Till now. "It really was an alien, a blob. It had taken on your dad's form. It looked like him, the same long arms and legs, the same suit, the same hair, but *it was not him.* If we cut him open"—the words flew from his mouth before he could even think about what he was saying—"we'd see it, that there's no flesh in there, no veins or bones. It would all be a green mass that can change its form." *Why green? That's ridiculous.* "They had hollowed him out; you said it yourself." Had Max really said that? *Yes.* Of course! He *had* said it!

Max took his arms out from between his legs, crossed them, and crushed them hard against his skinny body. He was shivering, his eyes squeezed shut.

"You're not listening to me," Till heard Max say.

HE isn't listening to me, hissed the voice in Till's head.

"You said it yourself, Max. I . . . it's not my fault. I had to do it, he . . . I couldn't be sure; he could have morphed anytime, couldn't he? You remember those waves under his skin? The alien could've suddenly ripped out of him, right here in the sewers. I didn't know what would happen. I mean I really thought he looked like a giant insect scurrying through the drains. He messed up my head. I didn't know if we were going up again or deeper and deeper down. I was scared; I couldn't trust him. He wasn't walking anymore; it was more like a high-speed crawl, or like scuttling or scrabbling, and I was scared that he'd get me with a stinger and poison me, that I wouldn't ever come back again and wouldn't even figure how much I'd changed."

Till had forgotten to breathe. He stopped talking, gulped for air.

"I made it up," Max mumbled, curled up as he was, his chin pressed to his chest, his arms crossed.

"WHAT? What did you make up?" Till screamed at him. *What had he made up?* The question cracked in his shaken mind like a whip. *What the . . . why doesn't he say something?!*

"The ward, man. The ward in the hospital."

Till's head was booming: *He made it up—but his father is dead. And I'm the one who killed him.*

At the same time, the waves of panic—*it really happened. I didn't dream it—it's not a game—it won't ever go away again—it'll always be there—it was me who slammed the door*—seemed to ebb, subside, evaporate, because another tide took hold of his consciousness. At first, he only sensed the power of it—and then realized what it was whispering to him: *He made it up.*

Till clawed his hands into the low wall left and right of his legs. He couldn't bring himself to look at Max. Instead, he looked straight ahead into the tunnel. "You made it up."

He sensed Max nodding beside him.

He made it up.

"The ward isn't there."

"I . . . Till, I couldn't stand it anymore. My father . . . he was practically killing me . . . I needed your help."

Till vaguely sensed that Max had turned toward him. "I wanted to tell you, but then it was already too late. And I was feeling really, really sick in the hospital. I thought my father . . . that he couldn't be like that, that . . . that something must've happened to him. I nearly believed it."

A yawning, black emptiness was opening up inside Till.

"I needed your help. I wanted someone to stand by me, against him. He would have squashed me, and I couldn't stand it. I . . . I tried everything, but . . . he wouldn't stop. He rolled right over me, or right through me. He didn't give a shit what became of *me* . . .

all he saw was himself and the kid he wanted for a son . . . I felt his shoes in my guts and didn't want to die . . . so I came up with the story about the ward. Could it really have been like that? That he was how he was because he wasn't himself anymore? Because they'd *replaced* him?"

"But that's not how it was." Till's voice was flat.

Max wheezed. "Of course not." His voice was tenuous, raspy. "Of course not. Because it isn't really like that. That never really happens."

But I really killed him.

"I never would've believed you'd go so far."

What have I done?

"I didn't want this."

Now it's too late.

Till got down from the wall. He felt numb. He had locked Bentheim—Max's *dad*—in that stinking hole back there.

Max was still sitting on the wall. "The deadline he gave me? At the end of summer vacation I had to decide what I wanted to do with my life? I didn't have a clue what I was supposed to say. But he kept coming back to it. And you know what would have happened?"

Till felt his knees trembling.

"Whatever I said to him, he would have sent me to a special school for it. But I didn't want to go to another school, Till. No way. Not now that you're going to be in my class. He would have split us up, Till, and I didn't want that. I wanted to go to *my* school with *you*. That's why I made up the ward in the hospital. How they cut open the people down there, how it's like a nightmare that's reaching out for you. Because I didn't want them to separate us."

TODAY

"It's impossible, sorry. He can't see you right now."

Ms. Bastian smiles. Butz always got on well with her. "Who's in there with him?" he asks, returning her smile.

Ms. Bastian, the chief of police's secretary, leans forward, visibly proud of the caliber of person her boss is meeting. "The mayor." She leans back to study the effect of this news on Butz's face. "That's why I'm still here."

"Wow." Butz puffs out his stubbly cheeks appreciatively. He thinks it over: *This could take a while. Should I sit here with Ms. Bastian and wait until the Chief has time?* In any case, Fehrenberg's desk and computer, both completely cleaned out, are something that he has to—wants to—report immediately. But languishing in the anteroom? He nods to Ms. Bastian. "Okay. I'll come back in a few minutes." He turns to go.

"Say hi to your girlfriend for me!" clucks Ms. Bastian.

Butz stops. "Has her application been approved, then?" Claire had been interested in being embedded with the on-call crime response unit for a few weeks as a photographer to take pictures for her Berlin book. Butz had submitted the application that Claire had prepared.

"Yes, yes, the application has gone through." Ms. Bastian pushes her hair into place with her right hand and looks at him, almost a little mockingly. "And she has even been in to pick it up. Didn't she tell you?"

Really? Butz nods briefly. No, she didn't. But it doesn't matter. The main thing is that Claire can take her pictures.

"I saw her just the other day," Ms. Bastian continues, and Butz notices the way her eyes light up. "Your wife—" She stops, interrupting herself. "Your girlfriend, I mean . . . it's great the way she does that."

"Does what?"

"Takes those pictures. I saw her at a boxing match, you know? She just went and climbed into the ring. You could see her jumping around among the men, all two heads taller than she is. But she wasn't about to let that stop her."

At a boxing match. Butz feels like a computer dredging up information from the depths of his hard drive.

Hadn't Claire gotten the tickets for the boxing match from Henning?

"So, you were there, too?" He nods somewhat absently.

Ms. Bastian's chest swells with the excitement of the memory. "The boss gave me two tickets." Her fingernails clack at the keyboard. "Here!" She turns the monitor a little so that Butz can see it from the other side of the desk. "*I took a few photos of my own!*"

The monitor goes black, and a few seconds later the boxing stadium appears, filling the screen. The seats are packed, and in the distance he can see the ring, two figures inside it, frozen in pose.

"Then I zoomed in," Butz hears Ms. Bastian say. "Here, you see? That's her."

Butz recognizes the back of her head, her dark-blonde hair flowing over her back. Her head is pulled down between her shoulders, her arms up, her body crouched like a tiger ready to pounce.

"Isn't she fantastic?"

Yes, she is, it occurs to Butz—as new slideshow images fade in over the old. Now he sees Claire jump onto an empty chair, duck between the ropes, and climb into the ring. Her face is glowing with excitement, fervid and alive, radiating the certainty that she was right where she wanted to be, doing exactly what she wanted to do.

"Here, look," explained Ms. Bastian beside him. "That's him. A great fighter. You should have been there . . . this Russian? He beat him to a pulp . . ."

Butz hears Ms. Bastian sigh—then stares at the monitor, where an image of a boxer fills the screen. His gloved hands are raised in triumph, his torso and neck muscles bulging. He is surrounded by his people, all in the delirium of victory.

"Barkar. Frederik Barkar." Ms. Bastian's hand points at the man's bare chest. The next photo is already fading in on the monitor: Claire, with her little Leica trained on the boxer from an angle behind him.

Butz automatically taps the spacebar on Ms. Bastian's keyboard. The slideshow freezes.

"Barkar, Barkar, Barkar!" He can almost hear the crowd in the stadium calling out the man's name—and at the same time, he realizes he has seen this face somewhere else.

At his house.

He swallows.

Delivering the drinks . . . the guy hauling the crates! Barkar came to their place to *deliver drinks?*

Butz's throat suddenly feels very dry. The man disappeared back into the pantry with Claire, he remembers. *Just a few minutes before she was standing naked and hot in front of me in our study . . . before I lifted her bathrobe over her ass and she looked so tempting I could hardly stop myself.*

She was alone back there with Barkar. Ten minutes. Fifteen maybe. What had she been doing with him just before she took a shower? What?

What?

43

TODAY

"Yo!"

Till hears it, but he can't turn his head. He's thinking, *Where did they get all the rats?*

"ANSCHÜTZ!"

He sees the animals' pinhead eyes as they tumble across the cement; he feels the softness of their fur as it presses against his pants; he feels the twitching of their bodies crushed between his legs.

The room is going to fill up with them, right up to the ceiling . . . it won't stop, ever, and the wall opposite will start to move in, and they'll squash us to death, compress us into a single block of meat . . .

Their squeaking fills the air and they are already brushing against his fingers—and when he lifts his arms up to free his hands, the teeming mass begins to swirl up his sides and surge across his stomach.

Till's head jerks and hits the wall behind him. The right side of his face burns. Then he sees him: the man with his mouth sliced wide has slapped Till across the face.

"Get it together and *come on!*" the guy orders him—dragging at Till's arm, hauling him free, shoveling the seething, squealing mass of animals aside—fighting his way forward to the door that he must have come in by: the same door through which Felix and the other dark figures must have left the room just a few minutes before.

The door is cracked open, but the man can't open it any wider. Too many rats are pressing against it; they are already tumbling, rolling, scrabbling, and screeching through the gap and into the corridor beyond the door.

Till feels the bodies of the animals writhing underfoot, edges his legs forward through the living wave, wading forward, using his hands to push through the swell of bodies swirling around him—and pushes through the cracked door.

"Fucking vermin!" The other man is also through, and he tries to ram the door closed behind him. The squeaking swells to a desperate, high-pitched scream, a death chorus, and Till thinks he can hear in it the terror of the rats: their misery at the devastation caused them by the man slamming the door so ruthlessly in their midst. The muck, the blood, the filth foams from beneath the steel edge of the door.

"Help me!" the man shouts to Till. Till grabs for the door handle, tearing at the door, doing his best to get it closed, hauling against the soft resistance blocking it, against the bodies of the rats that have had the bad luck to be in the gap, and fighting the repugnance and nausea rising in him.

When it clicks shut and the latch finally drives home, Till can still hear them scratching at the steel door with their claws, almost thinks he can hear the drumming of the tiny hearts in the bodies crushed against it.

"What . . . what . . . ?" Till wheezes. His lungs burn as he sinks back against the wall.

The man's extended mouth pulls wide. "Felix needs you. You know that."

"Did Felix know . . . about the rats . . .?"

The man turns away without another word and heads down the corridor.

"Wait!" Till catches up with him and they walk side by side.

"Where is Felix? I . . . I need to speak with him . . ."

"Don't sweat it. He'll be in touch soon enough. I'm supposed to take you to her first."

"To who?"

No answer.

Till ponders. *Who?*

They move on in silence. The man glances over at him, bares his gums. Almost like he's asking Till, *You want to touch?* At the corner of his mouth, where the flesh has been sliced back? And suddenly, he says:

"To Lisa. I'm supposed to take you to Lisa."

44

TWELVE YEARS AGO

For Lisa, the last two weeks of summer vacation had flown by. On Monday she'd be going back to school, but she wasn't thinking about that. In the last fourteen days, her world had turned upside down, had slipped, skidded, tumbled off the rails. Her father had never reappeared. For fourteen days there was no sign of him. It had been a day like any other. Till had been with them only a few weeks. Her father had said he would see them later . . . and she hadn't seen him since.

Lisa spent whole afternoons on her bed, lying on her stomach, her face turned to one side, watching the door. She had expected to cry, but nothing happened. She heard her mother crying, heard Max and Till talking, heard Rebecca and Jenna at work. But her father—his heavy tread on the stairs, his sonorous voice, his laugh—was missing. He hadn't come through her door or bent down to pick her up in his arms. There was no one fighting with Max; there was no one who her mother was happy to see come home . . . all there was, was a gap in the family that would never again—Lisa was certain—be filled. Her world had fallen apart.

If you looked at the outside, everything seemed the same. They still lived in the house, the cars were still parked in the drive, Rebecca and Jenna still came and went. Lisa's mother had changed, but you could see it only if you looked closely. She seemed to have aged a little, to have grown thinner, like a butterfly that has lost some of the dust that coats its wings. The shine of her hair seemed to have dulled, and someone seemed to have exchanged the 100-watt bulbs in her eyes for 60-watt versions.

Otherwise, things hadn't changed at all. Lisa would go back to school on Monday. Her mother had drummed into her what she should say if anyone asked: *Mom said I shouldn't talk about it.* Because no one knew the truth. Was her father dead? Had he abandoned them?

A few days earlier, Lisa had been eavesdropping at a door and heard her mother say to someone on the telephone that Xavier had seemed a little strange in the weeks leading up to his disappearance. Perhaps a bit more nervous, true, but otherwise? If there had been something else, Lisa would have seen it. But she hadn't noticed a thing.

The police had been there. They had searched the guesthouse in the garden and discovered a hatch in the basement leading directly to the sewer system. Her mother hadn't known anything about it, but the officers assured her that, in Berlin, it was nothing unusual.

The first few days had been hell. Lisa's mother hadn't slept at all and a strained atmosphere hung over the whole house. Since then, that tension—which at the start had felt like it might explode—had transformed into a grim, gritty persistence, and Lisa knew it would make all of them sick. But she also knew that they couldn't just shut it off, not easily.

For a while, she had whispered to herself, trying to speak to her father internally, in some vague hope that he would hear her and come home. She promised to work on Max and keep him from arguing so much with her father. The family would do anything to please him, if only he would return. She would make an effort; she would put in so much more effort than she had before. "Please, Dad. Please come back."

But it all came to nothing. It went on being quiet in the house, quieter with each day that passed. He was gone. He didn't call; he didn't write a postcard, didn't send a message. He was simply gone.

Lisa had no idea what had happened. She couldn't imagine that her father had simply forgotten her. She was certain that something had happened that made it impossible for him to contact them. He had to know they were worried. He wouldn't just leave them like that. Perhaps somebody had kidnapped him; perhaps he was lying in some cellar, hands and feet tied with a gag in his mouth. But then she rejected all these notions again. Who would kidnap him? And why?

The days passed, no one contacted them, and Lisa lay on her bed, unable to cry. Once, she had slipped into her parents' bedroom and opened the closet. That's where all the blue shirts were hung, the ones that her father always wore. She had taken one of them out, laid it out on the bed, and buried her face in its folds. It had smelled like washing powder, and for a short while Lisa felt a little closer to her father. But then she didn't know what else to do but carefully gather up the shirt and hang it back up.

✳✳✳✳

Summer's spine had broken. The murderous heat, 100, 102 degrees, was over. The rest of the year would be a slow descent into a Berlin winter, but for now it was still warm enough to swim in the pool.

Lisa pushed off from the edge of the pool and swam a length in a slow crawl. Someone had come to visit her mother about an hour before, and Max and Till were out somewhere riding bikes. Lisa dived down at the end of the lap, rolled over, and pushed powerfully off the wall with her feet, heading back up the pool. The water eddied behind her ears, under her arms, at the back of her neck, where she had tied her hair into a knot. She resurfaced, laid her head on one side, took a deep breath, turned her face into the water again, felt herself sliding through it rapidly.

But something was bothering her.

She turned and was about to swim the rest of the lap on her back when she noticed that someone had appeared at the side of the pool. A figure stepping calmly toward the far side of the pool, somehow liquefied by the drops of water still draining from her eyes. Lisa abruptly let her body sink into a vertical float and wiped the water and a few loose hairs from her eyes.

"Not too cold?" she heard the person say. She reached a hand toward the side of the pool.

"No." *Who is that?* "It's still okay."

She turned her head toward the man, who had come to a stop at the opposite side of the pool. He was wearing a fine, light-colored suit that fit as if specially tailored for him. He was substantially shorter than her father and his face seemed strangely lively, clearly defined, and delicate.

He squatted at the edge of the pool and dipped a hand in the water. "Hmm," Lisa heard him say. "Nice." He smiled at her.

He's wearing a ring, she thought. *But not one like Dad wears. It's got a stone in it.*

"You're Felix von Quitzow," she said. "You visited my mother."

Quitzow laughed. "That's right."

"Where is she? My mother."

"She still has to look through some papers I brought over."

"And you're waiting till she's done."

He nodded, withdrew a white handkerchief from his pants pocket, and wiped his hand with it, without standing up. "I don't think we've met before, have we, Lisa?"

He looked at his hand as he dried it.

"No, I think you're right." She held on to the side of the pool, treading water with her feet. Lisa felt awkward just hanging in the pool, but she wasn't sure what to do. Keep swimming? Get out of the pool? Talk with the man?

"I got to know your father over the last few months, Lisa," he said, and his words cut through her like white-hot wire. "He always talked about you, you and Max."

"Really?" She stared at the man, a knot in her throat. Did he know something?

"I can't say how sorry I am about what's happened." He pushed the handkerchief into his pocket again and looked over to her. His forearms rested on his knees, his hands dangling.

Do you think he'll come back? Lisa wanted to ask but couldn't find the nerve. "What did he tell you?" she asked instead.

"Nothing in particular . . ." Quitzow's face showed something like pain. "He always wanted to introduce his children to me, but then it never happened."

Lisa suddenly felt that the water was, indeed, a little too cold. She felt her skin tingle and goose bumps spread over her skin.

"What kind of papers does my mother have to look through?"

The man smiled, and for a second, she had the feeling that her question had taken him by surprise.

"Deadly boring stuff," he answered, standing up. "It's to do with the book that your father was working on last . . . ," he said, then hesitated. ". . . was working on when he disappeared." The smile was still on his face, but it seemed strained now.

Now! Lisa thought, and with three focused strokes she covered the last part of the pool and made it to the ladder. She reached for the round handrail, pulled herself up, and felt the water draining down her body. With one step, she was standing by the patio chair where she had dropped her towel.

"Quickly now," she heard Quitzow call to her with a hint of mocking in his voice. Then she wrapped the towel around her, buried her head in it, and rubbed her hair. The scratch of the towel on her ears sealed off all outside noise. She pressed the towel to her forehead and passed it over her head, sweeping it back from her eyes.

He was standing just a few steps away!

Lisa gasped slightly and heard her own quickened breath.

"School starts again tomorrow, doesn't it?" Quitzow leaned on the table standing beside the beach chair. She saw that the white shirt, the red tie, the beige suit were tailored from the finest material. A hint of a shadow on his chin and jaw, his thick, black hair looking at once unkempt and sculptured.

She nodded and went back to drying herself.

"You should come visit us at our offices," he went on. "We're the ones who make your father's books famous, you know."

I've never read a single one of his books, she thought—but she didn't feel any need to tell him that.

"I'd be very happy to show you the archive we've built up there," Quitzow said. "No library, no university in the world has as much of Xavier Bentheim's work as we do."

Lisa laid the towel around her shoulders and held it together in front with one hand.

"I have to go in," she said.

Quitzow smiled. "Of course."

She turned away. It was not easy for her to turn her back to him, but she had no other choice: he made no move to leave his place by the table.

To avoid hurting her feet on the gravel path, she tiptoed and, more hopping than walking, made her way toward the house.

"Oh, Lisa?" she heard him say behind her. She stopped and looked back.

He was still leaning on the table, a good-looking man—and he looked her straight in the eye. "If there's anything I can do for you, call me, won't you? I gave your mother my number. A pretty girl like you—I always look forward to that—it gets me all unsettled. Can you imagine that?"

Excuse me?

"Okay," she heard herself call back, and then she hobbled on toward the house. *"Unsettled"? What does he mean by "unsettled"?* Lisa felt the man's unabashed gaze following her. When she finally disappeared behind the door and into the house, where he could no longer see her, it felt like she'd moved into the shade, out of the blazing sun.

But the impression remained. The impression not only that Quitzow had spoken to her as nobody ever had before but also that he had looked at her as no man ever had before.

45

"What are you trying to tell me?" Lisa raised her eyebrows slightly and looked piercingly at Till. They were each carrying a paper bag containing bread rolls. They'd been to the bakery on this final Sunday morning before the start of school.

"I've been thinking about him a lot lately," Till replied. It was his last chance. He had to get it over with. He couldn't keep it bottled up inside. "About your father, I mean."

Lisa flinched, though it was barely perceptible. As if she had pulled her head down a little, as if she squeezed the bag of rolls against her body a little harder.

Flap, flap, flap, flap . . .

She was wearing a summer dress and her flip-flops smacked on the cobblestones. She had tied her hair back into a ponytail that bobbed with every step.

"I really liked him . . ."

Till suddenly jumped in alarm. Lisa had let out a little cry. She must have squeezed the paper bag too tightly: the paper had torn apart and she was trying to stop the rolls from falling out. But there were too many and they tumbled onto the ground.

Momentarily shocked, Till looked at Lisa's face and saw that she was fighting back tears. Then, in a fury, she stretched out her arms and let the remaining rolls fall on the ground as well. Lisa's shoulders shrugged high and she stood there as if she had suddenly forgotten how to walk.

Till kneeled, laid his bag carefully on the sidewalk, and began to gather up the fallen rolls.

"And where are we supposed to put them?" said Lisa, looking at him, her eyes at once angry and sad. But Till also thought he saw a flash of gratitude in there, gratitude because he was simply doing the sensible thing: picking up the bread.

Without hesitation, he pulled off his freshly washed T-shirt and loaded the rolls into it. Then he pulled the corners of the shirt together, stood up, and handed her the bundle.

"Thanks."

Till bent down and grabbed his own bag again. When he straightened up, she was already a few steps ahead.

"Lisa!" He ran to her, walked beside her. *You have to tell her!*

"I always liked your father, Lisa. I don't know why he was against Max so much . . ."

"He was not against Max!"

Till drew a quick breath. Lisa's vehemence caught him by surprise.

"Max is a dreamer, a lunatic," she blurted. "You haven't known him very long, Till. But Max is the kind of boy who just goes on running straight ahead. Once he's got something in his head, he doesn't know where to stop. There's no holding him back, and he doesn't care at all what happens to the others. He just keeps going his way—even if everything gets broken along the way. He has no sense of moderation, no shades of gray. Only one thing matters to him, and that's *him*. That's why he was always getting into fights with my father. Because Dad tried to protect him from the worst. He was worried about him."

She stopped, and her burning eyes swept Till's face. "I don't know what will become of Max now that my father is gone. Do you want to keep him in check? Do you want to take care of him? I can't. He doesn't listen to me, when it really comes down to it, and he doesn't listen to Mom, either. No one will be able to hold him back. And you know what the worst part is?"

Till shook his head.

"That the way he's going, he'll wreck himself," she spat, and Till saw the tears flowing unhindered over her cheeks.

"I . . . I'll try to stay by him," Till stammered. "I like Max; he's my friend, you know . . ."

How do you think you're going to help when they take you away? When they know what you've done . . . they won't let you stay in the family . . .

"But I don't want to talk about Max, Lisa. I want to tell you something else, I . . ." He struggled for air. "It's about your father, Lisa, not Max . . ."

"No!" she screamed at him. "NO! What do you want to tell me, Till? What do you *have* to tell me?" Her eyes were aflame, red from crying, and the hairs that had worked loose from her ponytail clung to her face. "*What?!*"

Till was at a loss for words. How was he supposed to tell her what was weighing so heavily on his heart? That *he* was the one, that *he* had slammed the door! He loved her. He loved her eyes, her mouth, her ears. He loved the way she walked, loved her when she cried, loved her voice, and loved what she had to say. He loved Lisa and now he was supposed to tell her that *he had killed her father*?

Then Lisa ran. Her flip-flops were left behind on the sidewalk, and she held his T-shirt with the bread rolls pressed to her chest. She ran down the street, which swept in a broad arc to the cul-de-sac where the Bentheims' villa was.

Till followed her with his eyes, saw her reappear between the neighbors' houses, turn into the cul-de-sac, and finally slow to a walk again.

He narrowed his eyes to slits.

In the last few days, a man who had introduced himself in passing as Felix and several of his employees had been going in and out of the Bentheim house, emptying out Bentheim's workroom in the guesthouse and talking for hours with Julia in the living room.

Now two of them—men with faces so expressionless that Till could never really remember them—were approaching Lisa on the street just outside the Bentheim property.

Till saw one of them take the T-shirt full of rolls from Lisa, while the other leaned down to her. Till thought he could see Lisa gasping for breath, then hesitating before abruptly turning around and pointing back down the street in the direction she'd come.

Till whipped his head around, following the way Lisa's gaze turned left and right, past the neighbors' houses. Then he turned back—and their eyes met.

The next moment, all he saw was the pavement flying by.

And Till was running.

Back down the street, head down, the bag of rolls tossed aside. His feet felt like they were barely even touching the ground.

Till didn't know if they were behind him, but he didn't dare to look back. Should he slip into one of the gardens he was running past and hide behind a hedge? What if they saw him there?

He ran. Crossing the street, he ran and ran until he reached the train station and ducked into the pedestrian shortcut under the railway embankment, his steps echoing through the underpass.

He could only hear his own steps, so they weren't close yet. He turned around and saw the end of the tunnel, a hundred feet behind him, as a cone of light; the cars, the trees, the street were washed out in the glaring sunlight like an overexposed photograph.

There they were. They were not running as fast as they could, but were still moving rapidly toward the underpass.

As quietly as possible, Till hurried deeper into the tunnel. A recess, an electrical cabinet! Just then he heard the footsteps of the men ringing behind him. With a jump he was on top of the cabinet, and then he slipped into the narrow gap between the back of the box and the rear wall. The space was just big enough for Till's slim body.

His pursuers' steps drummed nearer. Till squeezed into his hiding spot. A rushing noise filled his head . . . he could feel the cool metal of the electrical cabinet against his stomach, the soft vibrations of the circuits inside. And at his back, the grainy surface of the wall.

The steps paused.

Had they discovered him?

Till held his breath. And shuddered.

He could hear the two men speaking to each other quietly, but . . .

Their voices . . . *what was that?*

Hissing and gurgling. A sound that nearly made Till gag. It sounded like the rattle of dying insects.

Can they smell me? he wondered—and then he caught sight of them through the gap between the cabinet and the wall.

They were staring down the underpass; they had not yet noticed him.

Till was able to examine their heads from the side. They weren't wearing any masks that might cover their insect parts . . . but still . . . what came out of their mouths was a *hiss!*

Or was he just hearing the pumping of blood in his arteries, the suppressed gasp that wanted to escape his lungs at any cost?

And then the two men were past his hiding spot. Till heard their steps moving away. They had not smelled him.

Sweat was pouring over his naked torso. He waited until their steps had died away completely, and then he crept out from behind the cabinet.

****

"What if it's true after all?"

"I made it up, Till! How many times do I have to say it?" Annoyed, Max threw the stapler into his school bag and stood up. He had spread all of his school supplies across the floor and was trying to put it in some sort of order before school the next morning.

"Maybe I'm wrong about the voices of those two in the underpass," Till replied. "But still . . . what do they want in the house? What are they doing here?"

He had run back to the villa and up to Max's room without anyone seeing him.

Max let himself fall onto the bed. "They're picking up Dad's stuff. His manuscripts, notebooks, computer. Mom said that Felix explained it to her."

"Felix!" Till pulled his feet up onto the chair he was sitting on at the desk. "Who is that? Have you ever talked to him?"

"He said hello once."

"I don't trust him." Till tried to read the look on Max's face.

But Max didn't seem interested in Till's musings. "Let's just forget the whole thing as fast as possible," he mumbled. "In any case, it's too late to change anything."

Till shook his head. Had they ever been able to? "What if it isn't over? What if they got your dad first and now they want to keep going? You said yourself that . . ."

"Don't you get it yet?!" Now Max was genuinely furious. "I put that into your head because I thought you could help me."

"But it could still be true *anyway*!" Till had raised his voice as well. "Even if you just made up all that stuff about the hospital ward, Max! You must have come up with it for a reason! Okay, great, maybe the ward doesn't really exist. But all the other stuff? That your dad had changed? The woman we saw in the basement out there? The parrots? What he said to me when he showed me the two dogs?"

"Do you honestly believe he'd been taken over by aliens?" Max stared at Till in disbelief. "Sheesh, Till, settle down. You locked him in—and you shouldn't have done that! Don't try to talk your way out of it now by sticking to something that's just total crap. Wake up, Till. Wake. Up!"

He turned away stubbornly and refocused on his school things.

Till felt his courage deserting him. He wouldn't be able to count on Max. Was it true, what Max said? Was he really just making some desperate attempt to find an excuse for what he did? Of course, it was absurd to think that Bentheim . . . that Felix . . . that something could be coming. But there was something Till was still unable to pinpoint . . . something that had this family in its power, that was happening undetected, that explained everything that had happened around him . . .

But if he was just imagining all these strange things, then he had no choice: he had to own up to what he had done to Bentheim. The unrelenting logic of it struck him even as he thought about it. His forehead broke out in a cool sweat, and he stood up from the chair. He would talk to Julia. He would tell her what had happened down in the sewers. He would bring it to an end.

Up in his room, Till pulled on a fresh T-shirt. Then he ran downstairs. He assumed that Max's mother was in the garden and he didn't want to wait any longer.

When he entered the hallway on the ground floor, he saw Lisa standing out on the terrace with Felix von Quitzow. Lisa had her head leaned back slightly and was looking up at him.

Till stopped at the foot of the stairs and pressed himself to the wall, out of their line of sight. Till couldn't hear what they were discussing, and he couldn't see Felix's face, but he could see Lisa's. It seemed that Lisa didn't know which way to look. As if she wasn't sure what she was supposed to think and at the same time was fascinated by what she was feeling. As if she knew she was no match for the man before her but simultaneously enjoyed the warm shiver of excitement that his superiority triggered in her. As if she was enjoying the softness of a lion's mane, never forgetting that the lion could rip her apart any second. As if she knew that the pleasure of stroking the fur could only ever come at the risk of being torn apart.

Till saw her pull away slightly . . . had Felix reached a hand out to her? He saw how she inclined her head gracefully, moved past the man, and entered the living room, while Felix remained in front of the window and pushed his hands into the pockets of his pants. Till stepped out of his niche so that Lisa would see him. *What did you tell those two men?* he wanted to ask her, but he never got the words out because as soon as she saw him, she laughed.

"Till! Do you still want to say something to me?"

The sound of her voice disconcerted him.

"Do you know where your mother is?" he answered quietly, trying to push the picture of Felix and her out of his mind.

"Do you want to tell *her* now?" Lisa lowered her eyelids a fraction, and her eyes flashed.

Till hesitated. "Lisa, I . . . I—"

"What?" she interrupted, her voice just slightly shrill. "Is something on your mind, little Tilly?"

It hit him like a slap in the face. What was up with her? Was she ridiculing him?

"You can tell me everything." She reached her arms in the air as if she wanted to stretch, and then she lowered her voice to a whisper, which only reinforced Till's impression that she was laughing at him. "I won't tell a soul."

Instinctively, he reached out for her arms—he couldn't stand it when she stood in front of him like that—and pulled them back down, as if he wanted to transform her back into the Lisa that he knew. "What's wrong with you?"

"Ouch." She jerked her arms free of his grip, took a step back. But the derision was still there, in her eyes. "What do you want?"

"Lisa, I have to talk to you."

"With who, now? With me or Mom?" There it was again: that slightly shrill voice that Till had just heard for the first time.

"Lisa, listen. I know I can trust you. You were the first one I told that I'd been in Brakenfelde . . ."

She rolled her eyes. What had got into her? She was acting totally weird!

"Listen," he snarled at her—but it seemed impossible to get through this mask she had pulled on.

"Keep your stories to yourself," she hissed, and made a move to go past him.

"It's important. It can't go on like this!"

"Tell my mother. That's what you wanted to do in the first place!" she spat back over her shoulder. But the anger and disappointment was twisting in Till's gut. Without thinking, he grabbed her by the shoulder, jerked her around, and yelled at her: "What the hell is *up* with you? Is Felix putting weird shit in your head?"

It had slipped out of him. He had never spoken to her like that before—and its effect was not lost. Disgust flashed across Lisa's face. But for Till, it was if he spotted a crack in the facade she'd put on, as if, just for a moment, the Lisa he knew had appeared underneath.

"Sorry, Lisa. I didn't mean to yell at you, but . . . what's going on with you?"

She looked him in the eye. He drank in the sight of her, felt like he was almost losing himself in her . . . but it lasted only a moment, and then a virtually invisible membrane seemed to slide in place over her pupils and extinguish the shine of her eyes. As if the Lisa he had always trusted, with whom he shared a special bond, had escaped from the body of the girl in front of him in the space of a single breath and left no more than her shell before him. The shell of an eleven-year-old girl who, in the hour between now and when he had seen her last, had turned into something else.

He stared at her in dismay, but her eyes didn't move from his. She seemed to be completely aware of the effect she was having, to know the magnetic attraction she held for him better than she ever had before. The attraction she held for him seemed, in fact, to have inexplicably increased now that she was only outwardly the Lisa he knew. He felt as though it were anchored in the middle of his gut, as if he had always carried it inside him but until now had never sensed its presence. He felt a new sensation, a desire to take her in his arms, to wrap himself around her body, to explore the softness of her lips, which now slowly parted, right before his eyes.

For a moment, it was as if time stood still. Then Till saw her hand moving closer to his face, her fingers unfurling. Till felt her thumb touch his lips, brushing across them, but her eyes stayed dull, as if switched off, hard, blue, and distanced, as if she wasn't there with him in her head. As if she was calculating her effect on him instead, registering how the fire she had kindled in him was melting him, remolding him into someone who would never again be able to forget her.

Till could not help it. He took her hand, turned it up, and buried his mouth in the palm, no longer able to hold himself back, both confused and excited by the need to touch her.

But she was not about to let him.

"Go, Till. Run along. Didn't you want to find my mother and tell her something?" he heard her coo, and realized only then that he had closed his eyes.

She pulled her hand away. It felt as if she were ripping the bones out of his body. In the same moment, Lisa spun away from him and swept up the steps to the floor above.

Till remained behind. Stirred, confused, dazed. The feel of the palm of her hand still burned on his lips, and he tried as hard as he could, as long as he could, to hold on to the barely perceptible scent of her. But he felt it vanish, felt her slipping inexorably away.

He could not tell her mother. It would mean he could no longer stay here. And the thought of having to leave this house was unbearable. Not because he did not want to go back to Brakenfelde—or whichever home they'd stick him in—and not because he couldn't leave Max by himself. But because now he had to watch out for Lisa, too.

First, they had taken over Bentheim, and now Lisa was the one who had changed—practically right before his eyes. He could not let them take her. *That* was why he could not own up to what had happened to Bentheim. He had to be there for Lisa.

Till raised his head and looked out the window to the garden. He would be there for her, regardless of how much she changed.

****

50!! Not 100, not 200, not 80, not 60.

50.

If you go faster, something will happen.

BUT I HAVE TO . . . get onto the autobahn. I have to get onto the autobahn!

Go right, here.

50. You're not allowed to drive any faster than that.

Here's where it goes down. The on-ramp is up ahead.

Indicator on, deep breath, okay, now swing across. Good. 100.

You can't go faster than that. It's not permitted.

Aaaaahhhhhhh, this speed . . . everything else is unbearable, everything but acceleration!

Head out of the city, you have to get out of the city!

There's a stretch out there with no speed limit . . .

The number plates. Okay, they weren't expensive, but if anyone saw the car . . .

It's okay. No one would ever think they were Polish fakes . . .

100, no faster than that . . . just let him pass . . .

I'll call the car rental place tomorrow.

Today it's impossible. I can't talk with anyone now. And no one was looking in any case.

Right?

I checked the entire block.

There was no one about. Not just then.

(But she screamed—didn't you hear her screaming?)

Here. Now you can drive a little faster . . .

I heard her screaming!

(But I had the glasses and the cap on, back in the shop . . .)

I felt her skin, saw her eyes, her mouth, the teeth inside. I felt her naked ass against my stomach . . .

Now.

Here! The city limits. From here on, no more speed limit.

AAAAAAHHHHH . . .

120 140 160 . . .

Do you hear the swish of the wind, the motor purring like a music box, the fuel streaming through it?

180 200 220 . . .

She arched her head back—I was so aroused, my heart was pounding—she looked at me as I took her arm, the necklace glittering around her neck, her breasts nearly bursting out of the blouse she had on—and I could sense how confused she was, how she suddenly came up for air . . . came out of the hot frenzy she had already given herself over to. Her small hand had reached back to my belt—her lips were parted; her head lay at my throat—and she opened the buckle with a pull. Her hand slipped down to me, her fingers closing around me . . .

260 . . . 270 . . .

Do you feel how the steering wheel vibrates in your hands? One tiny motion and you'll be flying over the safety barrier, one unguarded moment and you'll roll . . .

280

No more! . . . the motor will break off its mounts and fly through the hood . . .

Her lips moved down over my chin, while her free hand lay on the necklace. She brushed against my ear and whispered something, which went through me, as if she had reached inside me. She could sense how she aroused me; she was acting on pure instinct, absolutely sure of herself, and rightly so . . .

Because everything in me was screaming to give her what she wanted from me, screaming *to take her, seize what she was offering, her body arching, stretching, caressing, nuzzling . . .*

But I couldn't give myself over to that; I couldn't have her—penetrate her—no, I wanted to prove it!

I watched the way she opened her straining blouse—and I grasped her arm and held it firmly.

Bent it, carefully.

She paused and looked at me.

Then I twisted. With all my strength.

It didn't break . . .

But . . . it cracked.

Suddenly, the car was filled with screaming . . . her arm was hanging slackly.

I threw the door open. I kicked her out.

I couldn't look at her face anymore . . .

(and should never have been allowed to. I wanted it—and I did it! But I'll never get over it.)

TODAY

Butz stares at the display on his cell phone as he strides down the barren hallway at state police headquarters. He needs to talk to Claire.

The phone shows 10:19 P.M.

Three weeks.

Three days.

Three hours.

Nonsense!

According to the pathologist, Anni Eisler died just after seven tonight.

The three hours have passed. And nothing has happened.

And just as this thought appears, he feels the phone in his hand vibrate.

RRRRRRINGG!

It feels like a high-voltage electric shock ripping through his nervous system.

"Hello?!"

"Mr. Butz?"

"What?"

"We've got something."

"What is it?"

"In Fehrenberg's apartment."

"Okay . . ."

"Best if you come here yourself."

He hears the beep of call waiting, a second caller. A quick glance at the display.

Claire.

"On my way," Butz rasps into the phone. He knows Fehrenberg's address. He taps a button to take Claire's call.

"Konstantin?" Her voice sounds harried. "You tried to call?"

"Yeah . . ."

"Can we talk later? Just now . . . is a bad time." Butz can hear her running.

"Listen, Claire, it's important; it's got to do with . . ." He wants to say *with the guy who delivered the drinks*, but he doesn't get to finish his sentence.

"No!" Claire's cry cuts him off. "They kept me in a goddamn holding cell the whole day!"

"Claire?"

His phone beeps. He jerks it from his ear and sees that the connection has been lost. And that a message has just arrived.

A picture. His assistant has sent him a photograph.

The slurry of pixels and colors on the display comes into focus, forms an image. And when Butz realizes what he is looking at, he knows in a heartbeat that what is happening here is more formidable, more far-reaching, than anything he has ever faced before.

TODAY

"After you."

Till steps past his companion and through the door leading out of the underground passage. The first thing he notices is the stink of old deep-fry oil.

While the man follows him into the shack and locks the door behind him, Till looks around. A deep fryer, a counter, refrigerators, cooking utensils—everything has been wiped clean, but it's still like they're saturated in the fat, the stench, the rancid reek of cheap fried food.

A wide pane of glass catches his eye, reflecting the neon tubes that light the interior. And he realizes he can see outside, through the pane, to a green-tiled passage running past the place.

Memory suddenly completes the picture for him.

It's been twelve years since he was last here!

The man accompanying Till pushes past him to the narrow door in the side wall and unlocks it. Two steps lead down into the passageway. The subway station at Alexanderplatz. It's the same place. Back then they had served Chinese food. Today they sell chips and sausages. It's the shack that Bentheim disappeared into, where Till had discovered the parrots in the trashcan . . .

They step out. The man slams the thin wooden door closed behind them with a dull thud.

"Okay, come on!"

The passageway lies empty before them. In the distance, Till can hear that the subway trains are still operating. He glances at his watch. Just after one in the morning.

The other man is already a few steps ahead.

Till quickly catches up with him. The man's face looks even paler than usual in the dim light; his scars seem to gleam. But he has turned up his coat's broad collar, and they are barely visible.

With everything that had happened in the last few hours, Till had been disoriented, but now his memory is starting to return: *How did he end up in that basement room where the woman was suspended from the ceiling?*

At the funeral! He had spent the entire day at the funeral! The bells from the chapel in the cemetery had rung as if Death itself were hurling the clapper against the bronze. Till had stared at the freshly dug hole as if it wanted to swallow him most of all.

All of them were there: Julia, Butz, Claire, Nina, Henning, Betty . . . it felt like they'd been standing beside the pit for hours, until each had stepped forward individually and lingered awhile by the grave. And then they had gone to a tavern near the cemetery. A huge hall had been hired for the mourners, and even though it was still early in the morning, Till had started drinking—more recklessly, perhaps, than he ever had before . . .

Until . . .

Until he woke up among the figures down in that underground hole, with a woman swinging on hooks from the ceiling . . .

Till sees his feet stepping along the subway tunnel tiles, sees the hem of his companion's overcoat at the upper edge of his field of vision, sees the man start to ascend the stairs ahead of them . . .

But he had seen her again! It had been two years . . . but when he stood opposite her at the cemetery, he felt unable to breathe. Lisa had looked so desirable, so familiar.

"Hey."

They have reached the top of the stairway. Above them looms the Fernsehturm, reaching up into the night sky covering the city. It towers over the huge public square, where the buzz of cars, trains, people sounds more . . . enraptured . . . than anywhere else in the city.

The other man looks around at him. He seems to have forfeited all his power up here, under the open sky. Inside his overcoat, his skinny shoulders are pulled up around his ears, his steps have taken on a stumbling quality, and his long-fingered hands are buried in his pockets. Till looks at him.

"You said you were taking me to Lisa?" The man lifts his chin. In his eyes, Till can read how little the man thinks they have in common. "Where is she?"

"Who?"

"Lisa!" Till tightens his stomach muscles. "Tell me!"

"At home. Come on."

But Till doesn't move. "And where would that be? Home?" *Dickwad!*

The man fingers the scars stretching back from the corners of his mouth, as if he has to think it over himself first. But then his reply comes so suddenly that it hits Till like a fist.

"Felix's place. Where else?"

ABOUT THE AUTHOR

Born in Berlin in 1966, Jonas Winner lived in Rome and the United States before moving back to his home city to study philosophy. As a reporter and television editor, he shot documentaries and covered cultural affairs. His experience informed his work on screenplays, and several of his detective stories and thrillers have aired throughout Europe. He released his debut novel in 2011, followed by the seven-part Berlin Gothic series, which became one of Germany's first e-book bestsellers. Winner lives and writes in Berlin.

ABOUT THE TRANSLATOR

Born in Australia but widely traveled, Edwin Miles has been working as a translator, primarily in film and television, for more than ten years.

After studying in his hometown of Perth, Western Australia, Edwin completed in 1995 an MFA in fiction writing at the University of Oregon. While there, he spent a year working as fiction editor on the literary magazine *Northwest Review*. In 1996, he was shortlisted for the prestigious Australian/Vogel Award for young writers for a collection of short stories.

After many years living and working in Australia, Japan, and the United States, he currently resides in his "second home" in Cologne, Germany, with his wife Dagmar and two very clever children.